Timeless
River

Marianne Petit

2020, Amore Moon Publishing
www.amoremoonpublishing.com
www.twbpress.com

Timeless River

Copyright © 2020 by Marianne Petit

Edited by Terry and Bobette Wright

Cover Art by Terry Wright
Images licensed from Shutterstock.com

Published by Amore Moon Publishing, an imprint of TWB Press, Centennial, Colorado

ISBN: 978-1-944045-66-1

"Thou art gone from my gaze,
Like a beautiful dream,
And I seek thee in vain
By the meadow and stream:
Oft I breathe thy dear name
To the winds floating by,
But thy sweet voice is mute
To my Bosom's sigh.

Acknowledgements

It's not every day an editor takes the time to answer a query letter let alone sends you suggestions that may lead to a contract, but I was truly blessed when I sent the query of "Timeless River" to Bobette. Thank you, thank you, for taking a chance on me.

Both my editors, Bobette and Terry, are wonderful to work with, and I can't thank you both enough for all your suggestions and insights.

Terry, I love my cover and my book trailer. Thank you for all your hard work in making this book the best it can be and for taking my concerns to heart.

A special thanks to my friend Loyd for reading through my manuscript and for your invaluable comments.

And finally a BIG thanks to you, the reader, for choosing my book from all the hundreds of stories out there.

Chapter One

Abby's premonition

I awoke, startled. Despite the warm room, an eerie chill prickled my body. I jolted upright, my eyes and ears alert.

What was that sound?

The hairs on the back of my neck bristled. My gaze darted around the dim bedroom then to the dark hallway.

Nothing. Just my imagination? Despite my impulse to bolt out of bed, I grabbed the bat off the nightstand, my ridiculous weapon to ward off any intruder. The doors were secured. The alarm was on. Not that locks would keep out a ghost.

Adrenaline tore through me like a freight train on steroids. Several deep breaths did nothing but make me lightheaded. Try as I might, I couldn't shake the feeling that someone stood in the shadows...watching me. Though I'd felt the presence before, it still creeped me out, especially in the middle of the night.

The bright illuminated numbers on my clock shone *2:00 a.m.* I groaned. After tossing and turning half the night, I'd managed to get three hours sleep. I should be used to the weird premonitions I get from time to time, and I'd sensed paranormal auras more times than I cared to count, and still they interfered with my sleep. The sense some earth-shattering event was about to happen began yesterday morning with my first cup of coffee. I couldn't shake that familiar feeling of dread I'd felt the night my mother died.

An unearthly tremor rippled down my spine. I recalled the freeze I'd felt earlier as I walked to my bedroom, the sensation that someone had passed right through me. Fighting a pulse-drumming panic, I bunched my pillow, drew my blanket more securely around me and my bat, and closed my eyes. I needed to get back to sleep, didn't want to worry about what was going to happen. If a ghost decided to haunt me, I couldn't do anything about it.

My stomach grumbled. I rolled over, tried to ignore the dread and thought about cookies instead, the cookies I'd been craving all day. Chocolate Chip. I imagined the taste, the sweet smell... I could really go for a snack...or a big fat piece of—

Tap. Tap. Tap.

My eyes popped open. Every muscle tightened.

Did I hear footsteps?

Something had crossed the hardwood floor outside my bedroom. Fear dug a hole in my chest, causing a lung to wheeze.

Is the ghost coming for me?

Tap. Tap. Tap.

In the corner of my room, creepy shadows leaned up the dimly lit wall. I lay perfectly still, afraid to breathe. Time hung suspended. Terror cut the air from my throat.

The tapping stopped; my racing heart did not. The bat felt worthless in my clammy hands. Ghost or intruder, I wasn't sure...but someone was at my door. I set the bat aside, slowly reached for my cell, my fingers groping along the nightstand, until I grabbed it like the Holy Grail.

Tap. Tap. Tap.

There it is again.

With nerve-rattled fingers, I dialed 9-1—

Something jumped on my bed. The mattress dipped under the weight. I gasped and dropped the phone. Panic drummed in my ears as I grabbed for the bat. I wasn't going down easy.

Meow.

Soft fur rubbed my arm. I exhaled. *Just the cat.*

"Matina, you scared me half to death." I patted the bed. Matina made herself comfortable, her presence comforting.

Snuggling into my cat, I closed my eyes.

The air conditioner groaned. I opened my eyes. A sliver of moonlight peeked through a chink in the curtains, casting distorted shadows on my walls. My breath hitched. *This is ridiculous. Why am I such a scaredy-cat?* My pulse was doing a Zumba routine in my neck. I rolled over, dragging the blanket with me, and tried to calm my breathing. *Relax. Sleep. Breathe.* The room was silent, except for Matina's deep purring.

Curled in a fetal position, I forced my mind clear, but an unexplainable sadness crept in. The unease subsided, but tears threatened, tears that came out of nowhere. I squeezed my eyes tight. Red, yellow, and orange pinpoints swirled before me, growing fainter and fainter...

"Mamma?" a girl's voice whispered.

I inhaled sharply, sat up, and flipped on my light. Matina flew off the bed and bolted out the door. An empty room stared back at me, a room that felt as cold as a meat locker. I brushed at the goose-bumps that made the fine hairs on my arms stand at attention. "Who are you?"

I knew from experience that spirits roamed this earth; I'd seen a few, but never did one talk to me. However, I had no daughter to call out to me, to call me mamma. So what little girl was calling for her mother...and why was she in my room? It must've been me. I'd fallen asleep. I must have called out to my mother. But why now, after three years since her death, was I calling for her?

Chapter Two

Abby and the Legend

I refused to believe the legend was true. As I sat with my best friend Cindi in her car parked at the river's edge, waiting for some of her old high school friends to join us for a swim, I could feel the ambiance of this area, its history during the California Gold Rush. Though I wasn't thrilled with meeting her friends, I liked it here, and to pass the time, we'd started talking about our town's prominent legend.

"She killed her children on the night of the blue moon." Cindi emphasized the words *blue moon* with a ghoulish flair in her voice and waved the porcelain figurine in her hands, a woman wearing a long red dress.

I disagreed. "I'm not so sure she killed her own kids."

With the air conditioner rattling, my mind traveled back to the gold rush when the legend of the Weeping Woman began. Over one hundred seventy years ago, hundreds of men camped at this very spot on the South Fork of the American River, finding or losing their dreams for a pinch of gold dust.

The nearby town was called Dry Diggins back then, now my hometown of Placerville, California. It looks nothing like it did back in 1850 after the gold rush began at Sutter's Mill, just nine miles downstream from here. There was a saloon in Dry Diggins, *The Boomerang Gambling Hall and Saloon*, where a woman who purportedly looked like the figurine sang for the miners, merchants, and gunslingers. One day, three outlaws were caught and hanged from a large oak tree on Main Street, earning the town the nickname *Hangtown*.

Today, families laid out their blankets and picnic baskets along the riverbank, and children splashed and squealed in the frigid shallows, just out of reach of the midstream current. I could imagine the men digging and panning for gold among the frolicking kids, as if the rushing water carried whispers of the past.

"Earth to Abby. You're zoning out on me again." Cindi handed me the figurine. "Lolita sure was beautiful."

I stared at the porcelain woman in my hand, her flowing black hair, Spanish green eyes, and golden brown skin, a most striking woman of her time. Her signature red cloak and red dress, the one they say she wore on the night of the murders, hugged her porcelain curves, and white pantalettes peeked out from beneath the gown. An engraving on the base read *Lolita* in sweeping letters, her stage name when she sang at the Boomerang.

"Cindi. They say her real name was Abigail, too, like mine, but I don't believe she was a killer."

"What makes you think the legend isn't true?"

"Some say she was seen dancing and singing at a party the night her children died, so she couldn't have killed them."

"Hashtag, that's only a theory." She looked out the window toward the dirt road that led down to the riverbank from the upper parking lot. "I'm hot. I want to go swimming. What's taking them so long, sis?"

We were like sisters, Cindi and I, and her endearment made me feel like I wasn't alone in this world. I curled a strand of crimson hair around my index finger. There were two beauties in the car, and I wasn't one of them. The term *beach blonde* fit my best friend to a T. She was slender, tanned by the California sun, and her figure would make Barbie Doll jealous. We'd been friends since middle school, though I didn't know what she saw in me. I didn't look like her, dress like her, figured it was just a matter of time before she'd tell me to get lost. It took a while to realize we both needed each other. She boosted my confidence on days when I felt down in the dumps about myself, and I encouraged her to see herself as more than a pretty face.

Still, I couldn't tell her the real reason I thought the legend of the Weeping Woman was wrong. Cindi would go completely nuts if I told her I'd actually seen the kids' ghosts, right here on this riverbank. Recalling that encounter still gave me the shivers.

It was the evening after I'd heard the little girl call for her mamma in my bedroom. I needed to get away from the house, so I drove here to think about that encounter and wonder what it meant. The setting sun colored the sky pink and orange and cast a golden glow across the swirling currents. From out of nowhere, two small children appeared on the riverbank, skipping along, throwing rocks into the water, and laughing like children at play. One was a girl, the other a small boy. Wondering what two children were doing out here by themselves, I walked toward them. "Hey, kids."

They abruptly stopped and looked at me.

"Where are your parents?"

"We can't find our mamma," the little girl replied.

Mamma? I've heard that voice before.

I approached them but oddly, though they hadn't stepped backward, my steps did not bring me any closer to them. "Who's your mamma? Maybe I can find her, give her a call."

"It's Abigail," the boy said.

His sister added, "The miners around here call her Lolita."

Stunned, I stopped. There were no miners around here. I had to have heard wrong. The little girl couldn't possibly be talking about Lolita, the Weeping Woman.

"Tell the lady," the boy said to his sister.

"Joseph, hush."

"Tell me what?"

"She didn't-"

The girl grabbed his hand, and they began to glimmer and glide backwards down the riverbank.

As I stood in awe, I realized I was seeing the spirits of Lolita's murdered children. "Wait."

They stopped.

"I wish I could help you."

"Be careful what you wish for," the girl said, and they shimmered out of sight.

Warm fingers of a sudden wind had softly stroked my hair, raising tiny dimples on the back of my neck. My sixth sense told me I would see them again.

Even now, I recalled how they looked. The little girl wore a blue Victorian dress and matching bonnet. The boy wore a white shirt and cut-off pants with suspenders. That night, I'd flicked through pages of a history book on the Gold Rush Era. A story about a lost gold claim interested me, gold nuggets just lying on the ground, right, but I read on and found a story about the Weeping Woman legend. There was an old sepia photo of the same children, dressed the same way, standing at the river in front of a wooden rowboat. They were real back then...ghosts now...but why did they reveal themselves to me? What was Joseph trying to say before his sister hushed him? She didn't...didn't what? Kill them? Right. My best friend wouldn't believe a word of it.

"Cindi, I believe someone else did it...the piano player, maybe."

"The piano player? He disappeared after the murders. What about her husband?"

I shuddered. "He ran off with another woman. Maybe she got all jealous and wigged out when he paid more attention to his kids than her, so she drowned them in the river."

"Maybe so, but Lolita could have been jealous of the new girlfriend, felt tied down, trapped, resented her kids for it." Cindi sighed. "Wouldn't be the first time a mother drowned her own children to be free of them."

"And maybe it was an accident that got blown way out of proportion. No matter what happened, Lolita mourned those kids night and day, wailing and screaming along the riverbank, searching for their bodies. Thus the Weeping Woman legend was born."

"Someone wanted her kids dead, but either way, their mother should have been there to protect them. I hate it when kids are neglected." Cindi waved her hand in a theatrical gesture. "She's guilty."

"It's hard to know what really happened, but I'm sure she died of a broken heart."

"You're always defending her."

"Why not? She's sexy, confident, beautiful, with a songbird voice and men bowing at her feet. A lot like you, I'd say."

"I don't sing."

"Lolita was truly a liberated woman for her time."

"Abby, you're such a romantic. She was a soiled dove."

"You're probably right." I grumped. My brain returned to my present-day problems. Cindi's Honda Civic smelled of coconut oil suntan lotion and French fries. I glanced at an empty McDonald's carton on the floor. How she managed to keep her amazing figure was beyond me. If I even looked at fried food, I swear, I gained a pound.

A Million Years played over the radio. Cindi switched channels. "Too depressing."

"Hey, I like Adele." I related to the part where she sang about missing her mom. Even after three years, my mom's absence still clung to every room in the house. Memories hit Dad and me every time we walked into the kitchen where she'd baked Christmas cookies, or the dining room where she'd served up evening dinners. The empty seat was a painful reminder. Dad escaped in his work at the hospital. I barely saw him. I knew she watched over us, but the thought did little to fill the void of her loving arms.

"Where are those guys?" Cindi let out an exasperated breath.

"At least we've had time to talk."

"I bet that silly legend never happened...just a fable told around campfires, but she's fun to talk about."

I shrugged. "I need something to fixate on. I'm a twenty-one-year-old virgin who can't remember her last date, and I'm struggling to lose ten more pounds." A nervous laugh escaped me. Even though we shared a lot about ourselves, admitting my lack of sexual experience heated my face. I hadn't dated much, not since the night of my senior prom. My high hopes for that date were dashed and put serious dating on my not-to-do list. "I don't care if I ever date again."

"Wow. Stop being so down on yourself." Cindi placed a comforting hand on my arm.

"Easy for you to say. You're gorgeous."

"Oh, stop. I'd trade my looks for half your smarts. The guys I date don't go out with me for my brains." Cindi said the words in a flippant manner, but I knew her well enough to know that bothered her.

"I'd trade half my brains for one-tenth of your figure." I would kill to have her body. Trade my soul to the devil. So maybe I was a little sensitive about my flabby middle, but what woman loved the way she looked one-hundred percent? *Well, except Cindi.*

"Don't be crazy. You've lost...like what, twenty-five pounds? You look great."

I didn't feel great. My black one-piece bathing suit cut into my crotch, and I felt like an encased sausage. "Just for once I'd like some guy to whistle, or trip over his feet, or do something to show interest when I walk by."

Cindi scowled at me. "No, you don't. You know what I go through."

I did. She'd been propositioned more times than I could count, especially in her current modeling gig, but I still envied her...and the Weeping Woman statuette. They were everything I was not, and everyone noticed them for their beauty.

"Anyway..." *Enough of the pity party.* "Reading about the other Abigail and her kids gave me something to do."

Cindi flicked her hand. "I don't believe in ghosts, little green men, or reincarnation." She studied me with a curious intensity. "Although, after all these years it still gives me the creeps when you answer the phone before it rings."

My sixth sense. I knew the problem well. At first, the sensations scared me. Then it became a game, a regular occurrence, a part of me I'd kept hidden from everyone. The bad feelings and festering sensations of doom were not fun, and ghost children really freaked me out. The nightmarish angst I'd felt the night my mom died in a car crash flashed cruelly across my mind. My stomach knotted. Prickling tears welled in my eyes. I thrust the memory away before I became a blubbering fool, and then focused my attention on the sound of a woman's laughter rising above voices coming down the dirt road.

When I looked out the window, I about suffered heart failure. The last person on earth I expected to see, didn't want to see, ever, was Wyatt Beaufort, especially with his old high school cronies, all dressed to go for a swim.

"Damn, that man is a hunk." Cindi sighed. "Can I get an amen?"

"For who? Golden boy?" I frowned, but he did look good, and so did his red Ferrari he'd parked on the dirt road. "If you like dumb jocks." He looked better than I remembered. The buzzed blond haircut gave his square-jawed face a tough-guy appearance. His lean and muscled body would fit well on a firefighters' calendar. Football pads, not needed, not with those shoulders. He wore colorful swim trunks, and the sun glinted off his gold Rolex. Okay. He was rich *and* good looking.

Cindi grinned. "You had a thing for him once upon a time."

I gathered my hair into a ponytail. "So did every girl back then." I tied the red strands with a rubber band and glanced at the big house sitting on top of the cliff. The Beaufort mansion, Wyatt's ancestral home. The opulent brick house with its two white columns towered over the river valley like a queen looking down on her subjects. That pretty much summed up the Beaufort family, wealthy socialites who thought they were better than everyone else. High school crush or not, Wyatt was one of them, and I should have known better than to trust him to show up for a date.

"Come on. Let's join them." Cindi pushed open the car door.

Sticky summer heat swirled in and slammed into me. A rushing sensation, like a dropping elevator, seized my stomach. "You go. I'll wait here. You know what he did to me."

"Of course, I remember," she said, her voice full of sympathy. "But you need to put that to bed. Really. That was over three years ago."

"Some wounds never heal." Foreboding nudged a thump in my chest.

Cindi huffed. "You need to get over it."

Get over being jilted? Did anyone ever get over that?

"And stop acting like a two-year-old. Besides, don't you want to show off your new bathing suit?"

"No." I shook my head as a subliminal warning persisted, raising the tiny hairs on the back of my neck.

"Isn't that Pam with them? I haven't seen her in ages."

The excitement in Cindi's voice soured my stomach. I didn't want to go swimming with them, but I wouldn't disappoint her. The pretty brunette walking next to Wyatt had linked her arm with his in a possessive manner. Pam's bright pink bikini showcased long shapely legs, and her round, perky boobs, obviously fake, looked like bocce balls on steroids nestled in frilly pink cupcake holders.

My own breasts felt heavy and sweaty. Feeling self-conscious, I flipped my white lace cover-up over my thigh that, next to Cindi's, looked like a side of rare beef. No matter how much suntan lotion I used, I still burned.

She pointed to my face. "You may want to wipe your nose. You overdid the lotion again. Anyway..." She glanced in the mirror, primped her hair, and wet her lips. "I don't want to go by myself."

"Now who's acting like a two-year-old?" I swiped lotion from my nose. The foreboding sensation in my chest chilled me, raising goose-bumps on my skin. Just a mixture of heat and air conditioning, I reasoned and pushed the creepy feeling away. "I'll go. But only for a minute. Probably be the longest minute of my life," I added under my breath.

Cindi's long legs were already out the door.

Not having any lip balm, I slathered some lotion on my dry lips. For better or worse, I wasn't sure, but fear made me want to slam the door shut and hide under the dash.

"You coming?" She popped a stick of gum in her mouth.

I took a deep breath, pushed open my door, and reluctantly stepped out to face the guy who had broken my heart.

Wyatt meets Abby

Walking toward the river, my friend, John, elbowed me in the ribs. "Hey, Wyatt. Check out the chicks. Some contrast, huh?"

I glanced at the tall, gorgeously tanned blonde walking toward us. Cindi Weaver. She was still as beautiful as I remembered. I'd dreaded coming home for the summer, thanks to my dad, but perhaps being here wouldn't be so bad after all.

Pam pinched my arm. "Put your eyeballs back in your head."

A shorter pale redhead hustled up beside Cindi. By the way she'd slathered on the lotion, I'd say she'd taken her dermatologist's UV warning a little too seriously. "Who's that?"

"O-M-G." Pam's mouth twisted into an unpleasant bow. "Don't you remember her? Abigail Stewart. She's the librarian over on Fair Lane."

"Vaguely." Actually, I didn't remember her but wished I did. I rubbed my temple to ease a headache starting to brew. Confronting my dad, as I had earlier about football, always ended with a migraine.

John laughed. "Casper spends most of her time with her nose in a book."

His comment about the redhead being Casper-pale made me want to slug him. If not for all the reading I did, I'd probably not be where I was today. As the women approached, I stopped under a shade tree and eyed the redhead. She had all the right curves in all the right places, cute as a bunny, and her hair trapped the sunlight in a crimson glow.

"Hi, Wyatt." Cindi took my free hand.

I felt Pam cling to my other arm a little tighter. "Cindi, you look awesome as ever."

"It's been a while," she cooed. "Do you remember Abby...er...Abigail Stewart?"

She didn't look familiar, but I nodded anyway. "Yeah, sure." I noticed Abby wore a frown and didn't make eye contact, a major turn-off, then I turned back to Cindi. "What have you been up to?"

"Enjoying the summer. I hear you got into Penn State on a football scholarship."

John looped his arm around my shoulders. "My man here was All American two years in a row."

"It's not a big deal." I shoved my hand into my swim-trunks pocket and jiggled the bottle of aspirin I'd grabbed from my car, a red Ferrari I'd parked up the road under a tree. The sports car was more proof of my father's gratitude for my football success. A full-blown migraine wasn't far off. Despite what others saw of the *popular* me, I wasn't comfortable in the limelight, even though I put up a good front for my dad and my coach and these clowns.

"We're all proud of you, right, guys?"

Everyone nodded except Abby. She remained silent, but

the look in those beautiful green eyes spoke volumes. The disgust aimed at me caused my stomach to clench like I'd been hit in the gut with a football. *What is her problem?* "Abby? Ah, Abigail...where do I know you from?"

She tugged at her cover-up then pulled the shoulder straps up to her neck. "I thought you said you remembered me."

"Well, you caught me there." I got the feeling her annoyance stemmed from more than a lapse in my memory. "Stewart. The name sounds familiar, is all."

Abby remained mute. Her intriguing green eyes squinted at me with a revulsion I didn't understand.

Gum cracked between Cindi's teeth. "Abigail's father is Dr. Stewart. He just became the head of the Neurosurgery department." She glanced at Abby, her brows at a quirky angle like they shared some secret girl language I wasn't privy to.

I really needed to meet her dad, maybe shadow him at the hospital because I wanted to be a doctor someday. Yeah. Like my dad would ever allow that.

Getting into med-school wouldn't be easy. I'd been taking pre-med classes on biology, anatomy, and emergency medical procedures, CPR and trauma care, in hopes of getting a head start. Herbal remedies interested me as well, but my dad wasn't behind me on any of this. *"Go Pro, my boy. Football is your future."* I saw a white gob on Abigail's mouth and reached out. "You've got some lotion..." I brushed my finger on the softness of her lower lip.

Her head jerked back.

I dropped my hand. Apparently, my touch revolted her. I wasn't sure if that pissed me off or intrigued me more. "Sorry. I didn't mean to startle you."

She scowled then rubbed the lotion from her mouth.

"High school, right? We went to the same school. I should have remembered your eyes." The emerald rings surrounding her pupils made her eyes as vibrant as the eyes of a Spanish maiden. "They're so...green." I wanted to say *beautiful*, but I doubted anything I said would deflect the darted gaze she flung my way.

"Yes." She pursed her lips, then: "El Dorado High."

I must've sounded like a jerk, talking about her eyes because she sounded annoyed.

She glanced down, adjusted her cover-up more securely around her middle, then crossed her arms over her stomach.

I couldn't help but notice, with all the tugging and pulling of her clothing, she appeared extremely self-conscious. Yeah. I could relate. I knew what it felt like to feel uncomfortable around the opposite sex. The quiet, shy boy no girl wanted to be with still haunted me. I'd worked hard to build the macho image everyone saw: weight training, karate, and of course football. I might have overdone it.

"Wyatt, darling." Pam tightened her arm around mine, and for the first time, I felt like pulling away from her. "I'm just dying to hear about your trip to Hong Kong. All that wonderful shopping. I'm so jealous."

Cindi cracked her gum. "When did you go to China?"

Pam flung her hair to the back of her shoulder. "The summer after high school. He went on a tour."

"That's epic."

Abby's gaze bounced restlessly around as if she was desperate to escape the conversation.

"Did you see the Great Wall?" Pam asked, her voice a little too syrupy.

"It was a real struggle to walk up all those steps to get to the top."

"Ah, come on." Pam ran her hand up my arm. "I find that hard to believe. You've got such great stamina." She squeezed my bicep.

Yeah. Pam had set her sights on me in high school, and I lapped up the attention like a puppy on an ice cream cone. She looked good on my arm, but as for anything serious, no way. Not gonna happen. She was too full of herself.

"An old Chinese woman had an easier time climbing the stairs than me. I gained a whole new respect for those people."

Abby's eyebrows were crooked, as if she were struggling to keep from telling me to shut up about China. However, an unexplainable need to impress her felt suddenly important to me.

"I wish I'd taken Chinese in high school along with my advanced Spanish classes. Would have come in handy in China."

Abigail's eyes widened with surprise, and a sense of satisfaction swept through me. Just because I'd gone to college on a football scholarship, women always assumed I was just a dumb jock. But then, whose fault was that? I never corrected the assumption. Seemed to me the redhead might appreciate a bilingual man.

John stared at me like I was talking Chinese. He had no idea how smart I was. Came from reading lots of books...like Abby. My mom knew how badly I wanted to use my education for something more important than football. My dad didn't care; he only wanted to live his fantasy football career vicariously through me.

Abigail turned to Cindi. "Well, it's hot. Are you going for a swim with me?"

"Do you mind if I hang out here?"

"I'm good."

Before I could invite myself to go with her, Abby walked away without so much as a backward glance at me. *What am I, chopped liver?* I took a step in her direction only to feel Pam tug my arm.

"She really should cut back on the burgers and fries." Pam's voice reeked of disgust.

I glowered at her. Abby wasn't like the anorexic women who threw themselves at me. "I like women who aren't afraid to enjoy a meal and eat more than salads."

Pam frowned. Salads were her food of choice. Out the corner of my eye, I saw Cindi smile then I glanced to the riverbank where Abby dropped her cover-up. Maybe she wasn't my type, a bit too quiet, a bit too angry, but her black swimsuit fit her body perfectly. Yeah, I preferred leggy blondes, and though Abby wasn't a blonde, she had a pair of shapely legs. And she'd challenged me with her hard-to-get attitude.

No, definitely not my type, but... I drew my gaze away from the woman who, for some strange reason, had piqued my interest and I glanced at my Rolex. *4:00 p.m.* Still time to cool off and get home before dad stormed in demanding to talk to me about football again. Didn't leave me much time to get Abby's phone number. "What do you say, guys? Let's all go for a swim."

Abby goes for a swim

Happy to be away from Wyatt and his groupies, I unstrapped my sandals and placed them side by side under my cover-up.

Thank God that's over.

Being around the old high school gang brought back the insecure geek in me. I'd felt like I was shuffling down those pea-green halls, trying to avoid classmates who made me uncomfortable. Those years colored my perception of life. Cheerleaders and jocks were the *in* crowd, and everyone wanted to hang with them. No one wanted to associate with the *nerds*, even though I was smarter than half the football team combined. The *geek* tag followed me after graduation until I was successful enough to break the stigma. I'd worked hard to put the past behind me and hated myself for regressing so easily.

Cindi, I noticed, laughed at something Pam said up on the road.

A pang of jealousy nibbled at me. How many years had I wished to be a part of Cindi's crowd? All those years I'd felt invisible while my best friend talked to the football players and sashayed through the halls with the other cheerleaders.

Memories, like tucked away ghosts, escaped from their hiding place; they clung to my thoughts. As a misfit who'd rather study than go to a football game, I never felt school pride. Not much had changed. My nose was still in books, and I still felt like an outcast.

As I plunged forward into the river, the cold water stung my freshly shaved legs. Frigid swirls lapped against my stomach, and the hairs on my arms prickled. The swift midstream current and white-water swells seemed a safe distance away.

Wyatt's husky laughter floated toward me.

Green eyes. Ha. Like he'd ever noticed my eyes in high school.

I dunked beneath the water, dragging that thought with me. As I returned to the surface, I swung my head to whip the water from my ponytail.

And why couldn't he just leave his fingers where they

belonged and not on my lip?

An ominous premonition washed over me, followed by a chill that had nothing to do with the cold temperature of the water. I had this undeniable angst that something terrible was about to happen, like the angst I'd felt the night my mother died.

Maybe I should get out and go home.

I looked back to the shore to see Cindi break away from the crowd. Wyatt's leering gaze followed her as she strolled toward the river. He was still the same jerk he was in high school, always drooling over a pretty backside.

Bitter resentment overshadowed my ability to enjoy the moment. Memories I didn't want to recall demanded attention. After three years of trying to get over him, I still held a grudge. Cindi was right, I should put it to bed...but I couldn't. Damn it. He hurt me, and it still hurt.

I dove and resurfaced in front of Cindi who stood waist-deep, rubbing her arms. "Damn, it's cold."

"Cindi..." I clenched my teeth to keep them from chattering. "He shouldn't be here." I tipped my head toward Wyatt. The muscles in his arms bulged as he pulled off his T-shirt, showcasing firm, sculpted abs. He ran to the river and plunged into the water.

"What can I say? You know, like, it's a free...river." Cindi shivered. "But it's a freezing river. This...is not happening." She trudged back toward the shore.

"Come on. I swear, Cindi," I shouted. "Don't be such a woose."

She slogged past Wyatt as he dove beneath the surface.

Damn. He's swimming toward me.

Not wanting to be anywhere near him, I turned, and with long breaststrokes, I swam upstream against the current to where the water calmed in another shallow pool. Treading water to catch my breath, I felt something scratch my foot. My heart lurched. Flutter-kicking to avoid the branch or whatever vegetation grew on the rocky bottom, I thought I was free of the annoyance when I felt the sensation of fingers grasping my ankles.

"Wyatt. Cut it out." Kicking, I glanced down, expecting to see him come up for air. Boy was he gonna get an earful.

However, he resurfaced a stone's throw away from me.

Hot panic stabbed my chest. I knee-jerked my legs up, flipped onto my back, and quickly swam backward. A safe distance from the plant or whatever had tried to entangle my ankles, I stretched out my legs and floated to calm my raging nerves. Maybe it was a snake...the thought that a snake might have slithered around my legs made me want to paddle for home. On top of that, a bigger problem was headed my direction.

Wyatt dove toward me, reappeared then dove again.

I refused to let him intimidate me. Cindi was right. I had to stop acting like a two-year-old. It was time to be more assertive, to confront him, to say what was on my mind.

I floated anxiously, my gaze to the sky. Without a cloud in sight, I watched a flock of blackbirds, heard a car door slam and an engine start. I glanced to the shore, saw children with buckets, digging in the dirt; a dog scampered out of the bushes with a ball in his mouth. As I floated downstream, I scanned the water but didn't see Wyatt. He should have resurfaced by now. What was he—?

Suddenly yanked under, I swallowed ice-cold water. Furious Wyatt would carry out such a childish prank, I thrust upward, scratched the surface, and coughed, kicking to stay afloat while thrashing my arms. Before I could cry out, he pulled my ankle down. I went under again. Air bubbles rushed out my nose.

What was he trying to do? Drown me? Fully intent on kicking him in the face, I was suddenly caught in the midstream current, which made fighting back impossible. I propelled myself above the surface and gasped for air as the swift current bulled me downstream. Wall after wall of white-water slammed into me. Tossed under, Wyatt's death grip on my ankle, once again, dragged me down deeper. I couldn't see through the bubbles and swirling whitecaps. My arm skimmed the smooth surface of a bottom rock as I fought the roiling current and Wyatt's grip on my ankle.

Fighting panic, I tried and tried to kick free. Twisting, struggling, I fought the burn building in my lungs. I stretched out my arms, trying to grasp some invisible ladder that would save me.

This can't be happening. No. I had to fight...to swim...

Pressure roared in my ears. I held my breath until my lungs demanded a spasmodic gulp that dragged water down my throat. I coughed. Gasped. More water spilled in. An oppressive pressure weighted my chest, heavy as any boat anchor.

Fatigue quickly took hold of my body...and the cold. The sunlight above began to fade. *God help me.* A silent scream echoed in my fuzzy brain. The burning sensation exploded in my chest then heat drained from the center of my core, leaving me numb. Delusions of survival sank as quickly as I did, like a stone into the cold depths. My strength gone, regrets bombarded me. Thoughts of my mother and father, of shared laughter, of our camping trip by the river at the Coloma campground mixed with the crazy question: when had the river gotten so deep?

Cindi. I don't want to die.

A strange calmness settled over me, and as my thoughts faded, one final question floated by.

Why did Wyatt drown me?

Chapter Three

Abby's new reality

Spiraling upward, I burst through the surface of the water, gasping. My lungs burned as I sucked in air that I thought I'd never breathe again. Choking, gulping, I swallowed then choked again. I coughed up water. Vomit rose in my throat. My body shook as I struggled to get my senses back. Oh my god. My chest and brain felt like a truck had run over me, but I was alive...

I heard Wyatt cough behind me.

Realizing I couldn't feel the bottom and fearing that he could drag me under again, I flailed my arms and, without looking back, swam through a haze of disbelief and confusion. My only thought: get to dry land and far away from him.

I set my feet down, dug my toes into the stony earth, relieved I could stand, relieved I could feel my toes. Icy water lapped against my chest. I was almost to shore. No thanks to him. My heart pumped wildly.

"Wait."

I didn't want to hear him. Didn't want to be anywhere near the murderous bastard. "I'm calling the police." Trembling, I stumbled, fell to my knees. Water lapped at my chin. My mind felt woozy. Something about the surroundings was dreadfully off. I didn't hear children's laughter or dogs barking, just incessant pounding reminiscent of metal against rock. I forced myself up to my feet and trudged forward. My heart thrummed like a drum against my chest. Fear cramped my stomach. *What happened?*

Cold fingers touched my shoulder. Panic snatched my breath away. Finding it difficult to breathe, to think, I swallowed hard.

"Will you stop for a minute? Just stop."

"Stay away from me." Not wishing to see the evil in his eyes I kept my back to him. "Keep your hands to yourself."

I had to get away. Call for help. I fought the current, the slippery bottom slowing my progress, impeding my steps, and I prayed he wouldn't catch up to me again.

A firm hand grabbed my upper arm. Before I could scream, he spun me around. "Lady, did you see her?"

"Let me go." I'd fight him tooth and nail, punch him in the gut, do whatever it took to break free.

He let go, stepped back, and stared at me like he'd never seen me before, his face scrunched, his mouth open, crazy-eyed like he'd gone mad. "Did you see a woman? Black swimsuit? Red hair?" Gasping, he darted his gaze about as though he was searching for me but couldn't see me.

"Are you nuts?" I backpedaled. "I'm not playing your stupid game."

He reached out and managed to grab my wrist. "Who are you?"

The guy was loony. "Cut it out." I jerked free. As fast as I could, I surged toward shore, now focusing my attention on the mossy, slippery rocks under my feet. "I'm getting the sheriff. You're going to jail."

Wyatt caught up with me. "What is going on?" he yelled at my back.

As I entered the shallows, my swimsuit felt heavy. My gaze fell, and what I saw stopped me. The white cotton shift and pantalettes I wore came down to my knees. *What? Where's my black swimsuit?* I was wearing undergarments from the Victorian era, the 1850s. "Oh, my God." I felt suddenly faint. As my legs gave out, Wyatt stepped in and held me up.

"I don't have time for this. I need to find Abby."

It felt strange how confusion sharpened the senses but dulled thoughts too shocking to register. My mind focused on one thing: Wyatt, how he held me with muscular biceps, how the golden hairs on his arms glistened under the sun, how at this moment I needed his strength. His raspy breaths alighted warm on my forehead, and I was keenly aware of the blood pounding in my heart, pounding not from fear, but from desire.

Desire? How can that be? I hated Wyatt. I pushed the longing from my mind and glanced down to see voluptuous cleavage too perfect to be mine. My chest tightened. I shivered. "What's happened to me?"

"Lady, you're freezing. Come on." He scooped me up as though I weighed nothing.

Too numb to complain, I wrapped my arms around his neck. My sopping black locks bunched on his shoulder. Black hair? That didn't make any sense. I was so cold I couldn't think straight.

Wyatt's face held a mixture of concern and bewilderment. His confusion confirmed what I suspected to be true but refused to believe. He didn't see me. He saw someone else. *Am I a ghost in another woman's body? I'd died and gone to hell, for sure.*

My thoughts were interrupted by whispers, snickers, and then peals of laughter from the men on the shore.

"What's their problem?"

"You're practically naked," I whispered.

"Naked?" He glanced down then back up at me. A frown creased his brow. "I'm wearing swim trunks."

"They're a bit skimpy for 1852."

I didn't know why I knew the year with certainty. I didn't know why he was dressed in the same swim trunks while I now wore another woman's clothes. Was my sixth sense playing tricks on me? If so, it was absurd. Comically absurd. A giggle erupted, an uncontrollable reaction that could only have come from total shock.

I glanced at the men who lined the river's edge, dressed in ragged, dirty canvas clothes, with gold-mining pans in their hands and buckets by their feet. My mind disputed that inherent power of perception that defied all logic.

This can't be real.

Through my wet underclothes, I felt Wyatt's hard pecs rub against my breast as he trudged through the shallow water.

Maybe I did die. But this is not hell. It feels like heaven.

How did this happen? How could it be? I rested my head on his shoulder and closed my eyes. Nothing made any sense.

The sun beat the top of my head, a sharp contrast to the cold wet hair on my shoulders, still black hair, not red; I'd lost the band that held my ponytail. My skin was the same golden brown as Cindi's California tan.

Slowly, my situation became clear. Though I didn't want to believe it, I knew what happened had always been impossible. Two worlds—one of the present, one of the past—and two women who shared the same name...had somehow merged in time. I doubted Einstein could ever explain it.

Sodden fabric clung to my body. I shivered, and he drew me in tighter. He'd stared at me as though looking at a stranger. Oddly enough, the woman's body I now shared didn't seem like a stranger to me. I'd read about her. Studied her. Investigated the charges made against her. Somehow, from my watery grave, my soul had emerged back in 1852, in the living body of the legend they called the Weeping Woman.

Wyatt's confusion

What just happened? Last I remembered, I'd reached Abby, put my arms around her waist, and fought the rushing water that was sucking her downward, and sucking me down with her. Something hit my head and I must've blacked out. Yeah. I thought I was a goner, but now I'm here and she is gone.

What happened to Abby?

Had this strangely dressed woman seen her? I needed to know. I needed to find Abby, but this raven-haired beauty in my arms was too angry to be of any help. With numb abandon, I pushed through the fast current, careful not to twist my ankle on the slippery rocks and odd crevices.

As I carried her to shore, I stared at the men standing on the riverbank, seeing them as though I was looking through an unfocused lens, seeing them in the past, miners, I guessed, and watching them laugh at me.

Naked? I wasn't naked. *This ain't nothing. They should see me in my Speedos.*

I scanned the riverbank. Where were my friends, the road to the parking lot, and my new red Ferrari? My heart pounded as I spotted the place where I was sure I'd parked it, alongside the road, beneath a tree. Now there was no tree. There was no road.

My car was gone. Whatever hit my head had left a big black space of confusion and apparently clouded my vision. As soon as I get home, my first phone call would be to the police to report my car stolen.

Shit. Dad is going to be pissed.

Voices, sharp and muffled, echoed across the water. I felt like I was standing in the middle of a football field, the crowd jeering and shouting, but this crowed looked like a rough bunch.

And who is this beautiful woman in my arms?

Damn, I'd better cut back on the booze. I must've had too much to drink last night at the poker game, but I didn't wake up with a hangover, though I did take a clunk on my head; no wonder my brain was pounding and I wasn't seeing correctly. I blinked several times, trying to focus. Still no car, no Pam, no John, no familiar faces, just those ugly-ass miners.

"You can put me down now."

Her words barely registered as I drunkenly trudged through the shallow water. As we emerged from the river, the men stared. I was used to women staring, but men...never. I focused my attention beyond their snickering faces, stepped past them, and picked up my pace toward the tree-line and shade.

"Put me down."

The agitated tone of her voice felt like a slap in the face. I had half a mind to drop her, but I let her down easy.

As soon as her feet touched the ground, she tossed her hair and straightened. Without so much as a glance back, she stalked down a pathway of flattened grass.

"Really?" *She's just going to leave me here?* I started after her. "Where are you going?" I rubbed the back of my neck to ease the tension only my chiropractor could relieve. *Where am I?* Nothing looked familiar. The pressure in my head and chest felt like I'd been tackled by six defensive linebackers. My gait was unbalanced, so I stopped to gather my composure and rein in the crazy woman I'd rescued. "Hey, lady. By any chance, do you have a cell phone? I gotta call my mom."

She swiveled around and stomped back to me. "There are no cell phones. They haven't been invented yet."

I was talking to a loon. "I need to find Abby..." I looked around. "And my friends." *If this is some kind of prank—* "And where's my car?"

"Wyatt, stop whining."

"You...you know my name? How..?" My next breath was like inhaling nails. "What's going on?"

Her lips narrowed, and she glanced at the ground then met my gaze. "Look. I don't know how...I...I don't know what, and I don't know why. I'm just as confused as you are."

"I doubt that."

"I'm dripping wet and cold. We can't stand here all night." She glanced at the men who'd gone back to panning for gold. "Just come with me."

"No way." I looked back to the river. "I have to find Abby."

"She's not out there, Wyatt."

Hearing this beautiful stranger say my name hit me like a gut-punch. It defied all logic. And last I saw Abby, she was in the river. "She has to be around here somewhere."

"Follow me and I'll try to explain." She sighed. "If there is an explanation," she mumbled then turned around and walked on. "I'm pretty sure she lives around here somewhere?"

"She..?" I hurried after her, hoping she knew what she was doing. A logical explanation could not come soon enough.

We hiked in silence up a narrow trail that broke out at a camp of tents all pitched haphazardly between trees, piles of rocks, and mounds of dirt, and there were a few log houses. The aroma of fried food hung like a glob of grease in the air. Hundreds of filthy men wearing outdated clothing, mostly unshaven, walked around or stood in groups, chatting. Curls of smoke wafted upward, its woody smell mixed with the foul odor of unwashed bodies. Scampering dogs barked. The high-pitched sound of a harmonica cut through the barking and chatter.

"It's unbelievable, isn't it?"

Her voice drew me to her face, and I took the moment to really look at her. Even in my dazed confusion, I could see she was beautiful. Black hair clung to her shoulders. Her flawless, golden complexion, high cheekbones, and Spanish green eyes gave her an exotic look. Her plump lips needed no lipstick. I found myself wondering if they tasted as sweet as they looked, an absurd thought given my predicament. My gaze went back to her green eyes, the color of freshly sod football turf. They seemed so familiar, Abby's eyes, but on the face of a stranger.

"Are you all right?" she asked.

I couldn't answer her, didn't know what to say, or what to think. My only hope was that I was dreaming. None of what I saw, not the beautiful woman before me, not the strange men or rustic campsite, could be real.

Abby meets the kids

As I stared at Wyatt's confused expression, I felt a pang of sympathy, which quickly faded. I wanted to hate him, not care, but something had changed. Maybe it was my sixth sense keeping me calm, or the little voice in my head telling me not to be afraid, but I was as overwhelmed by our new surroundings as he was. I was used to experiencing the unexplainable. The poor sap just came along for the ride. Somehow, I was going to figure out how to explain our dilemma, but like it or not, we were stuck here.

My thoughts flew back to the premonition I'd had in the river before I drowned, the feeling that something was about to go terribly wrong. I never would have guessed my identity and place in the world was about to change. Well, it had. This place was going to take some getting used to, and I was in someone else's body. If anyone should freak out, it should be me. Instead, I felt comfortable, like I was home at last.

I recalled the men on shore whose leering stares had made me uncomfortable. From the campsite inhabitants, I expected more of the same. "Come on." I placed a hand on Wyatt's arm and nudged him forward. My legs didn't feel as optimistic as my determination; they were moving a little too slowly.

Something in my head turned me toward what I knew was home, and as we entered the familiar camp, all eyes turned toward us. The stench of unwashed bodies, urine, and smoky campfires stung my eyes.

Catcalls and whistles pierced the air.

"Hey, Lolita. Where's yer clothes?"

I always wanted this kind of attention, but not from the

likes of this bedraggled bunch.

I heard a *snicker* inside my head and wondered where it came from.

The men's licentious hoots and whistles put more swagger to my steps. I felt lightheaded, somewhat out of control, but I liked it. "Just went for a dip, boys."

Why did I say that?

"Let me dry you off," a deep voice called out, followed by more whistling.

"Would you not just love that?" My voice dripped with a sweet Spanish accent that surprised me. However, thrilled by the attention, I flung my hair over my shoulder and smiled at them as I walked on.

A gruff-looking guy hustled up to me and matched my steps, backwards. "Wanna come on over to my tent?"

"Now, Roger, you know that will never happen." I playfully pushed him away.

Roger? How did I know his name?

Wyatt stepped in. "Beat it, Roger."

Someone shouted, "Strange looking duds on that fella."

"Looks like Injuns got his scalp."

Wyatt's hand flew to the buzz-cut on his head. His brows wrinkled with confusion, and then his cheeks reddened with embarrassment or rage, I couldn't tell which.

"I think he is cute," came out of my mouth.

I didn't mean to say that.

Wyatt looked at me and frowned.

The men's loud chatter bombarded me as I tried to control my thoughts and clear my lightheadedness. "Ignore them," I said to Wyatt. "They are harmless." My brave words did little to ease my taut nerves. I had a bigger problem. Where were my clothes, and why hadn't I worn them to the river?

I led Wyatt through the maze of tents, some round, some square, all with steeply pitched roofs, some with black chimney pipes, smoking. Interspersed among the dirty canvas quarters, makeshift plank huts were built with upright branches and interwoven stick roofs, which further cluttered the camp. Piles of chopped wood lay everywhere. Rickety outhouses and open latrines sickened the air. Covered wagons had been parked helter-skelter, *California or Bust* painted on the sides, and mule teams were tied up to nearby poles. Flags of different countries, brightly colored scarves, hangings of shiny silk, and strung-up laundry flapped in the hot breeze. I took it all in as I ignored the gawking smelly men who crowed at me.

When I came to a large tent, I stopped short to observe a dark-haired man standing shirtless before a wash bucket and a cracked mirror. A wet lock of hair fell over his forehead. With long slender fingers, he held a blade to his round face and scraped off soap and facial hair. His earthy brown eyes widened when he saw me, and then his surprise quickly changed to a smile. "Miss Lolita, I took the liberty of stacking some wood for you." He pointed the blade across the mud-rutted dirt track of a road.

I glanced at the pile of cut wood set beside a shack. Slats of misshapen timber formed the walls, a canvas cover served as a roof, and a hanging Mexican blanket served as a door. I instantly knew it was my home. "You are so kind."

He went back to his shaving.

"This is where I live," I told Wyatt and ducked inside.

I looked around the small space, at the dirt floor and the canvas ceiling where support branches crisscrossed at different angles. The hodgepodge of furnishings made the room feel claustrophobic. There was barely enough room to walk between the two uncomfortable-looking cots that lined one side of the shack and the wood table that sat in the middle of the room. My gaze was drawn to a trunk set in one corner. Excitement revved my pulse, but I didn't know why.

Wyatt had followed me in. "So you gonna tell me now, lady? Where's Abby?"

"My name is Abigail, but you may call me Lolita."

I couldn't believe I'd said that. And my voice came out all breathy and seductive. *What the..?* I had wanted to tell him I was Abby and to stop complaining.

"All right, whoever you are. Parading around in your underwear is drawing the kind of attention I don't need."

"It is not like they have never seen me in my undergarments before." Again, the words had flowed from my mouth, Lolita's words, smooth and sensual, annoying the hell out of me. I glanced around the shack for some dry clothing.

Dishes and cups set for three sat on a plank-topped table with three oddball crooked chairs around it. Cookware and leather bags of various sizes hung from long poles that served as the hut's upper frame. A hanging shelf held jars and cans, utensils, and a knife big enough to gut a deer.

"Well, apparently you love it."

I pivoted to Wyatt. "Love what?"

"The attention," he nearly shouted, his tone bitter. "And from the looks of this place, there doesn't appear to be many women around."

It figured that Wyatt would notice the lack of women. "Are you jealous of all those men crooning over me?" I breathed.

"No. I'm humiliated."

"Aw. Did I embarrass you?" I walked over to my wooden trunk and threw open the lid.

"They were making fun of me."

"Long johns would be the choice of swimwear these days, not what you are wearing."

"What are you talking about?"

I placed my index finger over my new pouty lips and tossed him a little kiss. "Personally, I like seeing your body."

His eyes bled shock. "You do?"

"No," I shouted. "I don't. I didn't say that."

"Yes you did."

"It wasn't me."

"Now's a good time for an explanation."

"Don't you get it? *She* said that."

"Who?"

"Let me think." How could I make him believe Lolita was in my head with me? I looked down at the open trunk of neatly folded clothing. I held up a long slinky gown. *Oh my god. This is too surreal.* The red dress of the legend. I fingered the silk, felt a chill as I held history in my hands. "We've gone back in time, Wyatt."

"Time travel? No way. I'm stuck in some kind of bad dream. But I don't know why."

Why? Breathe, Abby. Think. What am I doing here...in Lolita's skin? Am I here to learn the truth about the legend? Or

maybe change it?
I hugged the dress. "I think I was sent back here to change the past."
"Change the past? You can't do that."
"Why else would we be here?"
"It's a nightmare, I tell you." Wyatt stepped toward me, his brow furrowed.
I slapped his face.
He stopped and glared at me. "What did you do that for?"
"Still think you're dreaming?"
He rubbed his cheek.
Okay. I felt a little guilty, but I also felt a little satisfaction. "That's what you get for trying to drown me."
"I didn't drown you."
"You should have let go of my ankle."
"The current was dragging Abby down. I tried to save her, and now I find myself in this godforsaken place."
"I'm sure you're not supposed to be here. You're a mistake."
"Mistake? I'm a mistake?" Wyatt took a deep breath as if to corral his anger. "I'm nobody's mistake." He snatched the dress from my hands and threw it in the trunk. "Time travel is the mistake. You're talking like a nutcase."
Annoyed at him and frustrated with myself, I didn't have any answers that made sense. He had every right to think I was nuts. I couldn't argue, but I wouldn't let him deny the reality of our situation. I strode past him and pushed aside the Mexican blanket door. "Explain that." I pointed to the camp outside.
He looked out. "I can't." He huffed, claimed a chair, sat. "But if this is really 1852, and if you're really Lolita, you couldn't possibly know me."
"Wyatt Beaufort." I let go of the makeshift door. "You were all American at Penn State...two years in a row."
"Who told you about me?"
"Your friend John."
"You know him too?"
I stared into a somber, puzzled face. "I'm Abigail Stewart. We went to the same high school."
"No way. She's a redhead. I just met her."

"I may look different, but my father is Dr. Stewart, head of neurosurgery. He works at Mercy Hospital. You scored the winning goal for El Dorado High School's homecoming game, probably got you the scholarship to Penn State."

He put his face in his hands. "It's not possible." He shook his head.

I walked over to where he sat. "Look at me."

He looked up, his eyes glassy.

"Now I'm Abigail of the legend, the Weeping Woman. Lolita is my stage name."

"How..?"

"I can't explain it. Maybe it's because we share the same name, maybe because I've read everything I could find about her..." I shrugged. I couldn't tell him I'd seen her murdered children's spirits at the river. "I have this feeling I'm here because I cared."

Children's laughter erupted behind me. I spun around and saw them, a boy and a girl no older than five and nine, burst through the blanketed doorway. They stopped. Surprise widened their eyes. Dirty and scraggly, their black hair lay limp to their shoulders. Grass stains soiled Cattie's green dress, and Joseph wore dirty cutoff pants held up with suspenders, but no shirt. However, I knew they were the same kids I'd seen that day by the river, the spirits of the legendary Weeping Woman's children. My breath hitched. It took me a moment to realize the gravity of my situation. I was the only one here who knew they would both be murdered.

"Mamma."

Cattie's voice drew me from my thoughts. It was her voice I'd heard in my bedroom. I wasn't calling for my mother. The child was calling for her mother, the Weeping Woman. Now she was calling for me.

My heart was hammering. I gestured for them to come closer. Like two obedient, yet hesitant puppies, they obeyed but took the long way around the chair where Wyatt sat. I bent down and took their hands. "Hello, Cattie, Joseph. Where were you playing that got you so dirty?" I kept my voice light despite my thrashing heartbeat and roiling thoughts of salvation and doom.

Little Joseph nervously glanced at Wyatt sitting there barelegged and bare-chested in his wet swim trunks. He seemed especially intent on the gold watch Wyatt wore.

Wyatt held up his wrist to the boy. "You like it?"

Joseph said nothing.

"It's a Rolex. My dad bought it for me."

Joseph said nothing.

Cattie glanced at Wyatt then her blue eyes snapped back to me. "Who is he, Mamma?"

"His name is Mr. Wyatt."

"Where are his clothes?"

"And yes, he needs something to wear."

To my delight, a blush crept up Wyatt's cheeks. He didn't seem like such a big-shot now. I smiled. "Do either one of you know where Mr. Wyatt can get some clothing?"

"Yes, Mamma." Cattie's long black hair swayed behind her as she rushed to a small trunk behind the table, opened the lid, and pulled out a pair of brown pants. She skipped back and handed them to Wyatt. "They belong to my pa."

Wyatt's brows arched. "Thanks." He held up the pants for inspection. They looked ten sizes too big for him. He scowled at me. "You're married to this guy?"

My chest tightened. "He's gone." At least I hoped so.

Wyatt's narrow-eyed glare focused on my left hand. "Where's your wedding ring?"

"He took it with him. I never want it back."

As legend had it, Lolita's husband left town with his mistress. But if the story was true, at some point, they returned to get the kids. Was that when Lolita got rid of them? Or did the mistress get jealous and drown them? As long as he was gone, I figured the children were safe. But for how long?

"And I do not want him back either." That came out laced with anger.

Cattie glanced at Joseph, who was staring at the ground and shuffling his foot in the dirt. "Mamma didn't mean it, Joseph. Pa's coming back."

Wyatt waved the pants at me. "These won't fit me."

Lolita's husband was a huge man, probably weighed three-hundred pounds with that belly. How I knew that, I didn't know, but I cringed at the thought of having to lay with him. Another good reason for him to stay gone.

"They're too big," Wyatt whined.

"Do I have to dress you too?" Rummaging through the trunk, I found a checkered shirt, also too big for Wyatt, then pulled out a pair of cloth suspenders and calf-high miner's boots, size twelve. I handed the ensemble to him. "These will have to do for now...until you can buy something more suitable."

"Buy?" Frowning, he didn't move. "I don't have any money."

"Not my problem, rich boy." I pointed to the door. "Find someplace to get dressed."

"What's wrong with right here?"

"You can't dress in front of me."

"Of course he can," Lolita's sexy inner voice said to me.

"No, he can't. I mean...get out," I shouted.

"Where do you expect me to go? You got me into this mess, now you're kicking me out? No way." He dropped the clothing beside him. "I'm not going anywhere."

"You can't stay here," I insisted.

"But he's so muy guapo, gorgeous," Lolita's sweet voice said in my mind.

"That's not the point," I silently argued. *"He broke my heart."*

This was insane. I was arguing with the other woman in this body. I should get my head examined. "Get out, Wyatt. I want nothing to do with you." I pointed to the door.

"That is a lie," the sensual voice chimed in.

Wyatt's stubborn gaze locked on mine. "Well, that's too bad, 'cause I'm staying put." He folded his muscled arms across his chest.

"Let him take off his pants. I want to see what he has got."

"Yes. I mean no." The thought of seeing Wyatt naked shot heat to my face.

"Yes? No? What? You want me to undress right here, or not?" A smirk lifted the corner of his mouth.

"Leave." Again, I pointed to the doorway.

"What is wrong with you?" Lolita asked me. *"He is too good looking to throw him out."*

"I can't forgive him for what he did to me."

My temple began to throb.

"A body as caliente as his is worth forgiveness."

"Shut up. I don't care how hot he looks." I pressed my fingers into my temples in an attempt to quiet the voice inside my head.

"You have seen the men in this camp. This one is a prize."

"I don't like him...ah...I mean you," I blurted more harshly than I meant to.

Wyatt sprang from his seat. "I don't like you very much either, but I'm not going into camp with those old-timer rejects who think I'm from another planet until I figure out how I'm getting home. You're the only link I have to the Abby I know, so get used to my face 'cause I'm sticking around." He proceeded to slip his wet swim trunks down his hips.

I darted between him and my daughter. "Wyatt, the children."

"You better turn around if you don't want to see me butt naked."

The flutter between my legs caught me off guard. I turned so fast my head got dizzy. "Kids, let's go outside. He'll be dressed in a minute." I hoped.

My heart thrashing, I grabbed my red dress, ushered the children through the doorway, and let the blanket flap shut behind us.

What in heaven's name am I going to do with him?

"I know what I want to do with him," Lolita's soft voice offered.

"Keep your hands off, you tart."

Chapter Four

Wyatt believes

That Lolita woman was nuts. This whole situation was ridiculous. I didn't know if I should laugh or yell with frustration.

An intense headache pounded me. I massaged my scalp then the back of my neck. How could this have happened? Time travel, it was crazy. But then... I glanced around the rustic shack. Cramped, cluttered, and unsanitary. I couldn't imagine living in a place as filthy as this. Yet, here I sat, in some other man's clothing and boots. I felt ridiculous. I reached into my swim trunks pocket, pulled out the bottle of aspirin, and downed a pill.

The scene in the river played over and over in my mind. I saw Abby go under. I dove, but she was sinking fast. I managed to grab her ankle. Her eyes were shut; she appeared to be unconscious. I remembered struggling toward the surface but felt myself sinking with her. She'd said my hands had yanked her downward. I hadn't seen anyone else. Then I blacked out.

I glanced at the dirt floor then to the ceiling of interwoven branches, better suited for a pergola. What a hovel. I could only hope the canvas roof held back the rain, or it'd make a muddy mess in here.

I walked to the shack's doorway, drew the blanket aside, and stared out. The woman who tormented me stood in the road, talking to the children. She'd taken the red dress with her and slipped into it outside. A good six inches taller than the Abby I knew, her smoking hot body could rival any woman on any centerfold. Her glossy black hair fell to her waist, a waist I could span with my hands.

I shoved the blanket out of my way and stepped outside. I

had to find a way out of here. Perhaps the answer lay back at the river.

My feet flopped around in the big boots as I hobbled past Lolita, aka Abby, without a glance. She was the last person I wanted to talk to. Seemed she couldn't make up her mind about me. I stepped over a shovel and pickaxe, and my ankle twisted. I winced. Damn boots. Just my luck her absent husband didn't have smaller feet.

Three men sat on a plank of wood held up by two short upright logs. Their blue pants and high black boots were caked with a thick layer of dirt. Another man sat on a wooden barrel, smoking a pipe, while another read from a bible. Nearby, another group of men crouched around in a circle, playing a card game. The stench of body odor made me gag. I was used to sweaty teammates, but these guys hadn't showered in months.

One of the men shouted out, "Hey, Pike."

I walked past them.

"You, Pike. You deaf?"

I stopped and faced the group. "You talking to me?"

The big man with a gut like a barrel and a grungy beard straightened. "You sure dress like a Pike. Same snuffy brown pants and those suspenders." He whistled. "Them pants a little too big fer you, ain't they? Hey, fellas, what-da-ya think? He looks like a Pike, right?" He stepped closer and sniffed. "Sure smells like a Pike. Your feet a little sore? Walk here all the way from Missouri or Arkansas?" He poked my chest.

"You tell 'em, Hank," one of his crummy friends bellowed.

I had no idea what a Pike was, but if that guy poked me one more time... I balled my hand into a fist. *CIP,* I said silently, recalling my Sensei's teaching. *Courtesy. Integrity. Persevere.* I relaxed my breathing, gathered self-control.

"We don't like your kind here. Do we boys? Like you Pikes just about the same as those Greasers or Yellowbellies over yonder." He pointed to a section of the camp where a group of Mexicans and Chinese men were busy cleaning their picks and shovels.

His racist insults made me want to ram a fist down his throat. "I don't want any trouble." *Master circumstances instead of being mastered by them. Be the indomitable spirit,* my Sensei had drilled into my head. Right now, those words were hard to follow as I stared the big guy down. If he wanted a fight, I'd give him one. Besides, letting off a little steam would feel good right about now.

"You jest stay outta my way. I don't like no Pikes nosin' around my claims."

Shouts and a stampede of horses galloped full speed toward us. I backed up against a tree. My tormentor jumped out of the way as a group of drunken men rode by, whooping and swinging their hats in the air. Their horses kicked up swirls of dirt as they charged away. I rubbed dust from my eyes and brushed dirt from my pants.

The moron belched then stalked back to his friends who gathered up the tumbled cards.

"Jerk," I mumbled as I walked away. Guys like him pissed me off. Small-minded, prejudiced idiot. I'd like to teach him a lesson or two.

Slowly, I trudged to the river. A thin old man knelt in front of a small wood cradle filled with dirt. His stringy hair looked like it hadn't been washed in months. While he shook and rocked the cradle, his partner filled it with water from the river. I stepped sideways to avoid a gush of mud flowing out onto the ground. "What are you guys doing?"

Bloodshot eyes glanced up at me. "You really are new to these here parts, ain't ya?"

"Yeah." I shrugged. "But I've seen pictures of gold miners."

"Placer mining, boy. We's a look'n fer gold."

I peered closer, staring down into the cradle of rock, mud, and water. "Did you find any?"

Silent, he rubbed his fingers through his dirty gray beard then glanced at his partner. They could be twins if fashion counted. "Well, Judd, what d'ya think? We a bust or not?"

"Too soon to tell." Judd dumped another bucket of water onto the dirt.

I thrust out my open hand. "Name's Wyatt."

A bit taken aback when neither of them accepted my offered handshake, I lowered my arm. "How long have you guys been at this?"

Judd squinted at me then scratched his hairy jaw. "Can't rightly say, maybe two months. My cousin Ed here, well, he's been here a month longer than me."

"You see anyone unusual around here lately?"

Judd snorted. "Seen you in them short colored drawers. Ain't never seen nothing like that before."

"Did you see a redhead, about, oh..." I raised my hand to my neck. "This high? She'd be wearing a black—"

Both men shook their heads.

"Okay, well, thanks anyway." My emotions at war, I glanced around. Abby never made it out of the river, not in *her* body, anyway. The woman from my time was now the woman from this time. Shit. My time. This time. I was losing it.

I walked blindly past outhouse shacks, through trenches hollowed out from solid ground, and hordes of men swinging picks and shovels. My thoughts in limbo, I wasn't aware of a person behind me until a horse whinnied.

I pivoted, ready to fight, but what I saw nearly knocked my boots off. Raven-haired Lolita sat on a tall black stallion. Her red dress fanned down to a black boot in the stirrup. A light breeze flapped the red cloak draped from her shoulders. I blinked and relaxed my defensive stance. "What are you doing on a horse?"

"Cars haven't been invented yet." She slid off the saddle and damn near fell when she reached the uneven ground.

If I hadn't caught her, she would've busted her tailbone. Close like this, her long black hair smelled good enough to get lost in.

The horse snorted.

She abruptly pushed me away. "Why did you come back to the river?"

"I'm looking for a way out of this...hellhole."

"Good luck."

I sighed. "I'm really here, in 1852, aren't I?"

"And I'm really Abigail Stewart." She waved a hand down the front of her dress. "Inside this woman."

I smiled. "You made a good choice."

"Look around." Abigail gestured with a sweep of her hand. A weather-beaten old man walked past us. A pickaxe rested on his shoulder, and a trail of stench followed in his wake. He joined up with others just like him, and they shuffled into the smoky camp.

"This is what we've got to live with."

I huffed. "Is there any way back?"

"I don't know." She glanced at the river. "I wonder what Cindi is doing."

"Okay, I get it. You're really Abigail Stewart. But what about your real body? Is the other you lying unconscious somewhere back in our time?"

"I think I drowned."

"What happened to me?"

"I don't know. Maybe you're driving around in your new Ferrari, chasing blondes, you know, you being you."

"Time travel and body switching. I'm losing my God damn mind. Why did you come here as somebody else...and I'm still me being me?"

"I haven't figured out your role in all this."

"Role? This is insane." My head pounding, I cupped my face and rubbed my forehead. The sound of clanking metal and men's voices bothered me. "So, if I'm a mistake, as you so nicely put it, I shouldn't be here. This is all on you."

"Me?" Abby slammed her hand on her hip. Her beautiful face contorted with rage. "Oh, that's a gem. I'll just wave my magic wand and send us home." She waved her hand in the air. "Whoops. Nothing happened. Better yet..." She lifted the red dress and clicked her black boot-heels together. "There's no place like home." She closed her eyes then opened them in a flash. "Are we home yet?" Her voice dripped with sarcasm.

"Very funny. What am I supposed to do while you're off playing mommy? I don't belong here...wherever *here* is. I have no credit cards, no decent clothes."

"I don't care what you do. Make the best of it, Wyatt. Get a gold mining pan. Get dirty. See what you can accomplish without your *daddy's* help and a football." She turned away.

I grabbed her arm before she could walk off. "Where are you going?"

"I'm heading into town. Lolita has a job at the saloon."

"So why come out here looking for me?"

She glanced at the ground then tossed back her head. Locks of rich raven hair swung across her face. "I wanted you to go into town with me."

"So you do care?"

"I don't."

"Sure I do," her sexy voice said, and she slapped a hand over her mouth.

"So you *are* attracted to me."

"I'm not—"

"But you just said—"

"It wasn't me."

"You like me. I knew it."

She folded her arms across her chest. "Don't make me barf."

I smiled.

"Don't look so smug."

I had to laugh. My new Abigail had spunk. I liked it.

Abby doesn't care

I stuck my nose in the air and turned back to the massive stallion, hoping for a fast getaway. Problem was, I'd needed the liveryman's help to get on this horse. Now I wasn't about to ask Wyatt. I stood at the stirrup and looked back at him gawking at my backside.

This situation was so surreal. As much as I wasn't freaked out, logic dictated I should have been freaked to the max. How did we go back in time? How would we get back home? In my gut, I knew I was here for the children, but would saving them be enough to send us back to the future? Seeing ghosts was one thing, being dragged through some wormhole...with him...was another. What had I done to deserve this fate?

Wyatt crossed his arms in front of his chest. "Why should I go to town with you? You don't even like me."

"If we want to get out of here, we have to stick together, so let's start in town. Come on."

"There's no way I'm getting up on that horse," he said, his jaw tight with stubbornness.

What a wimp, and I thought he was such a tough guy: the man who had everything, who never stepped in dirt, and got things handed to him on a silver platter. The hero of the team. Right. Can't imagine what I ever saw in him in the first place. "Fine. You can walk." I managed to get my foot in the stirrup, but the horse shifted sideways. I lost my footing and nearly fell on my ass. When he caught me, my heart threatened to leap from my chest.

Wyatt laughed. "Do you know what you're doing?"

"How hard can it be? Lolita got me this far." My knees shook, but the need to prove to him I could do this on my own gave me a boost of courage. I grabbed the saddle rim and tried to hoist myself up, but my cloak slipped off my shoulders. Wyatt caught it, wrapped it around me, and tied the neck strings securely. The intimacy of his nearness, which seemed to linger a little too long, and the heat of desire that seared through me, hitched my breath and sprinted my pulse.

He released me. "Have at it." Then he stepped back.

"This isn't as easy as it looks," I mumbled, flustered, then eyed the beast who stood patiently before me. Next time I'd have the liveryman give me a small mare. I stabbed my foot in the stirrup and took a deep breath. Once again, I grappled with the saddle but failed to mount my steed. Maybe if I held onto the mane for support... As I reached for the mane the horse shook his head, startling me. I jerked back and, with a squeal, fell backwards, right into Wyatt's strong arms again.

"How am I doing?" Lolita's soft voice cooed in my head. *"I just love being in his arms."*

"It's all your fault?" I shouted.

"M-my fault?" Wyatt spat.

"Not you. Her."

"Oh, for God's sake, here." His hands grasped my waist. I stiffened, my heart pounding. His warm breath kissed the back of my neck just before he gave me a boost up. A sensual current rushed through me, warming every sensitive spot in my body. I swung my leg over the saddle, none too ladylike in a long dress. My pounding pulse and the tingling sensation in my stomach had to have come from Lolita's desires, not mine. *I'm just afraid of falling off, nothing more.*

"You are wrong," Lolita breathed in my mind. *"You want him as much as I do."*

"I'm afraid of heights, that's all."

"You are afraid of him."

"Shut up."

I couldn't, no I would not allow myself to feel anything other than repulsion for the man standing there, ogling my leg.

I clutched the pommel with one hand and wiped my sweaty brow with my other sleeve, and then flattened my dress over my thighs. I should be sitting sidesaddle, as proper women of this era rode, but I was too afraid I'd slide off. As I grabbed the reins, the horse shifted.

"Slide forward and move your foot. I'm coming up."

I inhaled sharply as my two-handed grip on the reins tightened.

Wyatt jammed his foot into the stirrup.

"No. Don't. You're going to make me fall."

He pulled himself up and settled in behind me. Hard muscles pressed against my back. He reached his arms around me and grabbed the reins. "I hope I remember how to steer one of these beasts."

Focused on the feel of his thighs against mine and the thought that his body was tucked tight against my buttocks, I flinched at the sound of Wyatt's voice so close to my ear. I leaned as far forward from his body as I could. Gripping the pommel with both hands for support, I suddenly tapped my heels into the horse's sides. The animal took off with a start, throwing me back against Wyatt's chest.

I didn't do that. Lolita did.

I heard her *moan* with pleasure.

"This could prove to be interesting." His warm breath tickled the tiny hairs at the nape of my neck.

I tried to lean sideways, but his strong arms held me solidly upright in the saddle. Once again, I was rocked against him as the horse trotted over the rough, rocky ground. Unfamiliar sensations heated my insides...thanks to Lolita, I was sure.

"Not as smooth a ride as my Ferrari." His low, sensuous voice sent my heart racing down the hill faster than the stallion we rode. "But this is much more enjoyable, wouldn't you say?"

His thighs fit snugly against mine, hard chest muscles pressed into my back, and I could swear I felt a bulge against my tailbone. Uncomfortably aware of his enjoyment, my face heated. I managed to find my voice. "Do-do you have to hold me so tightly?"

"You don't want to fall off, do you?"

The ground rushed past us. With every nerve in my body on fire, I closed my eyes and melted into his protective embrace. I imagined Wyatt gloating. I knew if I turned around, I'd see smug triumph on his face. Not giving him the satisfaction, I wrenched myself out of my sensual stupor and stared straight ahead.

I heard Lolita's titillating *laughter*. She was enjoying my torture, but deep down, I was happy to be with him.

By the time we arrived, my back and rear felt black and blue, and my nerves felt just as bruised. Wyatt dismounted, took the reins and tied the horse to a hitching post.

I eyed the ground and clung to the pummel for dear life. The last thing I wanted was to end up on my ass in front of the entire town.

"Let me help you." He offered up his hands.

I shook my head, afraid of falling into his arms again.

"Okay, fine. Stay up there all day." He pivoted.

"Okay. Okay."

He coaxed the horse closer to the boardwalk, stepped up, and took hold of my waist with his strong hands.

My breath held. My pulse did not; it raced like the roaring river. Did Wyatt sense the effect he had on me? I glanced away from eyes that could easily hold me captive. When the impatient horse shifted beneath me, I gulped and felt like I'd left my stomach back at camp.

"Don't fight me on this," Wyatt said as his grip tightened. "Relax."

"Easier said than done. You should try getting off this saddle while wearing a long gown."

"That could be remedied." He grinned, a quirky challenging smile.

The heated light in those baby blues sent unexpected yummy sensations to my stomach. "Just get me off this thing." I placed my hands on his shoulders.

"I can't guarantee I won't drop you."

"Gee, thanks." I hoped he was joking, breathed deeply, and leaned into him.

He lifted me a little too slowly and held me a little too close to his body. I felt his corded muscles bunch, didn't know if he felt the heat sparking, but if our auras were dipped in fluorescent paint, mine would have been glowing red hot. My breath held as his strong arms encircled my waist. Desire charged the air, and his close proximity stirred intimate feelings deep within me. His breath tickled my ear. My throat went dry. I couldn't form a coherent thought. The feel of the ground at my feet broke my trance. I exhaled then smoothed my dress.

I heard Lolita *giggle. "Was it as good for you as it was for me?"*

"My racing heart has nothing to do with Wyatt. Nothing at all. "

"Yes it does."

I was trapped in the body of a crazy woman. I took a shuddering breath. My ass felt like I'd been kicked and my thighs ached. "Thanks, Wyatt."

He tipped an invisible cowboy hat. "Welcome, ma'am."

On wobbly legs that felt like they would buckle, I glanced around a town alive with crowds of men kicking up dust as they walked down the main thoroughfare. On either side of the street, tables were set with wines and sweet cakes. Dried fruits and steaming hot meat pies made my mouth water. A group of men, one who wore a sombrero, sat on a multicolored blanket. Silver coins glistened in the sunlight. The rambunctious group played a game where they tossed money and gold nuggets into the center of the quilt. The tinny sound of a piano, the thrum of guitars, and the whine of fiddles mingled with the metallic twang of a banjo.

"Oh my god, Wyatt, this is amazing. It's so cool to be here, to see this, to witness history."

"I feel like I'm in an old western movie." He hooked his thumbs under his suspenders. "Think I'll mosey on down to the saloon."

"That's where I work." My heart jolted. I sang in a saloon. Men adored me. Sudden anxiety killed my enthusiasm. What if I couldn't sing like Lolita? What if the men wanted more from me than a song? I couldn't be one of those loose strumpets I'd read about. What had I gotten myself into?

"You-you're a saloon girl?" His lips pressed into a narrow hard line as if he disapproved.

"I'm not one of those *painted women* who sits on gamblers' laps and laughs at their stupid jokes." I fanned my clammy cheeks. "Lolita is a star, a singer, and all the men love her."

"This I've gotta see."

"Just wait. You will—"

"Excuse me, folks." A tall man with a dripping mustache stepped up to us. He wore a narrow-brimmed, dome-topped hat, a long brown overcoat, white vest and black pants, a rather dapper old-timer. "Sir. I have something here I think would interest you." He opened a satchel strapped to his shoulder. "Take a look at this splendid pair of brand-new boots." He held them out for Wyatt's inspection. "Cowhide, double soled, triple pegged, and waterproof. Your boots look a mite big for you. These are more your size, sir, and made just for you mud-splashers."

Wyatt's brow crinkled. "Mud-splashers?"

A pensive shade of uneasiness shadowed the stranger's eyes. "Didn't mean no offense, sir, but the way you're dressed..." He gestured to Wyatt's baggy attire. "I thought you were panning. Most men around here are panning, except me. Too much work for my likin'. Here. Take a closer look at the quality." He shoved the boots at Wyatt. "What do you think?"

"Sorry, mister." Wyatt stepped in front of me, blocking my view of the stranger. "I have no money."

I wanted to ask Wyatt how it felt having been the rich brat in town and now having nothing. Even though my father made good money, I never had a nice car or designer clothes. I never got things handed to me.

Wyatt turned around. "Abby—"

"Don't look at me. I'm not buying boots for you."

"But you've got a job."

"Get your own job." I sounded cold-hearted, but a heaviness settled in my chest as painful memories of what happened between us in high school pushed to the forefront of my mind. The fact he had no recollection of that night fueled my annoyance even further. My blood pressure rose as stormy blue eyes glared at me with disdain, but I didn't care. He was on his own. As I stepped away, he grabbed my elbow and stopped me. I scowled at his intrusive hand. Sunlight glinted off his Rolex. "Let go of me."

"Where am I going to get a job?"

"Pan for gold like everyone else. There's a river full of it out there. A little hard work might do you some good."

"You can't be serious."

I yanked my elbow from his grip. "I don't care what you do." I didn't mean to sound so bitter, but I had problems of my own. The thought of walking into the saloon made me want to retch. I had no idea what song to sing. "I'm going to work." I nodded goodbye to the stranger, picked up the hem of my skirt, and started walking down the boardwalk toward the old-time piano music.

"You'll see," Wyatt yelled. "When I strike it rich, I won't give you a penny."

"I don't want your money." I hurried my steps.

"Not one penny," he screamed after me. "Do you hear me?"

Oh, I heard him all right, the rich spoiled brat. As far as I was concerned, he could bury himself in gold. At least he'd have to earn it.

Wyatt and the Mexican boy

"Panning for gold. How hard can it be?" I mumbled as I turned to the salesmen. "How much for the boots?" I'd find myself a ton of gold. *That'll show her.*

"For you? Five ounces and a half. Just come up to my hotel room and we'll weigh out your dust."

"Sounds like a bargain." Of course, I had no clue if that was true. "You save those boots for me." I patted the stranger's shoulder. "I'll be back for them."

"Don't take too long," the salesmen called out as I walked

away. "Price goes up after dark."

Damn Abby. Why'd she have to be so stingy? The back of my heels hurt from rubbing against the worn-out leather of the loose boots that didn't belong to me. My oversized pants kept slipping; I tugged them up only to feel a draft waft down my waist. And damn Lolita, too. One minute I felt like she was into me, the next she was giving me the cold shoulder like Abby always did. I kicked a stone and sent it hurtling across the dirt street. Talk about weird. While I wore another man's clothing, Abby wore another woman's skin. I pressed my thumb into my temple. *Insane. This whole situation is insane.*

Not sure where to go, I glanced around. Simple wooden buildings, including a log cabin, and hastily built structures that a child could have nailed together, lined the street. An oak tree, with a thick chain around it, stood in front of a building where a crooked sign read: *Jail.*

There were men everywhere, but very few women. The population hailed from every corner of the world. I heard Chinese, Spanish, French, and Irish, a British accent, a Southerner, and a defiant New York accent. Every man carried a gun buckled at his waist or slung over his shoulder with no attempt at concealment.

Across the street, a store sign read: *Groceries, Provisions, Mining Tools.* Thinking that would be a good place to start, I stepped off the wooden walkway, and immediately, my boot squished into a glob of horse puckey. "Great. Just great." I lifted my foot from the foul slop and shook off chunks of brown crap and undigested grass.

Pissed, I hobbled toward the store, stepped up the uneven wooden-plank steps, and walked inside.

A clerk stood behind a long counter. His brown mustache looked like handles one tossed rings on at a carnival, and it was so heavily waxed it could have been used to buff a surfboard. He showed me a genuine smile. "Howdy."

I nodded back.

Shelves lined with bottles, cans, dried goods, and carefully folded clothing were neatly stocked. A beam of light filtered onto the dusty wooden floor from the only window. The room was badly in need of some paint and smelled dank. A clock ticked from a back wall.

"Seems like this is the place I need," I remarked casually, though my nerves felt like they were about to fry. I wanted to blink and wake up lounging in my backyard pool. "Thought I'd try my hand at gold mining." What choice did I have? Who knew how long I'd be stuck here? Abigail, aka Lolita/Abby, had made it clear I'd get no financial help from her. Just thinking about those two women made my head hurt. I selected a shovel then stepped up to the counter. "How much for the shovel?"

"Eleven dollars."

"Sounds fair. Problem is...I'm broke at the moment." Damn, I never thought those words would come out of my mouth. "How does a guy go about getting credit around here?"

The owner studied me for a moment then put the shovel behind the counter. "Guess you'll be diggin' by hand 'til ya come up with fifty bucks."

"You said eleven."

"Gotta have more than just a shovel if'n you're gonna try your hand at gold diggin'."

I shook my head, wrung my clammy palms together. Not having a dollar in my pocket, let alone fifty, made me feel like a loser. Then I got an idea and took off my Rolex. "Will this do for collateral?" My gut knotted with unaccustomed anxiety. If he turned me down, then what?

The clerk eyed my offering with skepticism then rubbed his chin thoughtfully. "I never heard a no Rolex."

"European. Very expensive."

"Sure is perrtty. I reckon I'll take your word fer it. Fifty dollars."

"That's all?"

He waved his hand around the store. "It'll buy what ya need." He set the shovel back on the counter. "Pay me in thirty days. I'll hold this here piece 'til then."

"Thanks." I picked up an ax and a wooden bucket and grabbed an apple from a crate on the counter. "Can I get some clothes that fit?"

"Yeah. Those ain't exactly proper wear for a fleecer. Here." The clerk set out a blue wool shirt, flannel long-johns, a wide-brimmed felt hat, black, and a pair of blue canvas pants.

"Kentucky's best, last pair in your size."

"I need some boots, too."

He stepped to a shelf of footwear, grabbed a pair of brown boots, and set them on the counter. "Size ten, right?"

"How much?"

"Ten dollars."

"How much is that in gold dust?"

"'Bout half an ounce."

That crook. I glanced out the window for the salesmen I'd met earlier. Scammers here were no different from scammers back home. "I'll take the boots. How about one of those wooden boxes? I saw some guys down by the river using one."

"A rocker?"

"You got one?"

"All out. Would-a cost you two dollars. Or you could build one."

"You got the wood?"

"Plum out. All you need to start is the pick, shovel, and this here pan." He reached under the counter and pulled out a dented twelve-inch tin pan. "On the house."

"Really?"

"Got it from a fella who gave up and headed fer home. Happens a lot around here."

Headed for home, like I have a choice.

"If'n you're lucky, you'll be needing this too." The shopkeeper placed a pickle jar on the counter. "Just need to add water so the gold dust don't stick."

"Wrap it all up." I grabbed the boots and the shirt. "Except these. I'm going to get a drink. Be back in a while for my stuff. You take good care of my watch."

Outside, I sat on the boardwalk fronting the store, removed the baggy shirt, and slipped into my new one. Then I pulled off the boots.

Men strolled by without giving me notice. Horses clopped down the street, kicking up clumps of dirt as they passed. The sound of raucous voices mingled with the tinny music from the saloon. Occasional laughter floated through the air. I stretched my legs, wiggled my toes, wished I had socks, and held up a new boot. *Ten dollars.* What a bargain for leather. Maybe hanging in the *good old days* for a short time wouldn't be so bad after all.

I was about to take a bite out of my apple when a scrawny looking kid wearing ragged clothing came out of nowhere. Toes protruded from his dusty, weather-beaten shoes. He stared at the apple.

"You hungry?"

"No hablo ingles." The kid, I guessed to be in his teens, raised his guarded dark eyes and scanned the area as if searching for someone then took a hesitant step forward. His clothes hung on his thin frame like a big suit on a scarecrow. He reminded me of me when I was a skinny kid. His mahogany-colored skin shined with sweat. Dark hair lay against his forehead as he studied me silently, hesitant, as if unsure of my intention.

I held out the apple to him. "Aquí. Here. Take it."

He bolted to me, grabbed the apple, bowed, then scurried away.

"Kid, wait. Dejar."

He stopped and faced me.

I couldn't see throwing out Lolita's husband's clothes. Her kids would probably want them back. I spoke to the boy in Spanish. "If you take these old boots and that shirt back to camp and leave them at Lolita's place, I'll buy you a new pair of shoes."

The boy got all bright-eyed and nodded. "Lolita, si."

"Un momento." I stood and headed back into the store.

The clerk glanced down at my bare feet as I walked in. "Them boots too small?"

"Gonna fit just fine. Do I have any credit left?"

"Depends."

"Enough for a pair of kid's shoes?" I pointed to the shelf of footwear.

"I reckon I can extend ya another five."

"Good." I grabbed a pair I hoped would fit the kid and left the store.

The boy tossed the apple core as I walked out.

"We got a deal, right?"

"Si."

I handed him the shoes.

A big grin lit his face. "Gracias, señor."

"You're welcome."

He scooped up the shirt and old boots and hurried away.

Mom would be proud. I slid a new boot over my left foot. Always give to those less fortunate, she'd say. Charity should be spread around like potting soil. *It's my Christian duty.* And everyone thought I was just a spoiled rich kid.

Abby goes to work

I stepped up to the swinging doors of the Boomerang Gambling Hall and Saloon then stopped to get up the nerve to go inside. I couldn't sing. The jitters in my stomach intensified. By all the boisterous noise coming from the men inside, I knew my audience was drunk. Maybe they wouldn't notice...wouldn't care that I couldn't carry a tune to save my life.

Footsteps on the boardwalk drew my attention to a group of women passing by, all dressed as if going to church, noses upturned to the likes of me. And men passed by, as well, venturing a wink and a leer in my direction.

Another worry struck me. Half-clad women inside the saloon would be passing around drinks, sitting on men's laps, or leading them upstairs for a bawdier form of entertainment. Saloon girls dealt with roaming hands, crude jokes, and God knew what else. I wondered if Lolita had stooped so low in order to survive, which earned her a bad rap with the townsfolk. I wanted to turn around and run away, but I had to see this charade through. The children depended on my actions, good, bad, or whatever they might be in the end.

Charged with determination, I placed my hands on the double doors, threw my shoulders back, and pushed my way inside.

The strong odor of eye-burning cigar smoke and unwashed bodies assaulted my senses, made my eyes tear up as I strode past tables crowded with rowdy men. A woman's shriek pierced the air, followed by hardy bass laughter. I watched a buxom woman remove herself from a man's embrace, crook her finger under his chin, and coax him toward the stairs.

I took a deep breath. *Be calm. You can do this.*

"No you cannot." Lolita *laughed* inside my head.

"Shut up." I hastily glanced around. The barroom was sparsely decorated: gaudy Carlton wallpaper, oil sconces, wood floor, spittoons scattered about. Cards, coins, and gold-dust pouches lay on wooden tables, some covered with green cloth. Gamblers sat on wood chairs, their guns and booze bottles in front of them. Some smoked. Some spit in spittoons. Some fondled saloon girls. Other women busied themselves serving drinks and fanning patrons. Heavy gold drapes lay against the back wall. In the center of the room, under a glistening chandelier, sat a raised wooden platform.

"That is my place," Lolita whispered to me.

"The stage." Three steps above these ruffians and prostitutes, at least I wouldn't be singing down here on the floor in the midst of all the commotion and groping hands. "Hopefully," I muttered, "with all the noise and activity, no one will hear me sing anyway."

"Oh, they are going to hear us just fine."

My throat tightened. I sashayed up to the rustic bar, not that I wanted to walk with such confidence. Lolita made me do it.

The bartender looked at me as if I were a bother.

"You seen Monty around here?" I knew the name from somewhere in the back of my mind but wasn't sure why Lolita needed to see him.

The bartender glanced across the room. "He's over there." He pointed to a table where an elegantly dressed man stood watching over a card game. His slicked-back hair, black as the three-piece suit he wore, shined like it was well greased, and his long face sported a thin mustache. He stood with self-confidence, thumbs stuck behind his belt, broad shoulders thrust back. My better judgment told me he was bad news.

"Thanks, Joe." I stood in awe of knowing the bartender's name until Lolita coaxed me to move toward Monty. I strode through the crowd, my ass swaying with each step.

"Stop it," I told Lolita.

"Look how the men enjoy the show."

I suddenly realized I'd wished for this very response from men. But Cindi had warned me...

At Monty's side, I grasped his arm. "Sorry I'm late."

"Lolita, my love, I was wondering when you were going to get here." He tapped his pocket watch. "I should be angry...but what does it matter? I could never be mad at you. You look great." He took my hand and kissed it lightly. "Benjamin has your music ready." He tipped his head to the piano player sitting on the bench in front of the keyboard, his fingers plinking out a lively tune.

I stared at him. *The piano player, suspect number one.*

"Suspect? How you mean?" Lolita asked.

I couldn't tell her that her kids were going to be murdered and that she'd go down in history as the killer. Now wouldn't that ruin her day? So I said nothing as I watched Benjamin play the old upright piano.

He was not exceptional but pleasant looking. Smooth olive skin, high cheekbones: his nose was hooked slightly. He'd parted his wavy hair in the middle, exposing a broad brow. Something about him looked familiar, but I couldn't place where I'd seen him.

According to the legend, Benjamin left town soon after the murders. My feet felt glued to the floor. My heart fluttered with the angst of actually seeing my murder suspect.

"Go." Monty gave me a light push. "The men are bored, and your lovely voice is the perfect excitement they need, not to mention my pockets could use my cut of your tips. Quite a few men have hit pay dirt lately. Let's see how much gold you can get from them."

I headed toward the piano.

"And, Lolita."

I stopped, my knees trembling. "Yes?"

"First, go backstage and change into the nice green dress I bought for you."

"What's wrong with this one?" I opened the red cloak to show him the full cleavage of my red dress.

"It's full of black horse hairs."

"Oh. Of course." I'd forgotten Wyatt and I had rode in on a horse. Quickly, I closed the cloak and scurried behind the gold curtain where I knew I'd find the back dressing room. A rack of gowns, each one gaudier than the next, had my name on it, all in my size. Another rack of clothes had the name *Daisy* on it. I wondered if I'd have competition on that stage.

With jittery fingers, I undressed, and as I pulled the green dress from the hanger, the rack teetered and nearly fell over. Finally redressed in green, I took a deep breath and looked down at my boldly revealed cleavage. *Wow.* I skimmed my hands down my slender drop-dead figure and admired the way the fabric clung to every curve. I'd damn near killed myself to lose twenty-five pounds when all it took was a trip back in time to give me the perfect body. Cindi would love the new me.

Benjamin started another tinkly piano tune, which jerked me from my self-adoration.

What am I going to do? I can't sing.

"Sure you can," Lolita said.

"They're going to die laughing," I muttered.

"You'll do fine, Sugar."

I turned to see a heavily made-up blonde, with daisies in her hair, had just walked in.

"You'll knock 'em dead, as usual."

"Thanks."

"Daisy," a loud voice bellowed. "Thar ain't a drop of drink in this here cup."

"Oh, don't get your whiskers in a twist. I'm coming."

She rushed out in flurry of petticoat lace.

Gathering my composure, I headed for the stage.

Three steps up, despite Lolita's reassurance, I felt like I was climbing the stairs to the gallows. The thought of all those men staring at me made shivers skitter up my spine. I should have been petrified, but I was too excited. My pounding heart echoed in my ears.

The piano music changed to a familiar intro. My brain went on overload as it sorted through the tune. Benjamin stared at me as if baffled, stopped playing. I realized I should have started singing. Again, he played the intro.

I gulped in air. My breasts practically spilled from my low-cut bodice. I tried not to stare at the men gathered around below me, but the excitement in their eyes was addictive. Feelings inside me blossomed into song. I threw back my shoulders and flung back my hair as the words to *Camptown Races* flowed from my lips.

"Camptown ladies sing this song. Do da, Do da..."

Startled by my rich, sultry alto voice, I was barely able to control my impulse to gasp. From all across the smoky room, everyone's eyes focused on me, on the stage, singing my heart out. Men began to slap their thighs and stomp their feet as lyrics fluttered from my songbird throat. The rich strains of Lolita's voice filled me, pushing away all doubts, all anxiety. I, like every man and woman in the barroom, was caught up in the melody. My feet were heel-toeing as if they had a mind of their own.

"Somebody bet on the bay," I sang.

When the song ended, a roar of approval erupted. Shouts and whistles mingled with the clinking of coins thrown onto the stage. I bowed, and a new, unexpected tingle of excitement surged through me. At my feet, pouches of gold dust joined the coins on the stage floor. A gold nugget the size of an almond bounced into the pile. They loved me.

The piano music changed to *Oh Susanna*. My light voice and the thrill of acceptance and admiration heightened my confidence. My spirit soared. "Oh, Susanna, oh, don't you cry for me, I've come from Alabama wid my banjo on my knee."

I pranced back and forth on the stage, fanning my dress and gesturing come hither with my hands to encourage the men to join in. Their voices blended and clashed with mine, but that didn't matter. We were having fun. "I had a dream the other night when everything was still; I thought I saw Susana a-coming down de hill."

Again, as the wonderful rendition of the song flew from my mouth, a thought entertained me. Lolita's talent had once again taken over. A flirtatious laugh erupted from my lips.

I caught a reflection of myself in the gilded mirror hanging over the back-bar. The sight nearly burst my heart with pride. I was the very picture of the Weeping Woman, straight out of the history books. A true Spanish beauty. Lord, now I was more beautiful than I'd first realized. I was more beautiful than Cindi and all those bouncy cheerleaders I'd envied for so long. I was perfect. True happiness must have gleamed from my eyes.

Cindi Weaver, eat your heart out.

My gaze traversed the singing, cheering crowd. I was looking for Wyatt, hoping he was here to witness this wonderful moment in my life. My heartbeat surged as I glanced at the men who stood looking up at me. They were enamored. They were smitten, but Wyatt was nowhere in sight. Suddenly I wanted to kick myself. What did I care if he hadn't been here to see me perform? After what I'd said to him earlier, he probably wouldn't even look at me. So what if I was the only person in the entire town he knew. Truth be told, he was the only person I knew in this century.

"I come from Alabama with my banjo on my knee."

The song ended. Benjamin stood and bowed to the raving crowd. More coins and gold nuggets flew to the stage. I bent down and began scooping them up then tossed them in a pouch I made with my dress. After I picked up the last of the gold, I sauntered down the steps and past the hoard of adoring men.

"Sakes alive, Lolita, you was great."

"Voice of an angel she has," Benjamin said.

I smiled, beaming at their praise.

Hoots followed me as I walked toward the piano. I couldn't deny the feelings of euphoria surging through me. It felt good to be hooted at and stared at for all the right reasons. For the first time in my life, I felt pretty. *And I'd just sang on stage.*

"I sang, not you, Abby," Lolita's voice insisted in the back of my mind.

"Don't rain on my parade, you witch."

"Now, now, be nice, Abby. You have only borrowed my body, my voice. I can take them back any time I want."

I squared my shoulders and threw back my head. *"What's stopping you?"*

"Well, your boyfriend, of course."

"Wyatt? He's not my boyfriend."

"Then he is fair game?"

"You can have him."

I didn't care if I wasn't me, right now. I felt ecstatic, alive. Wyatt was just an unfortunate mistake. He didn't care about me, just himself. Now I was the center of attention, and I was going to savor every minute.

Wyatt and the dead man

Piano music and a woman's sassy singing voice drifted from the saloon. Men were cheering with the enthusiasm of college football fans on Saturday afternoon. *"Oh Susanna, don't you cry for me."* Yeah. Lolita was pretty good.

I started to slip into the other boot, but before I could pull it all the way on, a blast of gunfire shattered the air. I lurched forward and dove to the street, damn near knocking the breath from my lungs. My neck crunched, and my face ate dirt. The boot had flown from my hand. *What's going on?*

A second shot pierced the air. A moan. A thump. Hands over my head, I waited for another round to go off. I felt no pain so I probably wasn't shot, but I lay frozen anyway, my heart pounding. I wanted to get up and run, but I was too afraid I'd be the next one to catch a bullet.

After an eternity, a murmur rose from the silenced crowd, and I realized the firing was over. Slowly, I raised onto my forearms and stared into the eyes of a downed cowboy. Blood stained his chest and flowed to the dirt in the street. A queasy feeling welled in the pit of my stomach. I would have vomited if not for the knot in my throat, formed from a single thought: a man could be shot dead as quickly as the snap of a finger, anytime, anywhere, and without prior notice.

I was glad it wasn't me who lay there bleeding in the street. Beads of sweat speckled his brow. His fingers curled into a fist.

He's not dead? I pushed to my knees and knelt at the man's side. My mind reeling, I recalled what I'd learned from my EMT trauma training. I yanked his shirt from his pants and ripped it open, scattering buttons to get a better view of his wound.

The man gripped my arm and raised himself up. "Damn varmint," he wheezed.

"Lie still." I eased him back to the ground then pressed his shirt on his spurting wound, hopefully to stop the flow of blood from a hole the size of a quarter near his heart. Survival didn't look promising.

The man grabbed my shirt with a bloody hand. His fist

shook. "He stole...my claim. Blast that cursed son-of-a—" The man's breathless voice cut off.

I glanced around at the gathering crowd. "I need help." I couldn't say, call 9-1-1. However, all the activity around me resumed to normal as if a man lying shot in the street was an everyday occurrence.

My heart thumped madly as I pressed my palms into his chest in an attempt to perform CPR. A clammy chill invaded my forehead. I wanted to be a doctor, but this guy needed a real doctor.

"Someone help me get this man to a doctor." My voice sounded strangled as I kept up chest compressions.

"What you doin' to him, boy?" a gruff voice said above me.

"Trying to save his life." I stopped CPR and placed my bloody fingers on the man's neck to feel for a pulse.

Nothing.

A boot-toe nudged the man's limp leg. "He don't need no doctor."

I looked up and saw a tall man, weathered face, star on his chest, gun on his hip. "An undertaker's more than likely what he's needing."

"Did you see what happened?" I managed to ask, though my throat felt as dry as the dusty street.

"Seen you drop like you was shot. You hurt?"

"No."

A heavyset bald man in a gray suit walked up, the undertaker, no doubt. "Whatcha got here, Sheriff?"

"New customer for ya, Thaddeus. He's all yours." The Sheriff turned back to me, "Well now, Sonny, you mosey on. We'll take care of this fella."

My mind numb, I stared at my blood-stained hands then hobbled to where my boot lay in the dirt.

Dead, just like that, and no one cared.

My new shirt was soiled and bloody, so I wiped my hands on it then jammed my foot into my boot.

High-pitched piano music filtered into my stupor. I needed a drink. A good stiff drink.

I staggered to a horse watering trough, rolled up my

sleeves, and washed blood from my hands and face in the cold water. Meanwhile, I breathed deeply to gather my composure. As presentable as I could be, I walked to the saloon, pushed through the swinging doors, and stepped inside.

I accidentally kicked a spittoon. It clanged against the wooden floor, rolled, and left a trail of brown spittle.

Men laughed. All eyes focused on me.

Heat crept up my neck. Feeling foolish, I squared my shoulders and made my way toward the bar, pressing through a crowd of shouting and laughing men.

"Greenhorn," someone shouted.

"Mud-splasher."

The need to knock one or two of the loudmouths down a notch had me itching for a fight. "Whiskey," I told the bartender. "Make it a double." I leaned on the bartop to look cool.

The bartender slammed down a dirty glass and poured two-fingers twice. "Four bits, pal."

"Run me a tab and keep that bottle handy."

He left the bottle in front of me and moved on down the bar. The roar of voices and the tinkling of piano keys accosted my ears. *Yeah. This is the freaking Wild West.*

Whiskey in hand, I scanned the room. Almost every man wore a weapon slung over his chest or hip. Guns rested on top of green-cloth card tables, just in case someone cheated, I surmised. I didn't like guns, had no desire to go shooting at the range, or hunt, like my dad and his macho buddies.

I took a swig of whiskey. An inferno burned down my throat and brought tears to my eyes. I coughed. Heat settled in the center of my chest. The sound of gunfire still ricocheted in my brain. I feared I'd need to get a gun. Without one, I could get shot, left in the street to die, and no one would care. Problem was, I didn't know how to shoot a gun.

I took another gulp of golden fire-water. My eyes teared up and I damn near choked to death. As for paying for this torture, I'd have to come up with some excuse why I had no money. Better be a good one or I might get shot over a bar tab. A gun to protect myself would come in handy...but I didn't think I could actually shoot a man. No way. Still, I should get a gun...just in case some fleecer decided to draw down on me. Karate was no defense against bullets.

As my eyes cleared up, I studied the dirty glass clutched between my fingers. One more swallow left. Damn booze could burn a hole in my throat. Back in college, I could party with the best of them. Modern aged whiskey went down a lot smoother than this 1850's moonshine.

Outside, whoops and gunshots disturbed the day. Horses whinnied and boots clomped on the boardwalk. The swinging doors burst open, and a big burly guy charged in. He held a canvas bag in one hand and a smoking pistol in the other.

Expecting to be shot, I turtled my neck and turned back to the bar.

"Hit me a nice payoff, fellas. Everybody's drinks are on me."

How about that. I slammed down my glass, grabbed the bottle, and topped her off. *Looks like I have a rich benefactor.*

The brute ambled up to the bar, stood next to me, holstered his gun, and set the bag of gold in front of the bartender. "Drinks fer everyone 'cept this here greenhorn." He spat tobacco chew on the shoulder of my new shirt.

"Hey. Watch it, mister."

"You look like a greenhorn...smell like a greenhorn ta me."

"Nate," the bartender shouted. "Don't start no trouble in here."

He shoved me aside. "Go back to your mammy's teat, boy."

Yeah. I had to get a gun.

Abby to the rescue

Before I reached the piano, and still cradling a skirt full of coins and gold, gunfire outside the saloon doors stopped me. A big bear of a man stomped in. He said something about buying drinks for everyone then stomped to the bar. That's when I saw Wyatt. My heart skipped. He must've come in while I was gathering up my tips. He'd rolled up the sleeves of a new blue shirt, showcasing the muscles of his arms. His back was to me, so the girth of his broad shoulders looked impressive.

The burly guy didn't look impressed. "Smell like a greenhorn ta me."

"Nate," the bartender shouted. "Don't start no trouble in here."

Wyatt glared at Nate, got pushed but held his cool. "No trouble." He slowly picked up a glass and downed the drink.

I could see the tight grip of his hand, any tighter and the glass would shatter. I noticed his watch was gone. He must've sold it to buy whiskey. Not very smart.

Monty stepped in front of me. "Lolita, my love. I believe you have something for me."

I glanced around my boss's shoulder, my attention still focused on Wyatt as he placed the glass on the bar and poured another drink from the bottle in front of him.

"The gold, Lolita," Monty said as he jabbed a collection basket at my bunched-up skirt.

Nate scowled, didn't look happy about Wyatt's calm demeanor. "I seen ya drop in the dirt like ya was shot out there." Nate pointed to the street then addressed the men gathering around him. "Fellas, funniest thing I ever done seen. This here greenhorn takes off his boots on the boardwalk." He turned back to Wyatt. "Didn't yo mammy ever teach ya never get caught dead without your boots on, boy?"

Wyatt straightened to his full height. Eye to chest, he stood before the obnoxious man, his fists clenched by his side. "I'm not your boy."

His calm tone surprised me, given the venomous glare Wyatt shot the big guy. Obviously, the word *boy* pushed an unpleasant button that tightened his stance.

"Lolita, the money." Impatience came out heavy in Monty's voice.

Focused on Wyatt, I spilled the contents of my bunched dress into the basket.

"And as for my mother..." Wyatt shouted. "I suggest you shut your ugly trap, because if I hear you talk about her again..." He poked his antagonist in the chest. "Your mammy will be weeping at your grave."

The man's face turned brilliant red with rage. He reached for the gun holstered at his side.

Panic shot through me. I had to do something...and fast. I hurried to Wyatt's side. "There you are, Wyatt, darling." I wrapped my arms around his neck. "I was looking all over for you." My heart pounded. I was crazy with fear. "Did you hear me sing?"

He glared at me, damn near cross-eyed.

"Why don't you buy Lolita a drink and tell her all about how pretty she is?" I unwrapped my arms from his neck then curled a strand of ebony hair around my index finger. My smile felt genuine as I batted my eyes at Wyatt's antagonist, his fingers poised over his gun. "Mister, can you shoot him *after* I get my drink?"

Slowly he dropped his hand. "Gladly, ma'am."

A surge of relief washed over me. I might despise Wyatt, but I didn't want him shot dead.

"Come." I grabbed his wrist and pulled him past his would-be killer. "Sit over here with me." Seated at the table, I leaned into him. "What's that guy's problem?"

"What do you think you're doing?" Wyatt's calm composure cracked.

Taken aback by his ungrateful statement, I stared at him across the table. His new shirt was soiled and bloody, with a brown glob of goo on the shoulder. I wondered who spit tobacco on him...suddenly it hit me. Bloody? I gasped. "There's blood on your shirt. What happened?"

"It's not my blood."

"But it could have been if I hadn't jumped in. I just saved your life."

His blue eyes darkened. "You made me look like a fool in front of everyone."

"You're a jerk." I caught a whiff of strong liquor on his breath. "This is the thanks I get for helping you?"

"I don't recall asking for your help."

Despite his anger, I noticed his gaze drop to the swell of my breasts, where he got a good look down my low-cut bodice. His stare lingered there for a moment then snapped up. "In fact, I'm a little confused."

"I'm not." My face heated, adding to my annoyance. "You're an ingrate."

"Perhaps you can explain why all of a sudden you give a damn about me. One minute you're telling me to go to hell, the next you're my guardian angel."

"I don't give a damn about you."

"Good." His gaze held mine long, hard, and unwavering. "Right back at you."

Wyatt gets drunk

The saloon patrons seemed to have forgotten the commotion at the bar, now happily drinking on Nate's tab. Piano music plinked and tinkled over the hawing and jawing of the riffraff.

The woman sitting across the table called herself Lolita, but I knew Abby was in there, a woman who hated me. Then there was *Lolita*. What a fitting name for a woman who appeared to be comfortable in a place as raunchy as this one, a place where I didn't belong, in a world I wanted no part of. Problem was, I needed them both to help me acclimate to this cesspool.

History was one subject I'd never been interested in. Science, languages, math, yes, but history...not so much. Abby had a pretty good insight into the happenings of this era. Sitting here in this bar, staring at a woman I didn't know, I realized I didn't know how to act and react appropriately for the times. I regretted not paying better attention in history class.

When I was outside, I'd heard her sultry singing, imagined her every seductive move; the way she would have swayed her hips and sashayed across the stage, and I could see all the slobs in this place drooling like hungry dogs. Oddly, that vision pissed me off. I came here to get drunk, not ogle over Lolita's bosom. The last thing I needed right now was to hook up with Abby's alter ego.

A blonde saloon girl with flowers in her hair delivered a drink to Lolita, a drink I didn't order, much less have money to pay for. I watched her strut off and figured the drink was part of the ruse to get Nate to back off.

Lolita didn't even look at the glass. "It's sarsaparilla." She stared at me as if my nose had fallen off.

So I stared back, my gaze traveling from her beautiful sun-kissed face, slowly down her slender neck, my eyes savoring every inch of skin all the way down to the creamy swells trapped in her bodice. I swore any quick intake of breath could cause those honeys to spill from her dress. I felt my body respond to that delightful vision in my head.

I was being absurd. Yeah. She was desirable, but I had more important things to do than proposition Lolita. I needed to survive, keep my wits about me, and figure a way out of this nightmare. Sex dulled the senses, complicated matters, but something told me Abby wouldn't let Lolita touch me with a ten-foot pole.

Her anger had turned those tempting, pouty lips into a hard pressed line, but her startling eyes pierced my heart, same as the moment I'd met her. I knew I was looking at the beautiful shell of one woman and feeling the anger of another woman within...and right now I was hot for both of them... *Never mind, Wyatt.* I had bigger problems on my plate, like getting home, or getting shot by some cowboy with an itch to kill a fleecer.

I glanced at the bar. The jerk I'd had the run-in with moments ago stood pounding down drinks. I'd like to have punched him to a pulp, but thanks to Abby's interference, I didn't get to teach him a lesson in manners. *Nobody calls me boy and gets away with it.* The neighborhood bully always called me boy. *Come here, boy. Give me your lunch money, boy.* I hated that guy, but if not for him, I may never have taken karate lessons. After I'd earned my black belt, he didn't call me boy anymore.

Yeah. I'd been aware of the gun at Nate's side and the way his fingers itched to pull it from the holster. Abby must've seen the gun, as well. In a way, I was surprised she'd had the guts to place herself in danger to protect me. The downside of that move: now everyone thought I was a coward hiding behind a woman's dress. "I can defend myself, Abby."

"He was going to shoot you."

"I need a drink." I stood so abruptly, the chair scraped the floor.

"Okay. Get drunk. That'll solve everything."

I slapped the table with an open palm. "I'm stuck in this

hellhole with two women..." *Well, one woman inside the other.*
"I've got no money. No idea when, how, or if I'm ever going
home. But, hey, maybe if I drink 'til I'm unconscious, I'll wake
up with such a hangover that my life will look better than it does
right now. What'd ya think? Got a better solution?" I didn't wait
for her reply; I didn't want one. I decided to get out of there and
stormed toward the door.

"Hey, mister," the bartender shouted. "You got to pay up
before you leave."

I stopped short of the exit. My palms began to sweat. I
turned to the bartender, though I had no excuse on my tongue.
"Look, I—"

"Skipping out without paying, huh, Swartwouter?"

"Yeah," some drunk guy chimed in. "He's a Swartwouter,
all right."

"He's skipping," another said.

Their hostile stares bored into me. *Swartwouter?* I didn't
have the faintest idea what the word meant, but I didn't like the
tone in their voices. Bullies, all of them. I took a deep breath.
Stay calm. The satisfaction of kicking some ass wasn't worth the
trouble, but it would relieve the anger gripping my chest. I strode
to the bartender. "How much do I owe?"

"Eight bits. Settle up."

"Yeah...about that. Hang on a sec." I returned to Abby still
seated at the table, her cold green eyes staring at me like I was
horse pucky on her shoe. "Can you spot me? Please?"

"Go to hell."

Damn, she's still pissed. I turned back to the bartender.
"Ah...I just bought a new shovel. How about a trade?"

"We don't take no trades."

"How about collateral for a loan?"

"No loans. Gold or jail. Should I send for the Sheriff?"

"Now, J-Joe," Nate interrupted. He was sloshed. "I
wouldn't want you...to send my good fleecer friend to jail, now
would I?" He walked up and drunkenly slapped his arm around
my shoulders.

I gave him a *remove-your-arm-or-else* glare.

He gave me a man-hug then stagger-stepped back to the
bar. "I'll cover his debt." He indicated his bag of gold on the

bartop. "And there's enough here for drinks...*hic*...for me and the greenhorn. Keep 'em comin' 'til one of us drops." He grinned at me.

I knew this wouldn't be just a friendly drinking game. He expected something in return for his generosity. I'd been up against guys like him before, bullies who got their kicks out of picking on smaller guys. What this jerk didn't know was, right now, I didn't give a damn if laying into him might get me shot. He was gonna feel my jabs. "I'm not drinking with you, cowboy."

"Ah come on...you against me. Barkeep, line 'em up."

"Not interested, but thanks for covering my tab." I turned my back to him.

"Well...fellas..." He turned to the men standing around. "Pay up. Looks like I won our bet. Told you this here boy was too chicken to try 'n drink me under the table."

"Boy?" That got me steamed. "I'm not chicken of nothin'." I stepped up to the bartender. "You heard the man. Line 'em up."

While Joe poured two whiskeys, I looked over at Lolita, saw the frown on her brow and figured that was Abby's doing.

Joe placed two shots of whiskey on the bar.

Nate grabbed the nearest glass with a filthy calloused hand and downed the whiskey. I did the same. Fire burned down my throat. Immediately, two more drinks were placed before us.

I raised my glass. "Salud."

An hour passed, or so it felt, as I leaned against the bar with an empty glass in my hand. The last thing I wanted to do was drink with this bully, but I refused to let him get the better of me. Even if it killed me, I was gonna drink him under the table. I slammed the glass on the bar. "Another."

After my fifth shot, the burning sensation disappeared; the booze went down like water. Yeah. I was sweating, but I was still standing, still coherent.

The plink of the piano and boisterous voices raised in song blended together in a tunnel effect. A woman's irritating high-pitched chatter sounded like fingernails scraping on a blackboard.

My drinking partner waved to Joe. "Per me another." Clinging to the bar, he could barely stand. His shoulders drooped, and his head slumped to one side. Drink delivered, he straightened. His hand shook as he held the new shot to his mouth, threw his head back, and dumped her in. Whiskey dribbled from his mouth as if he could no longer swallow. He dropped the glass. It shattered on the floor. He wiped his lips with his sleeve, staggered, then down he went, face-first on the bartop then he slumped to the floor with a thud.

It was the best sound I'd heard all day. The bully hadn't considered he was already drunk when the drinking game began. Battle won, I did the shoot-him gesture with my finger gun.

One for the good guy.

Abby's sleepover

I jumped up to cheer Wyatt's victory but caught myself before I acted like a fool. Suddenly, rough hands reached around my waist from behind. My heart lurched.

"Lolita, kin I sit down here with ya fer a spell?"

I twisted around, saw an old stranger had pulled up a chair. "Easy there, big fella." There was my sultry voice again. "Buy me a drink first."

"Lolita? What are you doing?"

"Having fun."

He started to sit down and pull me into his lap.

"Whoa." I pushed the chair back with my foot and wriggled out of his lecherous embrace. Good thing he was too drunk to hold onto me. "I mean...I can't. You can't buy me a drink."

"Sure he can."

His face wrinkled with a toothless grin. "Sure I can." He pulled the chair back to him and sat down. "Jest jack yer heels up and sit right here in my lap." He patted his knee, and before I could step back, he grabbed my wrist and pulled me into his lap. "Daisy," he called. "Hows about a couple beers over here?"

I tried to stand up, but this time the old goat had me in a death grip. A stab of panic tightened my throat. I shook my head to Daisy. "I don't drink beer." But she just smiled and sauntered to the bar. Damn. "Look, mister..." His foul breath, a mixture of rotten gums and liquor, sickened me. The jabber in the room intensified to a dull roar. Piano music stopped. I stole a quick glance to Wyatt. His victory had attracted two floozies, and he was too busy being fawned over to notice my predicament. *What a dick.*

The old man's hands began to wander; I blocked his every advance up my thigh while his whiskers itched my neck. "Stop."

"Come on...*hic*...give old Billy a little kiss."

"Lighten up, Abby," Lolita said in my brain. *"Let me have a little fun."*

"If you kiss him, that means I gotta kiss him, and that ain't happening." I shuddered at the thought of his grungy mouth on mine.

"It is either him or Wyatt," Lolita said breathily. *"What is it going to be?"*

"And you're not kissing Wyatt, either."

A warm hand settled on my bare shoulder. "Miss Lolita." The voice belonged to Benjamin. "I need you to come with me." He pointed to the piano. "We need to go over your next set."

"Oh, yes. Of course." I forced a smile for old Billy with the wandering fingers and loose lips. "Duty calls."

"Dang. I had high hopes fer yer favors, miss." He let me up and slapped my ass. "Go on, git."

"Ow, you jerk." I escaped the table with Benjamin, and we weaved through the crowd to the piano. "Thank you for coming to my rescue."

"It wasn't a rescue, Miss Lolita. You don't need *my* help with these drunken fools." He sat on his bench and stared at the sheet music before him. "How does this sound?"

As he plinked the keys of an unfamiliar tune, my thoughts went back to the legend. Had he been suspected of killing the children? Is that why he'd left town? He didn't look like a killer, but then the quiet ones were least expected to turn evil. However, just because he left didn't mean he was guilty.

A shy smile touched his lips then quickly disappeared. His fingers were working magic on the keys. That was when I recognized him. He lived across from me at camp. The man with the razor in his hand. No wonder he looked familiar. "For a minute there, I didn't recognize you."

He dipped his eyebrows questioningly, and I realized my words made no sense to him. As far as he knew, I was Lolita. He was my pianist. She would never not recognize him. I'd spoken without thinking. "I mean, without those soap suds on your face, you...well, you look different."

He stopped playing, looked at me head-on. "Are you feeling all right, Miss Lolita?"

"No. No. I'm fine." I glanced at his hands, noticed how long and slender his fingers were, how immaculately clean he'd kept his nails. "Why wouldn't I be all right?"

"I just supposed...well...after last night you'd—"

"Last night?" I blinked. "What about last night?"

"I didn't mean you any disrespect."

I hadn't been here last night. What did Lolita do? What had he done? "What are you talking about?"

He cleared his throat. "I don't believe anyone saw us, even under the full moon."

"Saw us? Doing what?"

Wait. Full moon?

"I put you to bed. Honestly, that's all."

I tried to concentrate on his words, on why he'd put me to bed, but all I could think about was the legend and the full moon. Was it a blue moon? "What happened? I don't remember."

"You were in no condition to ride back to camp. So I snuck you out of here and took you home in my buggy. Honestly, nothing happened." He placed his hand on my shoulder. "This morning you must-a had a hangover that'd kill a horse."

I stared at him. Lolita had been drunk...so stinking drunk she needed help getting home...so hung over she'd gone down to the river the next morning in her underwear...to sober up in the cold water.

"I do apologize for my, um, condition. Thank you for helping me get home...ah...but I forgot. What was the date yesterday?"

"The second day of June, Miss Lolita."

"Yes, of course. I must sound like a ditz."

"Ditz, ma'am?"

"Never mind."

A pained expression crossed his face. He was clearly

uncomfortable with the conversation, turned back to the keys and started to play.

Relieved, I now knew how to track the moon's cycle. Today was the third. The moon would be full again in twenty-nine and a half days. Thirty days in June, that meant the next full moon would land on the second night in July. Then the next full moon would occur on the thirty-first day of July. The second full moon in July. A blue moon. I had until the end of next month to stop a killer. We got here too early. What crummy universe was this?

My attention settled on Wyatt. A woman wearing a gaudy blue dress with feathers in her hair clung to him and whispered in his ear. Wyatt laughed.

I didn't give a damn. Didn't care if every whore in the joint wanted him. He was the same old cad I remembered from high school. I tried to look away but Lolita made her eyes search out his gaze. Even from this distance, a sensuous current of electricity hit me. I felt like that same breathless teen back in high school. I frowned. *How can I possibly be attracted to him after what he did?*

"I do not care what he did," Lolita cooed. *"I would take him in a heartbeat."*

"He has no conscience. No remorse."

"Neither do I."

Now she was just being cruel. I saw Wyatt whisper in the woman's ear, and then she walked away. His eyes never leaving mine, he headed toward me.

Anticipation kicked my heart into a rapid beat.

"Feel how my heart beats for him, Abby."

"Please don't."

"Ab-Abeee." His speech, though slurred, oozed of sexual overtones. "Can't take your eyes...off me, huh?"

"Come to Lolita," she made me say in her sexy voice.

He tripped over his feet and crashed into me. My arms looped around him as he leaned into me for support. He reeked of whiskey.

I turned my face away. "Get off me, you drunken lug. You're causing a scene."

"Don't care," he mumbled. "Don't care a bit. Bad dream,

that's all. Nothing's real. You got beautiful green eyes. Anyone ever tell you that...you got..?" He slumped in my embrace.

I struggled to hold him up. "Wyatt. Stand up. You're embarrassing me."

The piano music stopped. Everyone in the room stared at us.

"I've got to get you out of here."

He perked up and glanced around. "We're going home?" He fell back against me. "That's great. Anyone ever tell you...you got...eyes?"

"Miss Lolita," Benjamin said. "Maybe you should take him upstairs to a room."

"He is in no condition for Lolita's lovin'." My voice came out all syrupy sweet, but I knew what went on in those rooms, and it wasn't happening on my watch.

"No Lolita loving," I told the crazy woman in my head. *"No Abby loving, either. Just sleep, you hear me? He needs rest, so hands off."*

Benjamin grimaced. "He can't make it back to camp, and we can't throw him out in the street. He can sleep it off up there."

I glanced to my boss, Monty, standing behind a card table. Our conversation hadn't gone unnoticed. He watched us with narrow eyes, didn't look pleased having a drunk take up lodging in a room where his bargirls made him money by the half hour. "What do we tell Monty?"

"I'll worry about him," Benjamin said. "I've got to get back to playing, but if you need me—"

"I will be fine. Play. I got this," I assured him, but I had no idea how I was going to carry Wyatt across the room, let alone get him upstairs without dropping him.

Benjamin's brows arched as he turned to the keyboard. "I got this." He laughed.

Did my word choices amuse him? I needed to be careful to not use modern phrases. "Wyatt. Straighten up. Come on."

He pulled himself up and draped his arm around my shoulders. "Where...are we going?"

"Upstairs."

His face brightened. "Well, lucky me. Thought I'd lost my

charm."

"Don't flatter yourself. Just move."

The stairs seemed miles away. He dragged his feet. My boss was staring at me, and if looks could kill, I'd be a dead woman.

"Come on, Wyatt. Can you move a little faster?"

"Can't wait to get me upstairs, huh?" A silly smirk curved his lips.

I had a sound mind to drop him, the conceited jerk. Why did he have to get so damn drunk?

Groups of men played cards or stood at the bar. Several women flirted with rowdy, smelly men, while others busied themselves serving drinks. No one appeared to notice our clumsy struggle.

Wyatt's hip jabbed my side as he leaned into me. "Dreaming. Yup. All this'll be gone in the morning. I don't need a gun." He waved his hand in the air.

A gun? Why would he need a gun? I tightened my hold on him. I needed to help him. He didn't belong here, and this situation was my fault. Besides, I'd have to keep a close eye on him so he didn't do anything stupid like get himself killed. "Come on. Let's get you to bed."

We struggled up the stairs.

"Bed." He winked. "Good idea. We'll go to bed...naked."

"Not in your lifetime." Who was I kidding? Part of me liked the idea.

I want to tear off his clothes. No I don't. What am I thinking?

"I am doing the thinking, Abby. I bet he is gorgeous with no clothes. What do you think?"

"Nobody's getting naked, Lolita. You hear?"

Wyatt's arm lay draped over my shoulders as we struggled down a short walkway. A railing overlooked the saloon floor and all the activity below. With difficulty, I found a door ajar and toed it open.

I was hit with smells that made my nose tingle: dust, a mixture of mildew and musty carpet. A low burning kerosene lamp flicked distorted light on the dark green and gold flowered wallpaper. A plump pillow, a hideous shade of purple, lay canted on the single bed, and a white porcelain pitcher and washbasin sat on the bedside table. A wingback chair, its polished wood and poppy red color, stood vivid against the tired look of the other furnishings.

I didn't know if it was my imagination, but Wyatt's gait seemed less sluggish as we entered the room. He tripped over the edge of a worn throw carpet then straightened. "Damn."

The floorboards creaked as I dragged him to the hideous gold-satin quilted bedspread where I removed his arm from around my neck. As I plopped him down, the mattress sank under his weight.

He rested his head against the pillow and then stretched out his arms. "Come. Join me." He patted the blanket. A dazzling smile showcased straight white teeth.

I stepped back from the bed then stopped. No. I didn't want to stop; I wanted to walk out and leave him to sleep off his stupidity, but my feet wouldn't move.

"Lolita? What are you doing?"

"I want to accept his offer."

"What are you, some floozy who'd sleep with any man?"

"And you are Mother Mary, I suppose?"

Lolita took a step toward the bed. I stopped her. *"You can't be serious."*

"I am single. You are single. We can both do him."

"Legally, you are still married."

"I have not wanted a man since my husband left...until now."

"Sounds like a personal problem."

Grinning, Wyatt wiggled his fingers come hither.

"Wyatt, don't be ridiculous. There's no way I'm getting in bed with you."

"You're not gonna just leave me here," he whined.

"No. I will sleep with you," I said breathily.

"Lolita, stop it."

"I-I mean yes. I'm leaving." I turned to leave, heard the mattress shift, and quickly turned back to see him wobbling on his feet. I hurried to him. "Lay down, you drunken lug. You're going to break your neck."

Both his arms encircled my body. His face was inches from

mine. I couldn't breathe. I couldn't think. A fire burned in my belly, the heat rising to an inferno.

"Kiss him," Lolita breathed. *"I want to feel his lips on mine."*

"But I don't want to kiss him."

"Silly girl, yes you do."

I forced his arms to release me, and I pushed him back down on the bed. "Behave yourself."

"Okay." He lay back and stretched his legs out over the side. "At least help me take off my boots." He regarded me with puppy dog eyes.

I sighed. He had to be kidding.

"I will do it," Lolita sang.

"Fine." I stepped up, bent to his left boot, and grabbed the heel. New boots? Nice. The boot slipped off so quickly I stumbled backward, caught myself, and reached for the other boot. This one didn't budge. I pulled again. I swear he was curling his toes to make this difficult on purpose. I huffed, lifted my green dress then turned my back to him and straddled his leg.

"Quite a nice view."

Wyatt's mellow tone slid under my skin, making my cheeks heat. I gritted my teeth, grabbed the heel and toe, and pulled again. Then I felt his left bare foot push against my backside.

"Soft, too."

I gritted my teeth, felt his foot relax, and the boot flew off, pitching me forward. I dropped the boot and grabbed his bare foot to keep from falling on my face. I couldn't believe how my body reacted to holding his bare foot, the wave of heat exploding through me. Then again, I was sure the reaction was entirely Lolita's.

He sat up and gripped my hips. "You okay?"

"Let go." My face flaming, I dismounted his leg, smoothed my dress, and started for the door without looking back.

"Abby?"

I stopped, my back stiff with tension. "Now what?"

"You gonna make me sleep...in my shirt?"

I pivoted and glared at him. "It's already bloody and dirty.

So what if it gets wrinkled? Take it off yourself or sleep in it. Your choice."

He glanced down at his chest and shook his head. "Nope."

"What do you mean *nope*?"

"Too drunk to see the buttons."

I wished he'd stop ogling me. As his gaze traveled from my eyes to my lips, a provocative warmth settled low in my belly. His assessing glance slipped to my neck then slid boldly lower, as if he were undressing me with his eyes. I knew Lolita was enjoying this attention. She thrust out her bosom to show off her exceptional cleavage, creating an unaccustomed throb between my legs...I mean *her* legs.

"Take off his shirt, for God's sake, Abby, or I will do it myself."

Heat stoked every nerve in this body we shared. I didn't know what I would do if I got that close to him, to unbutton his shirt, to open his shirt, to slide his shirt off his broad shoulders. I was pretty sure I knew what Lolita would do. She'd run both hands over his pecs, rub his nipples then slide down to his abs, feel the strength and power in his every breath.

"Please stop, Lolita. You're turning me into a sex fiend."

She *giggled*. *"Look what we are doing to him."*

His lusty evaluation of me put a sparkle in his eye, a smile on his face, and I was sure there were other parts of his body going wild. His reaction was doing a rhythmic tap dance on my libido, and it wasn't the soft shoe; it was more like a full-fledged Tango.

"So..." With a curl of his finger, he gestured for me to come closer. The silly expression on his face made him look so boyishly charming, but I knew there was nothing boyish about his intentions.

"God. You're so damn helpless." I gnawed my lip, and fluttering anticipation rippled through me as I straddled his legs and went to work on the buttons. My fingers trembled. I started with the top button, leaned over to wrest it out of the buttonhole, and finally got it loose. As I spread the lapels to access the next button, a splay of fine blond hair peeked out at me. I had to ignore the throb between Lolita's legs in order to concentrate on the task at hand. Another button. Another glimpse of the treasure beneath. I had to distract myself or fall on him like Lolita wanted.

"I see you sold your watch."

"Collateral at the mercantile."

Another button slipped free. I took a deep breath and continued. Thanks to my traitorous new body, this simple task became more complicated than I'd ever imagined.

"What happened to your new shirt?"

After another button, more tanned skin became exposed. Smooth. Hard. Muscular. I swallowed to ease my dry throat while savoring the attraction between us, the adoration in his eyes, eyes that were looking at Lolita, not me. The feelings within me, I wished they were all mine, not hers, but I refused to let him get into my heart. I refused to let him hurt me...again.

"The shirt's not important." He reached up and caressed the side of my face.

I flinched. "Don't."

"Why do you hate me?"

"Lolita doesn't know you enough to hate you." There was that sexy voice again.

"Stop butting in, girlfriend, or you and I are going to have issues."

"Why do you torture him so?"

She didn't know what he'd done to me. Worse, he didn't recall what happened between us back in high school. Anger crawled up my neck. Now was not the time to get into past history. He was drunk, and I wanted him to be perfectly sober when I enlightened him. The dreamy desire softening his eyes was just unguarded drunken lust that would disappear in the morning light. Last button undone, the open shirt exposed his chest, and I knew Lolita was going to get me in trouble. "I better go."

His fingers curled around mine. "Don't. Don't go."

His softly spoken, seductive plea found a hot spot in my heart, revving up its rhythm. Why did he have to be so damn handsome? My gaze lingered on his square jaw. Those ice-blue eyes of his, though dreamy with drink, excited my senses and shattered my resistance.

He sat up, leaned closer, and my breath held. I stared at his lips. Kissable lips. Beckoning me. No. Beckoning Lolita.

I felt his hand on the swell of my back, gently edging me closer to his bare chest. A tremor ran through me, a wonderful sensation, quieting the alarms.

"*One kiss. Just one...*"

"No." I scooted back and fought Lolita's need. "If you don't want to sleep in your shirt, you'd better let me finish." I slipped the shirt over his head and let it fall to the bed covers. I had all I could do to keep Lolita's hands off him.

"Abby. I don't want to sleep." He drew me in closer, within inches of his sensual mouth.

"Wyatt, what are you doing?" I placed my hand on his chest, his hot wonderful chest.

"I'm trying to kiss you."

"You're drunk. I should go before I end up slapping you."

He leaned back. "It's too dangerous out there...and too late. You'll never find your way back to the camp."

"Lolita knows the way."

"And how are you gonna get off the horse by yourself?"

"Lolita knows how to ride."

"I don't want either of you out of my sight." He lifted me off his legs, set me next to him, skirted the edge of the bed, and stood. "Take the bed. I'll sleep in the chair. I promise I won't try anything."

Did I trust him to stay on the other side of the room? Did I want him to try something? Part of me didn't. All of Lolita did.

He yanked his shirt off the bed.

"I still want to know how your shirt got bloody."

"No you don't."

"Of course I do, you big lug."

"I told you, it's not my blood, so you don't have to worry about it."

I wanted to worry about it, but arguing with a drunk was fruitless. I watched him fold the shirt in half then neatly tuck in the sleeves. That's when it hit me. He wasn't as drunk as I'd thought. "You skunk." I grabbed the pillow and threw it at him.

"What?" He grinned. "Are you disappointed I'm not totally plastered?"

I wanted to flee from the room. I wanted to be mad, but I

couldn't take my eyes off his magnificent body, off the sensual lines of definition that angled down to his hips.

He slipped off my husband's baggy pants and stood in his swim trunks. My gaze fell lower to what I could only guess would fulfill every woman's needs. A rush of pleasure flowed through me. He was a woman's dream of perfection. Too bad he was such a jerk.

He plopped down into the chair and yawned.

I chewed my lip while debating my choices. Without Lolita, I had no idea how to get home, and the thought of getting lost or falling off a horse was a greater fear than being alone in this bedroom with Wyatt.

"Get into bed, Abby." A tired, honest expression softened the lines of his face.

I never thought I'd hear those words coming from him, even though I'd dreamt he'd said them three years ago. If he had, I was sure I wouldn't be a virgin today. Settling into the bed, I drew up the covers. "I don't hate you, Wyatt, but I'm still mad at you."

"Turn down the kerosene light, will ya?"

I reached to the table, turned down the wick, and we were thrust into total darkness. I was sure he could hear the pounding of my heart from across the room.

"Abby?"

"Yes?"

"I heard you."

"That I don't hate you?"

"Sing. I heard you sing. Beautiful. Just beautiful."

The compliment took me aback. That was Lolita's voice coming out of me, and right now I was very thankful for her talent. "Wyatt? Just how drunk are you?"

"Feeling a little mellow now, is all."

"Do you remember Ms. Patrick's class?" Since he wasn't drunk I could bring up the past. The cloak of darkness gave me a sense of security, as well, but I needed to know why he didn't show up on prom night. "You used to strut into class like you owned the room. You'd crack a joke, everyone laughed, including Ms. Patrick. You had her eating out of your hand."

"I was a jerk back in high school."

"I won't argue that." I waited for an irate remark; when none came, I felt emboldened. "Everyone noticed you. I noticed you. Every guy wanted to be you. Every girl wanted to date you." *Including me.* "Mister popular, I think, was written under your yearbook picture."

"Being popular isn't all it's cracked up to be."

"I find that hard to believe."

"It's true."

His admission surprised me. He'd made being popular look so easy. I plowed on toward the big question. "I sat behind you in class. You didn't even notice me."

He yawned. "Sorry. Like I said, I was a jerk."

"You went to the prom with Pam."

You were supposed to go with me.

"My mom and I spent the day shopping for a gown. That was the last time we'd spend time together, just the two of us. I remember the excitement of that evening, how it faded bit by bit as I stood by the door and waited an hour and a half for my date to arrive. The hope I clung to dwindled as I watched the clock, and when I gave up and shut the door, I burst into tears. Our perfect date lay crumbled, like my heart, at my feet.

"After my mother died, I hung onto the dress to keep memories of our shared laughter and bubbling anticipation alive, so I'd never forget the love I saw in her eyes when I put on that perfect dress. Then Wyatt Beaufort went and broke my heart.

"Why did you stand me up on Prom night?" My pulse pounded in my throat as I waited for him to answer my question.

His response was a resounding snore.

Chapter Five

Wyatt starts a brawl

Yanked from a hot stimulating dream to dim awareness, I awoke with a pounding in my head and the taste of whiskey on my tongue, not the sweet, berried lips of the Spanish dream-babe whose mouth was all over mine moments ago. I'd dreamt I was a gunslinger with two pearled revolvers hanging from my hips and a saloon girl in my arms. Her name was Abby.

I cracked open a bleary eye and was met with an unfamiliar room.

Where am I?

Disoriented, I found myself slumped in a strange chair instead of my familiar bed. I rubbed my eyes as recollection came back to me. The nightmare my life had become was still alive and well in 1852.

Shit. I closed my eyes and thought of Abby. I didn't want to get into a tug of war between what feelings were real and what feelings were fantasy. The feelings I had for Abby were real, but the way my body reacted to Lolita's touch was just as real. I pressed my thumbs into my temples. This splitting headache was definitely real.

When I looked around the rustic room, I saw how morning sunlight leaked through the shaded window and leaned across the bed. The sheets were askew, and Abby...well...Lolita was gone. If I lived to be a hundred I'd never get used to the two-women-in-one-body dilemma I found myself in. I'd always been one to be seen with babes, like Lolita, but underneath the showboating, a down-to-earth woman was more my type, like Abby. She might have been stuck in a gorgeous body, and she hated my guts, but she was my only link to get back home, the only hope I had to get back to my Ferrari and my goal to go to med-school.

One constant between these two women, Lolita had Abby's green eyes. So, if the eyes were the windows to the soul, then maybe Lolita's were the windows to Abby's soul. However, to get to Abby I'd have to go through Lolita, and anything I said to her, Abby could take the wrong way and think I was talking to Lolita. The problem was enough to give me a migraine. My head felt woozy enough.

I got out of the chair, dressed in Lolita's husband's pants and my soiled blue shirt, pulled on my boots and figured I'd buy a gun just to shoot myself.

As I descended the stairs, the noise level below was as loud as last night. Shrill piano music pounded my brain. I scanned the area for Abby...well, Lolita, and found her at the bar. Some bandito-looking Mexican had his arm around her.

"Come on, señorita. Vamos a tu cuarto."

The jerk was inviting himself to her room.

"Maybe later, sweetie." Smiling sexily, she touched his chin and giggled.

Fiery heat shot through my veins. I bolted down the steps two at a time, shoved through the crowd, and confronted the guy face to face. "Get your hands off her."

The entire room fell silent.

"Gringo, ocúpese de lo suyo." *Mind your own business.*

"She *is* my business," I replied in Spanish. An attack of possessive jealousy tightened my stomach.

Surprise arched his dark brows. "Si, amigo. Usted entiende Español. Good. Alejarse o morir." *Walk away or die.*

By Abby's look of confusion, I knew she didn't understand he'd threatened to kill me. "Let the lady go." I'd said it in English so everyone knew I meant business.

A few Mexicans in the room put their fingers on their guns. Other patrons, a few with drinks in their hands, a few men seated at card tables, watched in silence.

The bandito released her abruptly; she stumbled, caught herself, and moved back.

I was aware of the gun holstered at his hip and the knife sheathed at his belt. He outweighed me and out-gunned me, so

I'd have to rely on the best defense I knew, a good offense. I punched him square in the face. The blow knocked him backward, but the bruiser didn't fall. He just smiled.

"Oh shit."

I dropped into a karate stance, right knee bent, left leg straight back, my fists poised above my hips, thumbs up.

His face scrunched like he thought I was crazy.

I gestured him to 'come on'.

He charged for my throat. I caught his wrist with one hand, twisted my body into him, jabbed my other elbow into the side of his head and followed him down to the floor where I knelt on his shoulder, pinning him. With his free hand he pulled the knife.

I rolled away from the blade and jumped up.

For a big guy, he popped to his feet easily and jabbed at me with the blade. I parried with my left, striking his wrist, which sent the knife flying. He came back with a right hook.

I stopped his fist with an open-palm grab, sidestepped, and pulled his arm past my body then clubbed him with my other fist as he tipped forward. Now he was off balance enough for me to wrench his hand behind his back and scissor his neck in the crook of my free arm. The more he writhed, the more pressure I put on his throat. "¿Rendirse? Give up?"

He grunted.

I took that as a yes, shoved him over my extended foot, and he dropped to the floor with a thud.

Laughter roared through the barroom, but damned if he didn't jump to his feet and throw another punch.

I shifted my body weight backward, grabbed his arm, stepped inside, and let his momentum carry him over my shoulder. He landed on his back with my fist in his sternum, hard enough to knock the air from his lungs. I was having so much fun, I helped him get up. Stooped as he was, I kneed him in the chin. His head flew back and I belly-kicked him with my boot-heel. That threw his head forward and I popped him in the nose, not a knockout punch but bloody, nonetheless. He stumbled backward into a poker table. Gamblers jumped from their chairs as cards and money scattered across the floor.

Then a brawl erupted.

I didn't know how many men I'd laid out, or who punched

me in the jaw, but when it was all said and done, the room was in shambles. Splintered wood from broken chairs and tables lay strewn all over the floor. Tables were overturned. Someone had tossed a Mexican into the big mirror behind the bar, and cracks now webbed the glass. Busted bottle shards, mixed with liquor and beer and blood, decorated the bar-top. Men lay bruised and bleeding on the floor and draped over chairs. A clutch of saloon girls huddled in a corner, frightened out of their wits.

"You," a deep voice bellowed from behind me.

I pivoted to see a dark-haired man dressed in black pants, white shirt, and a long black coat, stalking toward me.

"I suggest you get out your gold, right now, and pay for the damages."

"Me? What about him?" I pointed to my attacker who lay belly-up on the floor.

"Pay up or jail. Your choice."

I held out my hands, wrists together. "Then jail it is. I've got no money."

"Monty. Wait." Lolita hurried up to us. "This should cover the damages." She dropped a tied cloth bag into her boss's hand.

I grabbed the bag from Monty and gave it back to her. "I don't want your money, Lolita."

"A little voice in my head insists," she breathed.

Abby, of course. I hated being dependent on her. I never lacked for money before. Between football and classes, I had no time for a job, so I never felt guilty taking my dad's money. But I'd be damned if I'd take her money now. She'd already turned me down twice, for the boots and the drinks. I stepped in front of her and faced Monty. "Let's mosey on down to the jailhouse now."

"Don't be an ass," she whispered in my ear. Not sexily like Lolita, but demanding like Abby. "Take the money. Rotting in jail will never get you home."

I doubted she had any idea how we were getting home, but I realized I didn't want to be locked up and miss the opportunity to blow this pop-stand. "Fine. Call it a loan, with interest." I took back the coin bag from her, pitched it to Monty, and stormed out through the swinging doors.

I retrieved my supplies from the merchant, and by some

miracle, I found my way back to camp, dragging the pick and shovel with one hand, and holding the bucket of clothes in the other. I carried the free gold panning pan under my arm and wore my new hat.

The long walk didn't cool my anger. My body felt stiff and bruised, but at least I felt satisfied I'd pounded the creep who'd accosted Abby. Actually, he'd propositioned Lolita, and she seemed to like the attention, but nevertheless, I defended Abby's honor in the process. A nice shower or soaking in a hot tub would do me good right about now. Yeah. Like that was going to happen. It was a cold bath in the river for me. Oh, well. My shirt needed washing anyway, but nothing about this time in history appealed to me.

As I walked deeper into the camp, I noticed three very distinct divides. In the center, a mainly Caucasian group mulled around, talking about their finds or lack thereof. At one end of the camp, I saw a colorful Chinatown. Men sat around smoking. Their long braided hair hung down their backs over silk clothing decorated with birds and dragons. Not remembering where Abby's house was, I aimlessly passed unfamiliar tents and makeshift huts. At this end of camp, brightly colored Mexican blankets flapped in the breeze. Men wearing colorfully striped ponchos played cards.

A few women wore flowing dresses and busied themselves stirring pots over campfires. The metallic thrum of a Mexican *vihuela de mano* clashed, off rhythm, with strains of a guitar coming from another direction.

"Señor." The kid I'd bought new shoes for ran up to me. "Me gusta mis zapatos nuevas." He pointed to his feet.

"I'm glad you like the shoes," I replied in Spanish.

"Hablas español bastante bien."

He said I spoke Spanish pretty good. "Aprendí español in la secundaria." *I learned Spanish in high school.*

"No hablo inglés muy bien. You teach?" His round face scrunched with question, and hope glistened in his eyes.

How could I say no? "Si...why not?"

My young friend pointed to his chest. "Emanuel."

"Wyatt." I set down the bucket and shook his hand.

"Ven." *Come.* He started walking.

Hoping he didn't think I would begin lessons now, I lifted the bucket and started after him.

Curious glances followed me, no surprise there. I got the feeling white men didn't enter this part of camp very often. A woman, maybe fifty, stood in front of a tent. Her long graying hair was woven into two impressive braids. She smiled as we approached her.

"Madre," Emanuel told me.

"Your mother," I replied.

"¿Quien es tu nuevo amigo, Emanuel?" she asked the boy about his new friend.

He introduced me to his mother. "Señor Wyatt."

"Yo so Camila. Sentarse por favor, Mr. Wyatt.." She indicated a crude bench in front of her tent then ducked inside.

I accepted Camila's offer to sit down, happy to set my supplies to the side. "She's very nice," I told Emanuel as he sat beside me, then translated, "Ella es muy agradable."

"Si. Very nice."

She came out and handed me a cup; its contents resembled thick hot chocolate. I lifted the steaming brew to my lips and inhaled the sweet aroma of chocolate and cinnamon. The beverage went down more like grainy pudding, but it was delicious.

"Bueno, Camila," I said between swallows. "Good," I repeated in English and gave Emanuel a thumbs up.

He smiled and returned the gesture. "Good."

"Champurrado," she said with a nod of pride.

I'd heard of this drink but had never tasted it. "You will have to teach me how to make this," I told her in Spanish.

"Si."

I stood and gathered my supplies. "Gracias..." then to Emanuel, "Thank you."

"Thank you," he repeated, then: "De nada."

"You are welcome."

"Welcome," he said.

I did feel welcome. And it felt good. For the first time since entering this crazy time zone, I'd met someone who didn't want to rip me off or kill me.

Chapter Six

Abby adjusts to her new life

After spending the night with Wyatt at the saloon and feeling guilty I'd left my children home alone, today I took Cattie and Joseph to the river to play. I was sure of my purpose here. It wasn't to be just a ride-along singer. It was the children. I needed to find out if Benjamin or Lolita had anything to do with their deaths. I couldn't believe she would kill her own kids, but no matter who had done it, I was sure I was here to stop the murderer.

Now, I never was much for science and astrology, fate and religion, but I wasn't naïve. I knew that changing the past could have dire consequences. The Domino Effect would probably create a time warp or open a worm hole and destroy the future, in part or in whole, in a chain-reaction of devastating events. However, I also knew there were forces of nature that no one knew a thing about. My sixth sense had always been plugged into supernatural phenomena that I couldn't explain. So, here I was in 1852, having traveled back in time, an event that no one could have expected or thought possible. I refused to believe there was no reason for this fantastic journey. Maybe I was supposed to save Lolita's children to correct a problem in the future. Why else would I be here if I wasn't meant to help them? I could only hope I was correct and wouldn't inadvertently create a paradox that couldn't be undone.

Because Wyatt had been protective of me, I no longer believed he had tried to drown me, but I couldn't ignore the grip on my ankle. Maybe someone from this era drew me here. Maybe it was Cattie, or Joseph, or both clinging to me. I'd heard her voice calling me that night. I'd seen their ghosts walking by the river, so it was reasonable to conclude they'd sucked me back in time so I could save them.

But why me?

I also had to wonder if solving this mystery would send us back home. Or would we be stuck here forever?

I sat by the sparkling river and watched the children dig in the dirt. Cattie barely said a word to me since yesterday. She had every right to be angry that I'd stayed at the saloon. Maybe that was a regular occurrence. Lolita loved her job, but what kind of mother would let her children fend for themselves? Maybe Lolita was a lousy mother. Maybe I wasn't any better. Cattie's aloofness made me wonder what else I'd done wrong. Joseph's sullen demeanor and his refusal to speak to me had me thinking about what Cindi had said. *"She's guilty."*

If so, why did her kids' spirits reveal themselves to me at the river? Maybe they wanted to prove their mother was innocent. I owed them a vow to do everything I could to solve the mystery. I just wasn't sure where or how to start.

I fanned my face. The bonnet I wore did little to protect me from the blaring afternoon sun. My long brown striped dress felt heavy and bulky. I'd thought it would be fun dressing up like women did in the good old days, but I never fully understood how many layers I'd have to wear.

After my entrance into camp wearing nothing but my underclothes, I thought it would be a good idea to stick with what a proper woman would wear. Under the dress, first came the pantalettes, leg coverings that went down to my ankles; God forbid someone saw any skin. A chemise, a fancy French word for shirt, went on next and hung to my knees. Then I'd struggled into a tight, uncomfortable corset. Why I needed to wear one with my tiny waist was beyond me, but I put it on, nevertheless. Several petticoats gave the long dress its bell shape. Lastly, a camisole covered my corset and padded the bone-stays that still cut into my abdomen. By the time I'd gotten into the dress, I was exhausted. With the hot sun and no breeze, I wished I'd rethought my wardrobe.

Still, being here was so serene. When I woke up yesterday morning, I'd forgotten where I was. Reality hit me when I walked down those stairs and got manhandled by a drunk Mexican at the bar. Lolita didn't mind, but I was appalled. Wyatt saved me from yet another man who felt he could have his way with me. I never realized what beautiful women dealt with, and for the first time, the jealousy I felt toward Cindi disappeared. I always sympathized with her when she complained about the creeps who came on to her, but deep down I really envied her.

Still, I liked my new skin. Being beautiful made me feel visible for the first time in my life.

My dad came to mind. Did he realize I was missing? How did one measure time from one dimension to the other? Time travel. No one would believe it possible. Well, no one other than Wyatt. Would we remember any of this when we returned to our own century...if we returned?

I glanced down the riverbank and saw Wyatt. Some Mexican kid was with him, wearing a sombrero. They were crouched by the water's edge. He appeared to be showing Wyatt how to pan for gold.

Wyatt's shirt was clean, he'd probably washed it in the river like everyone else, and he had rolled up his sleeves. I couldn't help but notice his corded arms, the way the knots of defined muscles bunched as he shifted a pan back and forth. The fabric of his new pants strained against his firm rear end. Sunshine highlighted the golden strands of hair on his arms, now slick with sweat. Damn him for looking so good.

I couldn't deny his being so close that night, in the same room, affected me in ways I could never tell my mother. I'd barely slept, listening to him snore all night. I kept wondering if he'd keep his promise to stay put in that chair. Part of me hoped he'd crawl into bed with me, the other prayed he'd keep his promise. As much as I rebelled against the ridiculous want inside me, I tried to shut out the memory of our night together, but the memory refused to leave me, how I'd tossed and turned, annoyed and wondering if he'd given up on me because I wouldn't kiss him. The flutters in my stomach hadn't helped matters, either, probably because Lolita wanted to lay under him. I just wanted to know the answer to my question: *Why did you stand me up on Prom Night?* I wasn't sure he'd heard me ask him, sleeping as he was. Come dawn, I'd scuttled from the room like a scared rabbit, afraid he'd wake up and I'd have to face him, ask him if he'd heard me or ignored me before he fell asleep. Maybe it was best

I didn't know his answer.

Now, my gaze lingered on him despite my desire to ignore his presence. I was surprised to see him working the river, never thought he'd actually take my advice, especially since he'd never done hard labor. Had he found any gold? I didn't feel like asking. I didn't care.

This morning, when he walked past me without so much as a glance in my direction, I figured he was still pissed that I'd forced him to take my money to pay the damages to the saloon. I wanted to thank him for coming to my rescue. Though Lolita was in her element, the Mexican's advances bothered me to no end. Sorry the saloon got destroyed in the process.

Suddenly, I noticed Joseph had waded into the water, and my heart kicked my ribs. Sure, the shallow pool there was safe, but not much more than a few steps farther out, the midstream current roiled by at a frightening pace.

"Joseph." I struggled to rise. My foot got caught in the hem of my long dress. The bones of my stays cut into my ribcage. I winced. Before I could get my footing, Cattie had steered him back to shore like a mother duck watching out for her little duckling. Always protective of him, she was more of a mother than Lolita. That had to change. Being a better mother and protecting those kids was now my responsibility.

As Cattie and Joseph returned to digging in the dirt, I settled down and went back to staring at Wyatt's magnificent arms. Cindi would have a cow if she knew I was here with him. Pam would probably slit her own throat. I wondered if they wondered what had happened to us.

"Git away from my claim, you lousy brats."

Startled by the angry voice, I jerked my head around to see Hank, a heavyset old man whose beard could house a colony of creepy bugs. A revolver hung from his belt. I didn't know Hank, but Lolita did, and I felt her alarm electrify my nerves.

I jumped to my feet. "Do not yell at my children."

He sneered at me. "They're digging on my claim."

"They are just playing." I stomped to the kids before he could lay a hand on them. "Children."

"You jest keep them young'uns away from here or else."

Or else? Hank had no tender spot in his heart. A character straight out of the woods, his serial-killer mug would be right at home on a Wanted Dead or Alive poster.

"Come, children. Let's go home."

Cattie and Joseph just stood there staring at me. "We don't want to go," Cattie said.

"We're having fun," Joseph said to Cattie.

"I said we are going." My shrill demand spurred them into motion. After I'd herded them a good distance from danger, I stopped them and bent down to their eye level. "I don't want you to go near that mean old man again," I said softly, regretting my earlier harsh tone.

Joseph said to his sister, "I want to play miner."

I straightened. "Sorry. It's not safe here today." I held out my hand.

Cattie took Joseph's hand, ignoring mine, and as they walked away, a tear formed in my eye.

"And don't come back," Hank bellowed.

I pressed my lips together, holding back a sharp retort that would only fuel his anger. For all I knew, he was the murderer. I tucked the thought into the back of my mind and followed the kids back to camp.

Wyatt pans for gold

A raised voice caught my attention. Some jerk was yelling at Lolita's kids. Bullies were bullies, no matter what time period in history. I stood to intervene, but the situation was handled before I had a chance to jump in, so I made a mental note to keep my eye on the creep. If he dared bother her or the kids, he was going to regret it. As much as I was annoyed at her right now, her safety was my priority.

My jaw still hurt from the sucker-punch someone laid on me in yesterday's bar brawl, but my aches and pains this morning were worth restoring my manhood when I rescued Abby. However, I hated taking money from her. It made me feel like a loser.

There goes my manhood again. I kicked a stone. It plunked into the water.

Emanuel looked at me from under his sombrero. "¿Estás bien?"

"Women!" I swatted a mosquito and scratched my arm.

"No comprender *women*."

"That makes two of us." I knelt, submerged my pan in the water, scooped up bottom sludge, and swirled the dirt and stones around like Emanuel showed me, but I bumbled the technique, and the contents, along with any hope of gold, dumped right back into the river.

My back and legs hurt from crouching for hours with nothing to show for it. I was jealous of the men who had rockers, who got to stand over the long wooden box and just shovel the dirt into the cradle and shake the mud down. I needed to get my hands on one of those, soon, or I wouldn't be able to walk within a month.

I'd been eager to start panning today, even after an uncomfortable night sleeping on the ground. Emanuel suggested I pan near the mouth of a shallow gulch and look for blue or red clay, a good sign I was in the right spot. After panning through the loose layers of muddy river-bottom, I started digging with my shovel and hands. Still, I came up empty.

The clank of pickaxes against rocks mixed with the guttural groans of men like me, I presumed they too had found nothing.

Emanuel slapped his arm. "Sakes alive, these here gallinippers are hungry today," he said in Spanish. If he was talking about the swarm of mosquitoes buzzing around us, I agreed. Every water-filled hole, abandoned for lack of gold, bred the nasty bugs, and I was red with bites and scratch marks.

"Bonanza!" The shout, followed by whoops and hollers, had men dropping their tools and running to a claim downriver. "Boys, lookee here." Judd held up a muddy rock that reflected shards of yellow sunlight.

Pandemonium broke out. Men started grabbing their tools and scurrying to find an unoccupied spot near Judd's while he and his partner zigzagged around trying to keep the horde of greedy men away from their claim. Not wanting to get in the middle of the chaos, I stayed put.

"Everyone is gold crazy," Emanuel said in Spanish. "If a

man lost his head, and it rolled across the ground, they would kick it from their claim, lest their gold be eaten."

"Tienes razón." *You're right.*

"Last week, I thought my jaw would hit the floor," he continued.

"¿Que pasó?" *What happened?*

"I had tailed a preacher and men who knew some dead hombre to a funeral." Emanuel made the sign of the cross on his chest. "The preacher, he was talkin' and prayin' over the grave, and I was thinking I got to get back to my claim. Someone yells *color* and points in the hole. The funeral was over, and even the preacher was up to his neck shoveling."

"You find any gold?"

Emanuel shook his head. "I moved outta their way. They don't like our kind digging with them."

"Your kind?"

"Greasers." He shrugged. "We're hated. Less than the Chinese but better off than Injins. Gringos use them for target practice."

"They're racist jerks. Don't listen to them. I'm happy you joined me."

"We sharing?" Emanuel crouched beside me and smiled.

"Maybe between the two of us we'll find something." I shoulder-bumped him. "Besides, I don't know what I'm doing."

We worked the site in silence, each of us hoping against hope we'd be as lucky as Judd.

I saw a glint in my pan. "I think I found something." I looked closer. "I did." My adrenaline pumped. "Bonanza," I shouted with excitement.

Men ran over to see what I'd found.

Emanuel tugged my shirt. "Señor Wyatt. No."

I was too excited to pay him any mind. I'd found gold. I was rich. Things were looking up. I could pay Abby back Lolita's money. I could get my watch out of hock. I could—"

"Well, don't this beat all." A hand reached into my pan before I could stop it. "Lookee here, he's done found a chispa of fool's gold. Gold for a fool," the toothless man shouted and dropped the worthless rock back into my pan.

Laughter and grunts of displeasure echoed as the crowd

dispersed like sprayed roaches. Excitement turned to humiliation.

Emanuel sighed. "Intenté decírtelo."

"Si. You tried to tell me no. I should have paid attention." I drew in a deep breath, used all my self-control not to toss the worthless pan into the river. "How do I tell the difference?" I asked in Spanish.

Emanuel picked out the rock from my pan. "Fool's gold is darker in color," he said in Spanish. "Looks like dull brass. Real gold is bright yellow and shines in the sun."

Okay, lesson learned. "Keep it." I dumped out my pan. "What is chispa?"

"A bit of shine." He pointed to a boulder near the rapids. "Try over there."

I waded to the rock, stuck my shovel into a submerged crevice, and dug out soggy clay.

"Red clay," Emanuel said. "A good sign."

Once again, excitement bubbled. I pushed aside gravel and we dug side by side. The current swept the clay from the growing hole. Suddenly, there at the bottom, shined bright yellow bits and pieces. My heart started to pound. I stepped back, not daring myself to believe. "¿Es oro?"

"Si. Oro."

We found gold.

A knot of dread twisted in my stomach. "Don't let the others know," I whispered in Spanish, having learned that lesson, too.

I scooped out several pieces the size and shape of barley grains. Finally, pay dirt. My mouth watered for oysters and brisket. "¿Cuánto cuesta?" *What do you think they're worth?*

Emanuel scratched his head. "Cinco dólares."

"Five dollars?" That was it? All that backbreaking manual labor under the blaring sun, and we only made five bucks?

I slumped against the boulder. I guessed it was fried pork, again, for our dinner tonight. I really wanted to go home, get a home-cooked meal...and I didn't mean back to camp. I meant back to Placerville in the 21st Century.

Abby and Lolita

With the kids down for a nap, I returned to the river to see if Wyatt had found any gold to pay back Lolita's loan. I sheltered behind a tree near him so I could watch without him seeing me. He was a total mess. Gone was the spoiled rich kid. His hands were dirty, as were his shirt and pants. There were streaks of dirt on his face that, damn my traitorous mind, I wanted to wipe clean with my fingertip.

I watched his muscled back and firm butt as he bent and picked up his shovel. Once again my inexperienced libido kicked my heart into rapid-fire. *No way am I attracted to him.*

"That is a lie, Abby."

"He's a cad. A womanizer."

"I know not of these things. I only know how I feel when I see him. Is he hung like a bull, I wonder?"

"Have you no shame?"

"I am a saloon girl with needs of my own."

"Keep them to yourself."

"What fun is that?"

Lolita planted racy images in my mind. Wyatt has me pressed against this tree; his strong hands are working up my thighs, his fingers find places no man's fingers have ever found. An unaccustomed fire throbbed between my legs...Lolita's legs.

"Stop."

The images faded, but the fire remained.

"You no like Lolita's needs?"

"No."

"You lie to yourself, Abby."

Maybe so, but I refused to let her or Wyatt get under my skin. Being jilted, even if it was three years ago, taught me a lesson I'd never forget. Trust no man. Was I bitter? *Damn right I'm bitter.*

"Bitter feelings will shrivel up your heart like an old chili pepper."

"My heart is slathered with suntan lotion to keep it from getting burned."

"I know not of this lotion, but I do know you would like to

see if he is hung like a bull."

"Oh my god. Stop," I shouted without thinking.

Wyatt turned and looked my direction. "Who's there? Lolita? Abby?"

Busted. I stepped from behind the tree. My gaze fell to his crotch. *Hung like a bull..?*

"You see anything interesting?" he quipped.

Humiliated, heat flamed my cheeks. He knew exactly what I was looking at and couldn't resist pointing out my indiscretion. "You're a jerk." In a swirl of petticoat lace, I pivoted to leave.

"Abby, wait."

I stopped and faced him. "What?"

Exhaustion dulled his eyes. "It's been a long day. What do you want?"

I wasn't sure. The Lolita part of me wanted to throw my arms around him, but I'd rather throw darts at him. Even so, he deserved an answer. "Have you found any gold?"

"I thought you might want to thank me for coming to your rescue yesterday."

"Lolita had that Mexican wrapped around her little finger, but you had to butt in and start a brawl."

"I figured since we're back in the good-ole days, a man's supposed to save the damsel in distress."

"I'm not a damsel."

"I am." Lolita's sexy voice came out of my mouth...well, her mouth. "You can save *me* anytime you want, Mister Wyatt."

Smiling, he walked up to us. "You girls had better behave yourselves."

I was touched by the concern in his voice.

He added, "Nobody can know about this predicament we're in."

"Predicament?" Lolita spat, her Spanish temper showing. "Half the time I am just along for the ride in my own body because of this mojigato."

"Abby's not a prude." Wyatt pressed me against the tree, his mouth so close to my ear I could feel the heat of his breath. "Just a little confused, but Lolita, you've made your point. Abby. I know you're doing the best you can, but don't take over Lolita's personality. People will notice something different about her."

My heart did a little flip. "But she's so...loose with men. Totally my opposite."

"Deal with it."

"If you kiss me I will deal with it," Lolita's sexy voice whispered from my mouth.

"Lolita, stop it," I begged.

Wyatt's lips brushed my cheek then pulled away. "I gotta get back to work."

I held his arm and stared into his eyes. I didn't want him to leave, but I wasn't going to ask him to come back to camp with me. Lolita would love it, but I had my boundaries. Still, I wondered where he'd stay the night. Back at the saloon? In a room upstairs? With one of the saloon girls? Jealousy wormed in my stomach, but I had to stay strong without being cold-hearted. I let go of his arm. "Be careful."

"You too." He turned to go.

I watched him walk back to the river. A stab of disappointment tightened my chest. *What's wrong with me?*

"You are stubborn like a donkey. He is going to get away, and we both lose."

Annoyance sharpened my mental tongue. *"Do you think I ever do anything right?"*

"Not yet."

I wished I could talk to Cindi. She understood me. A tear trickled down my cheek. God I missed her.

"We must get home to my children," Lolita said.

It was dinner time, time to put Wyatt out of my mind. I walked back to camp and stepped into Lolita's stifling shack. The kids were sleeping on their cots so I had to be quiet until I awoke them for dinner.

Earlier, Lolita had purchased canned turkey and all the fixings. I grabbed them off the shelf and set them on the table. She'd also picked up candied fruit and berry syrup, figuring she'd make pancakes in the morning. Her children loved pancakes. I wasn't much of a cook, but I could boil water and heat TV dinners in the microwave. No such modern conveniences here.

Starting a fire would have been a difficult task for me.

Thankfully, matches had been invented in the early eighteen hundreds. Rubbing two sticks together would have been disastrous. Good thing Lolita took the lead. She lit the wood stove, tossed in a couple chopped logs Benjamin had supplied, and closed the fire grate. It wasn't long before cans were opened and dinner was heating in a big pot.

I was about to wake the kids when a woman's voice resonated from the front door blanket. "May I come in?"

"Daisy. Of course."

She pulled back the blanket and strode through the opening, prim as a peacock. Blue feathers in her blond hair framed her round, overly made-up face. She eyed the stove. "Looks like you're making dinner."

"I was about to wake the kids." Not wanting Daisy to think Lolita had just landed from Mars, I let her carry the conversation. "They will need to go wash up."

"Let them sleep a little longer, Sugar." She claimed a chair at the table. "I want to make sure you're feeling all right. You got pretty drunk the other night."

"Thanks." I sat across from her. "But I am okay."

"I don't know how you did it, but last night you sang one of your best shows...like you were someone else."

"Thanks to your encouragement before I went onstage."

"Ah, that's what friends are for." She reached across the table and squeezed my arm. "But I have to ask...where did you dig up that new sweetie?"

"Wyatt?"

"He's a wild horse. Very protective of you."

"We're just friends," I cut in on the conversation.

"Friends? You act like you hate him, and that's not like you, Lolita. You're very attentive to men, especially the young handsome ones."

"Wyatt is complicated."

"And your husband? How long will he be gone? Have you forgotten Monty? I think you are the complicated one, Lolita."

I had to change the subject. "Would you like to stay for supper? I have to warn you, I am not a very good cook."

A puzzled expression scrunched her face. "I've enjoyed your cooking many times. It's wonderful...but thanks for the invitation. I'm on my way to the saloon. Benjamin is going to give me a ride."

"What do you think about Benjamin?"

"Keeps to himself. Not much of a talker."

"Do you think he's dangerous?"

"Sugar. All men are dangerous, especially when there's money to be made or a lady's favors to be taken."

That wasn't comforting.

"Why do you ask about Benjamin? You've known him a long time."

I shrugged. "The other night, he took me home. I was so drunk I didn't remember any of it. He says nothing happened between us. True?"

"He's a mystery, that one. I see how he looks at you when you're not looking."

"Not him, too? He seems so nice."

"He can't be trusted."

"What about Monty? Can he be trusted?"

"Lolita, are you blind? He's been trying to get under your skirt since you came to work at the saloon. How could you not know that?"

"I-ah...didn't think he was serious."

"You know he's buying a nightclub in San Francisco?"

"I didn't know."

"I'd love to go to San Francisco." She stood. "But here I am in Dry Diggins. I must go to work now."

I stood and hugged her. "Thanks for coming by."

She ducked outside, and standing at the doorway, I watched her negotiate the rutted dirt road to Benjamin's buggy. She wasn't Cindi, but having someone I could confide in lifted my spirits. I'd been feeling a little homesick. In a crowded camp where ninety-five percent of the population was male, having a woman to share things with was a godsend.

By now, dinner was bubbling hot. I woke the kids and sent them outside to the washbasins. A glance at Benjamin's tent across the way gave me pause. I made a mental note to keep an eye on him.

The heat of the evening was intense despite the setting sun. I tugged the bodice of my dress away from my skin and blew some air down between my borrowed breasts. Wearing a long dress in ninety-degree weather was unbearable. I would have loved a cool dip in the river, but the thought lasted less than a second when I remembered the lewd remarks and stares I'd gotten the day we arrived.

Children's laughter caught my attention. Cattie and Joseph raced each other around a bend in the camp road, playing catch me if you can. My heart began to pound with uncertainty for their future.

Chapter Seven

Wyatt loses his claim

I knew, by the thick stubble on my face, approximately two weeks had passed since I'd landed in this nightmare. Not having an electric razor, there was no way I was going to use a knife and accidentally cut my throat. Most men around here didn't bother to shave; the prospect of finding gold outweighed personal hygiene. Sweat dripped down my forehead, despite the fact I stood knee-deep in cold water. I removed my black felt hat and fanned my face. Where was a breeze when I needed one?

Hat on again, I waded to another large boulder. Fast-moving water swirled around it, and from what Emanuel had told me, gold carried by the current could become lodged under the rock. Standing upstream, I dug up a shovelful of river-bottom at the base and dumped it into my pan. I'd gotten pretty good at swirling the contents just enough to expel the dissolved mud, hopefully leaving gold dust or a nugget or two on the bottom.

Nothing. Damn it. Time and time again, nothing.

My face burned with frustration. Emanuel was going to be disappointed. The kid was studying today, and I missed his company. I liked him, liked having someone to talk to. If it weren't for his family's generosity, I'd have been sleeping under the stars. The mosquitoes at night were worse than during the day. I was grateful for the small corner in the back of Emanuel's tent where I had a makeshift bed of Mexican blankets. Though I pitched in and helped as much as I could: hauling wood, lugging heavy bags, carrying buckets of water, I felt like a third wheel. Staying with people I hardly knew made me uncomfortable, and I didn't like being a burden. I promised the arrangement was temporary. As soon as I found more gold I'd move into a tent of my own and pay them a bit for back-rent.

As I swirled another shovel's worth of nothing, Abby came to mind. Sure, I'd said I was going to keep a close eye on her, but I knew when I wasn't wanted. Not being wanted was a first for me. Lolita fit in quite well, so I was sure Abby was in good hands...body and all. She sang like an angel. The men adored Lolita, and Abby didn't appear to be as out-of-sorts as I felt around here. Unlike me, she was raking in the dough and didn't seem the worse for wear. And Lolita looked downright amazing. The low-cut dresses she wore hugged her tiny waist and accented her breasts. I was sure she'd seen me staring. I couldn't help myself.

As for me, I still hated this place, hated the long, tedious hours spent finding nothing, getting nothing but sunburn, blisters, and bug bites. I hated the filth, the crowds, the heavy greasy smell of fried slapjacks and pork. The stench of body odor, urine, and horse dung always hit me like a blast of heat in the face and made me gag. I didn't belong here, didn't fit in, and I didn't like feeling like a nobody. With each passing day, the hope I clung to, the unheard prayer that I'd wake up back in my own time, faded.

Judd and Ed worked their usual claim by the river. They hadn't said much to me after our first encounter. In fact, no one bothered to talk to me. I felt invisible, inadequate. I hated that too. A confident, no-holds-barred kind of guy, this feeling of not knowing what to do next, not fitting in, not being me... I wished I'd never taken that swim to get close to Abby.

My knees hurt from crouching. I stood and stretched and wondered if I'd ever carry a football again. Everywhere I looked, unwashed men squatted by the river, swirling pans with the hope of finding gold dust or better. Callused hands drove pickaxes into rocks, cracking them again and again. Chunks of rocks that yielded no gold lay in piles everywhere. The constant sound of clanking, grunting, and swearing made my nerves bunch.

The shadow of a nearby cliff offered some relief from the glaring sun, and I looked up to where my grandmother's house would be built someday. Damn. I still couldn't believe it wasn't there. No breeze rustled the small fir trees that would grow tall enough to shade her home in the future. I'd give anything to be swimming in her infinity pool that overlooked the valley. I swiped sweat from my brow and eyed the river turned murky by the miners upstream.

I picked up my tools. The last thing I needed was to have them stolen. I hiked to a nearby section of the river where the water was clearer. Stripped down to my swim trunks, I placed my shirt and pants over my boots, pan, and pickaxe, and then waded into the cold water. Goose bumps erupted all over my body. I dove in. Would this be the answer? Would swimming in this river send me back the same way I got here? I swam out until I could no longer fight the current, held my breath, and dove to the bottom. Nothing weird happened. I surfaced to hear an excited voice cry out, "Bonanza." Men were rushing to my claim. *What are they doing?* I swam to shore.

Curiosity mixed with anger. Once again, someone else had struck it rich, but why were they celebrating on my claim? Unless it was my gold. I dressed, left my tools, and with my hat on, I made a beeline to the group of men huddled in the middle of my diggings.

"Hey, you're on my claim." I rammed into the crowd, knocking men out of my way. "Get out of here."

A beared man's steely gaze met mine. I'd dealt with this bully before. In his hand lay a lump of yellow gold the size of a walnut.

"That's mine. Give it back." I lunged at him but got tackled before I could grab my gold from his hand. My chest hit the ground and men piled on. "Get off me."

The bully knelt next to my face and lifted my hat so I could get a good look at him. "Ya forfeited yer claim, Pike."

"What are you talking about?" Rage heated my face. "I've been working that claim all week. That gold is legally mine." A vein in my temple throbbed. "Let me up."

The mob released me.

I sprang to my feet, wanted to swing at the guy, knock out his yellow-stained teeth, but the barrel-chested thief brandished a shovel, daring me with narrow eyes.

"You have no right—"

"Don't see yer tools, Pike." A nasty sneer crinkled his weathered face. "Maybe our law hasn't come to yer ears."

"What law?"

"If ya don't leave yer tools at yer stake, anyone can jump your claim."

"Leave my tools...so you can steal them too?" Curses teetered on the tip of my tongue, but I bit them back. "I'll get the Sheriff out here. You're going to jail for claim jumping."

"Not so fast, Pike." His ratty beard framed the smug expression on his blistered lips. "Town law don't count for nothin' at the river. Camp law is the law out here."

"I don't believe you."

The men around me nodded.

"Each camp makes their own laws," a gaunt miner said. "No tools. No claim. Ain't that right, Hank?"

"Stops prospectors from hoggin' up the whole riverbank."

Damn. The lump of gold taunted me. As long as the law allowed for jumping claims, I'd never get rich.

Wyatt finds gold

After that antagonistic scene, I needed to get away. Go somewhere I could think. Be alone. I followed the winding river upstream, walked through the dark stands of pines and oak trees that dogged the shore. The pristine air was so clear I could see far into the distance. White and purple flowers dotted the valley. Under the blaring sun, the river shone like silver, a beautiful sight I hoped would relax me.

I'd been working an average of forty pans in a ten-hour day with nothing to show for it, and I'd lost a rich claim through sheer ignorance. Angry, I booted a rock into the river. I wanted to blame Emanuel for not educating me on the laws of the camp, but he would be as disappointed and angry as I felt. Okay, lesson learned. I still felt like a loser.

The little gold we did find was not enough to buy decent food, let alone pay off the store clerk and Lolita. I'd marked a pickle jar with lines. The top line read: oysters. Champagne, roast beef, and potatoes beneath that, then turkey with all the fixings. Plum duff, a foul-tasting pork pudding was on the bottom. Most days, the little dust I'd found never rose above the middle line, and I was sick of eating pork and beans.

Suntan lotion applied on my burnt skin would be a welcomed relief. I wished I could invent some and sell it. I'd make a fortune. That day by the river came to mind, the glob of lotion on Abby's lip, the mental joke I'd made about her overuse of suntan lotion. Never again would I belittle someone who was overly cautious.

I never appreciated the hardships people suffered, not until now. I stared down at my bruised knuckles. My dad would be appalled at the dirt under my ragged nails. If people thought they had it rough, they should take a step back in time. They'd think twice before complaining.

I sat under a giant oak tree and took in the scene from under my hat brim. Across the river, an elk grazed. He jerked up his head and sniffed the air as though he feared a predator was near, then he went back to grazing. A flock of ducks landed with a splash, causing the massive beast to, once again, glance my way.

Attempting to relax, I closed my eyes and began meditating. The air smelled pure and clean with a scent of pine. Water gurgled. Birds chirped, and trees swayed in a gentle breeze. Funny how the spot I always went to in my meditative mind was beside a river shaded by pines. I inhaled the earthy smell of green moss and the sweet scent of summer air. It took several deep breaths and frustrated exhales to center myself, to quiet the torment playing over and over in my mind. When my ass felt numb, and the tension eased from my neck and shoulders, I stood.

My throat dry, I walked to the river's edge and dipped in my hat. I was bringing the black felt to my lips, when a glint of yellow caught my attention. I squatted in the water and looked at the rock-bed beneath the surface. Nestled in a crevice lay a lump of what I hoped was gold.

Excitement revved my pulse as I picked up the nugget. *Fool's gold? No. It's bright yellow. Gold? Gold. Definitely gold.* I wanted to scream *bonanza*, but the prospect of a herd of men storming this spot before I'd staked my claim made me bite my tongue.

I dropped the nugget into my pocket, tossed my hat onto

the shore then bent over the water. Slowly, in an attempt to stir up less debris, I gently scooped out gravel and sand, stepped back on shore, emptied the soil into my pan, then I hurried back to the water. I raked my finger through the pan removing the larger rocks and gravel and fingered the dirt to break up clumps and make for a smoother texture. My pan at an angle, the way Emanuel taught me, I dipped, making sure the lip wasn't under the water, and lifted the pan with a backward motion, letting water and gravel run out. With each dip, lift, and swirl my heart pounded with anticipation. When there was very little water left in the pan and just black dirt, a good indication I'd find gold, I slowly rolled out fine sandy particles until specks of gold dust glistened.

I straightened so quickly with excitement I nearly lost my balance, and as I hurried back to shore, I came up with a plan on how to stake my claim. No way in hell was I going to lose this one.

Abby makes a list

I awoke breathing hard after dreaming about Wyatt.
Damn.

I sat up and rubbed my eyes, unable to erase the images of me, of Lolita, making love to Wyatt. It felt so real. I still throbbed with a want that, in my dreams, had held me captive in his arms. We lay under the bright stars and a crescent silver moon. I closed my eyes, picturing us intertwined on a blanket, his strong arms wrapped around me. I could still feel the heat of his skin against my naked body, the hard muscles that bunched as he drew me up on top of him. I groaned, as I had moaned in my dream. He savored every inch of me with his desire-filled eyes, his teasing hands, his lips, and in my dream, my body ignited with emotions so new, so uninhibited...

I threw off my blanket and got off the uncomfortable cot. Those sensual emotions were certainly not mine. How could they be? I was a virgin, and I never dreamed of riding on top of a naked man. No. Not me. But Lolita? I'd bet it was her dream of making love to Wyatt. Not mine. Besides, Wyatt had hurt me once. I refused to let him into my heart again. Several times I thought about confronting him, but I just didn't have the energy. Call me a coward, but it was easier to harbor my hurt feelings than face him. Since he hadn't brought up the past, I figured neither one of us was ready to discuss what happened that night of the prom.

Determined to forget and pull myself together, I glanced across the shack at my children who lay sound asleep nestled together on one cot.

Needing air, I quietly made my way outside. Dense gray fog hung heavy in the treetops, only visible by the glow of campfires. I wrapped my arms around my chest and listened to the chirp of crickets and the occasional deep throaty croak of a bullfrog.

Trying to divert my attention from my thrumming body, I watched high clouds float in a moonless sky. The new moon rose and set with the sun, leaving the night dark and starry. We'd been here two weeks. It seemed like an eternity.

Homesickness weighed heavy on my heart.

Every morning I got up and cared for the children, and I wondered how much longer we had together. I fought feelings for Wyatt, feelings that couldn't be mine; they had to be Lolita's. With each day, I worried Lolita would grow more tired of my prudishness, take back her body, and I would disappear. The thought sickened my stomach. I'd gone to the saloon every day, wondering if she felt like singing. Every time I stepped on the stage, I feared she'd be quiet and I'd make a fool of myself. Another knot formed in my chest. Lolita hadn't let me down yet, but I wasn't sure how long I could take her intense emotions battling mine inside of us.

In all the times I'd read about her, I never thought I'd actually be her. Now, every time I saw my reflection, I took a second look, not believing it was possible to see her looking back at me. Despite it all, I still felt wonderful in her skin.

When anyone reminded me how beautiful I was, how I sang like an angel, my confidence soared. It was a novel feeling, one I promised myself I'd work on when I got back home.

Every night I observed the moon, went back over the day's events and the people I'd met to see if any of them had a reason to harm my kids. It was June 17th and except for suspecting the nasty man at the river and the piano player, I had little evidence that pointed to the killer.

A light breeze swept through strands of my long hair. I brushed a lock from my face...well, Lolita's face. I was in someone else's freaking body. What else, besides her taking control of her voice, would pop out when I least expected it. Like that sexy dream of Wyatt. What's to stop her from making it a dream come true? I'd be caught in the heat of passion beyond belief.

I caught a chill that I blamed on the night air. Time to go back in and face my dreams. I pivoted and pushed aside the door blanket.

"I killed him...it was my fault," a familiar voice said behind me.

The raspy words stopped me short. I turned toward the sound coming from Benjamin's tent.

"I had no choice," he cried.

Who was he talking to? Making sure I wouldn't be seen, I glanced left, then right, then snuck across the narrow road separating our homes.

Who had he killed?

Careful not to lean too close to the side of his tent, I tilted my ear to the canvas and bunched my gown in my trembling hands. Barely breathing, fearful someone would see me eavesdropping or the people inside would hear me, I was rooted to my spot, not daring to move. I had to learn what Benjamin was up to. The normally welcomed silence that settled over the camp this time of night now jangled my nerves. A knot formed in my chest.

"Dangerous, very dangerous," came from the tent.

I shivered. My gaze darted around. Should someone notice me snooping... A sudden bloom of clammy sweat dampened my face. One movement, any movement, would give me away.

The approaching whisper of footsteps in dirt caught my attention. I straightened. Someone was coming. *Oh my god.* With uneven steps, I darted to my door and ducked safely inside.

While I recovered my nerves I wondered: Who was Benjamin talking to? Why wasn't that person responding to him?

What was dangerous? What was his fault?

Worry had me tossing and turning for the rest of the night. With the light of dawn, I was up, preparing porridge, laying out the children's clothes, and sweeping the dirt floor free of pebbles and leaves. Hours later, Benjamin's conversation was still on my mind. I had no clue where to start looking for his silent partner.

Pacing did nothing but make tracks in the dirt floor, so I decided to check out the camp store, pick up a few items, and hopefully a few clues. The money I'd made last week at the saloon would cover some much-needed clothing, and there was always next week's pay for other necessities.

I walked up the rutted road that wound around to a shed-like store, the façade made of rough vertical poles. Over the door, a large hand-painted sign read: PROVISIONS. As I walked in, an elderly woman studied me with judgmental eyes. I quickly averted my gaze.

The store boasted two windows, a luxury afforded by few. To my surprise, the temperature felt ten degrees cooler. An earthy smell of dirt and natural wood scents floated among specks of dust highlighted by the sun-drenched windows. Vegetables, potatoes, and various other produce lined the shelves. Cans were neatly arranged side by side. Tools and cookware hung from pegs. Bolts of fabric sat on a counter, and alongside a stove, a large pile of colorful blankets lay on the wood-plank floor.

Happy to see a few dresses hanging in one corner, I walked to them and chose a pretty blue one with black, orange, and purple plaid. Cloth-covered black buttons lined the front and sleeves, and the neckline was modest. With so many men in camp, I didn't want to attract any unnecessary attention.

"You will need these." The shopkeeper held out a pair of long white cotton leggings, a chemise, and a corset. As she eyed me, the expression on her thin mousy face was one of disgust. Some women didn't approve of Lolita's profession.

I hated corsets, and layering was uncomfortable in such extreme weather, but her condescending tone made me withhold any barbed comments of my own.

"Of course. Thank you."

She wrapped up the trio.

It boggled my mind every time I woke up in my shack or got dressed in clothing from 1852. I'd pinched myself several times. When I get home, when I tell this story, would anyone believe me? If I started spouting wormholes and time warps, would anyone take me seriously since I couldn't prove I was actually here?

"Perfume. Do you have anything nice?" I crossed my fingers.

"All the way from San Francisco." The shopkeeper bent down, rummaged in a box, and held out a small white bottle.

I hurried over, opened the top, and inhaled the aroma of honeysuckle. "I'll take it." Then I spotted a blue calico dress with a matching bonnet and decided Cattie had to have it. The color, against her black hair, so much like mine, would be striking. Then I spied a boy's white shirt the perfect size for Joseph. I opened my purse and took inventory of the coins. I'd be broke but purchasing something for Joseph was a must. I hated his quiet caution when we were together. Maybe if I bought him a gift, he would warm up to me.

On the next shelf over, books were lined up. Some were by Dickens, Pushkin, Hugo, and there was a small section for Children's books. Fairytales: Brothers Grimm, adventure: *Swiss Family Robinson*. The kids would love these...but I didn't have any more money. As I placed my purchases on the counter, I decided I'd have to ask Wyatt to buy the books.

"Such a shame it is, your husband leaving you with two small children and you having to soil..." She scowled. "I mean, leaving you with having to find the means to feed them."

I knew what she was referring to. I was a soiled dove. As far as she knew, I was a whore who worked in a saloon, someone lower than pond scum. "My songs put food on our table and allow me to buy all this lovely merchandise from you." I pushed the clothing toward her and smiled sweetly. "You do take soiled coins, right?"

"I didn't mean—"

"You should come into the saloon and hear me sing." I knew full well she wouldn't dare. "I'm sure you'd do whatever it takes to care for your children."

Agreement flashed in her judgmental brown eyes but

disappeared quickly. "Your husband is gone, what? One year now?"

"Time does fly, doesn't it?"

"You must be devastated, him just hightailing outta town like that." Her tone was one of distaste.

"Devastated? No." I tossed back my shoulders with confident authority. "I say good riddance. Who needs a good for nothing husband?" I grabbed my purchases and walked out the door, hoping to God if he came back he'd stay far away from us.

How could someone who looked like me lose a man? If the legend was correct, he'd abandoned me for another woman. Was I such a lousy person, or was it incompatibility? From the hoots, hollers, and attention I got everywhere I went, most men around here wanted me, and wanted me bad. Knowing that gave me a big boost in confidence.

My dad came to mind. Did he worry? Did he think I'd gone off somewhere without telling him? He was usually so immersed in his work and his patients, we spent little time together. He was always up before dawn and home after I was in bed.

Would the police find our bodies? Since Wyatt was missing too, would they think we'd run off together? Great. Just what I needed; my name linked to his. Cindi would deny any such suggestion. She knew how much I despised him, though I honestly couldn't say the same thing now. But what did Cindi think? Did she think we both drowned? Did anyone see us go under? Was one day here, a month in my time, or maybe a minute, or what? This whole mess was so complicated.

I entered my shack, dropped my packages into the trunk, grabbed a sheet of paper, then sat at the table.

Lately, I'd been so busy singing down at the saloon I'd had no time to look for a killer. But then, it wasn't like I could go around interviewing people about Lolita. They'd look at me like I was crazy. No solid clues had turned up yet, so all my thoughts were nothing but speculation.

I dipped my pen into the ink. On the top of the page, I wrote *Legend*. Centered under the title I wrote *Cattie and Joseph*. To their left, I wrote *husband*. He was the main reason Lolita supposedly went crazy and drowned her children, all because she was jealous of the attention her husband paid to them and not her. I found that hard to believe. Lolita loved her kids. Besides, she was seen dancing at a party on the night in question, so that version of the legend couldn't be right. But like Cindi said, she could have left the party, but no one had seen her slip out.

On the other side of the page, I wrote *Benjamin.* He left right after the kids were murdered, so as far as I was concerned, he was my main suspect. *Hank*...I couldn't forget Hank. He threatened my kids and was as likely a suspect as anyone else around here. Lolita came to mind. As much as I didn't want to write down her name, she was accused of the murders and became the nexus of the legend. I hesitated to take a breath, then at the bottom of the page I wrote: *Lolita.*

"Abby? Why did I write my name on this paper? And Cattie's and Joseph's. And Benjamin and Hank? What is going on?"

My heart hitched. If she knew her kids would be killed on the night of the blue moon, certainly she would take them and flee. There would never be a legend of the Weeping Woman. Though telling her the truth would save the children and accomplish my goal, her actions would change the future in ways I couldn't guess. I was sure it had to be my actions that saved them in order to fix a problem in the future, though I didn't know how. I just had to trust my sixth sense. So, no matter who had done it, I couldn't let her know what history had said happened that night.

"Abby? Are you keeping a secret from me?"

"It's nothing, just names of those I've met so far."

"But you have not met my husband."

"I don't know his name, but maybe I'll meet him soon."

"I hope not." There was that Spanish temper again.

I figured she'd bought my lie. Gnawing my lip, I looked over my list. If I didn't find the killer before the night of the blue moon, Lolita's kids would die, and Wyatt and I could be stuck here forever.

Chapter Eight

Wyatt and the bully

Emanuel was asleep when I returned yesterday. Last night I barely slept. Visions of finding more gold at our claim kept me tossing and turning. With the rising sun on the twentieth day of June, I got up and nudged my friend awake.

"Gold, look," I whispered

He sat up and crossed his legs on a brightly woven Mexican blanket. His dark eyes widened, and a big grin lit his face. "Veta Madre."

"Motherlode? Too soon to tell," I replied in Spanish. "But, shush. No one can know. The last thing we need is a stampede of claim jumpers."

"Si, jefe."

Ever since I'd asked him to join me in my pursuit of gold, he'd called me jefe. I'd told him I wasn't his boss. Then he'd call me boss. We were partners, but he persisted, and I gave up trying to correct him.

"I staked the site, but upstream whitewater is rapid. I'm praying my markers held."

"I pray as well." Emanuel made the sign of the cross.

"I think to be safe, I'll start out for the claim, and you watch from a distance to make sure no one follows me, then come ahead."

Emanuel nodded.

For the first time in days, I felt hopeful. Granted, I was stuck in this hellhole, but maybe things would start to go a little easier. With a lot of gold in my pocket, perhaps the men in camp would treat me with respect, or at the very least, stop making me feel like a loser. Money was power, no matter what anyone said.

I hated to think that way, but I liked the power. I liked feeling in control. Most people hung with me because I was rich. That bothered me from time to time, especially when it came to women. But not having any dollars in my pocket was worse than being concerned why someone liked being around me.

Abby came to mind. I had a feeling my wealth, or lack thereof, made no difference to her. She was a novelty that intrigued me. Most women wanted to hitch a ride on my popularity and get into my pants, hoping we'd be an item, which meant access to the lifestyle my money would buy. Abby was the first woman who showed no interest in me. When I was around her, I got the impression she was pissed at me, especially during our little sleepover.

Abby aside, I couldn't deny that Lolita was hot. And I knew that look, the dreamy eyes when women were interested in me. Lolita was definitely into me; but as tempting as she was, nothing could come of it. I needed to set my sights on boosting my image and gaining some respect in Abby's eyes.

Excited to start out, I stood. As Emanuel rose, his stomach grumbled. "Breakfast first," I said, even though I wanted to bolt to the river.

We sat outside the tent while Camila served sweet biscuits. Men stretched, belched, and scratched their scraggly beards, then picked up their tools and headed off to dig and pan. The rising sun blanketed the camp like a thermal heating pad.

"Emanuel, you have a novia...girlfriend?" I took a bite of hard biscuit. Despite being smothered in sweet butter, the dry lump scratched my throat as it went down.

"No, boss. Not many girls around here."

I began to divvy the gold pieces I'd found the day before into two piles. "¿Cuantos años tienes? How old are you?"

"Quince."

"Fifteen." Back in the day, that was old. What was the life expectancy? Thirty? Forty? If manual labor determined longevity, I'd be lucky if I made it to twenty-five.

"Someday I will have a girlfriend like Lolita...like you."

"Girlfriend? Lolita?" I tossed a gold piece in his pile. "Me? No."

Emanuel studied me, his carbon dark eyes steely. "Because

of her profession?" he suggested in Spanish.

"No."

His hard expression softened. "She sings like a bird, and her body is muy bien."

"We were talking about you. Not me. Here." I pushed his share of the gold toward him. "This is your half. Keep it safe."

Recalling Lolita's muy bien hot body was not a path I wanted to go down. I kept my distance; she was keeping hers, at Abby's request, I was sure, and that worked for me. Getting it on with one woman right now would be unwise. Getting mixed up with two would be suicide.

It seemed crazy thinking about Abby as two women. From what I saw, Lolita reacted the opposite of Abby. Every time someone flirted with her, she enjoyed it, but Abby would fight back. Lolita may have been a tease, but Abby had a tight rein on her, at least so I thought when she denied Lolita a kiss from me. The only time I noticed Abby enjoying Lolita's lifestyle was when she was on stage. That's when Abby, the star, came out.

I swallowed sweet biscuit. "How long has your family been digging?" I dumped my share of the gold into my jar.

"Since the last new growth."

Was he referring to last spring, over a year ago? My chest tightened. God. I hoped to be out of here before August. "Your papa find anything?"

Emanuel frowned. "A chispa."

"Not much, huh?"

"Your people make it difficult for my people. My papa says Gringos tax us more than anyone else. They take away our claims, leave us with little. California is our land, the land of Mexico, yet your people stole it from us."

"I'm sorry about that. The greed of gold makes men do nasty things, especially to people who are different."

"They treat you badly, like me, I see." Emanuel's face showed no malice, as if he'd grown accustomed to the hatred of those around him. "Where are you from, boss?"

How to explain? I didn't have a clue. I came from the mountain above the cliff where my grandmother's house would someday stand. I used to swim in the same river I now panned in, went to school in the same town two miles from here, Dry

Diggins, now called Placerville. Oh, by the way, I traveled here from the future. Yeah. I had to stay away from that question.

"We should start out before someone else—"

A man's painful wail pierced the air.

We jumped to our feet.

In the Chinese section of the camp, a group of men surrounded a small man. His quilted jacket hung ripped from one arm, and his short blue pants were covered in dirt. A white man landed a punch to the Chinese man's stomach.

"No sense kickin' about it. You done lost yer claim, yellowbelly." The beehive-looking cap he wore flew off. Other white men held his arms to keep him on his feet for the beating.

Appalled, I headed toward the ruckus. My stomach twisted with repulsion and drove me to a run.

"No, boss. Bad idea."

The white man yanked the small man's braided hair and brought him to his knees. A knife glistened in the sun.

"I wouldn't do that if I were you." I stared down the gruff, beer-bellied man who held a blade against his victim's long queue.

"Mind your own business, Pike."

"How about we even the playing field?" I kept my sight focused on the bully, but I was keenly aware of the position of every man there, moving in a circle, closing in around me.

"There's one of you and a dozen of us. I'm gonna gut you next."

"I suggest you let him go before you get hurt."

"Is that so?" A scrappy guy, who looked like someone from the nastiest part of camp, pointed his gun at me. "I knows your reputation, but your mouth is flying too loose for your own good."

The hostile crowd moved in closer.

I was ready. Years of training for this moment pulsated through my veins. I balled my fists. Adrenaline pumped. "I suggest you boys back off."

Hesitant glances darted between the two men. My guard up, my stance limber, I stared him down.

"You looking to eat a bullet?" Sharp little eyes challenged me.

I delivered a round kick to the gun; it flew from his hand. Then I dropped into a fighting stance, hands in front, position solid, I was ready to leap. "You looking to eat my fist?"

His smug, confident expression fell.

No one moved. All eyes were on me.

Nostrils flared. Hands were clenched, and a blade was still ready to cut the man's braid. I wasn't sure how I was going to kick the knife away without bashing in the small man's skull.

"Cut it. I dare you," I challenged the big guy. It would be my pleasure to pummel that nasty scowl off his racist face.

Abby cares

I heard all the commotion, heard Wyatt's steely voice, and ran toward the Chinese section to find out what was going on. Hank, the nasty man who had threatened my kids, held a knife against a Chinese man's long braid. Wyatt stood in the middle of a gang of rough men. I held my breath, watching the scene before me in horror.

I knew Wyatt could defend himself, but he was outnumbered. I saw him karate-kick the gun away. Why wasn't anyone helping him? I glanced frantically around the camp. A few men watched the confrontation. Others paid them no mind and kept clear.

Then Wyatt dared the burly guy to cut the braid. I wanted to yell, wanted to rush in and defuse the situation, but remembering his dislike of my interference at the saloon, I didn't move. The sound of picks pounding rocks and water-filled pans swirling pebbles mixed with the loud pounding of my heart.

Hank angled his head and spat.

Wyatt appeared calm as he glanced down at the spittle on his boot, but I was close enough to see one hand clenched at his waist. His other arm was up in front of him defensively.

My heart fluttered with pride, despite my fear of him getting hurt.

Hank lowered the knife. "Come on, fellas. Let's git."

Despite the indifference I swore to hold between us, a gush of breath escaped me.

"I ain't up to teaching this Pike a lesson right now." Hank kicked the small man in the back, knocking him face-first in the dirt, and the crowd broke up.

I hurried to Wyatt as he helped the man rise.

"You okay?" He patted dust from the man's back.

I wasn't sure if the Chinese man understood English, but he bowed his head.

Wyatt picked up the man's hat, tapped it against his thigh, and handed it back to him. "You better stay clear of those guys for a while."

The man scurried away.

I grabbed Wyatt's arm. "Are you okay?"

"What do you care?"

"That was very brave of you." My very own hero was standing in front of me. I felt my heart melting into a puddle of...ahhhh. Damn him. "And very stupid," I added to cool the heat building inside me.

Wyatt's brows shot up. "You're kidding me, right?"

"You could have gotten yourself killed."

He scowled. "I know how to take care of myself."

"I am impressed," I replied in Lolita's sexy voice.

His scowl softened. "Really?"

"Is your pulse racing as fast as mine?"

"Don't listen to her," I growled.

He reached over and ran his calloused finger against my cheek.

My breath caught.

"Thanks for caring." A smile softened the edges of his mouth.

Tingles ran down the length of me. "I don't care," I insisted, even though I knew I'd lied.

He stepped closer.

A rush of pleasure flowed through me. Or was it Lolita's reaction to his closeness?

"Ah, but I think you do care."

"That guy had a knife," I managed through a throat that felt like I'd swallowed dirt. I licked my bottom lip.

He studied my mouth.

Is he going to kiss me?

"Let him," Lolita prodded me.

My heart thundered. "If you get your stupid ass killed...maybe I won't be able to get home...without you."

"So, you need me. Is that what you're saying?" Blue eyes bored into mine.

"No...of course not."

"Yes I do," Lolita chimed in, sweet as could be.

I couldn't think.

"Ah, huh." His warm breath caressed my face. "You're not a very good liar."

"Well, it's...it's the truth." My hesitant tone didn't sound convincing.

He leaned in.

A hot flush crept up my neck. He was going to kiss me. Lolita's traitorous eyelids closed with anticipation. The sound of metal hitting rocks blended with voices in conversation and guitar music filled my ears.

His hand cradled the side of my face.

Time stopped. I could feel the pull between us, feel his breath against my lips. This was too surreal. Why would he want to kiss me? Maybe it wasn't me. Maybe it was her, Lolita. Lolita with the body men desired. Lolita of every man's fantasy. Maybe the yearning that pulsated through my body wasn't mine...but hers. My chest clenched.

He must have sensed my withdrawal, my impulse to flee, because he set his other hand on the swell of my back to hold me firmly against him. I clamped down on my doubts and allowed myself to remain relaxed. If Lolita wanted this, there was nothing I could do to stop it. *Relax and breathe—*

"I am relaxed." Lolita made me bend her head back, her lips slightly parted for the kiss we both wanted.

"Boss."

My eyes snapped open. I shoved Wyatt back, toppled over my feet, but he caught me. Disappointment flashed in his eyes. Shocked to be so close to him, I stepped back.

"¿Estas bien?" A Mexican kid rushed up.

"I'm okay, Emanuel. This is Abby."

The kid held out his hand without the slightest hesitation and shot me a wide smile. "Miss Lolita, of course. Everyone knows you."

"I've seen you at the river with Wyatt."

"He's my partner," Wyatt explained.

"Lolita, look." Emanuel pointed to his feet. "He buy me new shoes and teach me English a little bit."

"How nice of him." My mind a little clearer, I wanted to shake the boy's hand and say thanks, thanks for stopping the kiss that would have been a big mistake. Instead, I shook his hand and kept my feelings to myself.

"Gringo is loco." Emanuel made the finger-swirling sign by his ear. "Bad hombres."

"Yeah, he's crazy, all right." A soft spot opened in my heart. Perhaps Wyatt had changed from the guy I knew back in high school, that full-of-himself jerk who stood me up.

"Let's go." Wyatt cut into my musing. He actually looked embarrassed by all the attention.

I didn't want him running off so fast. "Wyatt, do you have a minute?"

He studied me then: "Sure." He turned to Emanuel. "Let's meet up later at the tent. *Reunirse en la tienda*." He moved toward me. "Now where were we? Oh, yes. I was about to kiss you."

Not wanting to repeat the sexually charged moment before we were interrupted, I backed up. "No." I put up my hand. "Keep your lips to yourself."

He fondled a loose strand of my hair and smiled as though he had no intention of doing any such thing.

My borrowed heart kicked my borrowed ribs. "You've been saving a lot of people around here." I didn't want to look like a total ingrate, but I stood my ground in front of him. "You should keep your nose out of everyone's business."

"I need something to do other than pan for gold all day."

"Just be careful of the Domino Effect. Besides, they don't call it the Wild West for nothing."

There it was again, that look of want in those gorgeous blue eyes of his. "I've noticed," he said softly. Once again, he leaned closer.

I was tempted to close my eyes and give in to the yummy sensations coiling low in my belly, give in to the emotional and physical need playing havoc with my body.

No. Those were Lolita's feelings. Her needs. Not mine. No way. "Wyatt. I need to ask you something."

Wyatt, the loser

"What?" Did Abby really have to ask a question now? I was torn between running off to meet up with Emanuel and the need to taste those luscious lips of hers. The desire to kiss her won, but the prize eluded me.

Damn, she was a knockout. Her jet-black hair shone blue-black under the sun. She'd piled it on top of her head, and my fingers itched to tug out those pins and run my hands through the silken mass. Even without a stitch of makeup, her eyes were stunning. No black outline or heavy mascara were needed on those long lashes. I'd sworn to keep my distance. Not get my heart involved, but one little kiss wouldn't hurt. My adrenaline was pumping from the tense confrontation of moments ago. I needed something to calm me down. A kiss would do just fine.

"Wyatt, why did you..." She bit her lip and studied the ground. I got the feeling she was debating with herself. "I want to buy the children some books." She blurted the statement as if it were an afterthought, and I wondered what was really on her mind.

"Okay." Once again, the urge to kiss her lit fires in my bloodstream. I leaned in closer to her lips. Her eyes lit up, but I felt her body tense.

Her breasts rose and fell with a quick, excited breath. There was no one here to stop us this time. No one to stop me from satisfying the need pulsating through my veins. I slipped my hands around her waist and pulled her closer. A sexy feather of breath escaped her. I wanted to press her up against me, let her feel my need, take her all in. She smelled like the honeysuckle that grew back home.

"Can I have some money?"

"What?" Her question sideswiped me. I stared, speechless.

"I was hoping-"

I kissed her neck, warm and soft against my lips. God, I

could lose myself in the scent of her skin. "Can we discuss this later?"

She backed up, and my arms no longer held heaven. "No. We'll discuss it now."

"Really? Right now. This instant?" I controlled my impulse to pull her back in and kiss her.

She glanced away then back at me. "They have books in the camp mercantile."

I took a deep breath then ran my fingers through my hair. "You have money...a lot more than I do."

"I spent it."

"On what?"

"I don't answer to you."

I knew she'd spent her money on her kids, but I'd let my frustration get the better of me. Still, I couldn't give her what I didn't have. The contents of my pickle jar was earmarked for food for me and Emanuel's family. Whatever else I was lucky enough to find by the river needed to go to the shopkeeper so I could get my Rolex out of hock. If I had any money, I'd give it to her. She'd bailed me out when the saloon got wrecked, but books? Damn. I felt like a heel, but still: "I can't help you."

She slammed her hands on her hips. "Can't, or won't?"

I crossed my arms. "Books are a luxury." Pride kept my true reasons from spilling out. Bad enough I was broke, much less admit it. Bad enough the miners thought of me as a loser, but I'd be damned if I'd admit that either.

Abby is propositioned

I was going to ask him about the night he stood me up, but the timing felt off. The feelings he stirred in me played havoc with my emotions, and I didn't want to ruin the moment; so I said I needed money for books. The ingrate had the nerve to tell me no. "You're being a jerk."

I didn't want to tell him I'd bought a new dress and clothing for the kids. It was none of his business. "And in case you forgot, my money went to pay for your barroom brawl."

"I'm saving to pay you back."

I held out my hand. "Pay me what you've got, right now."

"Go ask him for money." He pointed to Monty strolling in our direction. "You're cozy with him."

His pissed tone was clipped with a hint of jealousy. Wow. Who would have thought Wyatt would have that emotion?

"Maybe I will." I picked up the hem of my dress and strutted to Monty.

"Good day." He tipped his hat. "I hope I am not interrupting anything of importance."

"No. Not at all."

He glanced over my shoulder, and I knew he was eying Wyatt. "He was kicking up such a fuss," Monty said as he brought his attention back to me.

"He's just being his same argumentative self." I smiled.

"May I have the honor of escorting you on a stroll?"

I slipped Lolita's arm through his. "I would be delighted."

As we slowly walked away from the camp, I wondered just how close we were. By the way he held my arm and angled his body, a little too close for comfort, and from the interest in his glances, I wondered if he had already gotten under my skirt.

The farther away from camp we wandered, the more attentive he became: a pat on my hand, a tug on my body into his, even a wink that made me want to gag.

Edgy, I flicked my thumb from one fingernail to another. "What would you like me to sing tomorrow?"

We stopped. Monty stepped in front of me. "Whatever you choose will be delightful." He placed his hand on my shoulder.

My instinct was to back away, but Lolita wouldn't let me move her feet. I hoped she didn't want to throw her arms around his neck and kiss him, too.

If I bolted, what would he think? Were we in love? An item? I certainly couldn't ask him without sounding stupid. I stared into his dark eyes. Dark as coal. Coal pretty much summed up his hard features. Nothing about his face or his coloring was soft. His black hair lay slicked back from his broad forehead. He sported a mustache above his thin lips. Black clothes, black hat, and polished black boots made him look like a clichéd villain. Being alone with him, isolated, and him all touchy-feely, changed my first impression of him. If I'd met him in a dark alleyway, he would have scared the living hell out of me.

"You look exceptionally stunning today." He brushed a finger along my jaw.

"That is most kind of you to say," Lolita's sexy voice said.

Fighting Lolita's urge to run her fingers through his greasy hair, I clenched my skirt in her hands. "To what do I owe the pleasure of your company, sir?"

"I wish your permission to court you." He picked up my hand and kissed my knuckles. "I can offer you whatever your heart desires."

"While your offer is most kind, it is quite brazen, and until the day that I am a widow, for the sake of my children and my reputation, I must decline your affections."

I didn't say that. Lolita said it.

He grabbed my wrist.

My heart jolted.

"You know I cannot deny you anything," he said, his voice smooth.

Before I could open my mouth to reply, he pulled me close. I gasped. He was going to kiss me. My heart raced with angst and disgust.

If I slapped his face and we were lovers, then what? Would he fire me? If this was our first kiss, I'd be justified in defending my honor. My mind raced as fast as my pulse. *What should I do?*

Lolita to the rescue. *"Do not worry about Monty. I can handle him."*

He leaned in for a kiss.

Lolita placed her hands on his chest. "Monty. Someone might see us."

A flicker of annoyance crossed his eyes then disappeared as he straightened. "Your husband left you for another lover." He brushed his finger on my cheek. "A woman needs a man, you know, to take care of her."

Not him. No way.

"Relax, Abby," Lolita whispered.

I stepped back on wobbly knees. "But, sir. I am still a married woman."

"Without a man to see to your needs."

"I manage quite nicely."

I was impressed. She even delivered rejection with a sexy tone. Had she had this conversation with him before? Had they slept together? A knot formed in my gut.

"For now, I will abide by your decision."

I breathed a sigh of relief.

"I shall wait until you are widowed. Say the word and I'll have my men take care of him."

I reached up and touched his cheek. "That won't be necessary, kind sir." His casual words of murder turned my stomach. "The thought of you on the gallows would be too much heartbreak for me to bear." The words came out in a rush and I hoped he couldn't tell Lolita was lying.

"I am always careful."

What did that mean? Had he murdered before?

I eased my hand away. "We should return. My children must wonder where I am."

He nodded, offered his arm, and we made our way back to the camp in silence.

I needed to learn more about this man whose arm was linked with mine. Was he married? Did he have mistresses? How much of an item were we? Was he capable of murder?

With her husband out of the picture, Lolita would have no excuse not to hook up with Monty. But how did Monty feel about the children? Would he want them out of the way? I needed to find out.

Wyatt jealous?

I watched the two lovebirds walk arm in arm and wanted to run to them and tear the slimy bastard's limbs off. What was Abby thinking, going off with him into the woods alone? I didn't trust him. There was something about him that got under my skin. I couldn't put my finger on it, but he reminded me of a black snake slithering in the dirt.

I followed them, keeping my distance. I had to make sure Abby was safe. *For her protection. I'm not jealous. She's my ticket home.*

From my angle behind a tree, they looked a little too cozy. I knew the moves, the finger-brush, the lean-in. The kiss. That was next. Would Lolita kiss him back? Or would Abby? I didn't want to watch, but I had to know.

She stopped him with a hand to his chest.

All right. I wanted to jump for joy.

When she ran her fingers on his cheek I wanted to step in and ask what she was thinking. Thankfully, when I recalled there were two women in that gorgeous body, I stopped myself.

They headed in my direction. Satisfied they walked back toward camp and Abby was safe, I silently followed them back to her shack. Monty pulled open the blanket door. After a brief conversation, Abby went inside, and he left.

Why did I care if she liked the sneaky bastard? Well, I didn't care. Shit. I sounded like Abby. Fact was, we needed each other. If he was her choice, or Lolita's, I'd keep away, concentrate on surviving in this godforsaken century.

Abby had said the kids were the reason she was here. How? Why? I never gave the legend much thought. The only way I was going to learn more regarding this Weeping Woman was to stick by her. I had to get to know Lolita. Pick her brain. Observe her. See if she was capable of murder.

Did I hear myself? Loco. *I'm insane.* I was thinking about one woman with two personalities. However, despite Abby being Lolita, Lolita's thoughts had to be in there somewhere, so maybe Abby's already learned something that would help.

Emanuel was at our claim when I got there. We dug for a few hours, my thoughts still centered on Abby. If she had any ideas on how to get us out of here, she hadn't shared them with me. As far as I could tell, she hadn't done anything other than hang with her kids and sing at the saloon. I liked listening to her. What didn't sit well was the way all the men in the room stared at her like she was for sale. Didn't she understand the danger? Didn't she realize how her provocative dresses evoked carnal desires that could jeopardize her safety? If anything happened to her... I didn't want to think about what would happen to me.

Our hands and skin blistered from finding a few small nuggets, we called it a day. Emanuel left the claim ahead of me. The sun was setting when I walked back through the Chinese section of camp.

A little boy wearing a dirty quilted jacket, two sizes too big, tugged on my pants. Gaunt, he probably hadn't eaten anything substantial in weeks.

"You hungry?"

His dark eyes sheepishly focused on me.

I pantomimed the action of eating.

He nodded eagerly.

I reached into my pocket and pulled out a strip of beef jerky.

Angry Chinese words I didn't understand came flying at us. A woman, I guessed to be his mother, hurried toward me, swinging a broom. More words of reprimand, if the disappointed look on the little boy's face indicated anything, were flung at me. He hung his head in shame. Or was the mother reprimanding the boy?

"Whoa. Whoa. It's okay." I held out my palm. "I want him to have this."

The woman glared at me then her child. I could see conflicting emotions cross her face. It wasn't easy accepting charity.

"No one should go hungry. Please." I moved the offering in my hand a little closer, hoping she would understand.

She sighed then nodded.

I bent down. "This is for you."

The child's gaze flew to his mother. She smiled, and he took the meat. "Xièxiè."

That much Chinese I knew. "You are welcome."

I reached into my pocket, took out the small cloth pouch containing the gold dust I'd found and untied the string. A hand came over mine. The petite woman in front of me shook her head.

"Please. You need it more than me."

"No." She straightened her stance.

Too proud to accept my offer, not wanting to insult her, I nodded. But as I walked away, I vowed to help the kid and his family when all my debts were paid.

Abby and Daisy

Wow. First Wyatt and then Monty. All this attention was going to my head. I kinda liked it. Not that I wanted either of them to kiss me.

I sat with Daisy outside my shack and watched the sun sink behind the mountains.

"What dress should I wear tonight?" she asked.

I glanced at her. "I saw a light blue one with white lace on your dress rack that I think would look nice."

She wrinkled her nose. "You don't think it's too pale with this blond hair?"

"I think it will do you justice."

"I wish I was as tan as you."

I loved the color of my skin. The golden glow never burned despite the beating hot sun.

Tonight, soft lines of pastel, purples, and pinks blossomed on the horizon. I loved this time of day when the air cooled and the sky softened. Camp life settled in for the evening, the bustle slowed. Weary men, without a day's wage, lay aside their frustrations in song and drink and hoped for better luck tomorrow.

Daisy grumped. "Monty's been a little agitated lately."

Her words drew my gaze back to her. "Is he?" If he was upset that I hadn't kissed him yesterday, too bad. My first meaningful kiss wasn't going to come from someone who gave me the willies.

Recalling my limited kissing experience, I sucked in my lower lip. One date gave me a peck on my cheek and left me thankful that was over. The second was tight-lipped, and I felt nothing. The last was repulsive; he kissed like a suckerfish. Wyatt's kiss would be different. I just knew it. Despite my vow to keep him at arm's length, I would have let him kiss me, even though he was the rake who broke my heart. I needed to stop thinking about the *what-ifs* with Wyatt. There would be no more almost-kisses. I couldn't relive the pain of a broken heart.

"I wonder what caused our boss to be so distraught."

"Daisy, I couldn't say. Perhaps he fought with one of his

mistresses." I had no idea if he was seeing anyone, but I got the feeling he was the type of guy who would use a woman until he'd zapped the life out of her then toss her away like trash.

"Lolita, he doesn't have eyes for anyone other than you."

"We... Daisy, Monty and I... We've had our differences." I'd worried that we'd slept together, but now I knew he wanted to court me. And much to my surprise, he was quite the gentleman about it when I'd turned him down. "Do you think he's a family man?"

Daisy snorted. "Not likely."

"He likes children though?"

She shrugged. "Hell if I know."

"I guess he struck a rich load. I mean being the owner of the fanciest saloon in town."

An agitated look hardened her round face. "Monty wouldn't soil his hands digging. He's a gentleman. Brought his money with him. Knows important people, the kind who get things done."

Not wanting to sound like I knew nothing about the man who had his sights on me, I changed the subject. "What do you know about the man over there?" I pointed to the washbasins where mean-spirited Hank was cleaning up. "He threatened my kids and beat up an old Chinese man."

Daisy leaned in close to my ear, her tight blond ringlets tickling my cheek. "Hank? That ornery loon. Rumor has it he lost his temper, a fight broke out in a bar, and the undertaker was called in." She leaned back. "But some say he has a softer side."

I drew my attention from Hank, who, at last glance, was digging for gold in his nose, and wondered why he was a free man. "They didn't hang him for killing someone?"

"Don't rightly know why. Maybe he broke out."

"There should be a posse out looking for him."

"Now, honey..." Her head bobbed. "Half the country don't give a fig about the law when there's gold to be found."

"So a murderer walks around here free as a bird?"

Daisy snorted. "If you think he's the only one with a bounty on his head then look around. Half this camp is full of ruffians who'd stab you in the back, steal your gold, and not think twice about it. I thought you'd know that by now."

"Sometimes I just need a reminder."

"Watch your back, Sugar."

Cattie and Joseph bound around the corner, laughing and playing tag.

Daisy stood. "I better get back to town." She nodded to the kids. "Hi, darlings."

"Children, where have you been?"

They stopped. Cattie stared wide-eyed. Joseph said nothing. He never said a word. Not to me. Only to Cattie.

I didn't mean to sound so stern but knowing there could be more than one cutthroat in camp, I couldn't contain my concern.

Daisy smiled. "They're home safe so what does it matter? Right, darlings?"

Cattie nodded.

Joseph's gaze met mine then darted to his sister.

Was I such a horrible mother? Cattie hovered around him like a child protecting her most precious doll. What had Lolita done to make Joseph fear her?

"Joseph. What do you have to say? Were you out fishing, looking for frogs?"

Why did they both look so guilty?

"Cattie?" I moved toward them.

Joseph's shoulders slumped.

Cattie put her arm around him. "Nothing, Mamma. We were just by the river with Mister Benjamin."

My heart kicked into overdrive. "Doing what?"

Cattie stared at her feet.

"Stay away from Benjamin." I shook my finger. "Do you understand me? And I don't want you to go near the river." What was Benjamin doing with the children down at the river?

"But, Mamma—"

"I don't want to hear another word."

Daisy placed her hand on my arm. "Don't you think you're a little harsh? They're just children."

My eyes narrowed on the kids. "Go inside." I pointed to the doorway.

The river of all places. How could I keep these children safe with so many potential threats lurking outside our door?

Chapter Nine

Wyatt and the runaway wagon

On June 23rd, Emanuel and I dug out a hundred dollars' worth each from our claim. We were sitting pretty. It cost me $55 in gold, but I got my Rolex back, saved most of my share, and with the rest, I bought food for my Chinese friends. Knowing they wouldn't take charity, I managed to slip the fare into their tent without them seeing me.

All my debts were paid, including what I owed Lolita, which made me feel better. Ever since our argument over books, I'd felt guilty. I hated denying the children. Reading was such an important part of my life, but at the time I couldn't see past my annoyance and poverty.

The smaller streams were drying out. The hot, dry weather made for edgy, miserable men. Fights broke out. Deaths occurred over a loaf of bread and claim jumping. Very little gold was being found. I wondered if we'd depleted the area.

I decided to take a break from panning. Every day, I went horseback riding. In my younger days, I'd ridden at summer camps, so I was no expert cowboy, but I'd gotten pretty good, thanks to Emanuel's tips.

Today was one of those hot days made for a lazy man and a lazy horse. Jack, I named him after my grandfather, moseyed along, nibbling on grass. Emanuel helped me pick out the chestnut-colored beast and, just like that, most of my spare gold was gone. But a man needed a horse, or so Emanuel had convinced me.

The valley was hemmed in by lofty hills and draped in the shadow of a rocky mountain dotted with fir trees. The air smelled clean and pure. This California I could get used to, without all the cars and polluted air.

I reached down and patted Jack's neck. Not my Ferrari, but a nice ride. For the first time in weeks, I felt like my old self, relaxed, optimistic and confident in the belief that before long I'd be back home. Was my mother worried? Did my dad even notice I was gone? What did they think happened to me? I hated the stress Mother would be facing. She had enough to deal with living with my dad, who was overly demanding at home. Maybe I was in a coma, which wouldn't make life any easier for her, but it sure beat thinking I'd drowned. I'd wake up, and this whole place would be history.

Did my actions here change anything? Did breaking up that fight save the Chinese man's life and create a paradox? What would Emanuel's life be like in the future now that I'd befriended him? If I worried about it, I'd be too paralyzed to do anything. I wasn't going to—

A woman's scream pierced the air. Jack's ears perked. I pulled on his reins, gave him a slight heel kick, and we took off in the direction of the screams.

A football field distance ahead of me, a woman drove an out-of-control wagon. Her body was taut as she pulled on the reins with all her strength and leaned back into her seat. The horse paid her no mind as he continued his wild gallop, kicking up dirt clumps with his hooves.

I gave Jack a firm nudge, clicked my tongue, and our speed increased.

Jostled, as the wagon pitched back and forth, the driver's white bonnet flew off. Strands of long black hair loosened from her bun and fluttered behind her. "Whoa," she screamed. "Whoa."

A ways farther ahead, the road became rutted. I feared a wheel might drop into a deep groove and pitch the wagon over. Urging Jack to gallop faster, I stood on the stirrups to smooth out the ride while plotting how to stop a runaway wagon. I wasn't a hero, for god's sake. I was lucky to stay on the horse at this speed.

The wagon was getting closer to the ruts.

By the slacking rein, I could see the woman's strength was depleting. One rein had snapped and fallen alongside the stampeding big gray. It kept whipping the horse to go faster.

A few more yards, and with any luck, I'd pass the wagon and grab onto—

A big buck dashed onto the road.

"Shit." I jerked back on my reins. "Whoa."

Jack came to a dead stop. As I pitched forward, I grabbed the pommel to keep from flying over his head.

The buck bounded into the woods.

My heart pounding, I glanced ahead at the runaway wagon. By some lucky miracle, the wheels missed the ruts, and the uneven ground decreased the wagon's speed.

I still had a chance to catch up.

"Come on, boy. Let's go." I nudged my heels into Jack's sides. He understood, and we bolted forward. It took a minute, but we finally passed the wagon. I focused my attention on the broken rein thrashing alongside the horse. Squeezing my thighs against the saddle to keep my balance, I leaned over to grab it, but the damn thing kept whipping out of my reach. I had to move closer. Closer than I dared. If the big gray bumped into Jack, I'd be a dead man.

I nudged Jack nearer to the panicked horse. He fought me. I angled my body sideways, stood on the right stirrup, and reached out. My fingertips grazed the leather strap. The big gray veered right. The rein swung out of reach. I moved Jack beside him and tried again. Almost... I grabbed the line and re-centered myself in the saddle.

"Whoa." I kept my voice calm like Emanuel had taught me. "Whoa." Loud and firm. I eased Jack forward until he was running alongside the gray's head and pulled smoothly on the rein. Now that the gray could see us, he slowed. We rode together for a few moments until I could coax him to a stop.

"Good boy." I patted the animal's neck and turned Jack around to check on the frazzled driver.

"Abby?"

She stared at me with big wide eyes. Her breathing raced. She held her hand, fingers spread, against her chest.

I rode up to her. "What were you thinking? You could have killed yourself." I expected a snappy retort. She said nothing. There was something off about her. Was she in shock? "Move over. I'm coming up."

After dismounting, I climbed aboard and sat next to her.

"Sir, thank you for saving me. Handsome as you are."

"Yeah. You're in shock."

Confusion wrinkled her nose. Her excessive blinking made me shift into medic mode. I studied her pupils. Not dilated. Good. No concussion.

"Do you feel faint?"

She shook her head.

"Are you chilled?"

"No," she breathed.

"Give me your hand." If she was in shock, her skin would be cold and clammy.

"You, sir, may have my heart and much liberty."

Why was she talking so lewdly? Unless..."Lolita? Is that you?"

"Wyatt is now Lolita's hero."

"I just want to make sure you're okay?" And why was she looking at me as if she wanted to rip off my clothes? She must know Abby would stop her.

"I do not know how to repay you."

"Abby? Are you going to let her talk to me like that?"

"Abby is gone," Lolita breathed. "Now you are all mine."

"Gone?" Yeah. Now she was scaring me. "What have you done with Abby?"

She leered at me with those Spanish green eyes. Something about her mannerism was off for a woman who was just about killed. Her eyes, her face... All familiar, but her expression was sexy, Spanish maiden sly, and the way she held herself, straight-backed and her chest jutting out... Where was Abby to protect me?

Her arms flew around my neck, and before I could blink, her lips landed on my mouth, hot, sweet, all-consuming lips a man would die for. Shocked, I pushed her back. "Abby...Lolita? What did you do that for?"

Her shoulders slumped and she shook her head then looked at me with surprise-widened eyes. "Wyatt? What are you doing here?"

I took hold of her hand. "Abby. It's you."

She looked around in a panic. "Where am I?"

Abby or Lolita?

"Where am I?" I felt strange. Dreamlike. Wyatt was sitting next to me, his face a heavenly blur. Then I realized something wasn't right. "Why are you holding my hand?"

He eyed me with concern, or was it confusion? "Abby? What happened?"

"What are we doing in a wagon?"

"I was going to ask you the same thing. Why did you take out a wagon when you don't know how to ride a horse?" He let go of my hand, and for a split second, I was disappointed.

How did I hitch up a horse? When did I get in the wagon?

"Lolita? What did you do?"

I heard her *giggle*.

Giggle? My mind felt collapsed, confused. How could I explain the strange fear bulldozing through me?

"You almost got yourself killed. Next time ask me. I'll take you anywhere you want to go." The concern in his soft voice reached into my foggy brain and my heart.

Had Lolita taken control and blocked me out? She'd warned me she could take back her body at any time. I had no recollection of where I'd been or what I'd done. I began to shake. The chirping birds shouted at me, magnified as though I stood in the middle of an aviary with hundreds of cackling species. "I don't know what happened."

"Give me a minute." Wyatt jumped down, grabbed the harness of a horse munching on the grass nearby, and walked him to the back of the wagon. Once the animal was tied, he took off his sash, fidgeted with my horse's bridle then he got in. He flicked the reins, clicked his tongue a few times, and the wagon jerked forward. "One of the reins was cut. I had to tie it back together. Do you feel dizzy?"

"Just a bit shook up."

With languid eyes he assessed me as though he were an X-ray scanning my body. He nodded, though I suspected, by his furrowed brow, he didn't believe that was all that was wrong with me.

We rode in silence as I tried straightening out the tangled

web of my thoughts. Lolita must have taken over. Had I...did she do anything embarrassing? What did Wyatt see? Think? Did I act oddly? Sound different? I took a deep breath in an effort to calm my rattled nerves. "Wyatt. I can't remember how I got here."

"Good thing I was out riding and saw you."

"I think Lolita took over." I hoped he didn't think I was as crazy as I sounded. "She blocked me out."

"You're right. Whoa." He pulled back on the reins, and when the horse stopped Wyatt faced me. "I didn't know who I was talking to. I thought it was you...at first...but then I knew it was Lolita."

"Did she do anything stupid?"

"Not that I couldn't handle. Abby you can't let her take control of you."

"I don't know how to stop her." My hands shook. Worry raced my pulse. "I have no idea why she took over." I couldn't tell him that she had the hots for him.

"I sure don't like this Lolita person, but I really like the Abby I'm getting to know."

"But she's beautiful."

"She's just another Pam and Cindi."

Emotionally drained, his declaration pulled me out of my pity-party. *He likes me?* I never thought I'd hear those words coming out of his mouth.

"Did you hear that, Lolita? He likes me."

"Why would he like you? You are always mean to him. He must be loco."

Unsure what to say to him, I watched leaves dancing in the soft warm breeze. His captivating charm was luring me out of my comfort zone, breaking down my wall of resistance I'd vowed to hold up to keep him out of my heart. I fidgeted in my seat, not from the panic I'd felt moments ago when I found him holding my hand, but from the way he looked at me with sincerity, with kindness.

I needed a distraction. I needed to stop thinking about the way he looked at me. I needed to focus away from the bombardment of my disjointed emotions. I didn't want to dwell on the misery I felt over what happened on prom night or the fact

Lolita was strong enough to completely take over and swallow me up. My thoughts rushed back to the legend and the reason I was here. "There's a blue moon next month."

"You know, a blue moon isn't blue, but any moon can appear blue if there's volcanic ash in the atmosphere."

I tweaked a brow.

He scoffed. "Don't look at me like you're surprised I knew that."

"I'm impressed."

"Why? Because you thought I was just a dumb jock? I like to read. You got a problem with that?"

"Don't get so defensive." He was right. That was my first impression. *Dumb jock.* Guilt nibbled at the back of my mind. "Look..." I huffed, embarrassed we were entering a personal path I didn't want to go down. "I don't know you very well. You certainly don't know me at all. Let's concentrate on why we are here and how we can return to our century."

"If next month's blue moon isn't the right blue moon of legend, we could be here for another thirty-three months until the next one. That's two and three-quarter years." He frowned. "I don't want to stay here that long." He was clearly unhappy.

I couldn't blame him. "It's next month, for sure." The kids of legend were not three years older than they were now.

"And that's when we're going home?"

"I don't know."

He ran his fingers through his hair. "That means we have less than six weeks to find out."

"And there's more, but this is going to sound really bizarre."

"Nothing you say could surprise me." Wyatt gestured to our clothing.

"I don't think you pulled me under."

He gasped in mock surprise. "I stand corrected. I am surprised, and I can't believe you're admitting you were wrong." His brow raised. "Does that mean you owe me an apology?"

"Fine. I'm sorry. You weren't trying to drown me. You happy now?" As much as I wanted to hate the satisfactory gloat in his smile, it brightened his handsome face. The urge to lean in and brush away a stray lock of golden hair from his forehead tempted me. I was amazed at how fast his hair had grown in the three weeks since we'd arrived.

He gazed into my eyes so deep I thought he might fall in. "You're such a beautiful woman." His low sexy voice was turning me into melted ice cream.

"Are you talking to me or Lolita."

"I don't see why her husband would walk away from her."

"Maybe she was too much woman for him."

"That's highly possible." His playful gaze generated a flutter in my chest.

I ran my finger over his shoulder. "How do you like your women to taste, hot and spicy or sweet and tangy?"

I blushed. *"Lolita, why did you make me say that?"*

"That's easy to find out." He leaned in close to my mouth, and the faint scent of soap and leather intoxicated me.

Were these emotions gushing through my heart mine or Lolita's?

Let them be mine. Let me feel special. I wanted to be desired. *For once. For me.*

"Let me show you how it is done," Lolita whispered to my inflamed libido.

A gentle breeze played with his stray hairs against my cheeks like a feather massage. I closed my eyes with breathless anticipation. My heart thrummed in my ears, and a feverish awakening I longed for surfaced, but I didn't know whose, Lolita's or my own. As I waited for his lips to touch mine, I was fully aware of the intense desire that made my body feel alive in a dreamscape of his making. I wanted this, despite our past, despite all logic. I'd dreamed of the moment he'd take me—

The wagon pitched forward with a jerk, and the big gray whinnied.

Wyatt turned away and pulled on the reins. "Easy now."

Yeah. Easy, Abby. The mood broken, I swallowed a lump of disappointment. A soft sigh escaped me as I studied his muscled arms that controlled the startled horse. He was all man. I liked the golden stubble on his jaw, loved the long hair curling against his neck. And I suddenly realized how he looked like he belonged here. "Wyatt. You've adapted well."

"Oh, you mean the grunge look?" His eyes lit with

mischief. "I'm doing pretty well, seeing as how I was a mistake."
He smiled.

He was kidding, I knew, but a stab of guilt attacked my
chest. Still, he made a very handsome cowboy. I put my hand on
my heart and fluttered my lashes. "You are my hero," Lolita's
voice came out sweetly.

"Lolita, stop it," I demanded out loud.

She made me giggle like an innocent schoolgirl.

He laughed. "Just don't do it again." His expression grew
serious. "I mean it. You scared the hell out of me."

Lolita tossed my hair wickedly. "I cannot make any
promises."

"In that case, I'm gonna keep my eyes on you."

"I like the sound of that," she cooed.

A feeling akin to jealousy reared its ugly head. She was
playing me to get at him, and I wasn't any good at this lovers'
game.

Wyatt's first patient

The events in the wagon, three days ago, still played in my
mind. I couldn't imagine how Abby must've felt competing with
Lolita. And she had the power to obliterate Abby. It was bad
enough Abby wasn't Abby in appearance, but when Lolita took
command of her body, her *come-on* personality blew me away.
I've had women throw themselves at me before. I wasn't
impressed.

Yeah. I was getting to like Abby. When she came back in
Lolita's body, the confusion in her eyes and the dead stare
frightened me. I didn't know why she intrigued me, same now as
it was when we first met before that fateful swim. The
connection I felt had to have been more than the mutual secret
we shared.

I'm just glad she snapped out of it.

When I get home, maybe I'd study psychology. Split
personalities. I should write a paper on my experiences with
Abby and Lolita, not that anyone would believe me. Hell, who
was I kidding? No one had ever been in a situation like this.

Science fiction they'd say. Ah, damn. We didn't even know how long we'd be stuck here, or if we'd ever make it home.

I walked to the camp mercantile, pickle jar in hand. It was the twenty-sixth of June, and the supply wagons weren't due in for a few days. Staples, food, and books were on my shopping list. As patrons milled about, I saw pickings were more scant than usual.

I selected a half-pound of crusty cheese marked three dollars, and two pounds of bread marked seventy-five cents. I noticed, last week, Emanuel's mother had sliced up the last of her cheese, and she was due for more.

My mouth watered as I passed the oysters and roast beef. The price was prohibitive. The gold in my pickle jar only went so far. I'd never thought about the sacrifices poor people had to make when it came to putting food on the table. This experience was humbling.

I grabbed two chickens, one for my Chinese family and one for Camila. I tried not to impose on Emanuel's family when it came time to eat, so I often chose to sit outside and eat canned beans and dried pork. They'd been kind enough to let me stay with them until I could buy a tent or build something. A few men had built wood cabins, but that kind of *home* was too expensive for me. Still, I didn't want to overstay my welcome.

A strip of dried salted pork rounded out my grocery list, even though I was sick of the same old thing. When the day came that I started squealing and grunting like a pig, I was going on a starvation diet.

Then I came to the books, neatly lined up on a shelf. I thumbed through a few children's tales and found four I thought the kids would like.

A Native American walked in. All eyes focused on him. I didn't know enough about the Natives to know what tribe he belonged to, but I did know they worked inhumane hours for a mere pittance of food, booze, or trinkets. This man looked majestic, stood tall, maybe six-foot-three and had long black hair that fell to his mid-back. Seemingly not intimidated by the sudden quiet and unwelcoming stares, he moved silently as an elk in the forest. Dark brown eyes studied me as though he was sizing me up. I nodded an acknowledgment and smiled. He did the same then passed me.

After weighing out the remainder of my gold dust on a scale for the goods I'd purchased, I turned from the counter. That was when I saw the Chinese man I'd defended from Hank. He was picking up a jar of pigs' feet, and I nodded as I walked past him.

Emanuel rushed in. "Boss."

My pulse jumped. "What's the matter? Something wrong?"

"I very afraid, today." His English was pretty rough, but he was getting the hang of it. "My friend..." He shook his head. "Very sick. Very sick."

"Did the doctor see him?"

"No doc. Him away. I worried very mucho."

"He's away. I'm very worried." I corrected him by force of habit. "I'm not a doctor, but maybe I can help."

"You know medicine?"

"Some. I'll do my best."

We hurried to Emanuel's tent. I dropped off my supplies and picked up my leather pouch, the one that held the bottle of aspirin I'd had in my swim trunks pocket the day I damn near drowned, and scissors and bandages and the like.

As we rode our horses into town, I thought of the diseases prevalent in this era: dysentery, cholera, influenza, and the common cold. In the crowded mining camps, a virus could quickly spread and turn pandemic. Smallpox and scarlet fever were rolling epidemics in 1847. All I had to combat these sicknesses were aspirin and a little knowledge of herbal remedies. If my meager doctoring failed and someone died because of me, I didn't know how I would explain it. My gut twisted in a knot.

We got off our horses and tied them to a hitching post in front of a small house tucked behind the jail. Emanuel knocked on a door, not much more than a bunch of nailed-together boards. A woman, I guessed to be in her thirties, greeted us. Shadows lined her tired eyes, and her blond hair was disheveled. "Emanuel, what are you doing here? Thomas is sick."

"I know. I brought my boss to help."

She looked at me and frowned. "Are you a doctor?"

"No, ma'am, but I have some knowledge in medicine."

Doubt clouded her honey-brown eyes. "We should wait for the doctor."

"He may come too late to save your Thomas. At least let me have a look at him, see how bad off he is."

I saw hope in her eyes as she ushered us in.

The plank-walled room was sparse, a wooden table and bench in one corner, a few shelves with provisions near a cast iron stove and a chair. Dots of light spotted the floor from a few knotted holes in the wood walls. I figured a closed door on the far wall led to a bedroom.

"My boy is in here." She showed me to the far door.

"Emanuel, stay here." I pointed to the chair then followed her into the adjoining room.

Darkness enveloped me. Stale air and dust particles floated in thin streaks of sunlight streaming in through a shuttered window. I walked to the window and opened the shutters to let in a hot breeze.

A pale boy, in his early teens, lay covered in blankets. He opened his eyes. "You're not...Doc Wilson."

"I'm Wyatt. I am here to help you...if you let me."

He nodded.

I stepped to his bedside. "So. Thomas, where does it hurt?"

"My head. Mighty bad. And my throat is on fire."

The boy's forehead felt hot, at least a hundred and one. It would be difficult to control his fever without modern medicine, especially in this heat. "Any pain in your stomach?"

"No."

"Anywhere else?"

"My muscles." He sneezed.

"Do you have any shortness of breath?" I had to rule out pneumonia.

"None that I've seen," his mother said.

"Can you please bring me a lamp?"

His mother brought over the oil lamp.

"I need to see the inside of his throat."

She brought the lamp closer.

"Open your mouth, Thomas."

He did as I requested, and I was relieved not to see any severe inflammation, which ruled out strep.

"Your fever and sore throat are due to a bad cold. Thankfully, I don't see any signs of infection." I reached into my pouch, pulled out the aspirin bottle, and dumped four pills in my hand. "Have him swallow two of these, with plenty of water, and two again tomorrow. It will reduce his fever." I wanted to hand over the whole bottle, but I was afraid I'd need it at a later date, so I slipped it back into my pouch.

She examined the pills, her lips pressed together, her brows furrowed. She had every right to look at me as though I was a green alien with one eye in the middle of my forehead.

"I promise you they won't harm him." How was I going to explain modern medicine? "Believe me, they will help him get better."

She nodded.

"Next, do you have any honey?"

"Yes."

"Good. It will help his sore throat. Do you have garlic."

"Yes, but garlic?"

"It will help get rid of his cold faster. Crush it and give it to him in some soup."

She nodded. "Will chicken soup be sufficient?"

"Perfect. Thomas..." I smiled down at him. "You should be good as new in a few days, but you have to promise me you won't go running around outside for a while. You'll be contagious 'til you feel better."

He forced a weak smile.

I turned to his mother. "You need to make sure you keep your hands germ free."

Confusion crossed her face.

I realized the term germ-free might not be a prevailing science these days. "You must wash your hands frequently to prevent infecting yourself and your family with the virus. And you..." I turned to the boy. "Cover your mouth when you sneeze or cough or your momma will be the next one in bed with a fever."

He sneezed.

"And keep this window open to let in lots of fresh air."

"We understand. Thank you." She walked over to a chest of drawers. Her shoulders slumped, and a soft sigh broke out as she slid the drawer open then closed. "Please take this." She opened her hand to show me a gold nugget the size of a quarter.

I feared the nugget was all she had. As much as it would bolster my dwindling funds, I felt uncomfortable taking it from this poor woman. "Payment is not necessary."

"I don't take kindly to charity." She pressed the gold into my hand.

"I'll tell you what..." I closed her fingers around the nugget. "When you make Thomas's soup, save some for me. That's all the payment I need."

"I will be happy to invite you to dinner."

"Thank you."

Relief softened her features then she hurried to put the nugget back into the drawer where she made the sign of the cross over her chest.

I'd been right about that piece of gold being her last.

Chapter Ten

Abby the homemaker

F rustration was a feeling I was getting used to. Between working at the saloon and running a household, I had little time to figure out who might want to murder Lolita's children or why. As far as I could see, Hank stayed away from them, and I had found no reason to suspect Benjamin, though his confession to someone about killing a man still gave me reason for concern. I was beginning to wonder if his disappearance in the legend was nothing but a red herring.

It was the first day of July. Tonight, the moon would be full. And tomorrow night, too. In twenty-nine days, the full moon would return, a blue moon, on July 31st, and the facts about the legend would then be revealed.

I plucked feathers from a chicken and tried not the cringe. At least the shopkeeper did me a favor by snapping the bird's neck. I had serious thoughts about becoming a vegetarian.

Manual chores were starting to take a toll on me. I'd gotten better at starting a fire, but my back ached from hauling in firewood for the stove. Several times I'd burnt my hand when trying to haul the cast iron pot off the hot stovetop.

Sweat slid down my forehead. I swiped the moisture away with my forearm. Today was another brutally hot day. My clothes clung to my sticky body. I shifted my weight and leaned on the crude wooden table to relieve the pressure from the burning soles of my feet after so much walking.

Daisy hadn't visited me for some time. She was so busy hustling men, serving drinks, and God knew what else, that I barely saw her. Several times a day she'd saunter upstairs with a man on her arm. I knew I shouldn't judge her. A single woman needed to do whatever she could to survive, but I missed having someone to talk to.

The children were outside playing tag; I could hear their laughter. The sound should have lightened my heart. It had the opposite effect. Joseph had refused to respond to any of my questions; he'd just look at me, whisper something in his sister's ear, and Cattie would answer for him. It was extremely frustrating. I feared some awful event had traumatized him, or maybe he missed his dad and blamed his mother for him being gone.

"Knock, knock." Wyatt's voice came from outside. "I thought you could use more firewood."

I pushed the blanket aside. His arms were laden with chopped wood. Shirtless, the corded muscles in his arms looked more defined, the result of pounding rocks all day. I remembered how it felt to be held by those arms as he carried me out of the river. Damn if I didn't want him to crush me to his hard body and hold me again...kiss me...

He stepped in and stacked the wood next to the stove.

I watched the exquisite muscles of his broad shoulders and back flex and release as he worked.

"My, my, my," Lolita said in my mind.

He straightened and faced me. "That should hold you for another day."

I wondered how his hard, naked chest would feel pressed against my soft breasts. The veins in my neck began to thud. My eyes followed the fine thin line of golden hair that traveled down his firm abs and disappeared under his waistband. A throb between my legs brought heat to my face. Whether it was my throb or Lolita's, I didn't care anymore. I loved the way it made me feel. "Another hot day." I fanned my cheeks.

"What I wouldn't do for some air conditioning."

He looked exceptionally handsome today. Lightened by the sun, his blond hair curled around his ears. His tanned face made his blue eyes much more striking. I caught myself gawking.

"Good God, Abby, shut my mouth."

"I can't help it." I wiped my sweaty face with the back of my hand.

He stepped closer. "How are you and Lolita getting along?"

"Very funny."

"I don't want a repeat of that wagon escapade." His face grew serious. "Lolita got herself in trouble. I thought she was you, but she said you were gone and came on to me."

I inhaled. "How...what..?"

"She kissed me."

My heart jumped. "No."

"It was a quickie, but I pushed her back, more shocked than anything."

"How dare she do that behind my back?"

He shrugged. "At first I thought she'd set me up, but after I discovered the rein was cut, I realized she'd just taken advantage of the situation."

"I'll kill her."

Lolita's *laugh* came to me. *"You are jealous."*

"I am not."

"Do not worry. He did not have his heart in it."

"I'm not worried."

Wyatt took off his hat and placed it on the table. "Don't let her take over again."

"What can I do? It's her body."

"Don't do anything to piss her off."

I hoped I wasn't totally at her mercy. "But what if it happens again? What if one day you wake up and I'm not here anymore? She'll have you all to herself."

"Then I guess she'll be stuck with me."

"Oh, la la," Lolita said out loud.

"See? She likes that idea." I doubted neither of us could stop Lolita from getting what she wanted.

"It's not going to happen...oh...I brought something else for you." He darted outside, returned with a cloth bag, and pulled out a few children's books.

I blinked, astonished. Touched by his kindness, guilt choked my words. I'd told him I didn't want his money, and then I turned around and asked him for money. He must've thought I couldn't make up my mind. His gesture, books for the children, was so touching that tears filled my eyes. "Thank you."

His hand settled over mine, warm and gentle. "Are you okay?"

Sniffling, I swiped away the tears. "Okay is not a word either one of us should be using." Overcome with a sudden urge to kiss those enticing lips of his, to run my hands over his naked, muscled chest, I had to force myself to remember our past, well, my past. He didn't even remember what he'd done to hurt me.

He shrugged. "I should probably leave." He picked up his hat, and hesitantly, he turned to the doorway, but I really didn't want him to go, which was wrong, so wrong.

"Wyatt?"

"Yeah?" He leaned in, his lips just inches from my lips.

I inhaled his scents: woods, horse, and leather. He'd been riding Jack. Wow. He had turned into a real rooting tooting cowboy. The pulse in my neck sprinted. My body felt alive, every nerve dancing like the sun rays that bathed my face in the warmth of his aura.

"You have something to tell me?"

I was aware of the pulse beating in his throat, the way his desire-filled eyes seemed to reach into my soul and suck the last shred of resistance from a body now thrumming with need. My need. Not Lolita's, but I really needed to put an end to such wasteful feelings. Nothing would come of them, and I would be left brokenhearted again.

"Next time you come over...put on a shirt."

His response was a *humph*.

Wyatt feels at home

I stormed out of Abby's place, pulled my shirt off the saddle, slugged my arms into the sleeves, mounted Jack, and headed into town for a cold shower. The El Dorado Hotel had a place in the back where a pinch of gold dust would buy a bar of soap and privacy.

As I rode down the main thoroughfare, I noticed a layer of dust had covered my clothing. Good thing I had a change of clothes in my saddlebag. I hitched Jack to a post in front of the El Dorado and glanced at the jailhouse next door. All appeared quiet, so I grabbed my saddlebag and walked into the hotel lobby where I paid the clerk for a bath and a shave.

Soap in hand, I stepped out back and into a cramped stall with four walls, no roof, and a crooked door that barely closed. I hung my saddlebag on a hook, and with scarcely any room to move, I struggled to strip then tossed my dirty clothes over the door, which meant I wanted them laundered. I'd pick them up later. When I pulled the cord on a valve above the shower head, I got blasted by the ice-cold spray and jerked backward. My bare ass hit the door. I grabbed the sides of the stall and caught myself before the whole town would have something else to laugh at me about.

Steeling myself against the chill, I closed my eyes, and images of the woman I faced every day filled my mind. Lolita's long neck called for my lips to lay kisses on her bronze skin while her flowery scent intoxicated me. Her green golden-flecked eyes reminded me of soft moss and the sunrise I'd watch creep over the horizon, and those exquisite breasts rising over the cut of her gown, calling to me...in Abby's voice.

Yeah. Like that would ever happen.

I began to lather my neck and shoulders, trying to ease away the dust and sweat, trying to ease away thoughts of Lolita's body. Abby would be furious, but all I could imagine were Lolita's hands on me, her lips on me, her sweet loving a speedway to sweet ecstasy.

An hour and a half later, clean, dressed, and shaved, I thought about Abby as I walked toward the Boomerang Saloon. No woman had ever gotten under my skin like her. I hated to say it, I hated to think it, but I wondered who I was most attracted to, Lolita with the body, and she knew it, or Abby with the keen mind and caring determination for those kids.

I liked talking to her, didn't have to hide who I was around her. Riding Jack and panning all day, I wasn't doing anything to help get us home. At least Abby was making a list of suspects and plotting to expose the real murderer in hopes of saving the kids. I had to admire her for that.

I didn't understand why she was constantly pushing me away. What did I ever do to cause her to hate me so much? Granted, she'd been pissed when I didn't buy the kid's books, but eventually I did, and I still got the cold shoulder. There were times I felt she was into me; I'd catch a glimpse of her looking at me through lowered lashes when she thought I wasn't looking. Then she'd glance away. Her mixed signals were confusing. Was Lolita into me, and Abby not so much? Maybe they were both as confused as me.

The town, as usual, was bustling with activity. Wagons filled with mining equipment rolled over the rutted street. Filth-encrusted men carried axes, picks, and firewood. A tin pan hung from each of their belts. Worn leather knife sheaths hung at the hip while deteriorated clothes bore testament to the wearer's hours of hard labor.

I had to admit this gold-rush life wasn't so bad. I was just beginning to fit in. Every time I slipped some food, anonymously, under a tent or two, the satisfaction I felt chipped away my animosity at being stuck here. Seeing the choked-up gratitude on Lolita's face when I handed her the books made all my hard work worth the pain of Abby's rejections.

Back home, with all my money, I never worried about the hungry or how people survived day to day with so little. Returning the hospitality Emanuel's family had showed me was as rewarding as standing up to Hank, the camp bully. No matter our differences, everyone should have the right to work side by side peacefully. We were all equal. I couldn't do anything about the division of classes in camp or the way people were discriminated against throughout history, but maybe if men saw how I'd forged a friendship with Emanuel, others might follow suit and befriend *all* their neighbors.

I walked into the saloon. The noise level dropped to dead silence. With all eyes on me, I straightened my stance. My guarded gaze assessed those around me as I made my way through the throng of men. The strained muscles along my neck pulsated, but I kept an even pace and stopped at the bar. No one had a hand on their weapon. A good sign. But I felt like they were waiting for someone to raise a stink. I was ready. Ready for a fight if the need arose.

A glass of whiskey slid down the bar toward me. I stopped it with the palm of my hand.

"It's on the house," Joe said.

I nodded my thanks, not sure why the bartender thought to offer me a free drink.

Clapping and hoots erupted in the room. I spun around expecting some town hero to walk in through the swinging doors, but everyone's attention was on me. I turned to the bartender. "What's this all about?"

"Do you not know whose boy you cured?"

"Just a boy named Thomas." I downed the whiskey.

A hand clamped on my shoulder. I looked up into the cracked mirror behind the bar, ready to twist the guy's arm into a pretzel. Willie, one of the oldest prospectors, stood behind me. Rummy eyes edged by deep crow's feet studied me from a face like weathered shoe leather, and his chapped lips broke out in a smile that showcased tobacco-stained teeth. "That there boy you done fixed up is Sheriff Townsend's son...mighty well liked here in town, and you, my boy, done doctorin' good." He pointed to the bartender. "His next drink is on me."

I stared at him, my mouth agape.

More happy men moseyed up to the bar, offering congratulations and drinks. A few tossed some gold at me as a reward or payment for helping Thomas. I resisted their offers, but after much persuasion, and a few more drinks, I pocketed the gold. Talking about our successes and failures at panning, laughing at a joke or lewd comment about women, and bitching about the heat and working conditions, I felt like I was part of the good-old-boys club, and they made me feel right at home.

It was after midnight when I left the saloon with a stride much taller than when I'd entered. For the first time since I'd landed in this cesspool, I looked forward to tomorrow.

As I mounted Jack, I glanced at the sky. A full moon shone down brightly and painted silver linings around the clouds.

It was the second day of July, meaning the end of this month would come with a second full moon, a blue moon. Would it pass without murder, or would it be the blue moon of legend? Eager to get back to camp, I tapped my heals into Jack's sides.

Abby and I had only twenty-nine days to learn our fate.

Chapter Eleven

Abby stalks the gunslingers

Determined to do some serious snooping, and having finished my shift at the saloon, I strolled the boardwalk along the dusty street. It was the fourth day of July. Muggy afternoon air settled over me, making my chemise stick to my body. My stomach growled, and I realized I hadn't eaten breakfast.

A small wagon rolled by, kicking up swirls of dust. Two mules, loaded with mining equipment, trailed behind a packed cart. Every day more miners came to town in wagons and on horseback, men with enthusiastic hope in their hearts, some unaware of the hardships they would face. Blistered hands, wet feet, sore backs, fleas, and sunburned skin were just a few of the unpleasantries they'd encounter.

I stepped off the wooden platform and crossed the street toward a stand where a man sold his goods from a pushcart lined with canned foods, onions, potatoes, sweetmeats, and dried fruit. I picked up a chunk of sourdough and handed the merchant a Mexican coin.

As I bit into the bread, I thought about Wyatt. I had to collect my courage and speak to him. How much did he hear of my conversation before he'd fallen asleep that night we'd spent together? How could he not recall what happened between us, or did he not want to talk about it? The unexpected feelings I was having toward him were mixing terribly with our unsettled past. At times, my stomach was in knots, but I was uneasy, unwilling to ruin the gathering whirlwind of emotions that made it easier to talk with him, easier to be in his presence. I sighed. I wasn't ready to reveal the reason for my anger toward him.

Shoving aside my irritation, I walked past tables of liquor

bottles, soaps, and leather goods. Gaming tables were covered with red white and blue embroidered cloth, and a few men lined up, ready to toss their coins. Squealing fiddles, strumming guitars, and shrill harmonicas mixed in a crazy Western sonata while the steady sound of a fife and drum signaled the start of the Independence Day celebrations.

Two men stood out from the multitude of weathered and bearded men milling around. Clean-shaven, they wore wide-brimmed black hats that shadowed their faces, black vests over muscled chests, and gun-belts worn low on their hips. Fancy-handled pistols were holstered at their sides.

The sight of Monty's hired guns revved up my heartbeat. I watched as they strutted across the street like they owned the town; they looked like they weren't afraid of anyone. Without hesitation, I followed them, determined to find out what their plans were, hoping I'd learn something, anything that might indicate why Monty had hired them.

They walked toward the back of town through a hodgepodge of log and board-planked homes where the townsfolk lived.

I tossed the bread and followed behind them, zigzagging between the houses. Fearful they'd turn around and see me, I pressed my back against a shack then rushed to the next shed for cover. When they moved onto narrow crossroads, into the open, I wasn't sure how I was going to get close enough to hear them without being seen. After a pause, they continued on, and I quickly darted toward a horse that was tied to a post. The horse whinnied; the men turned, and I knew they'd seen me. Panic snatched my breath.

"What a beauty you are," I said to the massive animal as I petted its forehead. "What a sweetheart." My heart beat as though a hammer pounded my chest. The minute felt like an hour as the hired guns sized me up. My pulse thumped in my neck. My hands trembled, but I continued stroking the horse.

Finally, the men turned away from me and stepped between two houses. I breathed a little easier and stalked after them. They stopped in the middle of a wood-fenced corral where horses ate from buckets. I crouched down behind the fence and bushes at the near end of the corral, but I still couldn't make out what they were saying. I needed to move closer, but the open space left no cover. I chewed my lip and tried to come up with a plan.

A flock of birds took off from the rooftop behind me. The horses, spooked by the noise, started running around the corral. The two men jumped out of the way and looked toward me. One of the men opened the gate and headed in my direction.

Shit. Had he seen me?

Lolita gasped. *"You are going to get me killed, Abby."*

"Just be quiet...don't say a word."

My frantic gaze darted around in search of a hiding place, but I couldn't stand without being seen. My chest felt like an accordion squeezing the air from my lungs. I couldn't breathe. The sound of neighing horses and squawking birds couldn't overpower the thumping pulse in my ears.

"Hey, Slimbo." The other man bent down, but I couldn't see why. "I found an escudo." He stood and held up a silver Mexican coin.

Slimbo turned around. "Good for you, Buckeye. You buy the first—"

A hand slammed over my mouth and an arm grabbed me around my waist. Before I could gather a coherent thought, I was lifted and hauled from the bushes. I struggled against my attacker as he carried me behind the corner of a nearby house shaded by a massive oak.

"Shush," Wyatt hissed in my ear.

I stopped fighting, and when he uncovered my mouth, I spun around and glared into his face. "What are you doing here?" I whispered. Frustrated he'd interrupted my surveillance but relieved to see him, I couldn't keep the snap from my tone.

"Are you crazy? Do you want to get yourself killed?"

"That is what I said," Lolita put in with a huff.

I was pissed. "Why are you following me?"

"I'm shadowing those two thugs, hoping to learn what they're up to."

"Me too."

"Well...?"

"I didn't learn anything. Yet..." His arm was still around my waist, distracting me.

He pulled me into him.

I gasped as our hips and chests met.

He pressed his index finger against my lips to silence me.

Voices sounded clearer. The hired guns were close by.

Wyatt removed his finger.

My nerves kicked up like a sudden electrical storm. Any minute now, both of us would be in a lot of trouble. Wide-eyed, I stared at Wyatt, hoping he had a plan. The heat of his body radiated through my dress. I could feel his heart pounding, and I was sure he felt the wild rhythm in my chest. His warm breath breezed against my face. His lips unbearably close, I tried to focus on the shadow of the tree against the house, on the sound of approaching footsteps, anything but his lips.

One of the gunslingers said, "It don't feel right...and I ain't hanging for him." He had a deep, bellowing voice.

"Shut up. You were paid to do a job. You and Hardington are gonna finish it."

The voices sounded louder. They were walking toward us. Wyatt's grip tightened around my waist. There was nowhere to run. We were trapped.

"I was paid to take care of Gilles–"

"And you will."

I closed my eyes, as though doing so would somehow make me disappear, take us both away from the danger that was about to walk right into us.

"I'm good with settin' a fire, but I ain't gonna–"

"You're paid to do whatever our boss tells you to do."

"I ain't afraid of him."

"You should be. Colton's not as mild-mannered as he appears. You cross him...watch your back."

Wyatt looked at me. "Monty?" he whispered.

"Monty Colton, my boss," Lolita whispered in my head.

"They're going to set something on fire for Monty," I whispered.

"What? Where?"

"Shhh."

Footsteps thumped closer, accompanied by the jingle of spurs. I could see dust kick up from the men's boots. I held my breath to control the fear coursing through my veins.

Wyatt's lips tightened. A frown furrowed his forehead. I feared he'd jump out and start swinging on the killers.

The men's shadows slanted in front of us from just around the corner of the house. Two more steps and we'd be in a fight for our lives.

Queasiness hit like a bomb in my stomach.

"Slimbo. Buckeye," a distant voice shouted.

The shadows turned. "Yeah, Blackjack. You need something?"

"Monty wants to see you."

I glanced up at Wyatt. Serious eyes connected with mine.

Spurs jingled as the two men walked away. We remained silent until they were gone.

"Damn. I was hoping to deck those two clowns."

Unable to find my voice, my nerves bunched, I nodded and breathed a sigh of relief. "I'm glad you didn't have to."

Wyatt brushed his thumb over my lip. "You're trembling."

Heat rose from my bosom and up my neck. I stared at his mouth, wondering if he was going to kiss me.

"Do not wait for him to make the first move, Abby. Take what you want."

"I'm not like you, Lolita."

"Yes you are."

Adrenaline-heated blood pumped through my veins. As he leaned closer, the heat traveled down my body and pooled between my legs. How had I gone from sheer fright to sheer delight so quickly? Even so, I refused to take the lead and kiss him.

Dreamy blues gazed at me. He brushed his mouth lightly over mine, and wild sensations ran amuck in my heart: exhilaration, apprehension, relief, and pleasure. I wanted to smash our mouths together and let our tongues discover each other.

A flicker of desire crossed his eyes then disappeared as he released me. "We should go. They may come back."

I reined in my overheated emotions. "You're right." Disappointment chased away expectation. I stepped back and put distance between us. Unwilling for him to see the raw letdown I felt, I glanced to the ground.

He lifted my chin. Concern darkened his eyes. "I shouldn't have done that." He swallowed. "You, me...things are complicated enough without...you know."

I understood. I was Lolita, a married woman, alone, and I was Abby, single and free, except for my self-inflicted celibacy from an old wounded heart. We had to stop a murderer. Nothing could get in the way of that goal. "I get it. You're right. We should keep our distance."

He huffed. "The least you could do is argue with me."

Despite my irritation at his flippantness, I forced a smile I hoped would appease him. "What do you think Slimbo meant by starting a fire and taking care of Gilles?"

His playful expression hardened. "I don't know, but it didn't sound good. I wish their conversation hadn't been interrupted."

"We're no closer to solving the mystery than we were yesterday."

He ran his index finger against my cheek, and I swallowed a lump of emotion. "Promise me we'll work together, and you won't go off on your own again. We *are* going to figure this out."

I nodded and prayed he was right.

Abby and the wanted poster

"Lolita." Monty sat in a leather chair behind a fancy wooden desk and called me into his office. I felt cold and uncomfortable in his presence. I'd finished my Monday morning shift and was ready to go home.

A large picture of a nude woman lying on a green velvet couch hung on the wall behind him. I wasn't a prude, but nude paintings made me feel uneasy about my body. This one stared down at me with slumberous dark eyes, perky boobs, and wiry black hair in a place that should have been left to the imagination. Her face looked a little too much like mine.

"Darling, before you go home, deliver this to the Sheriff so he can take it to the post office in Coloma on his next trip." He held out an envelope.

I took it. "Of course." As I turned for the door, I wondered what was in the envelope. Did the message have anything to do with the hired guns? My thoughts flew back to Wyatt and our almost kiss after we almost got busted. I needed to get him out of my mind. We had more important things to do than play cat and mouse games with my heart. Being involved with him could be a fatal distraction. The lives of two children were on the line.

"Oh, and Lolita." Monty's flat, smooth voice stopped me at the door.

I turned around. Acutely aware of my low-cut bodice and how his eyes widened as he stared at my breasts, I bunched my dress in a fist and tried not to panic. I swear he was salivating. Not wanting my boobs to rise and swell over the top of my dress, I kept my breathing steady despite my pounding heart. A trickle of sweat slid down my neck.

Did Monty ever sweat? Not one wrinkle marred his pristine clothes. His lips were a hard straight line beneath a trimmed black mustache. The bold hunger in his eyes prickled my skin like invisible ants skittering down my arms. Did Lolita ever feel the same repulsion, or did she welcome his leering eyes?

"You look lovely today." His lascivious gaze rode me up and down like a slow-moving carousel ride.

Overcome with nerves, I didn't know how to respond. *What would Lolita say...or do?* Would she flirt? Sit on his lap? Slap his face?

"Why, Monty, how kind of you to say so," Lolita's sultry voice said as she waved the envelope. "I should post this."

"Nice save, Lolita. Thanks."

Before he could say another word, I headed for the door. As I left the office in the back of the saloon, I was sure Monty ogled my backside as I walked away.

The saloon wasn't as crowded as usual, probably because the streams were drying out, making gold harder to find. That didn't bode well for my tips. Usually, men stood in lines three or four deep at the faro table, and the mingled sound of victories and defeats, music and laughter roared throughout the saloon, as did the flow of gold.

At the swinging doors, I heard Daisy on the boardwalk, hawking to the passersby. "Come on in, all kinds welcome. A little mud on your hat and pants is no bother to me. Hey, fella. I'll handle that bulge for you as long as you got a little dust in your pocket." A low purr of seduction laced her voice. "Come on in, and I'll show you a good time."

I rushed outside into the blazing sun.

"Sakes alive, Sugar. Where you off to in such a hurry?"

My dress might have been cut low, but Daisy's was so low I could see a nipple's dark edge. Her white dress was so tight and sheer, it resembled a nightgown. Pink ribbons cinched the hem, bringing the length up to the top of her thighs, showcasing thick black stockings.

"To deliver a letter for Monty." I smiled.

"I plan to pay you a visit later. I have something for your little young'uns."

"You are always welcome anytime."

Her smile bewitching, she thrust out her chest. "Hey, big boy." She gestured to a large rough-looking man wearing miner's boots, a blue flannel shirt, and a scruffy beard. The massive guy could probably carry a hundred-pound sack of flour and a barrel of rum on his beefy shoulders and not break a sweat.

"Howdy, sweetheart." His brawn matched his deep bellowing voice. His arm reached out, looped around Daisy's waist, and he lifted her off the ground. "Don't mind if I do."

A moment later, I was crossing the street, dodging wagons and groups of men, laughing and talking and moving along, while the burly fellow carried Daisy inside for a quickie.

I made my way through the crowd, past a Mexican woman dressed in a brightly colored dress. Her arm was linked with her man whose colossal sombrero was big enough to shade both of them. I passed men who desperately needed bathing, and Native braves whose breechcloths barely covered their junk. The street was alive with every nation in all varieties of costume, Chinese silk shirts of gold and greens, black and red Spanish lace, and black French berets. Different dialects and accents mixed like cake batter churning in a blender.

I walked to the jailhouse and pushed open the door. Sheriff Samuel Townsend sat behind his desk with his booted feet on the desktop. "Mornin', Lolita." He dropped his feet to the floor and sat upright. "What brings you here today?"

"Monty would like this posted when you go to Coloma."

He stood and took the envelope from my hand. "My pleasure, ma'am."

I strolled past the cell bars to a bulletin board: *Wife wanted. Woman who can wash, cook, scour, sew, milk, spin, cut wood and make a fire, feed the pigs, raise chickens, saw a plank, and drive nails. Neither handsome nor a fright, age no difference, but old need not apply.* Good Lord. The advertisement was for a slave, not a wife. Reputation aside, thank God for my job at the saloon. Townsfolk could give me all the dirty looks they wanted. I'd take singing over feeding pigs any day.

A faded poster on the wall caught my eye. *Wanted, Dead or Alive,* then under a silhouette of a man's head: *the murderer of Madam Doble. $5,000 reward for information and capture.* What a shame the killer's name was unknown. Judging from how old the poster looked, the murder must've been committed long ago.

I turned and crossed the room. "Thank you, Sheriff."

"Good day."

As I stepped outside, Benjamin rode up in a buggy and stopped. "You needing a ride to camp, Miss Lolita?"

"Ah..." Hesitation stole my words, mixed with apprehension, and rattled my thoughts. He was a great piano player, but he was also a confessed killer, though I didn't know who he'd killed or who he'd confessed to. That had earned him a place on my list of suspects. Silent warning alarms blared in my head. If I wanted to learn more I'd have to spend time with him.

"Yes. Thank you." Perhaps now would be a good time to pull information from him, see who he was talking to that night in his tent.

He got down, helped me up to the bench seat, and a moment later, we were off.

As the wheels rolled over the uneven ground, so did my thoughts. What could I ask that wouldn't sound bizarre? I couldn't just come out and ask, hey, do you want to kill my kids? Pleasantries aside, working with him every day, Lolita would know where he came from and how long he'd been here. How could I bring up the overheard conversation I had no right listening to?

There was something odd about him. Putting the legend aside, his aura raised my internal antennas. Maybe Daisy was right. He couldn't be trusted.

"I understand you and my children were down by the river," I said casually.

"Yes."

"And what did you find to do down there?"

"I-um..." His shifting gaze refused to meet mine. "Joseph asked me to go with him to look for frogs. I couldn't say no. Cattie came too."

"How long do you plan on staying in camp?"

Legend had it, Benjamin left after the children were killed. Was he running or just moving on?

"I'm not keen on staying in one place too long."

"Why?"

He flicked the reins, and the horse picked up speed. "Been here in Dry Diggins longer than usual. Wandering is in my blood, just saying."

His words sounded a bit forced, like an afterthought, and I still wondered what part he played in the legend, if any. Nothing more was said as the trees whipped past us and I pretty much ate my hair.

In camp, as he helped me down, I noticed a nervous twitch in his eyes, like maybe he thought he'd told me too much. "Good day, Miss Lolita." He smiled, climbed back into the buggy, and rode off toward the livery.

I stepped into my home where Cattie was putting a bouquet of white roses on the table. They grew wild on the hillsides. She looked so grown up with her black hair braided and hanging across her shoulder.

"Hello, children."

Joseph glanced at me then went back to snapping twigs at the table.

Cattie glanced up. "Hello, Mamma," then turned to take dishes off the hanging shelf.

"Don't worry about setting the table. I will set it later." I hurried over to the trunk and pulled out two packages. "Come here. Both of you."

They dragged their feet over, uncertainty on their faces.

"Cattie, this is for you, and Joseph, for you." I handed each of them their package.

Cattie unwrapped her gift like it might be a priceless treasure. When she saw the dress, her eyes lit with happiness, and my heart lifted.

Joseph tore into his, shrugged, dropped the new shirt on the table, and picked up his twigs.

Cattie held her new dress up to her neck and twirled. "It is so pretty." She stopped and looked up at me with her big blue eyes. "Thank you, Mamma."

I'd hoped for a hug. "You are welcome."

She neatly folded her dress over a chair. "I will go get the firewood."

"I think we should all go out and enjoy this fine day."

"Really?" Cattie tilted her head, doubtful.

Made me wonder if Lolita ever played with her children?

"Yes. Come, Joseph." I held out my hand.

Joseph got up and took Cattie's hand.

I dropped my arm and sighed. Did I really think I'd win their affection with presents? Cindi's words came back to me. "*I hate it when kids are neglected.*" I was beginning to think Cindi was right. Lolita was a lousy mother.

Tears welled in my eyes.

Wyatt's new patient

On the ninth day of July, stifling air greeted me as I got up and did a few morning pushups. Emanuel and his family were already up and gone. I felt a little guilty sleeping in late, but I wasn't going to let my oversleeping, or the heat, dry up my good mood like it was drying up the river. I felt lucky. Emanuel and I were heading out to our dig. If the saying, itchy palm, money found, indicated anything, we were going to strike it rich today.

I pushed aside the tent-flap-of-a-door, stepped outside, poured water in a washbasin, and splashed the tepid water on my face. I wiped my forehead with a rough cloth. Out the corner of my eye, I noticed white stocking legs and shoes with thick soles worn by Chinese men in camp.

"Mister. I am Jiang." He held out a bowl of what looked like egg foo yung with a short wooden spoon sticking straight up.

"I'm Wyatt."

We shook hands.

Jiang still wore his queue with pride. A sense of satisfaction washed over me. Hank would have it for a souvenir if I hadn't stopped him.

"For you." He edged the bowl closer. "For saving my queue."

"It was nothing."

"You take, Hangtown Fry, very good eggs and oysters."

Did he see me eyeing the oysters the day in the camp store? "Not necessary..." The thought of eating something new made me lift the bowl from his hands. "But thank you."

As he turned and walked away, I grabbed the spoon and dug in. Scrambled eggs, crumbled bacon, and oysters never tasted so good. Yup, it was going to be a good day.

Across the way, Abby and the kids strolled to the edge of the camp. She held two big spoons in one hand and a couple bowls in the other. They plopped down in an area of mud and started to build mud castles. It was nice to see her taking time away from the saloon to be with her kids. Keeping them close would be an excellent start to keeping them safe.

Though I understood why she'd followed those hired guns, the unsettling thought that she could have gotten herself killed soured my gut every time I thought about it. Holding her close, seeing the fear that suddenly turned those sexy eyes into desire, made my head spin.

I hoped she understood why I didn't kiss her. Part of me wanted to, the other part reminded me we were here for one reason, to stop a murderer. What if a kiss screwed things up between us? Got weird? No. I'd made the right decision even though she was tempting in Lolita's body.

I pulled myself from my thoughts and took another mouthful of egg and savored the flavor of oysters. Gratitude never tasted so good.

I'd just emptied my bowl when Emanuel's mother walked up, a serious expression on her face.

"Camila? Is everything all right? Where's Emanuel?" I glanced around, hoping nothing had happened to him.

"My son is fine. But..." She raised her hands pray-like to her lips. "We heard you helped the Sheriff's son, and we were wondering if you could do your doctoring again."

I had no idea who she was talking about when she said we, but I nodded and placed the bowl on the bench. "Show me where."

We walked a few tents down and entered a small wood-framed shanty covered with old tarps that served as a roof. As we entered, a plump woman met us. Wrinkles creased the corners of her dark, sorrowful eyes. Gray streaks mingled with chestnut hair tied tightly in a bun at the nape of her neck.

"Camila, thank you." She hugged Emanuel's mother.

Uneven floorboards creaked as I made my way to a man whose dark skin looked sickly pale. Right away, I noticed the swelling of both legs below the knee. I suspected swollen legs might be a sign of scurvy, and given the lack of vegetables and fruit around here lately, a likely contender.

"Please open your mouth," I said in Spanish. Sure enough, bleeding and swollen gums. I turned to the woman whose worried expression far surpassed Camila's haunted stare. "He has scurvy."

She wrung her hands together, looked at her husband, then back at me. "¿Se va a morir?"

"No. He's not going to die," I replied in Spanish and explained further: "First you need to get him undressed and wash him down with cool water to help reduce his fever." What I should have said was he needed a good bath. "You need to boil some..." Lately, vegetables and fruits were so scarce that suggesting she buy some was out of the question. I racked my brain to think of what my herbalist friend told me about tree bark and herbs. "Willow." I knew willow trees grew in places along the river. "Grind up some willow bark. It will help defuse his fever and minimize his pain." I didn't have enough aspirin to go around. "Also, to improve his immune system, find some wild roses and boil them in water to make him a tea."

The sick man's wife hurried outside.

Camila placed her hand on my arm. "Gracias."

I nodded. "De nada."

As I washed my hands, I wondered how I became the camp doctor. I only hoped I wouldn't be faced with some deadly disease that spread around the camp and threatened the lives of people I'd come to care for.

Abby's husband returns

Daisy and I stood in the dressing room of the saloon between our wobbly racks of gowns. I searched through boxes of feathered hats and gloves, looking for the perfect combination to go with the red dress I'd selected for my next performance, black lace or white.

"He's back," she sang.

"Who?" *Wyatt?* I hadn't seen him in a while. Remembering our last intimate moment made my pulse erratic. The dangerous glint in his eyes had turned my mind to mush. The overwhelming need to kiss him hadn't only been Lolita's need; it was mine, too, but after what he'd done to me, I shouldn't even want him to touch me. I sighed. Even so, I had to wonder who he wanted to kiss, me or Lolita. He'd probably already forgotten I was just a frumpy redhead and not the Spanish maiden in his arms.

I turned, and Daisy began to lace up the back of my slim red gown.

"Are you going to see him?"

"See who?" Wyatt would just dump me when we returned home and he saw the real me.

Daisy pulled the strings, closing my dress a little too tightly. "Your husband."

I sucked in a breath and spun around. "Horace is here?"

"In the saloon."

The room felt void of air. My breathing became rapid, and feeling lightheaded, I gripped a nearby chair.

"Sugar..." She tied the strings. "You look like you've seen a ghost."

The pulse in my neck throbbed furiously. "No. He can't be back. Not now. What does he want? Why is he back? The children..." I rubbed my sternum, trying to ease the knot in my heart. I couldn't breathe.

Oh my god. He's come back for the children.

I heard Lolita *scream* in my head.

We were both terrified. A tingling in my feet began to travel up my legs, a sure sign they'd soon give out and leave me in a heap on the floor.

Daisy held me up. "He's dressed mighty fine. I'm thinking he struck a motherlode. Maybe he's here to collect you and your young'uns, take you all back to civilization and a life of wealth and privilege."

I stared at Daisy as though looking through a blurry lens. "I will not go anywhere with him," I lashed out with Spanish fury, the pain in my chest intense. "Not after he left us for that whore."

Daisy's eyes narrowed. The expression on her face was one of disgust, and I realized she'd probably taken offense to the word *whore*. "I did not mean you..."

She fluffed her hair and pinched her cheeks. "So what if I am a whore? I got no choice. But you do. And don't tell me you would rather stay here in this filthy town, singing for scraps and living in that hovel. If I were you, I'd hightail outta here with my man, if he's offering."

"Is that woman with him?"

"Not that I seen. Why?"

I couldn't tell her my fears, couldn't mention the legend, or tell her I thought Horace's mistress might be a jealous murderer. The bone-stays of my corset bit into my ribcage. I yanked the bodice, wishing I could free myself of the cumbersome fabric.

"Lolita. He's your ticket out of here."

"I do not care how much money he has. I do not want him." I knew I was speaking for Lolita, too. "I do not belong to him."

"Sugar, when he put a ring on your finger, you sure do. And the children are his, too, if he wants them."

"He took the ring back." I glared at her with annoyance, not wishing to argue, wishing I could tell her the truth and make her understand. If Lolita didn't kill her kids out of jealousy, his mistress surely could have. While he was gone, I'd figured the kids were safe from that theory of legend. Now that he was back, and the blue moon was coming in nine days, my mission just got more complicated than any kiss from Wyatt could have ever created.

"What is wrong with you, Lolita? Go out there and claim your husband. Your problems are over."

"My kids and I are doing just fine without him."

Something akin to annoyance flashed in Daisy's eyes. "Go with him willingly, or he'll take the children by force." She stepped past me and walked out the door.

"Abby, Abby, please. Help me. I will not let him take me." Lolita's voice sounded different, choked with emotion and fearful, for the first time. *"And he cannot have my kids. I will kill him first. Do not try to stop me or I will take back my body, and you will be gone forever."*

Lolita's words clenched my chest. Her threat was real and lethal. I had to stop him or I'd lose everything.

"We're on the same side, girlfriend." I stabbed my hands into the black lace gloves and stormed into the noisy saloon.

Daisy was already flirting with one of her regulars, a small man with a big bag of gold on the table and a silly grin showcasing only two front teeth.

Benjamin played a tune I didn't recognize, but Lolita would know it. A white and gray stray cat sat on the piano, flicking his tail.

"Where's that good for nothing escoria?" Scum.

My head began to throb, and a calming breath did little to soothe the anger churning in Lolita's stomach. My glance flew to the bar and I stopped. Lolita recognized the wide girth of her husband, no matter the fancy duds he wore. In my opinion, the light brown checkered suit coat made him look like a clown. My face burned crimson as I marched across the room. I stepped up behind the clown, my hands jammed on my hips.

He looked up into the bar mirror and our gazes met. "Hello, darlin' wife." He turned and faced me.

"Diablo." I slapped him across the face.

He grabbed my arm. "As beautiful as I remember. But then that's your only saving grace." His hand clamped me so tightly his fingernails dented my flesh.

"Devil." I tried to break free. "Get out. Go back to your whore." It wasn't me doing all the screaming. Lolita was standing up to this woman-abusing man. The pounding in my temples intensified.

"I see you still have a bad temper." There was no heat in his voice. His face was a mask of indifference. The only indication my demands had hit their mark was the dangerous glint I saw in his eyes.

"Let go of me, you big lug." I grabbed his wrist with my other hand and tugged in an attempt to break free of his grip.

"We are leaving right now." His composure was too calm for a man who'd just been slapped, though I knew him well enough to know the calm was for everyone else's benefit. Deep down, a volcano of anger was about to erupt.

"I am not going anywhere with you."

He picked me up and folded me over his shoulder.

As I struggled against his grip on my thighs, I kicked my feet while the patrons and gamblers broke out in laughter.

"This is how you treat an unruly wife," he bellowed as he pushed open the doors and stepped outside.

Chapter Twelve

Doctor Wyatt

After treating Camila's friend, we were called to another tent where a man was stricken with abdominal pain. Emanuel was working our claim, but so far nothing new was pulled out. It was probably time to move to a new area. I felt a little guilty leaving him alone, but he assured me that what I was doing was more important.

By curing the Sheriff's son and a few others who'd fallen sick with various illnesses, my reputation had spread around camp that I was a good doctor, and people started coming to me with all kinds of ailments. I wasn't qualified to practice medicine, but I couldn't turn them away. One look at a mother's desperate face or hearing the pleading tone in her voice, and I had to help them. My aspirin supply had whittled down to two, and I held on to them. I racked my brain, pulling all I could remember from the books I'd read to prepare me for pre-med school...when I wasn't playing football.

I removed my hand from my new patient's forehead. "You don't have a fever. The pain in your stomach might be from something you ate." At least I hoped that would explain his bellyache. Without an x-ray machine or a real doctor to examine him, the food diagnosis was the best I could do.

"Doctor, aquí, maybe this work."

"Camila, I'm not a doctor." I moved away from the bed where the man lay clutching his stomach and faced Emanuel's mother.

"Nonsense." She handed me a fistful of dried roots.

"What is it?"

"Sarsaparilla. My people use it for stomach pain," she said in Spanish. "It helps with digestion."

"Gracias."

I turned to the sick man's wife. "Boil this and make a tea. If you do not see an improvement, or if a fever breaks out, come get me."

She smiled, walked to a table, came back and handed me a jar of raisins. I'd given up refusing any means of payment and took the jar. I realized people didn't want charity any more than I did. And if anyone asked, my pickle jar was mostly empty all the time. I didn't have enough gold to last until the blue moon. In other words, I was flat broke but still happy to get a jar of raisins.

I placed the raisins in my new medical kit, a container that resembled a shoeshine box, set them next to my jar of water, roll of bandages, spare rags, and homemade remedies of herbs and roots. I used to kid around with my friend who'd studied to be an herbalist. She was always talking about leaves and bark and weird mixtures of plants for cures. I'd joked she was concocting salads, not medicine, but here I was now, grabbing the leather handle of my makeshift medicine box full of jars of crumbled twigs, leaves, and flower petals. I guess she knew what she was talking about.

As I stepped outside, the overbearing heat from a July summer sun slammed into me. I mounted Jack and he ambled toward our dig site.

Along the trail, a Native American sat slumped under a tree. Even from this distance I could see he was hurt. My throat went dry as I gave Jack a nudge, and he trotted to him. I jumped down and knelt at the man's side. "You need help."

Coal-colored eyes warily assessed me with a hint of recognition. He was the same tall and proud Native I'd seen in the camp store. His dark face was bruised and bleeding. Tree bark was mixed with blood in his long black hair. A swollen shoulder dangled low and limp. He'd been beaten badly.

"Who did this to you?"

"White man."

"We need to tell the Sheriff."

"Your law does not care about my people."

"Whoever did this can't get away with it."

He stared and remained silent. His eyes were void of emotion and his lips were pressed firmly shut.

I wanted to shake the truth from him, but I knew it was pointless. After rushing back to Jack, I grabbed my medicine box and returned to my patient. "Let me clean you up." I reached into my box, took out the jar of water and a clean cloth. I remembered what Emanuel had said, how the *Injins* were used as target practice. This guy was used for batting practice. I dabbed water on his facial wounds.

"You bring good medicine?"

"It's the best I can do out here in the middle of nowhere."

"You fix shoulder?"

"I don't know. I'm not a doctor...more like a medic."

"You...medicine man."

I went to work on a bloody abrasion on his cheek. "What is your name?"

"Soaring Eagle."

"I'm Wyatt." I cleaned under his swollen eye, careful not to press too hard, then reached into my medicine box for the aloe plant that a man from Mexico had given me. "This will help you heal." I sliced open a prickly green leaf and gently patted the goo on his skin.

"Now you fix shoulder." His dark eyes were full of determination.

"I've only seen it done once." What if I did it wrong? What if I made it worse? I picked bark out of the cuts then wiped away the caked blood. A real doctor would come in handy right about now.

I looked at his swollen eye, at a nose that would be forever crooked, and then lifted his arm a little.

He responded with a groan.

"Do you have any tingling, numbness, or weakness in your arm?"

He nodded.

Damn. That meant vital nerves and blood vessels could be compressed and cause permanent damage to his arm. Immediate treatment was required. I was his only hope. "I need you to lie flat on your back." Sweat began to dribble down my forehead as we got into position. I put his arm at a ninety-degree angle to his body and held his wrist then propped my foot on his ribcage. "I am going to count to three. Then pull." My palms felt clammy.

"Ready?"

He nodded and squeezed his eyes shut.

"One." I pulled hard and heard a pop.

Abby fights for her kids

I screamed as I pounded my fists into Horace's back. "You pig." He lugged me out of the Boomerang to a wagon and dumped me onto the bench seat. Lightheaded, I gripped the seat rail, praying I wouldn't faint and topple over. "Where are you taking me?"

"Home."

"I can't go home. I have to sing—"

"Shut up."

"Why are you taking me home?" What was he going to do? Images of being raped brought bile to my throat. "What do you want?" Cold sweat chilled my face.

"To see my children. They had better be there when we arrive."

"I..." I sucked in a shallow breath, then another. Was he here to take them away from me as Daisy had warned?

The trees we passed blurred into each other. My thoughts hit me as fast as the wheels churning across the uneven ground. What would he do if the kids weren't there? What if they were home? Did he plan on staying? Didn't he have a mistress? The legend said he had another woman...

What am I going to do? Oh God. Breathe, just breathe.

"If he touches my kids, I will kill him." Lolita seethed.

"If you kill him, we'll both go to the gallows."

"I will cut his throat anyway like the pig that he is."

I had no doubt she'd do it...to protect her kids. And legend had made her out to be their killer. Stupid legend.

When the wagon stopped, I wanted to bolt down, but before I could gather my full skirt and swing my body over the rail, he grabbed my waist and threw me to the ground. I was lying in the dirt at his boots. He stared down at me, his eyes hard. My heart thundered. My knees quivered. "Let me get up," I said with a voice resembling a pissed off Lolita.

He yanked me up. "Take me to my children." He gave me a shove.

I tripped over my hem but caught myself and ducked into the hovel he'd built for us, our family. It was the only home Lolita had known since he'd dragged her and the kids across the country to the California gold fields.

Cattie and Joseph were sitting at the table. My heart jerked, whether from fear or happiness, I wasn't sure. "Children. Your father..."

He pushed past me. "I'm here," he bellowed.

They stood and ran to him. He scooped them up in his arms. His big smile mirrored the happiness on the children's faces. My spirit fell. Their abundant joy smothered me. I dropped into a chair as tears clouded my vision. I felt Lolita's jealousy of his affection for them, and them for him, and he had nothing but loathing for her. Oh my god. The legend could very well be true. Cindi's words came back to me. *"She's guilty."*

"Go to the wagon," he told the kids. "I have brought you gifts."

The children ran outside.

Horace turned to me. "Pack up their belongings. They are coming with me."

I jumped from my seat. "I will be damned if you are taking my children from me." I yelled so loud I'd bet the entire camp heard me.

Horace acted like he hadn't heard a word. He plopped his big ass into a chair and kicked his feet up on the table. "You, dear wife, have no say in the matter." He studied his nails, dismissing me. "They're my children."

I wanted to scratch out his eyes and send him straight to hell. "They are my children, as well. They stay here with me." I stomped my foot. I was losing control. Lolita was trying to take over. When I grabbed the table for support, I saw the butcher knife on the shelf.

"Don't do it, Lolita."

Horace stood. Rage colored his bulldog face. "No law in this godforsaken land will stand up for you, a whore—"

"Whore? Whore?" I slammed my hands on the table. "I'm a singer." I saw the children hovering near the door, terrorized by our argument. "Run," I shouted to them. "Hide. I will find you later." When they were out of sight, I turned my attention back to Horace. "I am not a whore. I sing in a saloon to keep food on the table for my children. You left me with no money, no choice. For your puta."

Horace's eyes bulged. He threw the chair across the room and stomped toward me. Before I could back away, he grabbed my wrist and squeezed. "I'll not have you disgrace Sadie's good name with filth. She is a well-bred woman."

A new fear coursed through me, heating my limbs. I was out of control. Lolita had taken over. I could feel her overshadow me, suck up my thoughts as she spit venomous words in a language I didn't understand.

I tried to hold her tongue. I tried to stop her words, but the wild Lolita was loose and unstoppable. "Well-bred? The slut is sleeping with a married man. A whore is a whore. I will not have my kids live with a man who brings adultery into his home."

His grip choked blood from my arm. "You will give me those kids. I won't leave town until I have them."

I yanked free and stepped back. My face burned with rage. "Over my dead body."

He leaned into me with murder in his eyes. "That, dear wife, can be arranged." He stormed out, nearly tearing the blanket from the doorway.

I heard the wagon rattle away, grabbed a frying pan, smashed a pile of dishes then screamed at the top of Lolita's lungs.

Wyatt's redeeming kiss

Spanish words of obscenity flew from Abby's shack. I ran to her doorway, and not knowing what to expect, darted inside. The place was in shambles. Pots and pans and broken dishware littered the earthen floor. A chair lay on its side.

Abby stood in the middle of the room with a frying pan clenched in her hand. Fury crunched her face.

"Abby?"

Crazed eyes daggered in my direction. The pan flew from

her hand.

I ducked. The pan skimmed my head and banged against the wood-burning stove. "Shit, Abby. What happened?"

"Lolita no like men today. Get out." She pointed to the doorway. "Get out." Her shrill command could have rattled the rafters, it was so piercing and loud.

Oh, no. Not again. "Calm down, Lolita." My hands up in front of me, I edged closer. "Tell me what happened."

She picked up a cup.

The hesitation in her eyes gave me hope. "I just want to help."

"Lolita is angry."

"Yes, she is."

"Men are pigs."

"We can be...yes." I thought it best to agree with her.

"Horace...he is...he is..." The cup flew, crashed into a trunk and shattered. "A bastardo."

Who is Horace?

With my eyes fixed on her icy stare, I calmly inched toward her, righted the chair, and slid it to her. "Please sit and tell me who he is."

She didn't move. The veins in her neck throbbed. Doubt swirled in the depths of her green eyes.

I eyed the knife on the shelf and hoped she didn't go for it. "So, what did Horace do to upset you?"

Her hand reached to the shelf. The knife came up in her fist. "My husband, the pig, has returned." Her Spanish cursing came at me fast. "He demands I give my children to him and his puta mistress." Another string of curses followed.

The knife flew at me. I ducked as it whizzed by my ear. *Shit.* "Lolita. Stop." I put my hands up in front of me, palms out. "Did he take them?" Alarm colored my voice.

"No. They ran and hid, but the bastardo will return for them."

"Good."

Her upper lip curled. A frown marred her brow. "Good? Why you say good?"

"I mean it's good he doesn't have them. I will help you keep the children."

While she stared at me, her lips pressed together, I formulated a plan to get Abby back, but I'd have to kiss Lolita to do it, if I was right about what had happened on the runaway wagon. However, right now it would be like trying to kiss a pissed off cobra. Maybe I could rush her and grab her...or play on her oversexed ego. *That's it.* "You sure are beautiful when you're angry."

Suddenly, her whole demeanor changed. Her head tilted as she eyed me. Her shoulders relaxed and a seductive smile softened her expression.

She freaked me out. "Lolita? Are you all right?"

The exaggerated sway of her hips and the way her hungry gaze raked my body from head to toe as she sauntered to me, made it clear Lolita was still in the room. She tossed her hair and brushed her neck with her fingertips in a dramatic move meant to seduce me. This Prima Donna was definitely not Abby.

She reached out and pinched my collar. "You think Lolita is pretty." It was more a statement than a question. She swept the tip of her tongue over her plump lips.

I swallowed dryly. "Yes."

"Desirable, no?" Her fingers coiled a strand of her hair as she batted her eyelashes at me.

Standing there, letting her come on to me, left me feeling like a sex object, but I didn't want to face the crazy version again. *Best I appease her until I get Abby back.*

"Every man's dream?" she whispered as she leaned closer, her hot breath an invitation for love.

Her luscious shiny hair cascaded down her back to her waist. Skin the color of honey made her green eyes pop, a startling contrast. Her red low-cut dress accented her curvy bosom and would make any preacher drool.

"All men want Lolita," she purred.

Probably true, but right now she was a little too full of herself, too much like Pam, for me.

She smiled coyly. "You may kiss Lolita now." She pressed her breasts against me and looped her lovely arms around my neck.

Here goes nothing. I drew her in and kissed her like I meant it.

Abby fears Lolita

My arms were around Wyatt's neck, my breasts pressed against his chest. He was actually kissing me. Something inside me snapped and I pushed him away, horrified. "What do you think you're doing?"

"Abby. You're back."

Oddly, he looked pleased, smiling as if he was happy I'd caught him red-handed. Right. He was kissing Lolita. When I wasn't looking. I wiped my mouth with the back of my hand. "How could you?"

"It's not what you think."

"I know what I saw." The room spun.

Wyatt caught me. "I kissed her, yes, but she came on to me."

"She did?" I glanced around my torn-apart home. Tears flooded my eyes. "What did I do?"

"Don't cry," Wyatt whispered as he gathered me into his arms, his embrace comforting but dangerous.

I stiffened, inhaled his musky scent. Then I remembered. Panic shot through me like a rifle bullet. "Horace. He was here. The children? Did he take them?"

"They're safe."

My body trembling, I cuddled into him and sobbed. I felt so powerless. Lost. Numb.

"Abby, it's okay...you're okay."

Tears streamed down my face. I could taste the salt on my lips and took several breaths. "I'm not...I'm not okay. I-I don't know who I am...or who I think I am."

Gently, he lifted my chin off his chest. Our gazes met. "You're Abby. The Abby I've come to know." He thumbed a tear away, his touch so tender I felt more tears forming. "The woman who blushes when someone pays her a compliment."

I shook my head. "I'm two people squashed into one drop-dead body. Where do I start? Where do I end? And my alter-ego has a nasty temper. I'm afraid of her, Wyatt. She can destroy me."

He hugged me. His arms offered comfort and stirred a

whirlwind of need that made me cling to him. If only this wound on my heart would heal so I could love him.

"Nothing is going to happen to you, the real you."

"Don't you understand? If I can't control Lolita, if I'm not constantly aware of what she's doing, she could have done it, like the legend says she did. I know how she feels. I was there when Horace saw the kids. I felt the jealousy burn inside her, the way her kids greeted him, hugged him... By God, they were like traitors and she felt hurt to the core. Wyatt. She could be guilty. I can't stop her when I'm not in control."

"I can keep you in control. I promise."

I eased back and looked up at him as my tears tumbled. "You can't promise that. Lolita is powerful. I'm just along for the ride."

He took my hand and made me sit. "Before, when Lolita kissed me...in the wagon, you came back, almost instantly. And just now, when she put her arms around me and kissed me, you came back."

Heat seared my face. "What are you saying? I keep interrupting your fling with her?" I started to rise, but Wyatt placed his hands on my shoulders.

"I'm just trying to explain how I know I can help you."

I nodded, swiped a tear from my lip. "How?"

"A simple kiss. That's all it takes."

For a second, my mind went numb then my thoughts spun. Lolita and Wyatt kissing? What's next?

Wyatt must have seen the confusion in my eyes. "My kiss affects her. It draws you out and Lolita retreats. You and I are connected somehow, across time and space, and Lolita is the key." He chuckled. "For better or worse, you're stuck with me."

That has a nice ring to it.

"Do not let him get away, Abby."

"While I appreciate you looking out for me, you can't be with me night and day."

"Maybe I should move in with you."

I stared at him, dumbfounded, as a myriad of emotions ran through me: desire, dread, hope, and revenge. Never in my wildest imagination would I think to hear those words coming out of any guy's mouth, never mind Wyatt's. Having him close would solve one problem but created a whole new one. I was starting to like having him around.

I stood. "Wyatt, my husband is back and...oh my god, the children." I pivoted toward the door. "We have to look for them."

"They'll be back. Meanwhile, let's clean up this place."

I glanced at the mess that would take a good hour or two to sort out. Lolita's fierce temper must've sent Horace fleeing to safety in town. I was sure he'd be back for the kids, this time with reinforcements. Then what?

Wyatt's vow to Abby

Wow. Did I just ask to move in with her? That was a first. The offer slipped out of my mouth without me thinking it through. Now, standing here feeling vulnerable, waiting for Abby to make up her mind, yes or no, made me doubt the wisdom in my words.

"Wyatt. As much as I appreciate your offer, for the children's sake, you should just stay at Emanuel's."

I wasn't sure if I was relieved or hurt. No woman had ever rejected me before. With Abby, rejection was as sure as gravity. I pushed down the flash of annoyance rising in my chest. But this was Abby. She was different than the women I usually hung with.

Holding her in my arms moments ago, hearing her heart-wrenching sobs, all I wanted to do was ease her pain. For the first time since I can remember, I wasn't sure what to do, what to say. "Abby. If Lolita takes over again and I'm not here, you won't be able to stop her. I need to be here—"

"I know. I know." She touched my arm, her fingers warm against my skin. "But what will people say? My reputation is already a given. Now my husband is back. For all I know, he may think he has the right to sleep with me. Oh god." Her hand flew to her mouth like she was going to be sick.

"After the fight she just put up, I doubt Horace would ever get into bed with her."

I'd meant it when I said staying close was the best way to

keep Lolita from suppressing Abby into oblivion, but part of me wanted to stay for other reasons. There was no denying it, I was attracted to Lolita, but I felt Abby's presence in my heart. However, I knew getting caught between those two women might be hazardous to my health. Moving in wasn't such a good idea, after all.

"When he comes back..." Her eyes were wide with fear as she wrung her hands. "How are we going to stop him from taking the children?"

"Yeah." A deep breath escaped me. "He may bring the Sheriff with papers from a judge."

"What if the children will be safer with him?" Tears welled in her eyes. "If the legend is correct..." She sobbed.

My heart wrenched. "No." I placed a reassuring hand on her arm. "The legend is wrong. They belong here with you. If he had left with the kids, there wouldn't have been a legend. It might be dangerous, but I'll watch your back."

She wiped tears from her face. "Wyatt, you can't watch me twenty-four seven. I have a job to go to, children to take care of, a household to run." She shook her head. "You have your gold digging. It's not practical or possible to babysit me all the time."

"We have a murderer to stop." Sticking by Lolita was the only way I could keep her from showing her lascivious behavior. *Learn your adversary's moves,* Coach always said. How was I to observe Lolita if Abby didn't want me near her? Still, I respected her decision, but my bruised ego was making it hard for me to give in. "We have to stick together."

"Life has to go on as normal. If you're too close to me all the time, the family dynamics will change. People start acting differently, changing the future, maybe just in this camp, but we could alter the killer's behavior and change the future of the world."

"Fine." I wasn't going to beg, but I would keep an eye on that husband of hers. I shrugged, a little pissed by the rejection that bristled my spine.

"I've got to clean up this mess." She glanced around the disheveled room. "You better go."

"No. I'll help."

Surprise arched her brows. "You don't have to."

"If I had to, I wouldn't." I bent down and picked up a brass pot.

We worked in silence, sweeping, straightening and organizing. Several times I caught her glancing my way. Several times I wanted to gather her into my arms and kiss her, soothe away her fears. I wanted her to believe me when I said everything was going to be all right. I had to believe she'd be okay. We were connected, for better or worse.

Abby's fantasy gold

Shocked that Wyatt had asked to move in, my thoughts spun as he helped me clean up. Weeks of manual labor had changed him into the kind of man I could see myself loving. Caring, strong, someone I could depend on. Yes. The old Wyatt had stood me up. It wasn't something I would likely forget, and I wasn't ready to forgive him, but having him in my life now, and not antagonizing him, made sense. I'd bring up the past, eventually; the timing had always felt wrong before. Right now, we were connected across time in a bizarre place we needed to navigate together.

I believed the children would be better off with their mother, but I was afraid for them, frightened Lolita's anger and jealousy would surface, now that Horace was back, and prove the legend was true.

Wyatt folded a blanket over the back of a chair. "Abby?"

"I'm really sorry about this mess."

"I want to talk to you about a bigger problem. Pickin's are getting pretty slim around here."

"With the rivers drying up from lack of rain, is it any wonder? Attendance is down at the saloon. I'm barely making enough tips to buy food for the children."

"Emanuel and I just staked out a new claim, but we haven't found anything yet. It's not like gold is just lying around on the ground. We're going to run out of money before the blue moon."

"On the ground?" I chuckled at that joke then suddenly stopped cleaning the stove as the story in the history book came rushing back to mind. "Wyatt? I have an idea where we can get more gold."

He crossed his muscular arms and leaned against the table. "Shoot."

"I remember reading in an old history book the story of a lost gold claim up on the mountain, somewhere on your property—"

"My grandmother's land?"

"Where it will be built...in the future. As the story goes, an old miner came down from the mountain with his pockets full of gold. He'd found a vein that erosion had exposed, right on the ground. Just bent over and picked up the gold."

Wyatt scowled. "I'm not jumping some guy's claim."

"He hasn't found it yet." I felt like slapping him.

His brows arched. "Abby, he was meant to find it. Not us."

"True. He'll find it, but he'll never know we found it first and took just enough gold to get by."

Wyatt nodded, interested. "Okay. Where is it?"

"I don't know. The old prospector couldn't remember where it was. In his excitement, he'd forgotten to mark a claim or leave a trail back. They went looking but no one ever found it. All we have to do is go up there and find it."

"Great. We're supposed to go on some wild goose chase for a supposed lost claim? We need to stay right here."

"What do we have to lose?"

"We have no idea where it is, or if the story is even true. Besides, we may not even get back in time for the blue moon." He headed for the blanketed doorway.

"Just like that," I screeched. "You're leaving? End of our conversation? Period?"

"I'm going to get my pickle jar."

"Pickles? Oh, that will fix everything. I'm just craving pickles," I said with a bit too much sarcasm.

A deep breath escaped his lips. "Really? You're going to start talking like that?"

"I'm talking about gold, Wyatt. Gold."

"And I put my gold in the jar. What's mine is yours. I'll be right back."

"I can't take your gold."

"Why not?"

"Because it's yours. There's plenty more up on that mountain."

"Damn it. Don't be so pig-headed. We are not going. Period." The door flap swung in and out as he left.

"Yeah, we'll see," I shouted into the empty doorway.

Wyatt faces a lynch mob

The woman was nuts. Her demeanor had changed from quiet contemplation to a woman hell-bent on getting her way so fast I didn't know what hit me.

I made my way toward Emanuel's home.

No way was I climbing up the mountain to search for some supposed vein of gold just lying on the ground. Who knew what we'd encounter up there or how long it'd take to get back?

Yeah. Things at the camp were rough. Slim pickings flared tempers. Drunken fights erupted every night, but here there was safety in numbers. Up there we'd be vulnerable. Never mind the risk of getting lost, snake bit, eaten by bears, or killed by bandits. I'd rather take the chance of striking it rich down here where I knew what dangers I was up against.

How could we save those kids if we were gallivanting up the mountainside? What was she thinking?

Shouts of angry men came from the direction of the river.

I ran, leaping over fallen branches and dug up earth, until I came to a group of men standing in a circle under a tree. A rope hung down from a high branch. *Holy shit. A hanging?* I stopped short, not sure if I should take another step. These men didn't look very friendly. Some I recognized from the camp, others from the river, but some must've been first-timers. New faces poured into camp every day. Three men bent down and lifted a kid, his wrists bound behind him. Emanuel's ashen face was wrenched in terror. "No robar. No steal."

Emanuel? I bolted into the group like a bull, charging through the crowd, then grabbed his arm protectively. "What the hell is going on?"

That damn Hank strode up to me. "This here greaser stole my gold." He held up a nugget as exhibit A.

"No, boss." Emanuel shook his head. "I no thief." Then he explained in Spanish. "Our gold. On our claim."

"That there is gold in his hand. Ain't it?" A toothless accuser pointed out the gold in Hank's hand.

"Question is, whose gold is it?," I said. "Seeing how you are standing on our claim, that gold would be ours. You all better rethink your accusations before you go and hang a boy."

Hank puffed out his chest. "Seeing how's you weren't here, it's the boy's word against mine. I say it's my gold. Right, fellas?"

"Right," voices shouted in unison.

"Stealin' a man's gold is punishable by hanging. Camp law says so. We got every right. String him up, boys."

A tug of war started with Emanuel's body. Hands yanked me back. My grip on his arm failed. Two men looped the noose around his neck.

"In the name of God, how can you do this?" I shouted. "He's just a kid." My heart pounded. The horror in Emanuel's eyes pushed panic to my chest. Sweat dripped down my forehead. My gaze fixed on his face, a face twisted in terror, eyes wide, lips quivering. I could barely breathe. *This can't be happening.*

The Sheriff rode in on horseback. "Now, boys, let's all just calm down. I heard Wyatt yelling from down yonder at camp, rode out of my way to see what's got him all riled up. Hank, take that noose off the boy. What's the matter with you?"

Hank didn't move.

The Sheriff reached for his gun.

Hank complied. Toothless untied Emanuel's wrists.

Emanuel ran to my side and grabbed my arm. "Sorry, boss."

I breathed, relieved.

Hank wasn't done pressing his case. "Dang, Sheriff. He stole my gold."

"He pushed me," Emanuel protested in Spanish. "Tossed my tools off our claim. I found that gold."

The Sheriff shook his head. "That right, Hank?"

Hank's face paled. "You gonna believe the gibberish coming outta that greaser?"

"It's our claim, Sheriff," I said flatly.

"I believe you. Hank's been known to get away with claim jumping."

I scowled. "He got my last one. Stole it right out from under me. Something about camp law and my tools."

The Sheriff leaned forward on his saddle as he addressed Hank. "Should be you swinging from that tree. Camp law."

A murmur rose. The men turned on Hank. "String him up," someone said.

This was getting out of hand. "Sheriff, we don't want a lynching here. Let it go."

"I'm in your debt for saving my boy." The Sheriff tipped his hat. "Hank, if I see you making any more trouble, I'll haul your ass to jail. You understand?"

He nodded.

"And give him back his gold."

Hank glared at him, and a flash of gold flew at me. I caught the nugget. The bastard wouldn't even acknowledge our right of ownership.

"Break it up. Get back to your own business." The Sheriff turned his horse back toward camp, and the crowd dispersed.

Emanuel and I stood alone by the small hole he had dug.

"Thanks, boss. You save my life."

"Saved." Relieved, I tousled his hair. "You would have done the same for me." I peered down into the hole. "Any more gold in there?"

"We dig more."

"Yeah. I bet there's more where this came from." I held up the gold nugget Emanuel had found. I estimated it weighed four ounces. Twenty dollars an ounce. "You found it. This gold belongs to you." Eighty dollars would go a long way in feeding Emanuel's family.

He shook his head. "You, me, we partners. Fifty-fifty. You forget?" He grinned.

"Okay. Let's get to work."

After four hours of digging through clay and gravel, we pulled out a few more ounces then called it a day. After his narrow escape from the noose, I knew Emanuel, despite his insistence, was not okay, and I ordered him to go home. I stayed behind to wash up in the river. I was drying my face with a rag when movement in the bushes caught my eye. I stuffed the rag in my pocket and silently made my way to the cover of a big tree, wondering if someone was spying on me.

Two men, the hired gunslingers, milled around as though waiting for someone. I immediately noticed the guns slung low on their thighs. Pearl handles protruded from their holsters. Their fingers twitched, hovering at their sides, ready to pull out their weapons if the need arose.

The bushes parted. Their glances darted toward the movement. They drew their weapons and pointed.

"Put down the guns, boys." Monty strolled to them.

Hiding behind the tree trunk, I watched as one extremely thin guy twirled the gun and slipped it into the leather holster at his hip. I figured he was the gunman called Slimbo.

"So, Buckeye, did you take care of it?" Monty asked.

"Not yet, sir," the one dressed in all black answered with a sneer that clearly said he was pissed. An ugly scar marred his cheek.

"Why not?"

Buckeye looked at Slimbo. "Tell him."

"We don't do young'uns." Slimbo shuffled his foot in the dirt as though he was nervous.

"I don't pay you for nothing. Take care of those brats."

Shit. Is Monty talking about Lolita's kids?

Abby rejects her boss

Filled with trepidation, I got to work on time Monday morning, the twelfth of July. It had been three days since my altercation with Horace, and I was thankful he wasn't in the saloon. As I hung my red cloak on the coat rack in the dressing room, I heard the bartender call out, "Lolita. Monty wants to see you."

I walked past him and entered the back office. "You want to see me?"

"I hear Horace has returned." Monty didn't sound pleased.

"Bad news travels fast." I'd gotten very little sleep last

night, worrying when Horace was coming back for the children and stewing over the argument I'd had with Wyatt.

"You want me to run him outta town?"

I stared at him. His hired guns would do more than run Horace out of town. They'd make him disappear, permanently. I didn't want that on my conscience. "Thank you for your kind offer, but no."

He got up from behind his desk and walked up to me. "Your husband is a fool to leave you." He set his hands on my shoulders.

The hairs on my neck prickled. When he dropped his hands to my waist, I stepped back before he could pull me against him. "Monty, please." I placed my left palm on his chest. "It is not happening between us."

He leaned in against my hand and ran his lips along my neck. "But I can take care of you."

I pushed him back. "I am doing just fine."

He showed me a curled upper lip. "What's gotten into you lately?"

I had to say something. It took courage for those women who stood up for themselves against men who thought lewd advances were acceptable. The painting of the nude woman lying on the settee, hanging on the wall behind his desk made me feel like all women were simply sex objects on display for men to ogle. I needed to pull courage from deep in my soul to fight back against the sexism that was commonplace in this day and age. "You will act like a gentleman and treat me like a lady." The words flew from my lips. It felt good to put my foot down and demand some respect.

He laughed and stepped back. "Lolita, you are no lady."

That wasn't good news.

"Let me take care of you in the manner you deserve."

"And what manner is that, sir?"

"San Francisco. Come, sit." He offered me a brown leather chair. "I want you to be a part of my new business venture." His eyes were alive with excitement.

I wasn't going anywhere near San Francisco, but I wasn't sure how I was going to tell him no, so I let him talk while I figured an easy way to let him down. The last thing I needed was

Lolita to jump in and start another scene like the one with Horace. I had to remain calm. Monty was my boss. Screaming at him might get me tossed into the street.

"This place..." He gestured around the office. "Is a hovel compared to the saloon I'm going to open in San Francisco. And you'll be my star attraction. I'll set you up in the finest rooms. Give you the finest gowns and jewels befitting your style and grace."

I didn't want anything from him, but what if Lolita wanted to go? What if Lolita was in love with him? Then I realized that she didn't go to San Francisco, she was here the night her kids were killed, so I could say no and history wouldn't be changed.

"Monty, darling," Lolita's voice said with a sultry tone as she ran her fingertips lightly over her chin. "I am very happy here."

"Why? Because your cheating husband came back?" His tight-lipped expression hardened the lines of his face. "You gonna let him back into your bed?"

"Of course not." My breath caught.

"Is it true he wants to take your children back east?"

"Over my dead body."

He stepped a little too close to the chair for my comfort. "It will make things easier for us."

"I will not give my children to that bastardo."

He set his hand on my arm. "We don't need those kids. They'll only get in the way. We can travel, see the world. They'll be just fine with their father."

I jerked my arm away. "Where I go, they go."

Monty's face turned a nasty shade of red. "I will not have a mistress who drags children around like they are tied to her ankles."

"Mistress? I will not be your plaything."

His eyes narrowed. "You ungrateful..." He reared back his hand and slapped my face.

Cheek burning, I raised my hands to protect myself. Tears welled. "How dare you?"

"You came to me, begging for a job after your husband left you. You were nothing but a rejected housewife, but I let you sing. I made you a star. And now you turn me down? No one turns me down." He yanked me out of the chair and pulled me into his body, and leaning forward, he bent me backwards as he tried to kiss me.

I turned my lips away, but he grabbed my hair and cranked my head around to face him. I spit in his eye. He raised a fist—

"Monty."

I recognized Benjamin's voice. My first instinct was to scream, but I feared he'd slug me to shut me up.

"The men are calling for Lolita to sing."

The silence lingered an eternity as Monty's wild-eyed stare bored into the man who'd interrupted his abusive attack on me.

Benjamin cleared his throat. "Everything all right, Miss Lolita?"

Monty dropped his fist and shoved me toward Benjamin. "You can have her."

I hurried to the door.

Benjamin's gaze met mine. Anger stewed in the brown depths of his eyes.

"Lolita," Monty shouted behind me.

I stopped. My heart pounding, I didn't give him the satisfaction of uttering a single word.

"No one refuses me."

I stepped out. With Benjamin right behind me, we hurried across the saloon and stopped at the piano. I leaned against it and fought to regain my nerve.

Benjamin wiped his hand on his pant leg. His brows creased as he stared at his hand as though he'd thought to use it against Monty, then he shook his fingers and looked at me with concern in his eyes. "Did he hurt you?"

"I am fine...thanks to you...coming in when you did." Benjamin's compassion for me put a dent in my suspicions of him being the killer. My knees trembled; my legs felt like mud. How was I going to remain standing, much less parade around and sing?

His expression looked pained as he led me to the stage and walked me up. "You got this."

I nodded and waited for him to sit at the piano. He removed the stray cat from the keyboard, took a swig of whiskey then poured some on his hands and rubbed them together. All set, he glanced at me for a cue to begin.

The noise level was extremely loud. Voices bounced off the walls, and the large chandelier jiggled. A few men stood drinking at the bar while others stood in clusters around the poker tables, talking and laughing. Some wore brightly colored Mexican ponchos; some wore long black overcoats. Sombreros. Top hats. Cowboy hats. Conical hats. Soon all their eyes would be on me. I took it all in, my brain trying not to dwell on what had happened in Monty's office. One last big breath and I gave Benjamin a nod.

The music started, and I sang a familiar song, *Home Sweet Home*. How I wanted to go home. Tears burned my eyes. I missed my dad, my cat Matina, and my own bed. I missed Cindi and my job at the library. My tears overflowed as I sang with all the sadness I felt in my heart. The room stilled while my voice carried over the crowd.

I heard loud sobs, looked down, and saw tears flowing from the eyes of the bully from camp, Hank, his bearded face streaked with rivulets of sorrow. I suspected he missed his home and his family. Maybe he was having a bad day when he threatened the kids, maybe I was just feeling sorry for him, but I decided to take his name off my suspect list and replace him with Monty.

Chapter Thirteen

Wyatt buys a gun

The sun was barely up on the thirteenth day of July when I mounted Jack and headed into town. I wondered if I should tell Abby to add Monty to her list of suspects though I wasn't sure whose *brats* he was referring to. She might do something stupid again, like follow him and put herself in danger. And who knew what Lolita would do?

Once I arrived in town I rode straight to the mercantile.

"Give me that one over there." I pointed to a black gun with a brown handle and brass trigger.

"This one here is a Colt Walker. Forty-four caliber, single-action, black powder, cap and ball revolver." He handed it to me. "Careful. It's loaded."

I held the heavy weapon in my hand. "How much?"

"Twenty-five dollars."

"I'll take it." I poured out the remainder of my pickle jar. After the near disaster with Emanuel, I needed this gun, though I'd tried to convince myself otherwise as I headed for the saloon. I needed this to protect those kids. I shoved the revolver under my belt.

I walked through the saloon doors. My gaze met Monty's. For a moment, I froze, my hand on my new weapon, and stared him down. His glance dismissed me as he strode toward the bar.

Abby was serving drinks, an unusual occurrence. Daisy and one other woman entertained a few men. Usually, two or three other women worked, but I didn't see them.

"Lolita." I plunked my ass on a chair and clunked my boots on the table. "Bring me a drink. Whiskey."

She shot me a harried look and walked to the bar.

The gun pinched my waist. I pulled it out and placed my

new purchase on the table. A lot of good the damn thing would do me if the need arose. I had no idea how to shoot and was uncomfortable carrying the damn thing.

The stray cat jumped up on the table. I shooed it off.

Abby brought the whiskey. "What is that?" The glass hit the table with a thud as she stared at the weapon.

"What does it look like?"

"Why in the world would you buy a gun when you don't know how to shoot one?"

"I'll learn." So what if I wasn't a cowboy? Who cared if I couldn't twirl a gun around my finger and slip it into my holster? So what if I didn't have a holster? I'd get one, but leave it to her to make me feel like a city-slicker.

She sat. "Just don't shoot yourself in the foot."

My gaze zeroed in on the red mark on her cheek. A jolt of anger hit me. "Abby? What happened to your face?"

"Nothing."

"Something happened."

She cast Monty a horrified look.

"Son of a bitch." I started to rise.

"Please." She grabbed my wrist. "Don't."

The fear in her eyes hit my gut like a football. I sat back down. "Care to tell me about it?"

Abby shook her head. The cat jumped back onto the table, and she ran her fingers over the feline's back. It purred. A sorrowful expression turned down the corners of her mouth.

I took a swig of whiskey.

Daisy walked up to Abby. "Sugar, this here glass of port is compliments of that dreamy man over there." She pointed to a gambler wearing a blue beret. A cheroot hung from his lips and smoke wafted toward the ceiling.

Abby raised her glass to him. "Thanks, stranger."

The Frenchman lifted his identical glass to her, nodded, and smiled.

She brought the wine glass to her lips.

"Abby..."

She lowered the glass. "What?"

"I made you a promise...to look out for you."

She sighed, set down her glass, and put the cat on the floor.

"I told you—"

"If you're in danger, I need to know."

"I'm fine, really." She glanced over my shoulder to where I knew Monty stood.

I wanted to bolt from my chair and kick his ass. "There's something about Monty you need to know."

The white and gray feline purred at our feet.

A dreadful look came to Abby's eyes. "I don't want to talk about him."

"Fine." I reached out and lightly brushed her bruised cheek. "I don't like what he does to you or the company he keeps."

"I agree...but right now he's on my suspect list. What else can we do?"

I had no idea, but I couldn't just sit around and do nothing while she was getting beat up. Frustrated, I stabbed my fingers through my hair. Loud piano music started and rowdy chatter grated my nerves.

The cat jumped onto the table and knocked over the wine glass before Abby could grab it. "Shoo," she said. The cat jumped down as dark red wine flowed to the floor. She swiped at the front of her dress, trying to brush off the splatter that was sure to stain.

The cat lapped up the spilled wine.

Monty stopped at the roulette table, observed the game, then looked at me with hooded eyes. The guy was up to no good, and Abby was right in the middle of it.

A weird hacking sound caught my attention. I looked down, saw the cat lying in the pool of wine, convulsing and vomiting. It didn't take a moment before it stopped moving, dead.

Terror gripped my chest. "What the..?" I jumped from my seat, gun in hand, and looked for the gambler with the blue beret. He was nowhere in sight. "Damn it."

The patrons fell silent. Everyone looked in our direction.

Benjamin stopped playing. His face was a mask of cold dread.

I got a really sick feeling in my stomach. Protecting Abby would be much harder than I thought.

Abby's list grows

Blood drained from my face as I stared at the dead cat. Minutes ago, his gentle purring brought me comfort, now nausea rose in my throat.

Wyatt stood over me like a raving lunatic, his gaze darting around the room, one hand on a gun, the other protectively on my shoulder. "What the hell do you people think you're doing?"

My thoughts bounced around like ping pong balls in a room full of mouse traps. Stunned, I shook my head, trying to clear my confused mind. Why had the Frenchman tried to kill me? I glanced to Monty. His dark gaze bore into mine. *No one refuses me.* Did he poison my drink? I began to shake.

"Let's go." Wyatt pulled me out of my chair and scooped me up in his arms. I didn't complain. I rested my head on his shoulder and closed my eyes.

"Lolita. Where do you think you're going?" Monty yelled.

"As far away from you as possible," Wyatt replied, his voice sharp with conviction.

"She's got another set to sing."

"Oh, no she doesn't. And you've got a mess to clean up."

The poor cat. He was just a stray but he saved my life. I was going to miss the little guy.

Wyatt pushed the saloon doors open with his shoulder and let them swing shut behind us. "Do you think you can ride?"

I nodded.

He hoisted me up to the saddle and jumped up behind me. Hand around my middle, my head resting back on his chest, we rode slowly back to camp to the clip-clop of Jack's hooves.

In front of my *hovel*, Wyatt lifted me from the horse, and I wrapped my arms around his neck. I didn't need to be carried, but his strong arms brought me comfort. I felt drained. First Monty and then the poisoned wine, seemed the whole world was out to get me. I wanted to curl up into a ball and go to sleep.

Wyatt carefully laid me down on my cot. He knelt beside me and brushed his hand through my hair. His eyes were tender, his touch gentle. "You need to tell me what went on with you and Monty."

"Wyatt..." I sighed.

"I can't protect you if I don't have all the facts. Someone tried to poison you. Was it Monty?"

Shadows softened the edges of his handsome face. I stared into his blue eyes, so filled with concern. "We fought."

"Why?"

"He wanted me to let my husband take my kids."

"What does he care?"

"He wants me to go with him to San Francisco...to headline in his new saloon." I couldn't tell Wyatt that Monty wanted me to be his mistress. Too embarrassing. Made me feel like the soiled dove I was. "He thought the kids would be in the way, keep us from traveling around the world together." I could tell by Wyatt's frown he didn't believe I was telling him everything.

"And he hit you...why?"

I nodded. "I turned him down."

Wyatt scowled. "That son of a bitch. I'll kill him."

I reached out and touched his jaw. "Don't. If anything happens to you..." I swallowed the lump in my throat. "I'll be all alone." The thought tightened knots in my stomach.

"Who else did you piss off?"

"Just Horace."

"And the gambler who bought you that drink?"

"Never seen him before."

"What about Benjamin?"

"Wyatt, why would he poison me?"

"I don't know, but I'm going to find out who did it." He stood

"I-I can't believe it happened." Realizing how close I'd come to dying put a quiver to my voice.

"It must have been cyanide. That shit kills quickly. Did the wine smell like almonds?"

"Come to think of it, yes." I exhaled deeply. "That poor cat."

"Payback is going to be a bitch," Wyatt said, his voice hard. "God damnit. It had to be Monty. His hired guns are capable of murdering someone for him."

"He doesn't want me dead. He wants me..." I didn't want to tell Wyatt, but I had to tell him everything before he went off on a tangent. "He wants me to be his mistress. When I told him I'm not his plaything, he hit me, just once, but if Benjamin hadn't walked in, I'm sure there was more to come."

"That does it. He's my number one suspect, and I have to find the gambler with the beret."

"What are you going to do when you find him?"

"Have a little chat."

He wasn't telling me something. I could see it in his shifting gaze, in his locked jaw and hard tone. "If you kill him, you'll change the future."

"Nah. I'm just going to make him wish he was dead."

Wyatt confronts Abby's boss

I pounded my hand into my fist then slung the reins over Jack's head. Damn it. I wanted to tell Abby about the conversation I'd overheard between Monty and the gunslingers. They were ordered to take care of those brats. I feared Lolita would panic and do something crazy to protect her kids, maybe even put a bullet in Monty and change the future of the world.

Saddled up, I boot-tapped the horse into motion. The ground beneath me flew by as Jack galloped toward town. Chunks of dirt flew up behind us. I ducked a low branch that came close to swatting me in the face. I was getting pretty good at this riding business.

In town, I jumped off the saddle before Jack came to a complete stop in front of the saloon. After tying the reins to the hitching post, I pushed open the swinging doors so hard the wood crashed against the walls. The room fell silent. All glances followed me as I stalked toward Monty standing at the back wall by his office door. Two men leaned casually on the bar, but seeing me, they straightened. I recognized them as the two men I'd seen in the woods: Monty's hired guns.

I stopped in front of him. His two goons came closer, their hands near their gun belts.

With a flick of his wrist, Monty halted them. "If it's a drink you want..." He clicked his fingers at the bartender. "You better have money this time."

"I'm not thirsty."

"Then you have no business here."

"When you hit Abby, you became my business."

"Abby?"

"Lolita." I reared back my fist and punched him in the nose. His head hit the wall, and his knees damn near buckled. Blood gushed from his nostrils.

The two goons bolted forward.

Again, Monty raised his hand to stop them. "That's all right. Let him rave."

He eased a white handkerchief from his breast pocket and pressed it over his nose. "Do not think because I choose not to let them kill you..." He wiped blood from lips. "That you have the upper hand. I can assure you, you do not. You best leave before I change my mind."

"I'm not afraid of you, you lousy bastard." I clenched my fist in front of his face. "That's for Lolita." Using my peripheral vision, I registered the position of each one of his goons, calculated who could get to me first. That was before five men filed out of the back room. Dressed in black, like Slimbo and Buckeye, they wore their guns slung low on their hips.

Eight men counting Monty. Odds weren't so bad. But against eight guns, I didn't stand a chance. Getting killed wouldn't help Abby, but I had to stay on the offense. "You're scum." I spit on Monty's shiny shoe.

Guns shot out of holsters. Hammers clicked back.

"Easy, boys." Monty dabbed his bloody nose with the handkerchief. "Look around at all these witnesses, ah, patrons."

"Somebody tried to poison Lolita. I aim to find out who, starting with you."

"Me? Ruin a good port? You know how much that wine costs per bottle?"

Yeah. The tightwad probably didn't do it. I turned and strolled through the barroom, hoping a bullet wouldn't find my back while I glanced around for the guy who'd bought Abby the poisoned drink, the guy who smoked cheroots. Pissed he wasn't sitting at a table or standing at the bar, I decided to come back later. I stormed out and the saloon doors swung shut behind me.

Abby and Daisy go out

I couldn't stop shaking and hid my hands in my lap.

After I assured Wyatt I was all right, he flew out of here. Where did he go? After Monty? I prayed not. If he went back to the saloon, he'd have to confront those hired gunmen, too.

I got up from my cot and began to pace on unsteady legs.

Gun or no gun, he was outnumbered. What if something had happened to him? I chewed my lip. Could I get back home without him?

"Mamma, are you hurt?"

I turned to see the children had run in. Tears sprang to my eyes. Cattie looked concerned, and for the first time, Joseph showed interest in me. I quickly swiped the tears away and bent to their level. "I'm fine, really."

"What happened to your face?" Cattie asked.

"Oh, that. I ran into a door."

Joseph held up a wooden dog with wheels and smiled.

"Nice toy. Where did you get it?"

"Daisy gave it to him. She gave me a new ribbon for my hair." Cattie twirled around to reveal a pink ribbon that hung down her back.

"That was very nice of her."

"Knock, knock." Daisy entered the shack. "It looks good on her, don't you think?"

I straightened. "Your gifts are very thoughtful."

"How are you feeling?"

"Like a Mack truck hit me."

Her brows scrunched. "What's a Mack truck?"

"Sorry. It is nothing." I vowed to be more careful with my word choices.

Daisy's gaze darted around the room. I knew by her judgmental look she didn't approve of our meager dwelling. "Wouldn't it be nice if you didn't have to live like this anymore?"

"Home sweet home," I said sarcastically.

"I hear your husband is very rich now."

"He just wants my children. Not me. And I do not want

him."

"What did you do to drive him into another woman's arms?"

"Daisy. Shhh...the children." I grabbed her arm and pulled her away from the kids to the opposite side of the room. "It is not my fault that floozy ruined our marriage," I whispered harshly.

Why did I detect a flash of annoyance in her eyes? She was supposed to be my friend. My confidante. Not my critic.

"You haven't been yourself lately." She moved closer and leaned in. "I have an aphrodisiac for you."

"For me? I do not need help with my libido."

"Your what?" Daisy frowned.

I realized that too might not be a familiar term these days.

"I thought a few personal tips might get you back on track."

I didn't need to know what games she played upstairs in those rooms. "Thank you, Daisy, but it is just that I am a little put-off on men. Can you blame me?" My cheeks heated. If she saw my embarrassment, thankfully, she chose not to comment.

She shrugged. "Let's get out of this hovel and paint the town red. Just the two of us."

"I got the kids." I shook my head. "Maybe another time."

"Look, Sugar. There may not be a next time...I mean, you were almost poisoned. No time like the present to have a little fun."

She had a point. Right now, I was the one in danger, not the children. "I could use a little fun. But the children?"

She called to Cattie. "You're fine, right? We can go out for a short while."

She nodded while Joseph plowed his toy dog around the dirt floor.

"There is canned turkey and carrots on the shelf. Stay nearby and watch your brother."

"Yes, Mamma."

"I will be home before dark." I grabbed a shawl, and we headed for town.

Not wanting to be anywhere near Monty and his saloon, we chose the El Dorado Hotel dining room. All eyes and frowns were on us as we walked in. Women, even soiled doves, were a rarity in here, but they served us despite their distaste for our lifestyle.

The small room had four tables adorned with white linen and occupied by several men...and us. Though the room was not fancy by any means, it was clean. One picture adorned the wall, a river scene I found rather peaceful. Occasionally a bell would ding when someone walked up, or stumbled in drunk, to the concierge table in the adjacent hall.

The children were going to be safe, I assured myself as we sipped a second glass of champagne, compliments of two very fine-looking Englishmen.

Daisy nodded their direction then turned to me. "So why would someone want to kill you?"

"I have no idea." Maybe the legend was wrong. Maybe Lolita was the one in danger, not her children...but then again, there were the ghost kids at the river. They'd revealed themselves to me for a reason.

Daisy gulped her champagne as though she had a parched throat. "What happened between you and Monty?"

I shook my head. I didn't want to discuss the fight I had with Monty, but I was surprised she hadn't mentioned the bruise on my cheek. Maybe she'd taken a slap or two in her line of work and seeing a bruise or two didn't bother her.

"Well, Sugar, you'd better watch where you're stepping, 'cause whoever has it out for you ain't gonna stop."

"Gee, thanks." I frowned. "You ever see that gambler before, the one who bought me the drink?"

"First-timer."

"Seen him since?"

"No."

"So why would some guy I do not know, who did not know me, put poison in my drink then disappear?"

Daisy batted her eyes at the Englishmen. Two more drinks were brought to our table.

Maybe Monty hired the gambler, and considering we'd just fought, it was highly probable...but he wanted to travel the world with me, make me the star attraction in his new San Francisco venture. Still, he admitted my kids would be in his way, a perfect motive for killing them.

Daisy leaned toward me. "Keep a wary eye on Benjamin. He's no stranger to murder." Now her voice was a whisper. "Heard he killed a man back home."

"Where?"

She chomped on a biscuit. "Don't know, but he can't go back."

"Good afternoon, ladies."

I looked up at two Scottish redheaded men who stood at our table, their tartan plaid hats in their hands.

"Mind if we join you?" the bearded man asked with a hopeful look in his eyes.

Daisy smiled at them. "Sit those cheeky buns of yours down here." She patted the chair beside her. "I just love foreigners. That accent...yummy."

I could do without the company, wanted to talk more about Benjamin, but they sat without a second's hesitation. As it turned out, I enjoyed the conversation, ate up their compliments, and my worries, for the moment, were drowned in drink.

The door behind me opened with a rush of wind. "Abigail. You need to come home. Right now."

The familiar deep voice struck my heart with terror.

What was Wyatt doing here?

Wyatt reassures Abby

Abby sat at a table, flirting with two guys who were ogling her like she was gonna be their dessert.

"Come home, right now," I repeated.

She looked surprised as I strode toward her table. Daisy was stroking some guy's red beard. His gaze was glued to her breasts spilling out of her dress. I'd bet he had an idea for the evening's entertainment.

Abby looked like she'd been suddenly slapped back to reality. "Oh my God. The children." Her face paled. Worry widened her eyes. "Is something wrong?"

"It's Joseph—"

"What? What happened?" In a rush to stand, her chair toppled to the floor. "Is he okay? Is he—"

"He's fine. Now. Just a burn. I dressed it—"

"He's burned? I gotta go. Daisy, are you going to be okay?"

"Go. I'm fine. Right, boys?"

They nodded in unison.

"Let's go."

Outside, I got Abby up on Jack's saddle, climbed on behind her, and spurred him to a trot. It was a bumpy ride under a starry sky. "Abby," I shouted over the heavy tromping of Jack's hooves along the path back to camp. "Cattie said you were going to be back before dark."

"I'm so sorry, Wyatt. Daisy...she has an addictive personality."

"Apologize to your kids, not me." Abby and I weren't an item, not by any means, but I still didn't like the way men stared at her, or the jealousy her attentiveness stirred up in me. Yeah. I was jealous, but mostly concerned for her wellbeing. I'd promised to protect her. Nothing more. End of story. "I can't protect you when you run off on me like that."

"Can we go any faster?"

Since we were almost there, I spurred Jack, and a few minutes later we rode into camp at a full gallop. At her shack, she jumped down and rushed inside. I tied Jack's rein to a pole and followed her.

Cattie sat on the ground cross-legged by Joseph, who slept on their cot.

"Joseph—"

"Shhh, Mamma. He's sleeping."

A haunted look crossed Abby's face. "What happened?"

"I was cooking the carrots. He wanted to help. I told him no," she sobbed. "He grabbed the pot—"

"It's not your fault, honey." Abby's shoulders slumped. She blinked away once held-back tears. "It's my fault. I should have been here. I'm sorry."

I regretted my harsh tone with Abby earlier when I'd blamed her for not being home. She needed time for herself, but when I saw her flirting with those men, anger gripped my guts. Seeing her so distraught now softened anger's hold on my tongue. "He'll be fine." I stood over Joseph. "I put some Piñon on his hand and bandaged it. A day or two and he'll be tossing rocks in the river again."

"Piñon?" Abby glanced at me.

"My friend Soaring Eagle told me his people used it for burns. I made a poultice and applied it to Joseph's injury."

She sank into a crooked wooden chair, her demeanor deflated. "Thank you for helping him."

"No problem."

Again, tears sprang to her eyes. "I'm a terrible mother."

"You're doing great." I reached out and touched her arm, a move I hoped would comfort her. "You care."

Tears streamed down her cheeks. "You don't understand. I didn't think about them. I was having too much fun." She sniffed. "I wasn't worried because it's not the end of the month."

"I've never been a parent, but if you ask me, it's normal to want to let loose occasionally. Time slips by. You were caught up in the moment."

"Good parents don't get caught up in moments," she snapped. "They realize it's dark and their kids are home alone, hungry, worried. I wasn't. Don't you get it? Lolita loves being free. She loves the attention. Loves being single. What kind of mother would have those thoughts? I'll never forgive myself if anything should happen—"

"See." I knelt beside her and took her hand. "Listen to yourself. Listen to what you just said. Breathe, okay? Calm down. You're being a good mother to those kids. Lolita was the one who didn't watch the time. Not you. Not you, Abby." I hoped she believed me. I hated to see this torment in her eyes.

She jerked her hand free of mine. "What if something happens to them? I've done nothing to solve this mystery. Nothing." Her shoulders sank as the tears kept coming.

I stood and raked my fingers through my hair. I didn't know what to say. Women had cried in front of me before, but I never had a woman cry over something so heartfelt. "You made a list. We followed those guys. We haven't given up." A pent-up breath of anxiety escaped me. "Being here is a huge burden on both of us, but mainly you."

"You think so?" she said, her eyes glistening.

I bent to her and brushed a tear from her cheek. "I'm trying to make it as easy for you as I can, but you're not helping matters."

"Lolita has a way of making me do things I don't want to do. She's pretty sneaky...and subtle."

I smiled, hoping to see her smile too. "See? It's not all your fault."

"It's not easy when you go running off in a huff. What happened with you and Monty?"

"He says he didn't poison you...wouldn't ruin a good port. And the French guy who bought you the drink has disappeared."

"But why me?" She sobbed.

I knelt in front of her and placed my hands on her knees. "Don't fall apart on me now."

She put her open palm on her chest. "I want to go home."

"I know. Me too."

"The end of the month can't come soon enough. I hope I survive that long."

If something happened to her, I didn't know that I could survive either. I lifted her chin and stared into her alluring eyes. "I need you." In more ways than she knew.

Abby's search

He needs me? What did Wyatt mean? To get home? Those were his words, but the desire in his eyes was far from a ticket back home. Something akin to sexual want oozed from his sincere smile, sucking my heart toward him in a gathering windstorm. I wanted to kiss him. Wanted to feel his arms wrapped around me. The touch of his hand on my knee, his finger under my chin, the tenderness in his eyes, everything he did to me spun a whirlwind of emotions inside.

I'd sworn he had no heart, but here he was comforting me, again, making the guilt that was eating me alive, lessen. The wall I'd built around my heart to keep him out, the anger I'd harbored for the guy who wrecked my prom night, all my defenses crumbled a little more. He was not the boy I'd sworn to never speak to again. Now he was a man who was there for me; he protected me, looked after me. How had I been so wrong about him? Being here had changed him. Could I put the past behind me and give him a chance? Could there ever be anything more than this wall between us? I had to reach out and try. "Wyatt. You can stay here with us if you want."

He took a deep breath, and I figured by the way he glanced around he was considering the invitation. "I'm good for now. But thanks."

Rejection stung. Is this how he felt when I told him he couldn't stay here when we first arrived?

He stood. "I better go. It's late. Emanuel's probably wondering where I am."

"Right. Well... Thanks again for taking care of Joseph."

"Get some rest." He walked to the door, lifted the blanket and left. Part of me didn't want him to go. I wanted to call him back, tell him what I'd learned about Benjamin, that he'd murdered someone, to sit and talk and not be left alone. Physically drained by the day's events, I laid out my children's nightclothes and eyed my cot.

Cattie changed clothes for bed, and taking over the role of mother, once again, gave me a hard time. "I don't want to go to sleep. Joseph might wake up and need me."

"I'll watch over him." I tucked her into her cot.

I sat at the table, candlelight glowing on my suspect list, thankful there was still time to save them. Pen in hand, I crossed off Hank, the bully who threatened my kids. Anyone who got so tore up over the song *Home Sweet Home* was not a killer of children. I suspected he missed his home, his family, and took it out on everyone else.

Crickets chirped. Dancing light from campfires filtered in through cracks in the walls. Mumbled voices floated in the air. I left the door flap open for ventilation, and an occasional miner walked by and cast a shadow on the dirt floor.

I looked at the children's names in the center of the page then glanced at the cot where Cattie and Joseph slept soundly. I needed to spend more time with them, but between working and chores, they always seemed to come last. Guilt settled in the pit of my stomach, but I had to remind myself their wellbeing was more important than fun and games.

I underlined the word *Legend* then wrote *Horace* next to

husband. But he had no cause to hurt his children. I tapped my finger over *Monty's* name then drew an arrow from his name to the names of Cattie and Joseph. Monty wanted me to give them to Horace...give them away like old paperbacks. On top of his name, I wrote *hired guns.* Maybe he'd order them to kill the kids to get them out of the way so I'd be free to travel with him. An arrow linked his name to his goons and from his goons to the kids. I stared at Lolita's name. Someone wanted her dead. I shouldn't have taken it so personally, but still, I'd be collateral damage if someone killed Lolita. And where would that leave Wyatt?

I drew an arrow from my name to Monty and the word fight. *Stranger.* I couldn't forget the stranger I suspected of poisoning my drink. Then I linked my name to the children as their possible murderer. I added a question mark next to *Benjamin.* Even though he'd come to my rescue in Monty's office, according to Daisy, he'd killed a man, and I'd heard him confess that much to someone in his tent that night. However, I couldn't come up with a motive for him to kill me. We were a team on stage. Still, I wondered what untold role he played in the legend.

With so many unanswered questions, I barely slept. The minute the sun shone through the doorway, I started my morning chores: making flapjacks, boiling coffee, and straightening up.

Joseph was in pain. I cleaned his hand and reapplied the salve. He struggled to hold back tears by gritting his teeth and hissing. Seeing the red blisters on his hand brought another bout of guilt to the surface. I should have been here.

"Honey, it's all right to cry."

Cattie leaned in to look for herself. "Pa says boys don't cry." Her eyes were narrow, her lips pursed.

I knew she blamed me, and with good reason. "Well, your pa is wrong. Plenty of men cry, and it's perfectly all right to show your feelings, Joseph. There." I'd rewrapped his hand. "You'll be good as new in a few days."

Cattie patted Joseph's shoulder. "I'm so sorry you got burned."

"And I'm sorry I wasn't here." I swiped the tear from my cheek.

Joseph sniffled and nodded.

All morning, Cattie hovered around him, helped him dress, then she fed him breakfast so he wouldn't have to use his bandaged hand. My offer to help fell on deaf ears. I thought it best not to push. Apparently, Cattie needed to be helpful. I'd done enough damage and didn't want to upset her more than she already was.

Today, I was going to learn all I could about Benjamin. As soon as the kids left to go play, I lifted the door flap.

Glancing left and right to make sure nobody would see me, I crossed the short distance to his tent. I'd seen Benjamin leave this morning, and I prayed I'd have enough time to do some snooping before he returned.

Once inside his tent, I smelled garlic. Warmed by the heat, cloves of garlic hung from every hook and the center pole, cluttered the shelf, and lined the perimeter of the tent. Did he believe in vampires? Like the interior of my place, the floor was dirt, but Benjamin had blankets covering every square inch.

I moved around the cramped quarters as quickly and quietly as I could, careful not to knock anything over. Creepy little bones hung from the ceiling struts like morbid mobiles. A sadistic Voodoo ritual? Despite the overwhelming heat, I shivered as grotesque visions of Satanic sacrifices invaded my mind.

I searched amid the garlic cloves, plates, and behind a black cast iron pot. Nothing looked like it contained cyanide. I moved to the back of the tent where a table with shelves stood in the corner, and I started pushing aside the different spices and pickled fruits and dried goods.

Out the corner of my eye, I spotted a toy. My breath caught. Joseph's wooden dog lay on a chair. What was it doing in Benjamin's tent? Did he steal it? Perhaps he found it, but why keep it? Did he not think to give it back to Joseph?

A dog barked. My shoulders jerked.

Quickly, I rummaged through the stuff on the shelf, pushing aside bottles, desperate to find any evidence that he was a killer.

Nothing. I picked up a jacket and—

Footsteps.

I whirled around. Someone was coming. My heart sprinted. My eyes searched for somewhere to hide. The place was the size of a shoebox. There was no closet. I couldn't fit under the cot. I dropped the jacket. Oh my God, he was going to catch me in here. My pulse pounded in my neck. Blood drained from my face. I pivoted, stopped, then rotated like a rat in a box with nowhere to go.

"Benjamin." Wyatt's voice.

My heartbeat eased only to be shot into the stratosphere when I heard Benjamin's voice. "I don't want to talk to you."

Please, I prayed. *Talk to Wyatt. Don't come in.*

"Look, I won't push you, but man, you gotta give me something. What did you see in the saloon when someone tried to kill Abby...I mean Lolita."

Two shadows stood close to the tent's opening. I clutched my tight chest and backed to a far corner, afraid they'd hear my panicked breathing.

At any minute, Benjamin would either step in alone or invite Wyatt to come in with him. Either way, I was busted. What could I say? *Sorry for snooping. I thought you might have tried to poison me. Just checking. Oops, wrong tent.*

"I'll buy you a drink. You can tell me what you know."

The hesitation...the silence tightened my nerves. Moisture sat on my brow. Claustrophobia clawed at my throat.

"I didn't see anything."

The canvas flap began to part. A spasm of alarm shot through my chest.

"Come on, Benjamin. Lolita's life is on the line."

Silence. The tent flap closed.

"All right. What can I do to help?"

"I have a bottle in my saddlebag. Let's go down to the river, sit a spell."

Footsteps walked away and I breathed a sigh of relief.

Wyatt and Abby dance in the rain

It was the fifteenth day of July when heavy welcoming rain pelted me as I left the claim. I took off my black hat, closed my eyes, and let the long-overdue refreshing downpour drench my sweaty face.

Whoops and hollers echoed through the canyon. I ran to the center of the camp. Men splashed like children on the muddy ground, their faces to the sky. Some linked arms and danced a jig of some kind.

"A blessing," someone said as he sucked on his pipe.

I could feel the excitement, the hope of riches to be found, of better days to come. The shift in atmosphere, not so much the temperature, uplifted everyone's attitude. Men who hadn't had a kind word to say in weeks shared good will and back slaps.

The last few days I'd agonized over my inability to find the one responsible for trying to kill Abby. Only finding Benjamin and learning his secret allowed me a reprieve from my angst about him.

Now, as the sky opened up, so did my spirit, especially when Abby joined me. I slipped my arm around her waist. "It's raining. It's raining," I sang and twirled her around.

She laughed as water ran down her cheeks.

A guitar and a banjo strummed and picked along with a harmonica.

I tossed my hat. "Come on. Let's celebrate." I took her hand, and we ran into the open, muddy area where men danced together. The lack of women did not deter the festivities. Even grumpy Hank joined in on the fun.

"Looks like music soothes the heart and turns even the meanest beasts to puppies," Abby said as we sashayed into the fray. After a few twirls and do-si-dos, we stopped to catch our breath.

"Wyatt, are you still not open to the idea of going with me to find the vein of gold?" She pointed up the mountain, now shrouded in heavy gray clouds.

"It's raining, darling. That means river flow. That means water to wash away the soil, and that means gold dust in our pans."

"You and the men in this camp have depleted the riverbed. Why not move uphill?"

I didn't want to talk about it. Didn't want to have a debate or argue about a lost vein of gold. It was a waste of time. Abby wasn't going to change my mind. "Let's just enjoy ourselves."

She nodded, though I could see the hesitation in her eyes, mixed with a whole lot of this-isn't-finished-yet stubbornness.

I hooked my arm in hers, and we high-stepped through the mud to *Yankee Doodle*.

Soaked to the skin, Abby looked radiant. Her hair dripped in strings down her back. Her clothes, plastered to her body, hugged every curve. The rain did little to douse the sizzle of nerve endings all over my body.

My gaze focused on the sexy curve of her breasts. Taut nipples pressed against the fabric of her white blouse. The eyeful I got of wet skin made me need her as desperately as the rain. Her musical laughter and the gleam in her eyes was infectious. I felt all the hardships in this realm melt away, didn't analyze the future, the what-ifs, just let the music lead me.

We kicked up our heels to the strains of a fast-rhythm guitar and the clang of metal-bucket drums. Mud splashed up my legs and soaked my boots. It didn't matter. Nothing mattered but the woman in my arms whose eyes were aflame with happiness, a happiness I hadn't seen in days.

The heavily trampled mud was getting slippery, so I tightened my hold around her waist. We sidestepped together to the clanking of metal spoons against someone's knee. I twirled her slowly and watched her enticing hips sway. It was sensuous enough to make a man want to pull those hips up close and tight.

"Oh my God," she exclaimed breathlessly. "This is so much fun."

I twirled her around then drew her toward me again, but before I could catch her, she slipped, and we both went down in the mud. Laughter erupted, followed by tears rolling down her cheeks and mixing with the rain, then more laughter. Like idiots, we sat in the mud and laughed until my sides hurt.

When the laughter subsided, I helped her to her feet and pulled her to my chest so I could stare into those beautiful Spanish-green eyes. Neither one of us said a word. The rain splashed on our bodies in rhythm with the strum of a sultry guitar. A bass voice sang words of love in Spanish. We moved slow and easy to the song, our bodies close, hip to hip. It felt like only a second had passed from our romp in the mud, so fast I didn't know how we'd gotten to this moment, a moment I didn't want to analyze. She was here in my arms, so close I could feel her breath on my face. She rested her head under my chin, and we swayed back and forth. I could hear the thunder of my heartbeat as I focused on the soft feel of her body pressed against me, the feel of her wet hair against the skin of my neck.

"Wyatt..."

"Yes, beautiful?" I cradled her face in the palms of my hands and stared at her lips. As much as I desperately wanted to taste those lips, wanted to make love to her right here and now, taking that liberty might distract her from her mission to save those kids. Things were complicated between us. We were getting along. I didn't want to mess up by getting all mushy.

She drew back. "People are watching us."

"So? Let them."

"I'm married. Remember? What will they think?"

Damn. "You're right." A deep breath escaped me. The rain did nothing to cool the heat radiating from my libido. As much as I wanted to hold her, pretend that I didn't care what others thought, I had to stay concentrated on my mission, keeping an eye on her, keeping her safe. Nowhere in my job description did it say that I could love her.

Our happy mood was ruined. I could only glance around at the folks carrying on around us and wish they'd mind their own business.

"About that trip up the mountain—"

"It's dangerous," I insisted, annoyed the conversation had taken a turn back to her fantasy gold.

"If you come with me, you'll be there to protect me."

"Do you ever give up?"

She smiled.

"The answer is still no."

Tight lipped and teeth bared, she pulled up her sopping dress, put her nose in the air, and stomped off through the mud.

I hoped I wouldn't regret telling her no.

Abby confronts Benjamin

Wyatt had made me feel alive, a novel feeling that was becoming way too familiar. Then he got bullheaded again. I cried all the way back to my home. Though wet to the bone, every sensual nerve in my body felt betrayed.

Pulling off my wet clothes, I couldn't stop thinking about our dance and how it went so wrong. When his gaze locked on my lips, I thought he was going to kiss me. I couldn't breathe, couldn't speak, only imagine his lips traveling up my neck, butterfly kisses on my ear, his mouth on mine, how his tongue would send tingles everywhere. I wanted him to kiss me, which I knew was not a good idea, but at that moment, I hadn't cared. I would have given him everything his heart desired, *If only I'd kept my mouth shut about being married.*

"Abby," Lolita's voice said. *"It is your fault he did not kiss you. Why do you sabotage his every act of affection?"*

"He called me beautiful, but he was looking at you, your wet face, your wet hair, your wet skin. He wants you, not me."

"That is not what I saw. He was looking right past my skin, looking at you, seeing his fantasy image of you."

"I'm a frumpy redhead, a bookworm. Not his type."

"Maybe that is the kind of woman he wants."

"How can you say that?"

"Do not be idiota. I know men. You know nothing."

"I'm not you, Lolita. I'm Abigail Stewart, and Wyatt doesn't want me. He wants you."

"Very well. I shall take him."

"No. You're married."

"That only stops you, so who is the fool? Not me."

"Shut up."

There were times when walking in Lolita's shoes gave me confidence, but then, in Wyatt's presence, the insecure girl, the prom-date reject, clawed her way out, and though I wanted to hold her down, she always rose to ruin the occasion.

I slipped into my nightdress, lay down on my cot, and pulled the coarse wool quilt over me. Rain pelted the roof, a constant soothing patter. I closed my eyes, wishing my worry away and still felt Wyatt's arms holding me as we danced.

Tonight had started like a night of dreams, of letting go, of forgetting the past and living in the moment. What a memory, but that was all it could be. I couldn't allow myself to fall for him. At some point, we were going home. I didn't know when or how, but the day was coming, and when it came, I would return as Abigail the nerdy redhead. Me with my paranormal sixth sense. Insecure me, who couldn't carry a tune or pass up a good book. Wyatt would no longer have his Abby in Lolita's body. He'd disappear from my life faster than a cheap magician's trick.

Still gullible, still foolish enough to hope a man like Wyatt had feelings for me, the place and time might have changed, but the girl inside me had not. A tear welled. I pushed the emotion away. No. I refused to let him in. The heartbreak of being rejected again would damn near kill me.

The lone, soft strum of guitar music lulled me to sleep as tears slid down my cheeks.

The morning of the 16th brought sunshine and melancholy. I laid out the children's clothing, boiled some oatmeal, then watched them eat and run. I agonized over letting them out of my sight, but I couldn't lock them up. I needed to go to work. I had to do some snooping. The kids never went far, and I felt reasonably safe to let them go outside and play.

I sighed. Today, I would confront Benjamin about why he had Joseph's toy dog in his tent. Did he steal it? Why? It didn't make any sense.

I stepped outside. Steam rose from the wet ground. The air felt heavy and thick with moisture.

"Do you believe in fairies?" Benjamin's deep voice came to me from his tent. Curious who he was talking to, I stepped closer and listened.

"In my country of Romania, we have many legends of fairies who are good, but some can be wicked." His voice took on a sinister tone. "Ancient stories tell of a woman with an evil eye. She wanted what she could not have, so she wore revenge like a black cloak on her heart. One night, she went to the river and waited until midnight to call upon the devil. The devil came out of the water. *Why are you here? he asked. I am in love with a man who does not see me*, she said."

My heart lurched at his words. Like the woman in the fable, I was falling for a man who saw someone else when he looked at me. I leaned in closer. I wanted to throw up the tent flap, sit beside whomever he was talking to, and listen to his ghost story. Ask questions.

"The Devil told her he would make the man see her, but when she died, she would be cursed, and on the night of the blue moon her restless spirit would roam the river in search of the man she loved."

Blue moon? Could this be right? Was he talking about the legend? The history behind the legend hadn't happened yet.

"You must stay away from the river at night. It's dangerous. Here."

I heard movement inside the tent.

"To keep the evil spirits away from our homes we hang garlic around our windows and doors."

That explained all the garlic in his tent. Benjamin was a superstitious man, but that didn't mean he plotted to kill my kids.

"Is that why you have so much garlic...to keep out the bad fairies?" Joseph's voice asked.

Joseph's voice? It hit me like a slap of cold water to the face. I threw open the tent flap and stomped inside. The children sat at Benjamin's feet. In their hands, they held bulbs of garlic. All reasoning flew to the wayside as I recalled his words: *Devil. Faceless woman. Evil eye. Evil spirits.*

"Cattie, Joseph, go home," I ordered, my voice shrill. "Benjamin, how dare you talk of the devil and scare my kids?"

Benjamin rose. "I was only—"

"I don't want to hear it."

Cattie looked like she wanted to say something but shut her mouth. Joseph looked like he was going to cry.

"Home. Right now." I pointed to the door.

They hurried to their feet.

I grabbed the garlic from their hands and threw it to the blanketed floor.

As they ran out, I turned to Benjamin. "Why do you fill their heads with talk of evil?" I pointed to the bones hanging over my head. "Are you some kind of witch?"

His eyes widened with fear. His gaze fell on the garlic at

his feet.

"Don't go near my children again." I grabbed Joseph's wooden toy. "Stay away from them." I spun and stalked out then collided with Wyatt.

"Whoa. What's the hurry?"

"Benjamin...Ben... he's just—"

"Breathe, Abby." Wyatt ushered me inside my shack. "What's going on?"

Trembling with rage, I sat. Took a few deep breaths.

Not wanting the children to hear what I was going to say I turned to them. "Cattie, take your brother outside and play. Do not go near Benjamin."

"But—"

"Cattie, Joseph, do you understand what I'm saying? If he talks to you, you are to come right back in here."

They nodded, held hands, and shuffled outside.

"This. This." I showed Wyatt the toy. "I found this in his tent."

Wyatt's brows scrunched. "What were you doing in his tent?"

"Well, the first time, I—I was looking for poison."

Wyatt dropped into a chair. "Did you find it?"

"No."

"And today?"

"I overheard him telling the kids a scary story about fairies and devils and evil..." I felt annoyed that I needed to explain myself.

"Really? What's wrong with a good ghost story?"

"He was talking about the legend."

Wyatt clamped his mouth shut. His blank gaze was steady as if he was considering my words. He steepled his fingers by his lips. "What about the fairies?"

"It was a Romanian story about fairies, but it sounded too much like the Weeping Woman's legend."

Wyatt put up his hand to stop me. "He's a gypsy."

I gasped and hugged the toy dog.

"I had a talk with him, asked him why he looked so frightened that day of the poisoning incident. He said someone would blame him. He's always a suspect when things go wrong."

Wyatt leaned back in his chair. "He doesn't mean any harm to anyone."

"But he did kill a man," I blurted, still not convinced he wouldn't kill my kids and flee.

"Who told you that?"

"Daisy."

"Let me tell you what he told me. His girl, back in his country, was being harassed by some guy. Benjamin stepped in; a weapon was pulled. He survived the fight. The other guy didn't."

"So, self-defense."

"Not when you're a gypsy, and the dead guy is the son of the richest man in the county. He fled."

"And he can't go back."

Perhaps the story he told my kids was just folklore and had nothing to do with the legend. Since Joseph never said a word to me, yet spoke with Benjamin, obviously Joseph felt comfortable in his presence. I exhaled pent-up anxiety. "How did you get Benjamin to tell you he was a gypsy?"

"We had a drink together. Look, you can't tell anyone about our conversation. Men would turn on him if they knew he was not just some mild-mannered piano player. I swore I wouldn't tell a soul."

I looked at the wooden dog and turned it over. A wheel was broken. Maybe Benjamin was going to fix it. Frustrated we were no closer to identifying the murderer, I shrugged. "I think I overreacted."

"Stop sneaking into his tent. And don't interrogate him again. Tell him you're sorry. You still have to work with him at the saloon." Wyatt's lip pressed into a tight line. "Since Lolita can't be with them all the time, he's been trying to keep an eye on the kids."

"I should take him off my list"

"Yes. And apologize to the kids."

Great. The list of suspects was getting shorter, and Lolita was still my primary culprit.

Chapter Fourteen

Wyatt and Daisy

A fter a long morning of panning, I found a nice-sized nugget. Emanuel's father summoned me to a tent where five men lived. The close quarters stunk of body odor. Dirty clothes cluttered the small cots and were draped over chairs. Greasy dishes lay scattered on a table and the floor. The place reminded me of our frat house back at college, less all the empty beer cans.

I made my way to the cot where a man lay groaning. I could see he had a fever by the redness of his face and glazed eyes. No appearance of scaly, dry, and brownish skin, and after a quick examination, I found no signs of swollen or purple gums, so scurvy wasn't the diagnosis. I knelt and put my ear to his chest to see if I could hear any signs of congestion. Bingo. I checked his pulse and found it quick.

His tent-mate said, "He was act'n mighty strange last night." He was a gap-toothed fella with hollow cheeks and a sharp nose. His pants were so loose I wondered when he'd last eaten.

"Acting strange? How?"

"Talk'n crazy."

Delirium was a sign of influenza.

"Any coughing?"

He nodded.

I reached into my medicine box and pulled out a small bottle of Camphor I'd purchased at the mercantile. Between Emanuel's mother, Soaring Eagle, and my new friend Benjamin, I'd learned a lot of interesting treatments and remedies. I'd even found a worn book of home remedies at the store.

"Put a few drops on a hot cloth and place it on his chest. It will help with the congestion in his lungs and..." I pulled out a bulb of garlic, compliments of Benjamin. "Crush this and give it to him in his tea. It will help."

I stepped outside, confident the guy would be all right if they followed my directions.

Different shades of orange sunlight sank into the horizon as I headed into town. My medical supplies were running low, and I thought to find out a little more about Monty. Daisy would be the best person to hit up for information. I walked into the saloon and found her at a poker table.

"Hey, Darlin'. Can I buy you a drink?" I slipped my arm around her and escorted her to a vacant chair where I sat and plopped her on my lap.

Across the room, a heavyset woman served drinks. I gestured her over while Daisy settled on my lap, wiggling her ass more than necessary. I tried to ignore her seductive attempt to attract my sexual attention.

"Two whiskeys," I said.

She nodded and waddled away.

"You're Lolita's flame," Daisy cooed. "Why am I sitting on your lap?"

"She's just a friend."

"Can I be your friend, big boy?" Daisy batted her heavily made-up eyelashes. Between the shiny green dress with its frilly yellow collar, and her chalk-white face and cheeks smeared with rouge, she was the perfect barroom floozy of the California Gold Rush. Her attempt to seduce me did not succeed.

Her drinks arrived, and I handed her a glass of whiskey.

She poured the amber liquor down her throat like a sailor on leave then ran her hand over my chest. When I stopped her, she pouted her full red lips. "Don't you like what you see?"

"I'm here for information about Monty." I noticed the way her eyes became guarded.

She shrugged. "What's to know? He's my boss." Again, she ran her hand over my chest.

This time I let her, figuring if I played her game, I'd get more information out of her. "You strike me as the kind of woman who knows everything that's happening around town."

"I suppose..."

"How did he get the money to buy this joint?"

"How should I know?" She undid one button on my shirt.

"He doesn't look like the type to prospect for gold. Not a speck of dirt under those manicured fingernails."

Another button came undone.

"Monty's a man of many means. He's a smart businessman." She ran her fingers over my bare skin. "Knows a lot of people."

"And likes his women." *Abby to be exact.*

Her fingers stopped. A stone-like expression sat on her face then softened. "What man doesn't want a woman between his legs?" She moved her round bottom back and forth in my lap.

I swallowed hard, her point taken. "He's not a family man then?"

"Now, Sugar, what difference does that make?" She picked up the second drink and gulped it down.

"Lolita told me Monty wanted her to give the children to Horace. With them out of the picture, he could take her to San Francisco and travel the world with him."

"Some girls have all the luck."

"Jealous?"

"She can have him."

"Lolita doesn't want to go to San Francisco. She won't take her husband back... By the way, how well do you know *him*?"

Daisy brushed a lock of lackluster blond hair from her cheek. "What do you want to know?"

"Where he's staying? What he's doing?"

"Don't matter. She'll never let him take those kids."

I didn't need to hear that. Maybe Lolita sooner murder them than let Horace take them away. Been known to happen. So I had two murder suspects. I knew where to find Monty, but not Horace, which gave me an idea.

"Daisy. I want you to keep an eye on Horace. Tell me where he goes and who he's with." I placed a gold nugget in her hand. "There's more where that came from."

Her bright red lips showed me a smile.

Abby's jealous performance

A gypsy? Benjamin? Who would have thought...no wonder he left after the kids were murdered. The entire camp would have blamed him. And Wyatt believed him. Relieved that part of the legend was right, I felt hopeful for the first time. Optimistic. I understood how he felt. How odd. How afraid he'd be that people would look at him differently, and in these times, blame every mishap on his heritage. I certainly didn't want to endanger him further.

Figuring it was time I went back to earning money, I grabbed a black shawl. The preacher was in camp and offered me a ride to town. Big mistake. After he spent the journey preaching about how I should repent and give my soul to Jesus, I couldn't wait to get to work and do some sinning.

Hoping I wouldn't run into Monty or Horace the minute I stepped inside, I walked into the saloon and glanced around. Smoke wafted in my face along with the stench of body odor I'd never get used to.

Benjamin sat at the piano, his fingers running up and down the keys in a happy tune. The roulette wheel whirled while the little ball bounced, round and round. Samantha, one of the *girls*, dealt out cards. So focused on their game, the men at her table barely glanced at her deep cleavage.

I hurried toward Benjamin and stopped beside the piano, which must have startled him.

He stopped playing. "Miss Lolita." His gaze went to the sheet music propped up in front of him. "What do you think?"

I bent over and read the title: *Sweet Betsy From Pike.* Familiar with the song and its quick cadence, I felt confident the verses would come from within me the way Lolita would sing them. "Benjamin, I'm sorry for my outburst. Your story frightened me, is all."

"You must know I had no intention of frightening the children. You are a different person somehow. You forgot those kids are special to me. They remind me of my family back home."

"Why did you tell them that particular story?"

He shrugged. "No reason other than to keep them entertained. It's just a fable of ours. I didn't mean any harm."

I placed a reassuring hand on his arm. "I know that now."

"Miss Lolita, we live in a dangerous camp in a dangerous time. And your children are very independent. I don't want anything to happen to them. I keep an eye on them when you're not around."

"Thank you—"

"Lolita." Monty's voice rose above the loud chatter. "I pay you to sing."

"I should get ready."

He nodded.

As I crossed the saloon to the dressing room, I recognized Daisy's laugh. I looked across the barroom, saw her on Wyatt's lap, rubbing her hand over his chest. My blood temperature shot to a boil. His poker face expression irked me. I wanted to run over and pull out Daisy's hair, but I knew Lolita would never do that to her friend. Overreacting would draw unwanted attention. I hurried to the backroom as tears clouded my eyesight.

A whore was a whore. Right? I threw my dress over a chair and struggled into a skin-tight cream dress with red roses jutting out from the bodice, right over my nipples.

Same old Wyatt Beaufort. Can't let a pretty face go unconquered.

"He can conquer me anytime," Lolita cooed.

Another tear slipped by. I swiped my face. What did I see in him, anyway? My temple began to throb as I slipped on black stockings and gaudy red shoes. I yanked up the front of my dress, exposing my upper thighs, then pinned flowers at my hips to hold it up.

I'll have Wyatt eating out of my hand then I'll...I'll... I'll toss him away.

"Do not be stupid, Abby."

"I'm only protecting my heart, Lolita." I pushed up my bodice until my breasts nearly spilled out, and then left the room in a huff.

Monty stood near the stage and announced my entrance. "Watch out, boys. Lolita is in the house."

"Lolita is here," I shouted and waved. "Boys, loosen up

those purse strings." With a seductive sway of my hips, I stepped up to Monty and ran my finger up his arm. I should have been repulsed. I should have felt a lot of things, but my mind felt woozy. I tossed him a smile then moved to the piano.

"Benny, my love...play me a song." The look of excitement in his eyes barely registered as I turned to my gawking audience.

Lively piano music began.

I started right on key. "Did you ever hear tell of sweet Betsy from Pike... who crossed the wide prairies with her lover, Ike... with two yokes of oxen and a one-spotted hog... a tall Shanghai rooster and an old yellow dog."

As I sang, I walked past men who stopped playing cards and grinned at me with lust in their eyes. Heightened by their approval, I continued, "That morning they stood on a very high hill... and with wonder looked down into old Placerville... Ike shouted and said, as he cast his eyes down... 'Sweet Betsy, my darling, we've got to Hangtown.'"

I bent over and kissed a bald man on the head. Hoots and whistles followed me as I moved forward with one purpose in mind. When I reached Wyatt, Daisy got off his lap, and I placed my foot on his thigh. Desire sprang to his eyes as he stared at my leg. He eased his gaze higher, and I knew he could see up my dress. Lolita loved the tease, loved the idea he wanted what I wasn't going to give him. Caught up in the role of Lolita, I knew what I was doing, but I saw my actions as if I were watching from a distance.

"Long Ike and sweet Betsy attended a dance... where Ike wore a pair of his Pike County pants... Sweet Betsy was covered with ribbons and rings... Said 'Ike, you're an angel, but where are your wings?'"

I fluttered my fingers near my breasts, offering them to Wyatt, then extended my arms to my sides like I was unfurling wings. A muscle twitched in Wyatt's jaw, and his mouth showed me a smile. I leaned forward, my breasts so close to his face, if he wanted, he could bend in and taste me. Every nerve felt alive, yet a part of me felt detached from my body as though Lolita was pulling my strings. I juggled my breasts, let the fabric roses tickle his nose. His eyes were inflamed with sexual torment, and his reaction tightened the tips of my nipples.

"This Pike County couple got married, of course... but Ike became jealous, obtained a divorce... and Betsy, well satisfied, said with a shout... 'Goodbye, you big lummox, I'm glad you backed out.'"

I pushed Wyatt back in his chair, straightened, and gave him a nasty once over. "Take that, you big lummox."

His expression went from a confident smirk to a sudden realization that scrunched his brow. Lolita and I were a team.

I turned away from him, bowed deep and low to hoots and cheers as gold nuggets and Mexican coins skittered across the floor. Satisfied Wyatt got a good look at my ass, I straightened and, with a beaming smile, walked away from him, as he well deserved.

Wyatt's confused...Abby? Lolita?

Holy cow. What just happened? I wiped my forehead. My body in overdrive, I sat there trying not to think of Abby's stimulating ass that, a moment ago, flashed before me.

One minute, she was all sexy and alluring, the next she nearly spat in my face. It took me a moment to understand. She was pissed. And jealous of Daisy.

As the song ended, I got the impression Abby wasn't Abby, but Lolita instead. Lolita had a way about her, a confident, there's-no-one-sexier-than-me demeanor that shouted in my face. Her bewitching siren eyes shined with self-satisfaction and shouted she was a goddess no man could resist. If she thought I'd fall like a puppet at her feet, she was gravely mistaken...but she did have a nice ass.

I watched her hips move seductively toward Monty. The woman who now stood so close to the man who'd hit her was definitely not Abby. She'd never crawl back to such a slime-ball. I pushed from my seat, marched across the room, and stood near the stage, my eyes on her, my ears tuned to their conversation.

"Your disagreeable words pained me to no avail," Monty said as he brushed back a lock of her hair. "I do not care to have the strength of my affections tested."

"I would very much like to consider your proposition, but I

am worried about my children."

Did she just say she was thinking about going away with that creep?

"You hold a great value to me," she said as her fingers crept along his arm. "But, Monty, now is not the time to discuss such private matters."

That had to be Lolita talking. Had to be. Out the corner of my eye, I watched Monty nod then walk away. Anger flared in my gut. I wasn't going to let Lolita take Abby anywhere.

I strolled up behind her and smacked her ass. Her shoulders jerked in surprise, but before she could cry out, I grabbed her arm, spun her around, pulled her close, and planted a powerful kiss on her lips. Just as quickly, I released her.

She slapped my face.

I guess I deserved it, but it was worth it just to see her shocked expression and know Lolita hadn't taken over her body again. Then realization lit her eyes. For a moment, I thought she would say she was sorry, it wasn't her but Lolita who moments ago had made sexual innuendoes toward me. However, she offered no such explanation. It was Abby all along, the woman I had kissed, and the woman who just slapped me.

"Wyatt, go suck up to Daisy and leave me alone."

"Abby. Let me explain."

"I don't want your excuses." She turned and walked away like I was no better than any of the riffraff in this joint.

I wanted to follow her, explain why Daisy was on my lap, but ordered a drink instead. Let her stew in her jealousy for a while. Maybe when she calmed down I'd explain. Or not. But at least Abby had not lost control of Lolita.

Chapter Fifteen

Wyatt's best friend

Two days later, I still hadn't spoken to her. She was avoiding me. I certainly wasn't going to crawl to her. Instead, I got Emanuel to show me how to shoot my new gun. We bought a bag of lead balls, a can of gunpowder, and a tin of primer caps, and he showed me how to load the revolving cylinder. I refrained from telling him that bullets would be invented someday. All in all, I got pretty good at hitting what I aimed at, but my quick draw needed a lot more practice.

I'd also purchased a wooden cradle. As I shoveled in dirt, Emanuel poured water on it from a bucket. Then we rocked the small box to wash away the loose debris, hoping gold would shine up from the bottom.

"Hey, boss. That was some tormenta."

"Storm. Yeah. It rained all night."

"You think Lolita's anger will blow over?" he asked in Spanish.

I stopped sifting and looked up. "How did we get from talking about rain to Lolita?"

"A storm is a storm." He smiled, his dark brown eyes glimmering. "Like Lolita."

"I wouldn't know." I went back to sifting. "Ain't seen her."

"Si. Nice ass."

"How do you know what happened in the saloon?"

"Se corre la voz." *Word gets around.*

I studied the honest expression on his face, the way he held himself straight and proud. His arms were defined with muscle from digging and hauling rocks. Yes, I could see the man lurking under his youthful, innocent face. He was a boy on the edge of manhood that was forced upon him too soon. Boys his age should be out playing basketball, hanging with his pals, and picking up girls, not digging in the dirt for hours upon hours with work-blistered fingers.

"Let's break for lunch."

We sat in the dirt and pulled our lunches from the shade of a bush where we'd stashed them. I unwrapped a small iron pot. Inside, ground pork, peppers, and onions were smothered with golden baked cheese, tomato, and cilantro.

"Queso Fundido Del Grito," Emanuel said then spooned a big helping into his mouth. "My madre makes the best."

"Muy bien." I savored the pork and spices. I was surprised the dish was still warm even though she'd baked it hours ago. Back in my time, I wouldn't touch anything sitting out without refrigeration for hours. I gobbled the delicious meal, thankful for a full belly.

Emanuel wiped his lips with the back of his sleeve. "I got my eyes on a cute filly," he said in Spanish.

"Did you check her teeth?"

He stared at me like I was speaking French. "Why would I check her teeth?" Emanuel frowned.

"To make sure she's healthy."

"I ain't gonna ask her to open her mouth so I can look inside." He shook his head.

"Oh...a girl filly." I rapped his arm. "You little stud."

"Stud? No comprendo."

"I thought you were talking about a horse."

"A caballo?" Emanuel burst out in laughter. "Oh, boss, you need to go visit your lady friend."

"Never mind my lady friend. Tell me about your novia."

"How you say bonita in English?"

"Pretty."

"Pretty. Long black pelo...hair. Eyes like shiny black stones," he finished in Spanish. "And when she smiles, my day looks brighter."

"¿Cual es su nombre?" *What's her name?*

"Singing Waters."

Emanuel had found himself a Native girl. "Bueno for you."

"Si. I will meet up with her esta noche...tonight." As he

reached for the canteen of water lying in the shade of the bush, he screamed and jerked his hand back. "Una serpiente de cascabel!"

That's when I saw the rattler.

Abby's dilemmas

I didn't understand how I could act the way I did in the saloon. Pacing the floor of my home for over an hour didn't make things any clearer. I knew what I was doing...but I kind of didn't. One minute everything I did was clear, the next, like I was walking in a thick fog, hearing everything echo back at me, seeing everything at the end of a dim tunnel. I felt slightly repulsed by my actions and kind of excited, too.

Wyatt must think I'm a whore.

"No, Abby. He thinks I am a whore. He thinks you are a goddess."

"No way. I'm a pain in his ass."

"I will not argue with that."

I slumped into a chair. I didn't know what Monty thought of me, either, or how I was going to explain I had no intention of going anywhere with him despite what Lolita had said. Was Lolita going to give her kids to Horace, or did she have a deadly alternative?

I plopped my elbows on the table and covered my face with my hands. Daisy. I didn't want to confront her about her loose display with Wyatt. If I burned that bridge I'd miss her company, miss someone I could talk to. She was my Cindi. Lolita was my Pam. The similarities across time astounded me.

But who was I? I felt like I was losing myself in this body. My gaze dropped to my breasts. They didn't belong to me. As perky as they were, I missed my own sweaty boobs. I didn't want Lolita's anymore. Not if it meant losing myself in her promiscuity.

I chewed my lip. Cindi was right. Lolita was not the woman I thought she was. What a waste of energy, wishing I was pretty like her. Idolizing her legend. Wishing I was her. Now I wished I wasn't. I wasn't cut out to be a seductress. Life was easier when I was invisible. Less complicated. Men were complicated. My feelings were complicated. One minute I was drooling over Wyatt, the next I was slapping his face for a stolen kiss. I wasn't sure whose emotions I felt, hers or mine.

"Knock, knock. Sugar, can I come in?"

Daisy. Great. Just what I didn't need right now. "Sure."

"I came to apologize if I stepped on your toes. I had no idea you had set your bonnet on that big strapping fella." Her syrupy sweet tone rang false. "He told me you two was just friends."

Just friends? That lousy... "I certainly have no designs on him."

"In my line of work, I take 'em when I can, Sugar. He offered his lap, I took it, and two drinks, to boot. Good for my commissions, but I didn't sleep with him, though, if he was willing, I might a paid *him*."

"I do not care who he sleeps with."

"Well, good for you. Better to concern yourself with singin' in case your husband comes calling. We wouldn't want him to think you crossed over to my line of work, now would we?" She smiled like that was some kind of private joke.

Daisy was right, but I still wanted to smack that smirk off her face. However, it was good to know that Lolita hadn't cavorted with men while she was married. I didn't know why Horace had left her and hadn't come back for the kids, or why he hadn't been seen around town, but I was thankful he'd stayed away. Probably only a matter of time before his kind of trouble found me again. Meanwhile, I'd continue fighting off horny men who thought I was a whore—

A woman's wail shrieked through the air. My heart lurched. Daisy and I ran outside and headed toward the loud commotion coming from a corner of the camp where I saw Wyatt hobbling in, holding Emanuel up, helping him walk. Both men's faces were pale with worry. Emanuel grimaced in pain and gripped his wrist. Camila was crying and screaming.

I ran to Wyatt's side. "What happened?"

"A rattler bit him." Wyatt's tormented eyes met mine briefly.

Alarm, tight and deep, pained my chest.

Camila crossed her body with the sign of the cross. "Mi bebé pobre."

I didn't need to know Spanish to understand she spoke of her son, her *poor baby*. I followed them into a tent.

Wyatt laid Emanuel on a bed of Mexican blankets and covered him with one.

"Camila, consigue mi caja," he said and Camila ran across the tent, picked up a wooden box, and hurried back to Wyatt's side. He pulled out a bottle of...aspirin?

What? It traveled back in time with him? If someone got hold of it, what kind of damage could that paradox create?

Wyatt shook the bottle and the last two pills fell into his palm. "Take these." He handed the pills to Emanuel. "With sarsaparilla."

Camila ran out and brought back a glass of the root-beer-like drink.

I was sure aspirin wouldn't save Emanuel from snake venom. "Wyatt, we should send someone into town to get the doctor."

His expression grave, his forehead furrowed in deep thought, he watched Emanuel drink down the pills.

Camila set an old hand on my arm. "Wyatt es doctor."

"What?" I looked at the heavyset woman studying me as though I'd just landed from Mars. "Wyatt? Is she for real?"

"I've seen a few patients, but I'm not sure what to do in this case." He rattled off something in Spanish.

After darting a glance at me, Camila gave a curt nod.

When had Wyatt become the camp doctor? How had I not heard? He couldn't know enough about medicine to help Emanuel. "Is there anything I can do?"

"I don't know." Wyatt jabbed his fingers through his hair and took a deep breath, exhaling the tension I heard in his voice.

"Did you try to suck out the poison?"

"That only works in the movies. More likely get the wound infected, besides, who wants rattlesnake venom in their mouth?"

Emanuel puffed out his cheeks as if holding back a scream. His hand was the size of a catcher's mitt, so red and swollen the skin looked like a thin balloon that might burst. And the swelling was traveling up his arm, blood vessels and lymph nodes enlarged and creeping to his shoulder like some kind of god-awful snake growing under the skin.

Camila knelt over him and held his good hand. Tears glistened in her eyes as she murmured in Spanish, words of reassurance and love, if I had to guess.

Sweat dotted Wyatt's brow. "The only thing they talked about in trauma class was to not suck on the snake bite and get anti-venom treatment within an hour."

"Where can we get some?"

"It won't be readily available for another hundred years."

"Oh, no."

The front flap of the tent thumped open. All eyes went to the tall, majestic Native who strode in and stopped beside Wyatt. "How is he?"

"I don't know what to do." Wyatt lifted the blanket off Emanuel's swollen arm.

Soaring Eagle grimaced at what he saw. "Put this on the arm." He handed Wyatt an old tin of salve.

"What is it?"

"Coneflower. White man call it Echinacea. Good for snake bite, but might be too late for the boy."

Chapter Sixteen

Wyatt's failure

I stayed by Emanuel's side throughout the night of July 19th, watching him toss and turn, become conscious then drop off. Each groan felt like a dagger to my heart. With each worried pace of his mother, I felt the need to apologize. I had no idea what I was doing. I insisted someone find a real doctor. Emanuel's father rode into town but came back with bad news. The traveling doctor wouldn't be back for a week.

After the aspirin wore off and cups of hot water infused with coral root did nothing, Emanuel's fever spiked. His hand, despite the salve Soaring Eagle gave me, looked more swollen, redder, and turning black in places. The skin was beginning to crack and ooze dying meat.

I pinched the bridge of my nose and closed my eyes. *What if the salve doesn't work?* The prickling sensation of tears stabbed my eyes and welled in my throat. *It must...the ointment must work.*

I looked at Emanuel who, for the moment, slept peacefully thanks to a tablespoon of syrup of poppies I gave him. I just couldn't stand seeing him in such pain.

He was my only real friend in this otherwise lonely place. I swallowed a lump and glanced at the single oil lamp casting shadows on the canvas. *I can't lose him. I just can't.* I rubbed tears from my eyes and glanced at his parents who, after much convincing, were resting. They'd put their trust in me, me who played doctor with their only son, me who held his life in my hands, me of all people on earth. What if the fever didn't break? What if he got worse? What if I had to cut off his arm? *How can I look them in the eyes and say I don't know what else to do?* I leaned back against the tent wall and stared at the ceiling until the sun came up.

Camila handed me a cup of steaming coffee. "You need rest," she managed in English.

I took a sip and shook my head. "I'm not leaving him."

Emanuel stirred. She bent over him, spoke in soft, reassuring Spanish words, words only a worried-sick mother could say. I could hear my mother, see my mother's worried look, wondering what happened to me. I got up and walked outside to give her some privacy. Moody gray clouds hung heavy in the sky, like my heart in my chest.

Was that how my mom felt worrying over my whereabouts? Where was I back in my time? Missing? Dead? Did my mother cry herself to sleep like I'd heard Camila last night? Were her motherly prayers as heartfelt as the ones I'd heard here? Prayers repeating over and over until exhaustion set in.

I paced. My legs and body were tired. I wanted to close my bloodshot, tired eyes and forget...escape.

"Wyatt?"

I quickly knuckle-swiped a teardrop from my eye and pivoted toward Abby's concerned voice.

"How is he?"

"Sleeping."

"Did the fever break?"

"No."

"Sorry. I brought you these." She held out a basket.

"What is it?"

"Biscuits."

"You baked?" I wasn't hungry, didn't even want to look at food.

"Cattie did, I'm embarrassed to say." She shrugged. "I have no idea how she does it. I'm a lousy mother."

"And I'm a lousy doctor." Tears burned in my eyes. I gestured she sit. While her attention was on arranging herself comfortably on the bench in front of the tent, I turned, wiped a tear from my cheek, then sat beside her.

"Have one." She held up a biscuit. "They are quite good."

"Thanks. Maybe later. I don't think my stomach could handle anything right now."

"I understand." She set the biscuit in the basket then placed her hand on my thigh, her reassuring gesture comforting. "A doctor, huh? Why do you let your friends back home think you're just a dumb jock?"

I shrugged. "Just never felt the need to correct their impression...until I met you." I probably shouldn't have blurted that out, but it was the truth. I thought back to the day at the beach. I wanted to impress her then. I still felt the need.

"You're obviously talented and smart."

"Smarter than you thought?"

"Well, yes. But that's your fault." She smiled slyly.

"You're right. I didn't want them to know I was a book nerd, or that I was headed toward being class valedictorian. I had a macho image to uphold."

"Seriously? Being popular was more important than being yourself?"

"Pathetic, I know." The words came out harsher than I intended. "I lived in a world where I had to pretend to be somebody I'm not. But here in this place..." Did I really want to spill my guts to her? Why not? What could she do to me, send me back to the Stone Age? "With you...well. I don't know. I feel like I can let my guard down, be the man I really am."

Abby opened her mouth but didn't say anything, as if she struggled with something on her mind. Her gaze kept shifting. Her posture tightened, and her brows furrowed.

"Sorry if I'm making you uncomfortable."

"No. It's just..." She shook her head. "You know what? Forget it." Her tone was brittle.

Whatever she wanted to say, but didn't, agitated her. I could tell by the way she looked off to the cliff rising beyond the river...where I would live in the future. I didn't want to press the issue for fear of what she had stuck in her craw.

"Does your dad know you're up for valedictorian?"

"Nope. He's only interested in football." I didn't want to delve into my family dynamics, didn't feel like explaining.

"Well, I don't doubt your skills as a doctor."

My chest hurt. I was so tired it was an effort to keep my head up. "You don't know anything about my skills."

"You don't know anything about me, period."

She was right. I accepted her challenge. "You got any brothers? Sisters?"

"Just me."

"Me too. I always wanted a kid brother."

She sighed. "Me too. A sister."

We had something in common after all. "What do you think your mother is thinking about right now? I mean with us being gone."

Her gaze lowered, and when she glanced up, I saw sadness in her green depths. "I don't think she worries about anything...up in heaven."

"She's gone. I'm sorry. I didn't know."

"Car accident. Three years ago."

I rubbed my fingers across my scalp. "I wonder if my mother thinks I'm dead."

"We are going to get home, you know."

I studied her face, wanting to believe her. Although I saw determination, doubt peeked through. "Right." I glanced at the tent where Emanuel lay. "I should check on him." I stood, helped her up from the bench, and opened the tent flap. "Bring the basket."

She nodded, and we stepped inside.

Camila held a wet cloth on her son's forehead.

I put my fingers on his wrist. His skin was hot to touch, and I could barely find a pulse.

"Did you try to give him more liquids?"

"Si."

Emanuel's father put on his hat, shook his head and stepped outside. The look of hopelessness on his face cut me bad. I didn't know what else to do. Didn't know what to say.

I sat by Emanuel while Camila and Abby kept themselves busy, straightening, sweeping, folding and refolding blankets. They'd hang up a pot then switch it around, all mindless chores to keep their minds off the sick boy lying deathly still.

Emanuel's shallow breathing was not a good sign. I clenched my fists, frustrated. I felt so helpless. Sitting around. Waiting. Doing nothing.

"Boss?"

I rolled up onto my knees. "Emanuel." His eyes were

lusterless but open. A good sign. I forced a smile. "Don't call me boss." I felt his forehead. Scalding. *Ah, shit.* My chest felt like a football was lodged under my ribcage. "I may have to cut off your arm, my friend."

"No. What good miner...one hand?"

"But you might live."

He began to shake...then he vomited.

I rolled him on his side so he wouldn't choke on his own bile. His mother and Abby ran over and cleaned him up.

The next hour was a repeat of the hour before, and the day dragged on as I reapplied salve and kept him as comfortable as anyone in severe pain could be. We tried to force liquids down his throat as he wavered from consciousness to unconsciousness. His vital organs were already shutting down. Hopelessness and helplessness increased with each passing hour as I watched my friend suffer. I was mentally and physically drained.

As evening approached, I knelt by his side. Staring into the darkness, I listened to his shallow breathing, held his cold, clammy good hand as tears streamed down my face.

"I don't know what else to do," I whispered in prayer. "Please forgive me." My head dropped against the scratchy wool blanket that absorbed my tears. "I don't know what else to do."

A hand touched my head. Jolted from my prayer, hopeful, I looked up. "Emanuel?"

"It...okay...boss." His voice was a raspy whisper, strained, breathless, painful to hear. What little hope I clung to burst, a painful stab to my heart."Mi amigo," he muttered.

Before I could argue it wasn't okay, to tell him I was so sorry I failed him, to beg God to save my friend, the light died in his eyes.

A flood of tears burst from my eyes, clouding my vision. My chest hurt as if a hot bullet pierced my heart. Pain shot from my back straight through my breastbone. My brain felt numb. I stood on feet I knew were there but couldn't feel.

I failed as a doctor, and because of me he's dead.

A shadow moved in the corner. Emanuel's mother came to me, sobbing. A second shadow took her into his arms. I walked outside and didn't realize I was standing under a tiny sliver of moonlight until a coyote howled.

Through my stupor, I recalled Abby's words. *We're going to get home, you know.* I wished I was dreaming. I needed to wake up. I punched my palm. Hit it again. I had to wake up from this nightmare.

Chapter Seventeen

Abby's fear

I t was the twenty-fourth day of July. Three days had passed and I had no idea where Wyatt had gone. He'd disappeared right after Emanuel's burial. I'd spoken with Camila every day, and she hadn't seen him either.

A tug of war battled inside me. Maybe it was the thought of being alone and facing the unknown without him. He'd been there for me on more than one occasion, and I realized I needed him. I missed him. I worried about him. If Wyatt was anything like me, he was doing the *what-if* blame game over Emanuel's death.

The morning sun was barely up, and already the air felt thick and sweltering as I trudged to Camila's tent. She greeted me with teary red eyes.

"Is Wyatt here? Ah...Wyatt aquí?"

"No." Camila pointed to me then to her eyes. "Ve a buscar a Wyatt."

"Go find Wyatt?"

"Si. Yo cuidaré de tus niños. I watch."

"Gracias." Thankful she would take care of the children, I hurried back home, but as I looked at Cattie and Joseph's sleeping forms, guilt nibbled at my soul, for once again I was leaving them in someone else's care.

I wrapped my shawl around some food and water, wore my sturdiest walking shoes, and headed out of camp, upriver to where I hoped he'd be panning.

I picked up the hem of my skirt and stepped over mounds of dirt and shallow holes as I passed man after man, their hands and faces sun-weathered, their clothing torn and filthy. Metal pans, picks, and shovels littered the ground. Some men squatted at the riverbank, others stood over wooden boxes, shoveling in dirt and dumping in water. Everywhere I looked, men dug, some buried up to their necks in a hole; but no Wyatt, not unless he'd dug so deep I couldn't see the top of his head. I glanced down into every ditch, hoping against hope I'd see him on his knees, picking through pebbles for those illusive yellow nuggets.

Shielding my eyes from the sun, I glanced across the roiling river and its white-water swells to see the same frantic activity on the other side. I hiked farther upriver past the spot where we'd entered this era in history. I hoped he'd be there, sitting by the river, contemplating what we'd have to do to get home. I certainly wasn't doing much of anything to accomplish that goal. I kept promising myself, tomorrow; tomorrow I'd continue sleuthing, but my life was so hectic I had little time to narrow in on a killer.

As I searched the dug-up area, the sun's blinding silvery path shimmered on the frothy water. Dismayed Wyatt wasn't there, I headed upslope from the river toward the property that would be Wyatt's family home in the future. Maybe he would be there. The ground, dotted with blue and white wild roses and groves of evergreens, made for a photogenic moment. In the distance, the Sierra Nevada rose its craggy head from a dense forest. I made my way uphill over an uneven path miners had made, careful not to twist my ankle on a stone or fallen branch, and I stopped now and then to catch my breath.

I didn't know how much farther I could go up this worn path, but I kept at it until I came to a cliff where a chunk of ground had been broken off by an ancient landslide. I'd either have to turn back or move forward across the narrow ledge that remained.

I stared into the distance, beyond the ledge, and saw a hunched man kneeling on a boulder, his back to me as he looked over the edge of the cliff. I recognized the blue shirt and brown pants.

"Wyatt?" I called out.

He didn't turn around.

"Wyatt."

He didn't move, just stared over the edge. Maybe he couldn't hear me. I'd have to get closer.

On my left, a rocky wall shaded the narrow, treacherous cleft leading to the boulder. On my right, should I fall over the steep edge, the river below would claim me once again, if I didn't die of a heart attack first. Why did he have to find a perch so damn high? I set down my bundle. Held my breath. Took a wary step onto the ledge.

Loose rocks shifted under my feet, sending a cascade of stones down the face of the cliff. My heart hitched. That could have been me.

Slowly, I edged along the narrow precipice, my back hugging the cliff, my hands feeling their way across the rock-face. Sweat trickled down my forehead, got into my eyes. My breaths came in short bursts. Tunnel vision set in.

Blinking, I focused on Wyatt. Staring over the edge as he was, he didn't see me. I wanted to scream his name again, but I feared I might startle him. He could lose his balance and fall over the cliff. My mouth went dry. I clamped down on my molars...took another precarious step.

When I reach him, I'm going to give him a piece of my mind.

"If you do not get us killed first."

"Shut up, Lolita. I'm trying to concentrate. Can't you see I'm afraid of heights?"

"Do not look down," Lolita cried.

What was he thinking? Why had he knelt so dangerously close to the edge? My gaze glued on Wyatt, I took another cautious step and forced my mind not to think of anything but reaching Wyatt. My heart thudded so loudly I feared the vibration would cause an earthquake.

At this dizzying height, my brain started playing tricks. Being so close to eternity mesmerized me, made me think I could step off into the abyss. No problem. I could fly. It would be one step I could never take back. I wondered if Wyatt could be mesmerized in the same way, contemplating that step so intently that he didn't hear me.

A sudden bloom of panic made my forehead break out in a cold sweat. What was his frame of mind? Emanuel was dead. He thought it was his fault. Could he be thinking of suicide? A tremor of fear traveled up my thighs from my quivering feet that felt unstable. My pulse hammered in my neck.

Determined to continue, I inched forward, willing myself not to look down. *I'm almost there... almost...* A spray of loose rock tumbled down the steep chasm.

I froze. I slammed my eyes shut as if doing so would somehow make the danger go away. My fingers dug into the wall's crevices as I clung to them for dear life. When my breathing calmed, my gaze dropped, and so did my stomach. *I can do this... I can...*

"You better," Lolita made me shout in her fiery Spanish voice.

Wyatt turned. "Abby? What are you doing up here?"

Finally, he noticed us. "I'm worried about you."

He stood up on the boulder. "Don't. I'll only fail and let you down." His voice was unmistakably flush with tearful emotion. "You're better off without me. Look what happened to Emanuel. He's dead because of me."

I teetered a bit on the ledge. "You were his friend, a friend he never would have had if not for you."

"But I couldn't save him. What kind of doctor does that make me?"

"Patients die. My dad says it comes with the job. Besides, you saved him once...from the hangman's noose. If not for you he'd have already been dead. It was a mistake to save him and change the past. The snakebite corrected your mistake."

He looked around and took a breath. "You may be right, but I don't have to like it."

"Stop feeling sorry for yourself and come back to camp."

"I'm not feeling sorry for myself."

"Then come home. The kids miss you."

"But not you?"

I didn't want to say no. He might jump. "Well... Maybe."

"Good enough." He started to work his way across the rocks toward me.

When I looked back along the ledge, I saw chucks had fallen. The way back was impossible, I was sure of it. By the time Wyatt reached me, I was frozen with fear.

"What are you waiting for? Let's go."

"I can't move," I managed through a tight throat.

"What are you talking about?"

"I'm afraid of heights." I wheezed. "Don't come any closer." My high-pitched command echoed back like a slap in the face.

"Abby, this is crazy. We can't stay up here forever. Let me get around you."

"No. No. You'll fall."

"I'll be okay."

"Give me a minute. I need to breathe."

"Relax." He crossed in front of me so close to the edge I could feel his breath on my ear. I couldn't look down, but I knew if I did, I'd see his toes on the ledge and his heels hanging over dead air.

Slowly he passed me and stood next to me with his back against the rock-face. "Give me your hand. I won't let you fall." He held out his hand. His fingers interlaced with mine. "Now look at me, Abby. Just look at me. Nothing else."

I turned my head to face him and stared into eyes reminiscent of a sunlit cloudless sky.

"We're gonna take it nice and slow...one sidestep at a time."

With his help, I was going to make it.

We stepped sideways in unison.

"How did you know where to find me?" he asked.

"I didn't."

"Just a woman's intuition?"

"Something like that."

Out the corner of my eye, a large black bird flew in the distance. My gaze dropped to the river, as did my stomach.

"Abby, don't look down."

Keep it together. I can do this. I took a deep breath and redirected my attention to those gorgeous blues of his.

Step by step, we inched our way back in the direction of the miners' path until we were standing on level ground, far from the dangerous crossing.

Whew. I made it.

"Do not ever do that again, Abby." Lolita sounded breathless too. *"I thought we were going to die."*

Wyatt picked up my bundled food and water and led me

down to a tree by the river and gestured we sit. I took a few deep breaths.

We sat in silence, listened to the creaking sway of tree branches, and watched passing clouds beam down shadows on the rugged slopes around us. The gurgling river and Wyatt's comforting presence soothed my shattered nerves.

"That was pretty stupid of you." Soft sunlight bathed his handsome face and body in golden shadows, accentuating every muscular ripple.

I shrugged. "What were you doing up there?"

"I used to sit on that boulder, when I was a kid, for hours at a time, thinking about stuff...and now life and death, time-travel, and trying to come to terms with Emanuel's death."

"You did your best." I barely knew Emanuel, but my heart ached for him, as well. "I know how you feel...like with my mom."

"You had no control over a car accident."

"But I kept thinking...what if I'd gone with her? What if I asked her to help me with my homework? What if—"

"Yeah. I was playing the *what-if* blame game too." He levered to his feet. "What if I'd tried to suck the venom from his hand? What if he would have let me cut off his arm? What if I did it anyway? Could I have saved him then? Looks like we both have crosses to bear." He strode off toward the river.

I struggled to my feet and followed him to the riverbank. "Where are you going now?"

He stopped, bent behind a log, pulled out a cloth pouch, and dumped the contents in his hand. Gold nuggets of varying sizes, some the size of orange slices, glistened in the sun. "Look at this." Beneath a light stubble, his jaw quivered. "This was our dream, Emanuel's and mine." He sucked in a breath. "Now that I've found it, it-it means nothing to him." His words shuddered with raw emotion. He dumped the gold back into the pouch and glanced away.

I knew he was hiding tears he didn't want me to see.

He looked up to the sky. "I miss you, my friend."

I touched his arm. I really wanted to hold him, comfort him. "I'm so sorry."

"Emanuel had a new girlfriend. A whole future ahead of

him." Wyatt sat on the log and dropped the sack of gold at his feet. "You know what's ironic? I have my whole future ahead of me too. My dad wants me to go Pro, but I have this foolish idea I want to be a doctor."

"That's not foolish."

"Doesn't matter. My dad's right. I should go Pro. Maybe I'm not cut out to be a doctor. Losing a patient...it sucks."

"Would you give up football if you lost a game?"

"Of course not."

"You can't win them all. You can't save them all. Don't give up on being a doctor."

"My dad will never go for it. He has my football career all figured out."

I looked directly into Wyatt's sorrowful eyes with as much self-assurance as I could muster. "Then make him understand that saving lives is more important than scoring points."

"You don't know my dad. He wants what he wants, and there's no having it any other way."

"Unless you make him understand it's your future, not his. Besides, Emanuel would want you to be a doctor. Don't give up your dream."

He smiled. "Why do you always have to be right?"

Wyatt's future

I glanced at Abby. She was amazing and I was happy she was here. She gave me the kick in the ass I needed. Standing up to my father was gonna be a challenge, but it was time I took control of my own future.

She reached for her bundle. "When was the last time you ate something?"

I drew in a deep breath. "I don't know."

She poured water into a tin cup and handed it to me. "Drink."

"Yes, ma'am." I saluted and took a gulp.

"And eat." She handed me a stick of beef jerky.

My stomach grumbled. I'd been gone on my pity-bender longer than I'd intended. I chewed a bite off the tough strip of dried meat.

"Did you get any sleep? You look like shit." A smile curved her lips.

"You look pretty damn good." The color had returned to her face. Her eyes were brighter. "Since I've been gone, have you gotten any closer to finding the murderer?"

"Nothing."

"Did Horace come back for the kids?"

She handed me an apple. "Not yet."

The jerk probably saw past his wife's beauty, saw Lolita for who she really was, a woman in love with herself, a woman with a wicked temper. Maybe that drove him into the arms of another woman, so he left, got his life together, and then came back for the kids. Then after facing Lolita's temper again... "Maybe he'll never come back. I asked Daisy to keep an eye out for him."

"You did? When?"

There was that jealous glare again. "I got her to sit in my lap. Had to buy her a couple drinks, but she agreed to help us out. She doesn't want him to get your kids either." I chomped into the apple.

"Whatever he does, we know he doesn't get the kids. Somehow, Lolita won that fight."

Yeah. She was powerful, demanding, and a dynamo when she sang. "Lolita needs to tone her temper down a notch."

Heat colored Abby's face. "I have to apologize for last week...in the saloon. I..." She glanced down then back up, clearly embarrassed. "My behavior was deplorable. I wish I could say it was all Lolita."

"You saying a bit of her is rubbing off on you?"

"Part of it was her, yet I knew what I was doing. And I was having fun until she walked up to Monty. I hope you'll forget that performance."

Forgetting that sexy ass, the way she'd come on to me, that would be hard to erase from my mind, especially if Abby had her hand in it. I pictured her as a redheaded dynamo back at home. Smart *and* sexy, whoa. I had to put a lid on my imagination to stay on track. Monty presented a new problem. "There's something you need to know about Monty, but you have to promise me you won't get in a tizzy over it."

"Tizzy? Wyatt, I don't do *tizzy*. Spill it."

I couldn't just *spill it*. We didn't want Lolita to know her kids were going to be murdered, *so I have to be very careful here*. "I overheard the slime-bag talking to his goons about getting rid of a couple of somethings we've been worried about."

"Somethings?"

"Don't be dense, Abby. It's code for something little. Two of them."

"Oh." Her brows dipped. "Do you think he wants Lolita to go to San Francisco with him that bad?"

"I think he'd stop at nothing. He's still on your suspect list, right?"

She frowned. "He's our number two suspect. I'm still number one."

"Yeah. As for who tried to poison you, anything new?"

"Even though I fought with Monty, I don't think he'd poison me. Horace. I fought with him too."

"Lolita's been doing a lot of fighting lately."

"In a roundabout way, Horace threatened to kill me after I told him he'd get the kids over my dead body. Then there's the gambler."

I took a gulp of water from the tin cup. "I think Monty could have hired him."

"Or maybe he's just some guy from Lolita's past, a little payback for some perceived slight."

"I think the cat would disagree, nothing *little* about that payback."

"We know I live, according to the legend, so I'm not worried about someone killing me."

"I am. We might have already changed the future just by being here. I'm not leaving anything to chance."

"Then let's go catch a murderer." She hurried to repack her parcel.

I finished the apple and tossed the core into the river. The fish would appreciate the snack. I picked up my pouch of gold.

"Where did you find the gold?"

"Top secret." We started back for camp.

"Are you rich?"

"It's enough to last us until the end of the month. After that, we won't need it anymore. I hope." I stopped, glanced at her. "Meanwhile, I don't want you to go back to the saloon."

"Wyatt, I have to."

"It's too dangerous."

"I don't care. That night, some say she was dancing and singing at a party, probably at the saloon. I need to be there."

Abby was right, but I didn't like it.

Abby's heartbreak revisited

We followed the river back toward camp. Silent, I watched torrents splash and swirl against the boulders. Moss, lichen, and pine scented the air.

Thinking about my performance in the saloon, and how Lolita had the power to come and go as she pleased, irritated me. I felt as though we were always under surveillance. She was always watching. Always listening. Always playing buttinski between Wyatt and me.

I glanced at him.

He was brilliant. Handsome beyond any woman's wildest dreams, even more so with the five-o'clock shadow on his square jaw and the blond hair curling over his shoulders. His California tan had deepened, making his blue eyes appear more intense. He wanted to be a doctor. Boy had I misjudged him...again. I wanted to hold on to my grudge, it was so much a part of me, but now it didn't feel right. Cindi had told me to put it to bed. *Time to put my hurt heart in the open. Say my peace to Wyatt. Let the chips fall wherever they land. Put it to bed. Move on with my life, one way or the other.*

"Wyatt. We need to talk."

I saw that wary look every man wore when a woman said she needed to talk.

He stopped at a pile of dirt. "I thought we were talking."

"This is different..." Facing him, close as I was, I felt hesitant to delve into the past when we were getting on so well. I saw the need in his eyes. I liked the need in his eyes. No one ever looked at me that way, so I chose to believe that look was for me and not Lolita. "Ever wonder why I'm mostly mad at you?"

"Always. And I don't understand why."

"How could you not remember that you never showed up for our prom date?"

"Prom date?"

"You broke my heart, Wyatt."

"Now wait a minute." He cupped his chin. "I think I'd remember if I ever had a date with you." He looked at me like I was talking a foreign language. "I never asked you to the prom. I didn't even know you."

"Then let me refresh your memory." I tried to keep my voice calm. "Pam walked up to me in the hall and told me you wanted to take me to the prom, but you were afraid to ask me yourself."

"Me? Afraid—"

"You told her, *hell hath no fury like a pissed off redhead.*"

"I did not."

"She told me you didn't want to be embarrassed if I turned you down to your face, so you sent her to ask me to the prom."

"I'd never ask a girl to set me up on a date with another girl."

"You were standing behind her, a few yards back. I could see you, clear as day. She said if I agreed to go, I should just look over her shoulder and smile at you. You'd wave and pick me up at seven, my house. I smiled. You waved."

"Waved? I never waved at you. Somehow, Pam set you up. Those cheerleaders were known to get on their *bad girl* pants."

My heart jumped. "You mean...it was a prank?"

"It had to be."

"Pam?"

"I wouldn't put it past her."

Anger crept up my neck and burned my cheeks. "That bitch."

"I had no idea. I'm so sorry." He wrapped his arms around me and brought me in close. "Abby, really, I am."

My throat felt tight. I leaned into his chest, finding comfort in his warm embrace as years of pent-up hatred for him began to melt away. What wasted energy. Wasted resentment. My hardened heart had kept me from getting close to any man for fear of being stood up or dumped again.

All because Pam found pleasure in hurting me.

Wyatt brushed his hand over my hair. "When we get home, I'm going to give Pam hell."

"I was such a fool." I sobbed on his shirt. "I should have known you'd never go out with someone like me."

He eased me back and looked into my eyes. "I'd have been honored to go out with you. You're amazing."

"You're just saying that because I'm in a beautiful body."

"Why do you think I swam out to you in the river? I wanted to be near you. Know why? Because I thought you were beautiful. I hoped to get your phone number, wanted to get to know you. I didn't realize it would take a trip back in time to do it, but here we are."

I wiped tears from my face. The honesty in his eyes gave me hope. "I'm sorry. My tears soaked your shirt."

"You can cry on my shirt anytime."

"We should be going. It'll be getting dark soon."

He nodded.

As we walked hand in hand, I wondered what he thought about me spilling my guts to him? What was going through his head? Part of me felt relieved it was finally out in the open. The past no longer put a wedge between us as big as the Great Wall of China. The other part of me felt a little nervous. I was so used to my great wall, now I felt naked, vulnerable. A fragile heart could easily be broken.

We entered the camp to crackling wood fires that illuminated men's faces as they chewed tobacco, and an occasional wad of spittle hissed in the dancing flames that sent swirls of smoke into the night sky.

Wyatt took hold of my arm protectively. "I'll walk you home."

"Where are you going to sleep tonight?"

"I'm hoping Camila will still let me stay there."

"Wyatt, you can stay with me." Just saying it set butterflies aflutter down low.

"What about your kids?"

"Camila is watching them," I said softly.

"Sounds like an offer I can't refuse." He smiled slyly.

We walked past a row of tents and turned the corner leading to my home. A group of men with torches stood like a wall near Benjamin's tent, blocking our way.

My breath hitched. My mind raced with fright.

The Sheriff stood tall, his shoulders back, his metal badge glistening in the torchlight.

"What's going on, Sheriff?" Wyatt asked, his voice calm though he tightened his grip on my hand.

Was the lawman here to arrest Wyatt for Emanuel's death? Was this a lynch mob? An overwhelming sense of dread bloomed in my chest. "Oh, no."

"Have you been waiting for me? Benjamin? Soaring Eagle? What are you all doing here?"

More faces came into view. I recognized the Chinese man Wyatt had saved from Hank and his group of hooligans. Why had these people turned against him?

"It's about time you came home." Camila stepped out of the crowd. She looked angry enough to kill him.

Wyatt pulled me in close, his body taut.

I jumped to his defense. "It wasn't his fault, Camila."

"He ain't no doctor." That came from Hank himself. He had a loop of rope hanging from his shoulder.

Visions of Wyatt hanged by the neck until dead on the Main Street of Dry Diggins struck terror in my heart. The town wasn't called *Hangtown* for nothing. "He did the best he could."

The Sheriff stepped forward. "We know."

"But he's the best doctor we got." Hank cackled like the old rooster he was.

Camila touched my shoulder. "We want to thank him."

"No hang white medicine man," Soaring Eagle put in.

The crowd cheered.

"You saved my boy," the Sheriff said.

"You healed my husband," a woman's voice put in.

"My boy too," someone else added.

A Chinese woman I'd never seen before stepped up. "You feed my family. You think we don't know?"

"My partner, too," a deep voice chimed in.

I stood stunned. Wyatt had helped all these people? I had

no idea. Joseph's burned hand should have been my first clue. He'd done a professional job of treating him.

"You bring good medicine to this camp," Soaring Eagle said as he rotated his shoulder then crossed his arms in front of his bare chest.

I looked at Wyatt. His face was a blank mask.

Benjamin said, "We are indebted to you, Doctor Wyatt."

He blanched. "You people don't owe me anything."

Benjamin moved back, and the crowd parted. "This is your new home."

Alongside Benjamin's tent stood a small log house with a real wood roof and wooden door. Approximately ten by twelve, the building looked straight and sturdy.

"You built this for me?" The stunned expression on Wyatt's face was precious.

The group cheered.

"Why?"

The Chinese man flung his long braid over his shoulder. "We don't want you to leave camp again."

Wyatt shuffled a foot in the dirt, looked uncomfortable and never looked more handsome. He was a hero to all these people. He was my hero, too, and now he was my new neighbor. Almost made me want to never leave.

Almost.

Chapter Eighteen

Wyatt meets up with Daisy

P eople were patting me on the back and shaking my hand. All their accolades made my head spin. The gratitude I felt by my friends' kindness overwhelmed me, and by the time everyone left, I felt emotionally drained.

I stood in my new quarters. It had all the luxuries: a small table with a few dishes and cups, a bed with a woven red and blue blanket, and a wooden armchair. Firewood had been stacked in one corner near a black potbelly stove around which cooking utensils hung.

As I sat on the bed and pulled off my boots, I realized how close Abby and I had come to sleeping together. Camila brought the kids back, and I had to try out my new digs. Seemed to me that fate knew our time was yet to come. I couldn't imagine how she felt being stood up on prom night. Pam was definitely getting kicked out of my circle. I knew she was superficial, but I never knew how cruel she could be. No wonder when I first met Abby she'd shot me dagger-eyes. Her disdain for me made perfect sense now. Still, I felt bad for all the tears she'd cried over me.

I yawned and drew up the blanket.

Abby's safety was still my top priority. Horace was still in town. Benjamin had seen him purchasing children's clothing and toys. It was only a matter of time before he'd return to Lolita's place and demand his kids. Good thing I'd bought a gun and learned how to use it.

Up at the crack of dawn on the 25th of July, I saddled Jack and rode into town. I secured his reins to a hitching post and stepped into the Boomerang.

"Morning, Daisy." I tipped my hat as she approached.

"Aren't you a pleasant sight." She set her hand on my arm.

"You got any information on Horace for me?"

"I could use a drink."

We walked up to the bar, ordered, then sat at a table in the corner of the room.

"Let's have it."

"Sadie is not happy."

"Who is Sadie?"

"Horace's mistress."

"What's her problem?"

"She didn't know he was married, let alone had them young'uns."

"Really?"

"She was mad as a hornet. Threatened to kill Lolita."

Had Horace tried to poison Abby to appease Sadie, or did Sadie try to kill his wife? "How did you learn this?"

"I overheard them arguing. Seems they fight a lot, and loudly."

"When did you hear this loud argument?"

"A while back."

Frustrated, I stared her down. "How long ago, a day, a week? Before or after Lolita was almost poisoned?"

"Before."

My face heated. I took several deep breaths to keep my anger at bay. "Why didn't you tell me back then?"

"I didn't have your gold in my hand."

If Daisy noticed my flaring nostrils, she said nothing as she gulped down her whiskey.

At least this information put a twist on the legend. Sadie was going on the suspect list. "Anything else?"

She wiped her mouth then held out her hand.

I dropped a nugget in her palm.

"If I hear anything else, I'll let you know."

"Thanks." I stormed out of the saloon. The doors swung shut behind me with a bang. My boots pounded the wooden walkway as I stalked toward the jailhouse to talk to the Sheriff. If there were any lawyers in town, he'd be the one to ask. I knew nothing about the law here, or if a woman could get a divorce, but I needed to find out. I had no proof Horace or Sadie had tried to poison Lolita, but killing her would serve two purposes:

eliminating the wife would satisfy Sadie, and he'd automatically get the children. At least with them out of the picture, Lolita wouldn't be jealous and wouldn't kill her kids, if that part of the legend were true.

Across the street, Camila held Cattie's hand as they walked up to the mercantile. Joseph rushed to the door ahead of them. Camila pulled him back by the suspenders when he almost bumped into Monty who was walking out.

"Watch where you're going, boy." Annoyance scrunched Monty's long face. "You should keep those kids on a tight rope."

"Lo siento." Camila mumbled an apology and ushered the kids to one side, allowing him to pass. Abby walked out the door, and my blood pressure rose. What was she doing in the store with that bastard? Torn between my mission and curiosity, I continued walking toward them and the jail beyond, but I kept my attention on her.

The minute Abby stood by her kids, Monty's face lit up with a forced smile. "Fine children you have." He patted Cattie on the head. I wanted to twist those fingers from his hand.

"Abigail. Camila." I tipped my hat to them as I stepped up, and dismissing Monty's presence, turned my back on him. Knowing what a bastard he was, I wouldn't put it past him to pull out a gun and shoot me in the back. "Good morning, ladies."

Abby snoops

"Good morning, Wyatt." I felt like I was looking at him with a fresh pair of eyes. The grudge I held toward him for the past three years no longer stood between us. He wasn't to blame for my broken heart; Pam was, but all was not roses and honey. I figured, when we returned to our own time, Wyatt would go back to his house on the hill and his fancy college. I wouldn't fit in his inner circle, which was okay, because I didn't want to hang with his snooty friends anyway. Would that leave us romantically barren? Maybe we could just be friends. Who was I kidding? I wanted to be more than his friend. Our unknown future hurt my heart. "Did you sleep well in your new home last night?"

"Better than I thought I would." The deep timbre of his voice sent flutters to my stomach.

I won't let my heart take the lead. That's a dead-end path.

"*Follow your heart,*" Lolita whispered in my head. "*It can be the path to heaven.*"

Wyatt reached into the small familiar bag at his waist and pulled out a gold nugget. "Hey, kids. Take this and go buy yourselves something inside."

They looked up at me, and I nodded.

Monty sidestepped Wyatt, knocking him in the shoulder to get to me. "Lolita. Might I suggest we share a meal tonight?"

Wyatt's jaw clenched. "The lady is eating with me," he said sternly.

Monty turned to face him with narrow, challenging eyes. "I don't recall you asking her."

"I asked her yesterday." Wyatt squared his shoulders and gave him an *I-dare-you-to-argue* look.

Both men looked like they were about to unload on each other.

Monty stood tall. "Lolita is in my employ. She will do as I request of her."

Wyatt stepped around Monty and linked arms with me. "Lolita has just punched off the clock."

Confusion crossed Monty's face. "What does that mean?"

I suppressed a smile. Wyatt really had to stop using our modern terminology.

Monty stepped to my other side and slipped his arm around my waist. "Lolita, I would suggest—"

"I would suggest you unhand her." Wyatt's voice was steely.

Neither man moved.

Someone yelled, "Fire. Fire."

Everyone's attention shifted across the street to the building next to the saloon. Flames leaped from the windows. Monty released me and ran toward the fire.

"Camila..." Wyatt yelled. "Keep the kids in the store." He took my hand, and we hurried to a bucket line already forming.

Men were already tossing buckets of water into the building.

I broke from Wyatt's hand and hoisted my skirt so I could run. "I'm going to make sure everyone is out of the saloon."

"No, Abby. It's too dangerous."

"I'm going." I ran to the saloon before he could stop me and pushed in through the swinging doors. I had to dodge men who were running out.

Acrid smoke drifted in and smelled like kerosene.

"Joe. Is anyone upstairs?"

The bartender looked up at me. "I think everyone has left."

Good. This would be my chance to do some snooping in Monty's office. "They could use another man out there. I'll go upstairs and check."

"Be quick about it." He stepped from behind the bar and raced outside.

I ran upstairs and yelled, "Fire. Everyone out," while flinging open doors. In one room, a naked man jumped out of bed and ran around the room, grabbing his pants and shirt as my harried co-worker struggled into a robe.

Satisfied the upper floor was empty, I followed them down the stairs and broke off toward Monty's office, praying time was on my side before flames spread to the saloon.

I didn't know what I'd find, or what I was looking for, but Monty had hinted way too many times at murder.

After shutting the door, I sprinted to his desk and thrust aside blank parchments and writing utensils, hoping I'd find something about the gunslingers he'd hired, anything that might finger the person who had tried to kill me.

"Abby," Lolita shouted in my head. *"What are we doing in here?"*

"Looking for evidence." Nothing in the top drawer. No bottle of cyanide. No incriminating notes.

"The place is on fire. Are you determined to get me killed?"

"Us killed," I reminded her. *"Monty is up to no good, and I intend to find what he's hiding."*

I slammed shut the top drawer, and pulse pounding, I opened the second drawer. I didn't have a lot of time. If the fire spread, Monty would rush in here to save whatever he could. I'd be in big trouble.

Smoke seeped in from under the door. My mouth went dry. My fingers trembled as I shuffled through more papers: bills, receipts. Vouchers signed by Monty Colton. Nothing to incriminate him. I pulled on the bottom drawer. It wouldn't budge. *No way? Locked?* Panic drummed in my ears as the room began to fill with smoke.

I glanced at the door, fearful at any minute it would slam open, or worse, burst into flames. I yanked on the drawer with more force and it opened. It must've been jammed. Frantically I rifled through handwritten notes with mathematical figures that looked like ledgers for the saloon. Disgusted, I was just about to slide the drawer closed when the name Doble caught my eye...on the deed to the Boomerang Gambling Hall and Saloon. It was signed *Monty Doble. Odd.* Everyone knew his last name was Colton. I slammed the drawer, hurried to the door, and opened it a pinch. No one there. No fire. Just a little smoke now. I stepped into the barroom. *Doble. Doble. Why did the name sound familiar?*

Perplexed, I took a deep, calming breath as soot-covered men hurried back inside. Monty followed behind them.

"Is the fire out?" I asked as nonchalantly as I could, while my heart rapidly thudded, and I prayed I didn't look guilty of doing anything wrong.

Monty barked out orders. "Open the windows, boys. Upstairs and downstairs. Get the smoke cleared out."

Wyatt pushed through the doors. "Drinks are on me."

"Saved as much as we could," someone said and raised his glass to Wyatt.

"At least the whole building didn't burn to the ground," someone else said. Murmurs of agreement rose as men made themselves comfortable at tables and saloon girls got busy spending Wyatt's money.

When his gaze met mine I asked, "Where are the kids?"

"I sent them back to camp with Camila."

"Thank you."

"Where did you go?"

I forced a smile. "You've got a bit of soot here." I brushed it off his cheek. God, he was handsome. It was a sin to look so perfect, even with black streaks on his face and hands. He'd rolled up his sleeves, showcasing his thick muscles. His shirt clung to his chest from what I guessed was sloshed water from a bucket missing its mark. I couldn't help but stare at the open front where light blond hair peeked out.

As my touch left his face, he grabbed my hand mid-air. I recalled how annoyed I felt when he'd wiped the lotion from my lip. Did he remember? I studied his face, waiting for a frown. I'd been so rude. Who would have thought I'd be craving his touch now?

Silently, our gazes held us captive. Amid all the commotion and noisy conversations going on around us, nothing mattered, not my disappointing lack of evidence, not my diminishing fright from moments ago. No animosity darkened his caring eyes, no frown marred his handsome face.

He brought my fingers to his lips and kissed them.

A contented sigh escaped me.

"Abby—"

The swinging doors banged open. "You son of a bitch." The angry curse silenced the patrons. All attention focused on a bony red-faced man who stormed through the barroom like a raving lunatic, his fists raised as he charged toward Monty. His shaggy beard extended down to his belly, and ash clung to his mottled face and blue flannel shirt. "I swear I'll kill you."

"Get control of yourself, Gilles," Monty ordered. "There'll be no killing in my establishment." At the flick of his fingers, his hired gunmen stepped out of the crowd.

Gilles stopped in front of Monty. "You did it."

Monty's two nasty-looking gunslingers marched up and stood on either side of him. Their fingers were poised over their guns.

Gilles pumped his fist. "You set fire to my place."

Wyatt's gaze met mine and I feared he was going to rat on Monty, tell what he'd heard. I shook my head. Now was not the time to confront him, not now with his gunslingers standing at attention and ready to shoot the first man who opened his mouth.

"Now, Gilles. You don't know what you're talking about. Why Mistress Lolita can attest, I was with her when the fire started."

Lust-filled glares settled on me, as if they thought Monty

and I spent the afternoon in bed. Heat flooded my face.

"Isn't that correct, Lolita?" Monty asked.

"We were both with her," Wyatt said.

Great. Now they think we were having a ménage à trois.

Fists balled, Wyatt turned toward Monty. I grabbed his wrist. With my best attempt at pleading with my eyes, I begged him to sit down and not say another word. I jerked my head toward Slimbo and his partner and hoped he noticed he was outgunned.

"We were at the mercantile together when the fire started." Then Wyatt took a chair.

I mouthed a silent *thank you.*

"I don't give a damn where you were," Gilles shouted. "You wanted my building to expand this place. Didn't like my refusal to sell out, so you burned me out. Damn it, you know I can't rebuild. I got young'uns to feed."

"I'd stop making false accusations. You're upset. Have a whiskey on the house." Monty clicked his fingers, and the bartender poured a drink.

Gilles spit on Monty's boot.

"I suggest you get out of my saloon, or I'll have my men escort you out."

Gilles turned, his posture hunched, a man defeated. Slowly he ambled toward the exit. He was about to push open the doors when they swung inward. The Sheriff entered, and it hit me. Madam Doble was the name of the victim on the wanted poster... *Monty has a dead wife.*

Wyatt warns Abby

I got out of the chair. "Abby, I need to talk to you."

"Not now. I've got to talk to Monty."

"You need to stay away from him." My gaze crossed the saloon. Monty wore a look of satisfaction on his smug face. "Do not go out to dinner with him."

"Wyatt, now is not the time to be jealous."

"I'm not jealous."

"Then take the sneer out of your tone."

I wasn't fooling her. Even though I knew in my gut Abby wanted only information from him, Lolita, on the other hand, might accept his invitation to San Francisco and take Abby away from me. Either way, I didn't like him, and I didn't like it when Abby was with him. "Fine. Go," I snapped, annoyed Abby wouldn't listen to me. "I'm gonna talk to the Sheriff, tell him what we heard about Monty's hired guns setting something on fire."

"It'll be your word against the most powerful man in town. We have no proof. Saying something at this point will only make you Monty's next target."

"I don't care. He can't get away with burning that man out of his building."

"You're right, I know. Look..." She sighed. "I'm going to tell him I don't feel like working this afternoon. Wait here. I'll be back. I have something important to tell you."

I shrugged as relief eased the tension from my shoulders.

"Wyatt..." Her voice softened. "I would have chosen to eat dinner with you...if not for the fire interrupting us."

Despite my annoyance, I forced a smile and watched the sexy curves of her hips sway as she strolled away from me and toward that bastard Monty.

As Abby talked to him, he toyed with her hair. It took all my self-control not to punch him in the jaw. When she finished her conversation and made her way back to me, I unclasped my fisted hand.

"You have to buy me a drink."

"What? He won't give you time off?"

"I'm supposed to look like I'm working." She sat and arranged her red gown neatly around her chair.

By the steely look Monty shot at me, I didn't think I was the person he wanted Abby to be with, regardless of the amount of money I'd spend at the bar.

I sat across from her, pulled my chair closer, and leaned in. "I've got something to tell you."

"So do I," she whispered with trouble in her eyes.

"You first." My gaze dropped to the creamy swell of her distracting breasts then quickly rose to her eyes.

"I think Monty killed his wife."

"He had a wife?"

"There's a wanted poster on the jailhouse wall for information leading to the murderer of Madam Doble. That's his last name," she whispered in my ear. "Monty Doble. There's a five-thousand-dollar reward. Why let everyone think his last name is Colton unless he's guilty?" A sly sneer formed on those tempting lips.

"He's hiding something, or from someone."

"Every document I saw is signed Colton except one, the deed to this saloon."

"How do you know?"

"I...well..."

"Abby, what did you do?"

"I went through his desk when no one was around."

"There's always someone around... Shit. You snuck in during the fire. Are you crazy?" Seemed like I'd never talk any sense into her. "You could have gotten trapped in there and burned alive."

"I know. I know. But I thought maybe I'd learn if Monty tried to poison me...find the bottle of cyanide, I don't know. Maybe I'd find something about what his hired guns were here to do."

"For starters, arson. And we already decided he wouldn't want you dead. He wants you in bed." I didn't mean to sound so jealous.

"Say it louder. I don't think the entire place heard you." A charming flush colored her cheeks.

I clasped my hand over my mouth and breathed deep, giving myself time to calm down, then: "If anything, Monty wants your kids out of the way. Not you. If he gets his way, you're going to San Francisco and Horace gets your kids."

"I wouldn't go with him. Kids or not."

"You wouldn't but Lolita might."

"She never left this town. The legend is perfectly clear."

"Daisy told me Sadie wasn't happy that Horace was married and had kids. Guess they had a loud argument about you."

"I do not want my kids to have anything to do with that Sadie whore." Disdain soured Abby's face, but I knew it was

Lolita who'd voiced her anger. Her body grew taut, shoulders back, chest puffed out...

Oh, yeah, that chest... I placed my hand on hers. "We've got this, Lolita. Don't go ballistic on us."

"I do not know what is this ballistic."

"Just stay calm, Lolita," Abby said and flashed me a disapproving glare.

Her posture softened. She took a deep breath. "So now what?"

"I'll keep my eyes out for Sadie."

"And I'll keep tabs on Monty."

"You be careful."

"Wyatt, I work with the man. He thinks we're going to be an item some day. He doesn't want to kill me."

"But somebody does, so watch your back."

Abby's close call

Later that afternoon, I sat in the shade of an evergreen and watched my children toeing the water at the river's edge. Cattie wore the new blue Victorian dress and bonnet I'd bought her; Joseph had on cut-off pants with suspenders and his new white shirt. I thought how well they played together.

Then my thoughts turned to Wyatt. He was jealous. I smiled. Did my feelings for him show? Every time we were together, every time he stood up for me or worried about my wellbeing, those hopeful feelings grew stronger. He hadn't played a part in Pam's scheme, so the wall I'd built to keep away hurt started to crumble. Still, I clung to the remaining bricks. I was afraid. Plain and simple. Afraid to give my heart away just to have it trampled on. Without some kind of wall, I wouldn't know who I was anymore.

Wyatt wasn't looking at me. He didn't see me. No one except Cindi ever saw me, the real me in my protective shell. He only saw Lolita. Her hourglass body and tiny waist, her perfect boobs, and gorgeous face, I knew her beauty enticed him. Part of me wanted to let Lolita out. Let her out so I could give in to the desire coursing through her body when we were together. With him living so close, it would be so easy to slip into his home and lay with him. I could blame these spiraling emotions on Lolita. He wanted her. What man didn't? But making love to him, wondering who he was kissing, touching, would make matters worse. I was an illusion. I had to remember that. As close as I'd come to sleeping with Wyatt, I now knew it wouldn't have been fair to either one of us. Pent-up anxiety knotted my chest. Not wishing to lose myself in depression, I watched the birds, sparrows, maybe finches, splashing in the river. They'd dip in, fly up, and perch in the trees where they'd flap their wings dry.

Someone had dragged a wooden rowboat to the shallows and tied it to a rock. It was lunchtime. Men sat around munching on hard biscuits or digging into earthen bowls. A photographer came along, set up is boxy camera on a tripod and took pictures of the men on their dig sites. He swiveled the camera to Cattie and Joseph as they stood by the rowboat and snapped their picture, the same picture I'd seen in the history book. A strange sense of déjà vu hit me. I missed my library, my books...my own body. I stood and waved thank you to the photographer.

Someone tossed out some biscuit crumbs, and birds darted in and squabble over every morsel. The photographer moved downriver. Cattie met up with another little girl. Joseph foraged for rocks. The rowboat bobbed in the water. Life went on as if I wasn't even there.

Joseph ran up to me, eyes wide with wonder. I knelt to his level. "Yes, darling?"

He held out his hand. A shiny black rock rested in his palm.

"How pretty."

He moved his hand toward me, suggesting I take it. I didn't know why Joseph wouldn't talk to me. Was it something I did? Was his father's abandonment the cause? Did he blame me that his dad had left? I wish I knew.

"For me?"

He nodded.

A tear formed in my eye. "Thank you. I shall treasure this forever." He went back to the riverbank to look for more pretty stones.

Cattie walked up. She looked like she'd been crying. I took

her hand and we sat on a patch of grass. "What's wrong?"

She looked at me with sad eyes. "Maria says I'm ugly."

"Is she blind?"

"No."

"She must be. You're a beautiful little girl." I wiped a smudge of mud off her face. "Under all this dirt." I wanted to bolt up and find Maria and give her a piece of my mind. Any minute now, the tears in Cattie's eyes would mirror mine. I sniffled, trying my best not to cry. I knew how she felt. How cruel some people could be. I couldn't let Cattie suffer from the same low self-esteem I did. I ran my fingers along her face. "Maria is just jealous."

"She says no one loves me. That's why Pa left."

"Oh, honey, no." I wrapped my arms around her and felt her stiffen. "We both love you."

"Adults are hard to understand."

"Kids too. I don't understand why Joseph won't talk to me."

"He's afraid he'll say the wrong words and you'll leave us too."

"No. No." I gasped. "He thinks it's his fault Pa left? Something he said?"

"I guess."

"There's nothing you guys can say that will make me leave."

"Then why did Pa leave?" Cattie's voice was on the verge of tears.

"He went somewhere to make lots of money so we can have a better life." I knew that wasn't true, but I couldn't tell her about the other woman. I placed a comforting hand on her arm. "I know he loves you and Joseph, in fact, he came back to get you."

"He did?" Hope welled in the depths of her eyes.

"Yes, honey. He wants you to live with him, but—"

"Are you coming too?"

"He doesn't want me to go with you."

"Then I'm not going."

Tears dripped from my eyes as I hugged her tighter. This time she melted into my embrace. "Mamma?"

"Yes?"

"Just tell Joseph you love him. He needs to know that."

Distant shouts caught my attention. I looked up. Benjamin and Wyatt were running in our direction, waving their arms.

"Lolita. Cattie," Benjamin hollered.

I'd vaguely caught a glimpse of a boulder crashing down the mountain. As I shot to my feet, still clutching Cattie, my foot caught on the hem of my dress, made me stumble, but I managed to thrust myself forward enough to propel us out of the way. We landed in the dirt, and I shielded Cattie with my body. Seconds later, the boulder thundered past us, followed by a stinging shower of gravel, dirt, and dust. I looked up and saw Benjamin and Wyatt emerge from the maelstrom at a full run as the giant boulder crashed into the river.

Wyatt skidded up on his knees and fell on top of us protectively. "Are you all right?"

"We're fine."

As the dust cleared, he helped me up. Benjamin took Cattie then sprinted toward Joseph downstream. Wyatt grabbed onto me and locked his arms around my waist. "You were almost killed."

Breathless, I looked up into concern-filled eyes. His chest heaved against my breasts. His wrists pressed into my back in a death grip, clasping me against him as if my life depended on a solid hold. Our bodies breathed as one. My throat dried. I couldn't think straight. Potent untamed stimulation shot between us, making a lie of the promise I'd made to myself not to succumb to these feelings. Silently we gazed at each other. All sounds and surroundings seemed nonexistent except for our quick breathing and our pounding hearts. I studied the lines of his tanned face, the five o'clock stubble on his square jaw, the way a lock of blond hair fell over his brow. My gaze lingered on his serious lips.

Kiss me, I begged silently. *Kiss me, you fool.*

For the moment, I didn't care about what had almost happened. We were alive. More than alive. Arousal ravished my body stronger than the hot sun beating down on us. I couldn't think. I didn't want to. I just wanted to feel his love.

Wyatt's suspicions

Everything around me was a blur except for Abby's incredible hypnotic eyes. Her soft curves against me sprang every nerve to attention. The desire shining in her eyes, and the sweet scent of honeysuckle all stirred my senses. Her glossy hair caressed her back and kissed the back of my hand on her waist. Aroused, I couldn't think of anything but the need to taste those full lips, to run my mouth along her slender neck. Her full breasts, pressing against my chest, inflamed me, and like an addict, I wanted more. I wanted to feel her naked body against mine. I needed to touch her satin skin. I wanted our bodies entwined like the vines of a heavenly vineyard. I sucked in a quick breath. What was wrong with me? Now was not the time or place to be having such thoughts. Shit, she was almost killed.

Strangers stood around us, gawking.

"Abby, we have an audience," I managed with difficulty, holding back a surge of desire that rolled over me like a runaway boulder.

She glanced sideways, "We...what? Oh."

I released my grip on her waist. "We should—"

"Right."

I took a moment to center myself, collect my composure.

Benjamin and the kids ran up to us. Both children threw their arms around her. Joseph was the first to cry out. "Mamma, are you hurt?"

His words brought tears to her shocked eyes, and I realized that was the first time I'd heard him say anything to her. I had a feeling, by her reaction, it was a first for Abby as well.

She reached down and lifted him up. "No, honey, I'm fine."

Her glance shifted to the boulder lying in the shallows by the rowboat, and her face paled. "I-I saw it just in time."

A group of miners gathered at the boulder and looked upslope to the path of destruction it left behind: shattered rocks and splintered trees.

"That big rock didn't come loose on its own," I told Abby as we trudged back to camp.

"It wasn't just nature being nature?"

"Doubtful." I gnashed my teeth to stop the curse about to spill out. "Thank God Benjamin happened to see the rockslide." The thought of Abby's close call tightened my chest. "That's the third attempt on Lolita's life."

"Third?"

"Yeah. The cut rein on the wagon, the poisoned wine, and now this boulder. Someone wants you dead."

Abby didn't look worried. "Whoever it is doesn't succeed. The legend is clear about that."

"I don't like it one bit."

We walked to Abby's home. She bent to the children. "Please go inside and get ready for dinner."

They ducked inside.

"Miss Lolita..." Benjamin held his tent flap open. "I need to ask you something."

She stepped into his tent and I followed. For a woman who had come close to death, she looked rather calm as she took a seat. Between my relief that she was all right, my fear that someone had tried to kill her, again, and the bolt of desire her body had aroused in me, my heart felt like a punching bag.

Benjamin pulled a chair in front of her and sat. "How did you sense the danger?"

"Ah... It happened so fast. One minute I was talking to Cattie and then...then...I saw it coming out the corner of my eye."

"That's not possible. It was still rolling down the mountain behind you." He looked at her with a tilt to his head. "You jumped in a panic before you could have seen it coming."

"Looked like a close call to me," I put in.

Benjamin scoffed. "Miss Lolita, with all due respect, you haven't been yourself lately, not the Lolita I've known for the past year."

She looked at me then Benjamin, her expression fearful, eyes wide, chin quivering. "Okay. I admit..." She clasped her hands in her lap. "I haven't felt like myself for quite a while. These weird feelings come over me out of nowhere. I must've seen the boulder in my mind's eye."

I frowned. "What's that mean?"

She turned her gaze to me. "Wyatt, I have a sixth sense. I get premonitions."

I stared at Abby as though she'd just told me she could fly. My expression must have been mystified as I plopped down on the rug-covered floor. "Why haven't you told me this before?"

"I wasn't sure how you'd react." She stabbed two fingers to her temple and rubbed. "I know it's hard to believe..."

I reached up and rested my hand on her arm, wondering why her premonitions hadn't revealed the killer but decided not to say anything in Benjamin's presence. Besides, Lolita would find out why we were here and complicate matters.

Abby took several quick breaths. "Do you guys believe me?"

"Don't look at me." I squeezed her arm. "I'll believe anything you say." After time-travel, her sixth sense was a breeze to believe. However, by the bent on Benjamin's brow, I figured he was skeptical, but I had to wonder if my warning to her had saved her from being killed. Or had Benjamin's warning actually saved her? Or had Abby's sixth sense saved Lolita? We knew Lolita wasn't killed by a boulder, but still, maybe our mere presence here had already changed the future in ways we couldn't have anticipated.

Abby's good friend

Wyatt looked really worried, but I knew we couldn't discuss our dilemma in front of Benjamin. I'd done enough damage for one day. "I should check on the kids."

"I'll do it." Wyatt stood, opened the tent flap. "You two have a lot to talk about." He left me alone with Benjamin. Too overwhelmed by the fact I'd told Wyatt my secret, I didn't want to worry about what comes next between us. If I were him I'd run for the hills.

"He is concerned for your wellbeing." Benjamin's voice drew my attention.

"He thinks that loose boulder was no accident."

"What's your sixth sense tell you about that?"

"Nothing. All I know, Wyatt is a good man." That was the

truth. He'd come to my rescue more than once. At first, I'd misjudged him. We were both hiding: me from my sixth sense, Wyatt from his father. I'd watched his shocked expression when I revealed my secret. The thought of him looking at me differently now soured my stomach. No one knew about my ability. I hadn't even told Cindi out of fear I'd lose my best friend. Now I may have frightened Wyatt away. I pressed my hand into my chest and rubbed, easing the knot brought on by stress.

"Are you all right, Miss Lolita?"

"I don't know what to do." I glanced up at the ceiling, saw the dangling bones, like some kind of god-awful wind chimes. "What's with all the bones?"

"Bat bones."

"Gross."

"They ward off evil spirits." Standing, he walked to a wooden bowl and came back with something in his open hand. "Would you mind if I give the children these to wear?" Two chain necklaces with blue-eyed stones rested in his outstretched palm. "The Greeks wore this symbol to fend off evil spirits." He looked at me with kind eyes that touched a soft spot in my soul.

"Sure. Better than bat bones. Thank you for caring for my children."

"My pleasure, Miss Lolita."

"You're a good friend." I stood. "I should go."

He nodded.

I stepped outside and looked up to a waxing crescent moon. In seven days, the moon would be full, a blue moon, the blue moon of legend. Time was running out, and my sixth sense hadn't been any help pointing me to the killer.

My pulse raced, pounded in my throat. Who wanted to murder my children; who wanted to murder me, and why? Who should I watch? Was it Lolita? Was it Monty? What about Sadie and my husband?

I'd stayed away from Horace and his mistress, only bumping into her once in town. That encounter provoked heat in my stomach from a sudden burst of Lolita's anger.

"Are you jealous?" I asked her.

"Lolita never is jealous of another woman."

"Then what's wrong?"

"She wears my wedding ring. Horace is a pig to give it to her."

I'd complimented Sadie on her ring, and she'd covered it with her other hand and moved away. Snooty bitch. I was glad Horace wasn't with her that day, showering her with attention, calling to the children and ignoring Lolita. She would surely have taken over and clawed out his eyes.

I thought of all the different stories associated with the Weeping Woman's children. Were they victims of an accident? Jealously? Revenge? Neglect? And now some mystery person had tried to kill me for reasons unknown. Nowhere in all the stories did it say Lolita was in danger. However, now I was in danger, as if just being here had already changed current events and maybe history itself. Some astronomical force brought me back here for a purpose: to save those kids, I still believed.

I stepped inside my shack. The children were drawing with sticks on the dirt floor. But no Wyatt. *What is he up to now?* I needed a distraction to calm my nerves, spotted the children's books he'd bought. I walked to the shelf, picked up one, and sat on my cot. "Come, children. Come read a book with me." I opened the book by Hans Christian Andersen, one of my favorite childhood authors.

While the children made themselves comfortable, my thoughts intruded. Would the identity of the murderer be revealed in time? I knew Lolita wasn't killed. If so, there would have been no legend of the Weeping Woman.

"Mamma. We're ready."

"Oh, sorry." I opened the book. "In an underwater kingdom, a little mermaid lived with her father, the king of the sea..."

Again, my thoughts strayed. To their father. Horace may have wanted me out of the picture, but he would never hurt his children. Sadie may have wanted the kids out of the way. Monty too. We were on better terms lately, at least I pretended to be agreeable. He didn't want me dead, but he wasn't fond of my kids, either. After what Wyatt had overheard about the brats, Monty was high on my list of suspects. And then there was his wife. Had he murdered her? We needed to find out. Nothing was mentioned of Monty in the legend, but folklore was just that, stories told over and over throughout the century. Characters could have been omitted from the legend or changed along the line of a thousand retells.

I glanced at Cattie and Joseph. A sigh escaped my lips. The thought of anything happening to them made me sick with dread. I wished I had something substantial to rely on instead of speculation. If I was wrong about the killer, the children would die, and I would have failed to protect them.

Chapter Nineteen

Wyatt makes a plan

Still concerned over yesterday's incident, intent on finding the person responsible for pushing loose that boulder, I stuffed my gun in my new holster, threw a saddle on Jack, and headed into town to see the Sheriff. Anger and frustration fueled a burning inside me, a no-no in the philosophy of karate. I flicked the reins with a fury that blinded me. Crazy dust swirls rose up from the street as I pulled back on the reins and stopped before the jailhouse. I dismounted and took a deep breath, exhaling slowly. At times like this, years of karate classes went out the window. Sensei would not be happy.

The Sheriff walked out and I hurried to meet him on the boardwalk.

"Wyatt? What's all the rush about?"

"Can we talk, Sheriff?"

He tipped his hat. "You can call me Samuel. I think we are past formalities. I want to thank you again for saving my boy." His calloused hand clasped mine in a firm grip. "Come on in."

I followed him into the jailhouse. "Thomas wasn't going to die. He was just sick."

"You tell it your way, I'll tell it mine."

My gaze went to the single jail cell. Behind the bars stood a flimsy, filthy cot covered with a faded-green blanket. "Have you heard about the boulder that came—"

"A near disaster at the river." Samuel dropped his hat on a clutter of papers that obscured his desktop. "Good thing no one got hurt."

"Is that a normal occurrence, boulders the size of a stagecoach just crashing down on their own?" I took off my hat as I walked past the desk to take a look at the wanted poster, the one Abby told me she'd seen.

"If it rains enough, could happen."

I doubted any amount of rain could loosen that monstrous rock, but without proof of a deliberate act, this conversation would go nowhere. I pointed out the poster. "Did Monty put up the reward money for this?"

"Not that I know of. Why?"

"It's his wife...or should I say ex-wife?"

Townsend stared at me like my hair had turned purple. His forehead furrowed. "You're saying Mr. Colton's last name is Doble?"

"Yup."

"You got proof?"

"Check the deed to his saloon. It's signed Doble, not Colton."

Samuel scratched his jaw. "Interesting." He put a pinch of tobacco behind his lower lip.

"And I overheard him order his hired guns to take care of Gilles."

"You see them strike that match?"

"No, but—"

"Monty is a very influential businessman in this town." Samuel spit into a spittoon. "I wouldn't go around raising a fuss without proof...not if I was you."

"I'll bet he was behind it, for the record. If you find me dead, you'll know who to interrogate."

"I will keep that in mind."

"Also...well, I'm curious about divorce."

"You asking for yourself?"

"No. No. I don't know the laws around here, but I was wondering how a friend could go about getting a divorce."

"I'm not an expert, but if there's justification and both parties agree, the judge might grant one without a big fuss."

Judges traveled from town to town during these Wild West days. "Will he be here anytime soon?"

"Tomorrow soon enough?"

"Perfect." I plopped on my hat and walked out. As I put my foot in the stirrup, I heard loud voices coming from an open window of the El Dorado Hotel next door.

"Please don't be angry with me," a high-pitched woman's voice pleaded. "I did it for us...for you."

Did what? I mounted my horse and moved closer to the window.

"Us? You're only thinking of yourself." The deep male voice sounded unfriendly.

"Getting rid of her will make our life easier."

Getting rid of her? Were they talking about Lolita?

"My children could've gotten hurt. Did that ever cross your mind?"

Cattie and Joseph? My fingers clenched the pommel.

"Horace, I would never harm your kids. Please believe me."

"Try another stunt like that, I'll beat you to an inch of your life. Who else knows what you did?"

"Just Hardington."

"How much did you pay him to pry that boulder loose?"

"I gave him the ring."

"The engagement ring I gave you?"

"The wedding ring you gave your whore wife first. Oh, you think I didn't know?"

"Nonsense."

"We crossed paths in town. The slut eyed my ring, told me it was very nice. I knew by the look on her face that she'd recognized it. It was the wedding ring you gave her."

"What does it matter?"

"How fitting it should pay for her death."

"You better hope Hardington keeps his mouth shut or I'll have to shut it for him...for good."

Excitement coursed through my veins. I had to get that ring from Hardington, one of Monty's hired guns. If Abby confirms it was Lolita's old wedding ring, I'd have leverage against Horace to run him out of town. I slapped the reins and nudged Jack forward as a plan bloomed in my mind.

Chapter Twenty

Abby's divorce

Threrising sun attacked my eyes and sent a sharp stab to my temple. I groaned and pulled my blanket over my head. Lolita wanted me to get up. I could feel her pushing. The skin on my arms felt sensitive, like pins were pricking me from the inside. My mind was in a fog, and I fought the urge to give in to her. I didn't want to face the day. Didn't want to play mommy. Didn't want the chores. Didn't want the backbreaking labor this wretched life demanded. But the kids were up.

I peeked out from under the covers. Cattie handed Joseph a spoon and they ate what smelled like porridge. Weren't they sick of those oats by now? I was. Champagne...how lovely it would be...and fancy cakes. I got out of bed and stretched.

The children ran over and hugged me. I pointed out the familiar necklace around Cattie's neck and noticed Joseph wore the same blue-eyed stone. "These are very nice."

"Mister Benjamin gave them to us."

"I hope you thanked him for such a fancy gift."

Cattie nodded.

"Go about your chores and have this place tidied up before I return home."

"Can we go down to the river?"

I scowled. *The river is too dangerous.*

"Mamma?"

I blinked and looked down at Cattie. "Of course you can go to the river...but only after you finish your chores."

Why did I say that?

Lolita nudged the back of my mind. *"They love playing by the river. What is the matter with you?"*

I couldn't tell her. Didn't dare take the chance that she'd change history. She couldn't save her kids. I had to do it...and I also had to get to work.

I drove the wagon into town.

Hoots and whistles greeted me as I tied the horse to the hitching post in front of the Boomerang. Delighted, I sashayed past the men, my breasts bouncing. "Hey, boys. You just gonna stand outside or are you coming in to hear Lolita sing?" I puckered my lips.

"Sure thing, darlin'."

"Wouldn't want to miss yer sweet voice." A big strapping fella slapped my ass.

I pivoted around and hooked my finger under his chin. "Now, Tommy boy, you just save all your energy for later."

Really? Really? No way. My mind revolted against Lolita's flirtatious behavior.

"Abigail."

Horace?

I spun around. "Hijo de un burro." I had no idea what I'd just screamed, but the frown on Horace's face told me it wasn't a pleasantry. By his side stood his whore, Sadie, a prissy looking Southern Bell with dove-white skin and curly brown hair. I rushed toward her, my nails poised to yank out her hair. More Spanish words flew from my mouth, profanities I assumed by the tone. Lolita was in full attack mode, yet, thank God, I was aware of my actions. If someone didn't stop me, if I didn't stop Lolita, Sadie's perfectly coiffed hair, neatly tucked beneath a yellow bonnet, was going to look like she'd been through a wind tunnel. As I charged at her, her eyes widened with fear.

"Abby," a familiar deep voice bellowed.

My fingers were inches from Sadie's bonnet when a strong hand locked around my arm and stopped me.

Wyatt calmly lowered my claws. "Take it easy."

Horace looped his arm around his mistress and snatched her out of harm's way. Out the corner of my eye, I watched him softly speaking to her.

Wyatt released my arm. "Abby. Horace has something to tell you."

A stabbing throb attacked my temple. "I do not care what

that pig has to say. He is not taking my children."

"Lolita, just shut up and listen."

My heated gaze bore into Horace.

He straightened and thrust back his shoulders. "Abigail. I am granting you a divorce."

Shocked. I stood there staring, not sure if his words made me want to scream with anger or scream hallelujah.

"How dare he leave Lolita for another woman?"

"Come on, Lolita. Divorce means you're free."

"No man walks away from Lolita."

"But he's a pig. Just shut up and let me handle this."

My next words came out in Lolita's voice. "I will give you a divorce but not my children."

Horace shot Wyatt a nasty look. "Don't worry. I'm leaving town. Without them."

"Why the change of mind? Why leaving town? What does he think, I am sad? Hijo de un burro."

I shook my head to shut out Lolita's jabbering, but the tantrum spinning in my head made me dizzy. I leaned into Wyatt's chest for support.

"Abby, breathe slow and easy." Wyatt's strong hands on my hips kept me on my feet. "He's doing the right thing."

What did Wyatt know? What did he do? Horace wouldn't just get up and leave without taking those kids with him, but if he did, he'd change the future in devastating ways.

"Just say yes. The judge will be in town tomorrow." Then Wyatt whispered in my ear, "You know what this means, right?"

I took a deep, calming breath. "Yes, of course."

"He is not getting off so easy. I will put a knife in his gut, stick him like a pig."

"Stop." I pushed Lolita aside. With Horace out of the picture, the kids were safe from Sadie, anyway, but I feared a murderer still lurked in the background.

Wyatt and the gunslinger

It was over. The judge granted Lolita a divorce. Horace and Sadie hightailed it out of town.

"How did you do it?" Abby twirled a lace umbrella over her head.

"Sadie confessed to attempted murder. She hired a guy named Hardington to push the boulder down the mountain, paid him with your wedding ring."

"I thought I recognized it, but how did you know?"

"I overheard her and Horace arguing. An open window is not good for private conversations. I told the Sheriff. He made a deal with Horace to keep Sadie out of jail. Grant Lolita a divorce and leave town without the kids. Problem solved."

"But why did she want me dead?"

"Sadie was jealous. She wanted you out of the picture so Horace had a free path to getting the kids."

"So she had no motive to be on the list."

"Dead end there."

"Lolita did love him...once. He had a way about him. She felt cherished...once."

"Horace is a fool."

Her crestfallen expression nipped at my emotion. Maybe Lolita had a heart after all. Horace's abandonment took a toll on her. And the kids. I wondered what she was like before he'd left her. Was she just tired of chores and job? I knew how hard and long Abby worked, and then she came home and took care of kids that weren't really hers. I admired her strength.

I took her hand in mine. She remained silent, closed her eyes, and pinched the bridge of her nose. "Well, I can take Sadie off the list."

"And Horace...ah...was he on the list?"

Abby nodded yes. "So, Benjamin is off, Hank is off...that leaves Monty."

I ushered her down an alley between the mercantile and the hotel. "I've got the Sheriff looking into the possibility that he'd murdered his wife. I hope he will lock that bastard up once and for all. End of threats."

"Did you talk to him about the fire?"

"I told him my suspicions. He's looking into Monty's hired guns."

"Yet he hasn't done anything. I still see those nasty men walking around town."

"Look..." I gave her arm a little squeeze. "Don't worry about them. Samuel's a good man. I bet he's working on arresting them right now."

She licked her lips. "Wyatt?"

"Yes?" I studied the delicate curves of her mouth.

"Thanks for caring about Cattie and Joseph."

"Heck. Those kids are great."

"And for me too."

"You got me there." I thumbed her cheek. I did care. A whole lot. *When we get out of this mess, I'm going to tell her how I feel and see where it leads.* I couldn't tell her now, not with Lolita staring at me. "You have beautiful eyes. Anybody ever tell you that?"

"Some guy I just met back home noticed my green eyes." She fluttered her lashes.

Yeah. I was too chicken to tell her they were beautiful. Gently, I tilted up her chin, and her dreamy, wistful gaze met mine. "Did you know the color green connotes empathy and compassion?"

"And your blue eyes...what do they mean?"

"I'm direct, forceful, and someone with the gifts of insight and observation. But that's not really me. You're the one with the premonitions."

"Blue eyes should mean you're protective, caring, and confident."

Her words hit a soft spot in my heart. "You may be wearing Lolita's body, but I'm looking into *your* eyes, Abby. I see you in there."

"I don't feel like me. Sometimes the line between where she starts and I leave off is blurred. I feel all jumbled."

"I know the difference," I reassured her. "You're nothing like her. Lolita is wild and unfettered."

"And gorgeous."

"Her looks are overrated, especially when she flaunts it." As I said the words I hoped would comfort Abby, I realized I'd changed. Looks were the first thing I judged when I decided if I'd go out with a woman or not. God, what a shallow jerk I'd been.

Yeah. Abby had gotten under my skin. The redhead with

the adorable smudge of lotion on her mouth, the woman with exotic eyes that could see into my soul, she'd captured my heart from the beginning, dragged me across time, and made me see the error of my ways. No other woman could judge me, badger me, or understand me the way she did, even encouraged me to be a doctor, no less, to follow my dream, not my father's.

"We should go. Someone might see us."

"Not that it matters. You're a divorced woman now."

"Is that all I am to you?"

"Wouldn't you like to know." I wasn't willing to reveal my feelings to Abby. Lolita might think those feelings were for her. Besides, my emotions were screwed up. Standing here, wanting to kiss her, I'd have to pull Lolita into my arms, and that would only confuse our emotions more. If we got hot and heavy now, what would happen when and if we made it back home? I'd go back to college; she'd stay at her library job in town. Where would that leave us? Would a long-distance relationship last? Maybe she'd get tired of waiting and find someone else. I'd lose my concentration, thinking about the what-ifs between us, and I'd need to study hard to keep up my grades. Becoming a doctor was a high bar to set for myself. However, with Abby, anything was possible.

We stepped out of the alleyway and made our way to the wagon. A gunshot blasted the air. I grabbed Abby, shoved her behind the wagon, and spun to face the gunman standing across the street.

A lean man, dressed from head to toe in black, shoved his pistol into the holster at his side. "I hear you're lookin' for me." He adjusted the black-brimmed hat on his head.

"Depends. Who are you?"

"Blackjack."

"Nope. Never heard of you." I began to turn away, hoping he'd shrug and walk off.

"You Wyatt, right?"

Damn. I faced him again. "Wyatt Beaufort. The one and only."

"Then I got the right fleecer." He strode across the street in my direction.

I eyed the weapon at his side, the way his fingers played

with the pearl handle. "What do you want?"

"Let's just say I'm gonna settle a score for someone who don't like being blackmailed into leaving town."

Horace. I should have known he wouldn't leave peacefully. "I didn't blackmail anybody."

"Not what I heard."

Folks began to scatter. Faces peered behind windows. Huddled figures stood in doorways.

"Guess you must be Hardington."

"So you *have* heard of me."

"I've not been looking for you, but seeing as how you found me, I think you got some confessing the Sheriff might like to hear about."

"Now why would I want to do that when all I got to do is shut you up for good?"

"Sounds like a threat, to me." I took a step toward him and felt a hand on my arm.

"Wyatt, no."

"Abby, go back behind the wagon. I got this."

"He's got a gun."

"So do I." I patted the colt at my side. I hated wearing it, but reality being what it was in the Wild West, it became a necessity. I'd bought the weapon to deter a fight, not with the intention of actually shooting anyone.

"But he's a gunslinger."

"Yeah. He'll probably kill me. Abby, go."

The anxiety in her eyes made me want to stop, gather her close, and tell her not to worry, but I couldn't lie to her. I had no place in a gunfight.

Blackjack stopped in the middle of the street. "You gonna talk to that whore or face me like a man?"

I fisted my hand and took a deep breath. "The lady and I are not finished." I turned my back to him.

She squeezed my arm. "Wyatt, please—"

I placed a kiss on her forehead. "Go back to the wagon."

She stepped back and took cover.

As I walked toward Blackjack, I noticed the street was completely clear of people and horse traffic.

"That's far enough," he ordered.

I kept walking, my hands in the air, my pistol holstered. "Let's settle this man to man. See what you got." I stopped. Slowly, with two fingers, I pulled the gun from my holster and placed it on the ground. A playing card landed at my feet, the Jack of Spades.

I straightened. "You fixin' to play cards? I'm all in."

"If you don't pick up your gun, I'll drop you where you stand."

I remained still and tried to come up with a plan to take his gun away. "Let's talk about this—"

"You got a death wish? I'd be mighty happy to oblige." He pulled out his pistol and pointed it at me.

My chest clenched. Over my thudding pulse, the silence unnerved me. All eyes waited for me to make my move. I held my hands out to my side. "You just gonna shoot an unarmed man? I'm guessing that's a sure path to a hanging. Drop the gun, and we'll settle this with our fists."

"Pick up your gun, you coward."

If I moved closer, he'd shoot. If I didn't reach for my gun, he'd shoot. Even if I did attempt to participate in a scene straight out of the old west, I'd be a dead man. As sweat slid down my forehead, I looked down at my gun. I'd been practicing. I was pretty good, but against a man with years of experience under his belt...

I bent my knees, kept my eye on Blackjack, and picked up the gun.

Abby and the gunfight

Helpless, I stood behind the wagon, my stomach rolling with dread. I wanted to run into the street. Stop Wyatt. Stop the foolishness. My feet wouldn't move despite my best intentions.

Unable to look at the gun pointed at Wyatt without feeling sick, I watched a gust of warm wind pick up strands of his hair and whip them across his eyes.

Sunlight glimmered on the gunslinger's gold belt buckle. Sharp metal spurs and dusty worn boots looked as rugged as the man wearing them. A black bandanna hung around his neck and a wide-brimmed black hat shaded his eyes. He looked the part of a killer, a man with no morals. Another gust of wind blew a tumbleweed across the street.

As Wyatt picked up his gun, tension clenched my chest like a ton of bricks had suddenly crushed my lungs. I opened my mouth to suck in a gulp of air and scream, but a soothing thought silenced me. This was not our time. Not our time. He couldn't die.

Wyatt returned his gun to his holster.

Blackjack holstered his gun, stared at Wyatt with narrow eyes, hand now poised to draw.

If either one of them got killed, the consequences would be permanent. Whatever happened here today would change every tomorrow hereafter. Tears welled as I contemplated a world without the man I deeply cared about...maybe even loved. My head spinning with dread, I broke cover and ran before Lolita could stop me.

"Abby, no."

"Shut up and let me fix this."

I stopped between the two men, arms spread, palms out. "Wait."

Both men scowled at me.

"Abby, get out of the way."

I turned to face Wyatt. Nothing I could say would make him back down from this gunfight. Everyone's attention was on him. Pride allowed him no escape. I ripped off a lace cuff from my sleeve then brushed back a lock of hair from his face.

"Abby, are you crazy?" He grabbed my arm. "Go back. You're going to get hurt."

"The sun is in his eyes, and the wind is coming from your right." I reached up, my hands trembling, and gathered his shoulder-length hair together. "Your hair keeps blowing in your face." Though I tried my best to hold them back, tears clouded my vision as I tied his golden locks into a ponytail.

"Hey, you coward. You gonna hide behind a woman's skirt or draw?"

Blackjack's malicious tone tied a knot in my windpipe.

"Abby, please—"

"You can't die."

Marianne Petit

He thumbed a tear from my cheek. "If I don't make it, take care of the kids."

I leaned in and brushed my lips against his cheek. "And you can't kill him," I whispered.

"I know." Wyatt drew me to his chest and kissed me, a kiss of passion, or fear that this would be his last chance. I clung to him, my tears streaming down. I felt his body tremble as he released me as abruptly as he had drawn me closer. "You're one hell of a woman."

There was nothing else I could say, so much I wanted to say, but our fate, and the fate of the world, awaited the outcome of a single gunfight on a dusty street in Dry Diggins. I gathered the little stamina I had left and carefully backed toward the wagon.

"So, greenhorn. That pistol hangin' there for decoration or you gonna pull it on me?" Blackjack's fingers twitched over the butt of his gun.

Wyatt stood tall. "Well, now, seeing how you're the expert gunfighter, you first."

A pang of fear attacked my chest. I held my breath.

The cowering townsfolk remained silent.

The wind intensified. Santa Ana's robust, breathy air lifted the hem of my skirt and billowed Wyatt's blue shirt. Blackjack's hat flew off.

Gunfire banged through the air. My shoulders jerked. I squeezed my eyes shut, afraid to look.

Please don't let Wyatt be dead. Please...

"This is all your fault," Lolita shrieked. *"Open my eyes so I can see if he is dead."*

"I can't."

Gunsmoke reached my nostrils. Nausea roiled in my stomach.

Movement and chatter filtered into my numb brain.

"Do it, Abby. I have to see."

Gathering my courage, I opened my eyes and sought Wyatt out. He was still standing. My heart jolted. I ran toward him as he holstered his gun. "Wyatt. Wyatt. You're okay."

A pale face with haunted eyes stared back at me. "I shot him."

I glanced at Blackjack who stood there holding his gun arm. Blood dripped from his hand to the gun lying in the dirt. The wince in his eyes projected pain and anger. He dropped to his knees. "Ya shoulda killed me, greenhorn."

"The lady wouldn't let me." Wyatt rushed to him, kicked the gun out of his reach.

Blackjack struggled to rise but Wyatt shoved him to the ground and jammed a knee in his chest. "Give me the ring, you bastard."

"I don't know what you're talking about."

Wyatt brought his fist to Blackjack's face. "The ring Sadie gave you to send that boulder down the mountainside. Give it to me now."

"You're crazy."

Wyatt slugged him in the nose. "The ring."

"All right. All right." He spit blood. "My shirt pocket."

Wyatt moved his knee from Blackjack's chest to his stomach then fished the ring from his pocket and stood. "It's not yours."

The Sheriff strode to us and yanked Blackjack to his feet. "I warned you about causing trouble in my town."

Wyatt faced me. "This belongs to Lolita."

I noticed him grimace as he handed me the ring. Blood drained from my face as I stared at him. "Oh my God. Wyatt. You've been shot."

Wyatt's bullet wound

Though I wanted retribution for his part in the plot to kill Abby, I felt no satisfaction, only revulsion at having shot Blackjack. A weird wave of heat, a sticky wet sensation on my left shoulder broke through my anger.

"You're bleeding." Abby stared at me with wide eyes full of horror.

I looked down at the blood stain on my shirt. The excruciating throb felt like I'd been speared by a red-hot poker. Nothing I'd ever experienced compared to the intense burn. I lifted my arm and cringed; the pain made me light-headed. "I can't believe I'm not dead."

Abby slipped under my good arm and supported my weight. "You need a doctor."

"Shit." I felt like a walking zombie as Abby led me toward the wagon. Nothing seemed in focus, but I could make out the Sheriff walking toward us.

He was holding Blackjack by the scruff of his shirt. "The doc's back in town. You both need to see him."

I stopped short of the wagon. "Have the doc tend to Blackjack first. I'll be all right for now."

Abby huffed. "Don't be absurd."

I took a deep breath, fought dizziness and the sensation I was about to pass out. Staggering forward, each step was absolute agony. "Whiskey. I need whiskey." I turned Abby toward the saloon.

Benjamin met us as we stepped up on the boardwalk. "What happened?"

"I should've never bought that gun."

The Sheriff approached from the doctor's office. "Take him over there." He pointed to his jailhouse. "I've got some questions for him."

Another wave of pain shot through me. "Ask Blackjack why he wants me dead."

"Doc's patching him up. I'll get to him later."

"How much trouble am I in?"

"Depends on why you shot him."

I grimaced. "He shot me first."

"Sheriff, do we have to do this now?" Annoyance hardened Abby's voice.

Drawing strength from her presence, I straightened my stance and bit back a wince. "Let's just get it over with."

Benjamin and Abby helped me lumber to the jailhouse where they sat me on the flimsy, filthy cot in the jail cell. I hoped the bars around me wouldn't be permanent.

The Sheriff drew up a chair. "What's this all about?"

"Abby, show him."

She opened her hand and held out the ring, the evidence I needed to show just cause. "You're looking at the payment he received for helping Sadie take a crack at Lolita...with that boulder."

"Why are you telling me this now instead of earlier?"

"With Horace gone, I thought Lolita would be safe. The matter was closed until Blackjack Hardington called me out. Now he can hang for his part in all of it."

"Still don't answer why he came gunning for you."

"Horace hired him to kill me...some kind of payback for you running him and Sadie out of town."

"Well then, looks like justice was served." He stood. "I've got some business to attend to. Lolita, my apologies, but the doc will take a look at him pretty soon."

"Thanks for opening your jail to us."

He tipped his hat and walked out.

"Abby, take a look at my shoulder."

Scowling, she opened my shirt. "Benjamin, where can we get some hot water?"

"The saloon."

"Clean towels, too."

"Be right back, Miss Lolita."

She reached under her skirt and tore off a length of her slip. "You're a bloody mess."

I drew my gaze to her face, a face filled with concern. "I'm not supposed to hurt people. I'm supposed to heal them."

"It was you or him. You had no choice, you damn fool." She pressed the strip of cloth on the wound.

I took a deep, painful breath. "There's always a choice, but no, I had to play gunslinger when I should have tried harder to reason with him."

"He didn't come to talk, Wyatt."

"When I saw him challenge me, saw the townsfolk scatter, when I stood in the street with the dusty ground beneath my feet, with the blazing sun beating down on me, I felt like a real cowboy who just wanted to punish the man who tried to kill you. *Western justice* I guess. I couldn't run. I couldn't back down."

"I know."

Benjamin placed a bowl of water and a towel on the cot and offered me a bottle of whiskey.

I grabbed the bottle, pulled the cork out with my teeth, and downed the booze. My throat burned, but nothing as fierce as my shoulder.

"How does it look?" Benjamin asked Abby.

"The bullet went in and out through the meat." She dipped the towel in the water and rubbed the wound.

I gasped and held my breath so I wouldn't scream. "Get the doctor. Get the doctor."

"Too late." Benjamin showed me a curved needle threaded with catgut. "He got called out to Cold Springs for a birthing gone wrong. Gave me this on his way out."

I ground my molars. "Abby, you've got to sew me up."

"I can't."

"I'll tell you what to do...talk you through it."

"But I'll only hurt you worse."

"I'm used to pain." Yeah. I'd taken my share of hits in the dojo and on the football field, but this... "Just do it, Abby." I shook my head in disbelief. "We're running out of time." I took another swig of whiskey and ignored the burn.

She grabbed the bottle from me and poured whiskey on the wound.

I gritted my teeth and fought for internal peace. The burn tightened every muscle in my body. If I looked, I was sure I'd see flames bursting from my shoulder. I needed to center myself, focus somewhere far away from the pain and clear my mind of gunslingers and murder.

Abby's in love

Tears clouded my vision as I sewed pieces of Wyatt's flesh back together while trying not to gag. I'd almost lost him. I still could. I did my best to make sure the wound was clean, and my needle was sterilized in a candle flame, but in these crude conditions, I was justified to worry. An infection could be deadly.

Several times I felt his bloody flesh cringe beneath my shaking hands as the needle penetrated his skin and the catgut tightened when I pulled. Several times I hesitated, only to have him order me to continue spearing his flesh and lacing the wound tight.

The room felt stifling. Sweat slid between my breasts and dotted my face. I wiped my forehead with the back of my arm.

Between pouring whiskey over his wound and him drinking several gulps, the bottle was almost empty.

Wyatt was exhausted as I pulled the needle through the final piece of ragged flesh and knotted the catgut. He fell over on his side. I lifted his feet to the cot, covered him with the green blanket, and let him rest.

Benjamin, my surgical assistant, looked like he'd just witnessed a car wreck. He stood. "I've got work to do at the saloon. Let me know if you need anything else."

I sat there all night, waiting, watching Wyatt for any sign of fever. I couldn't sleep. Occasionally he would groan, and I'd jump from the chair and place my fingers on his forehead. I'd almost lost him in a crazy gunfight, now the threat of infection could snatch him away. Tears ran down my face. I wished I had Cindi's shoulder to cry on. I'd already lost someone I loved: my mother. I couldn't lose another.

I had an epiphany that night, prompted by Wyatt's close call with death. Love. Did those feelings spring up from the fear of being alone in a world so foreign from the one I was used to? Did the need to cling to the familiar overshadow reason, or had the emotion been lying in wait, awoken by a greater fear, the one of losing Wyatt forever?

I didn't know how love between a man and a woman felt. I had nothing to compare it to. If the thankfulness I felt with every stitch, and the swell in my heart with every breath he took was love, then I was smitten. If the tears blurring my vision, and the worry ripping my heart as gunfire rattled the air was love, then I was besotted.

My gaze lingered on his magnificent body. I wondered if the scar my nervous fingers inflicted would follow him back to our time. How much of what happened here would stick? How much of what happened here would we remember? Would this feeling of love carry back with me or will all this feel like a vague dream? Maybe it would be better if we never went back home.

With teary eyes, I tenderly ran my finger through the light golden patch of hair on his sculpted chest. He had to get better.

He just had to.

Wyatt tossed and turned all the next day. Samuel's wife brought me a washbasin and I placed cool compresses on Wyatt's feverish skin. He'd wake, I'd feed him soup, then he'd fall asleep. I couldn't eat much; grabbed a catnap when I could.

The clock on the wall chimed five times. Slumped in a chair, I watched dust particles float in streams of evening light that beamed in around the window shade. Wyatt slept peacefully on the cot beside me. I reached over and put my hand on his forehead relieved to feel warm skin against my palm. No fever.

My gentle touch roused him. He patted the blanket, and I gladly settled in beside him. Careful to stay away from his wound, I laid my head on his good shoulder. I sighed, content to be close to him.

"Such a heavy sigh. What's bothering you?" he asked softly.

A lot worried me but now was not the time to get him riled up. "I'm afraid I did a lousy job."

"I'm sure you didn't." He caressed my hair. "Any wound your fingers touch will heal like magic."

Heat crept up my neck at his compliment. I wanted to ask about the kiss before the gunfight? *Did it mean as much to you as it meant to me?* Instead, I asked, "Are you in pain?"

"Nothing I can't handle, now that you're in my arms."

Could it be he felt the same as I did? Hope lifted the uncertainty of my mood. It felt like heaven lying here, feeling his heartbeat against my cheek and his light breath against my forehead I wanted to stay in the crook of his arm forever.

He hugged me. "I didn't mean to put you through such worry."

I lifted my head and looked into eyes so etched with torment that tears, once again, let loose. "You've gone through so much these past few weeks. It's all my fault."

He shook his head, a stubborn frown on his brow as he brushed aside my tears. "I'm grateful you're here."

I shuddered. "If I hadn't gone for a swim, neither one of us would be here."

"And we wouldn't have found each other." He released his loving hold on me and began to rise. I sat up, missing his warmth, an empty feeling taking control of my emotions. "Slip this on." I'd fashioned a sling from a Boomerang towel.

He swung his legs off the cot and stood. "See? Look. Good as new."

"We should check on the kids." I slipped my arm around his waist. "Just in case you get woozy." I needed to feel him close beside me.

Wyatt drove the wagon, left arm in a sling and all, despite my insistence that I drive. Streaks of orange and pink cut through the soft blue of a fading day. Tree shadows stretched across the ground. The winds died, leaving a comfortable freshness that cooled my heated body. Each of us lost in our own thoughts, the words I longed to say never made it out of my mouth. I couldn't decide if I was afraid to say I loved him in fear he wouldn't feel the same or if I hesitated because I was afraid of my own feelings. If I said the word out loud, it would be out there in the universe permanently. If I gave my heart away, it could be broken again. My thoughts were as taxing as the bumpy wagon ride. I stared at the swaying horse's mane as he trotted along the uneven ground. Maybe it wasn't love. Maybe what I felt was overly charged attraction or latent infatuation. I didn't know, but blaming my swinging emotions on Lolita was a copout.

We found the children in Benjamin's tent, playing with wooden toys I didn't recognize. They ran up to me, their little arms surrounding me in a big hug. Their warm greeting lightened my heart.

"I am so happy to see you guys." I kissed the tops of their heads. "And you have new toys."

"Daisy brought them over," Benjamin said.

"Look at my new train," Joseph chimed in with pride.

Hearing his words addressed to me still surprised me. "It's lovely." Perhaps the fear of my death prompted his speech to return. I'll never know for sure, but I was grateful he'd come out of his shell. "I love you both."

Benjamin eyed Wyatt's shoulder. "You're looking a little better." The color returned to Wyatt's cheeks, but his eyes still had a haunted look to them that worried me.

"I had an angel watching over me."

Our gazes met. I smiled. "You need to take it easy. I have

no desire to repeat my lousy sewing should you rip open my fabulous stitches."

He stepped up to me. "Really, Abby. Thank you. I know how difficult that surgery was for you." His gentle tone relaxed some of the angst brought on by hours of worry. I breathed a little easier.

"Can Mister Benjamin and Mister Wyatt stay for dinner?" Cattie's face looked hopeful.

"I don't see why not."

"Let's all eat at the hotel," Wyatt said. "It's on me."

We all piled into the wagon. Benjamin took the reins.

Abby meets the brothers

The El Dorado Hotel dining room was more crowded than usual. Rich strikes were the topic of conversation. Monty sat at a table, picking at a plate of food. He looked up as we passed by. "I see you lived," he snarled at Wyatt with contempt.

I smiled sweetly, despite my annoyance. Beside me, Wyatt tensed. I had the feeling a sharp retort wasn't far behind. I shot him a pleading look and breathed a little easier when he took hold of my elbow and guided me to the far corner of the room.

We ordered roast beef and potatoes. The kids were starving. As we ate, my gaze darted to Wyatt who was eyeing me. Was he thinking about our kiss, the kiss that turned my world upside down? I'd always refused to let him get that close, but now the emotional floodgates had opened. I smiled at him and forked a potato.

Midway through our meal, Monty strolled up. "Lolita, I expect you back at work tonight. We have much to talk about."

My dinner turned in my stomach. What did he want to talk to me about? Had he heard that I was now divorced? What would he expect of me? He already thought he owned me. Now he wouldn't stop at getting what he wanted: me sharing his bed.

"One hour, Lolita." He tousled Joseph's hair. "See you then."

Wyatt pushed his chair back and stood. His hand rested possessively on my shoulder. "She'll be there when she's ready."

"It is okay, Wyatt. I will be there with bells on." If Monty had heard the sweet sarcasm in Lolita's voice, he didn't show it.

A satisfied gloat twisted Monty's lips. He turned and headed for the door.

Wyatt shot me a killer look.

"Before you say anything, I'll be there because I have to be there to keep an eye on him."

"I still don't like it."

"It's the only way to..." I tipped my head toward the children fixated on their plates. "You know."

"I can keep an eye on our boss," Benjamin said.

I leaned toward him. "I can get closer to him than either one of you."

My words did little to appease both men. Wyatt's displeasure was apparent in the tight line of his mouth and the tick in his strong jaw. Benjamin shook his head and rubbed the back of his neck, relieving the tension I was sure my stubbornness had induced.

"Monty Doble?" a gruff voice bellowed, silencing the diners.

Monty stopped short of the door. His shocked expression quickly withered to aloofness.

A man in his late twenties and built like a refrigerator puffed out his chest and glanced around the room. "Where the hell is that damn Monty Doble?"

Wyatt pointed at Monty. "He's the man you're looking for."

Monty spun around, his gaze piercing Wyatt like poisoned arrows. "He's delusional, folks. Everyone knows my name is Colton." His menacing stare traveled over the patrons. As if fearing they'd ordered their last meals, they nodded.

The stranger's round face was mottled with rage. "Me and my brothers been lookin' for you."

Monty stood firm. "Might I ask...who the hell are you?"

"Lawrence Christen. We never met but I'm sure you know my brother."

The door swung open, and in walked a smaller man, elfin in stature but broad across the shoulders and hostile fire in his eyes. If not for his angry yet confident stride, one would think him a pushover. He stood fast beside his brother and glared at Monty. "You're the son-of-a-bitch who killed our sister."

A murmur reverberated through the dining room.

Monty huffed. "Well, well, well, if it isn't the family runt, Eunice. I thought you were dead."

"You thought wrong." The brothers poised their hands over their pistols. "Time to die, Monty."

Eunice had no sooner finished voicing the threat when Monty's gunslingers stepped in, guns drawn on the brothers.

I shot to my feet, pulled the kids from their chairs, and hustled them into the kitchen where I watched at the door. Wyatt had gotten to his feet but hadn't charged into the showdown, as I would have expected. Maybe he realized he was definitely outgunned.

"You boys are a mite over your heads," Monty barked. "Best go back home to your mamma."

The brothers looked at the gunmen fearfully... then backed out the door.

Monty laughed. "Good job, boys. Keep an eye out for them to come back."

The gunslingers stepped outside.

Monty stepped to the bar and ordered a double whiskey.

I rushed back to our table. "Wyatt. Are you crazy? You're looking to get yourself killed. How many close calls are enough for you?" My words rushed out faster than I could think.

He retook his seat. "That bastard needs to be behind bars."

"You shouldn't have fingered him. Now you're on Monty's radar. He's going to send his hired guns after you to find out how you knew his last name was Doble." I laid my napkin over my dinner, my appetite gone. "Then they're going to kill you."

"Within a week, the Sheriff will find the evidence he needs to lock him up, either for the fire or the murder of his wife."

"And how's that supposed to help? We have three days until the blue moon."

The question charged the air between us. He had no answer, just stabbed his roast beef with a fork and went back to his meal as if nothing had happened.

Chapter Twenty-One

Wyatt's intentions

Two days passed since the showdown in the street, and when I closed my eyes, I still saw myself fire the gun. I saw the smoke, felt my fear, and saw Blackjack drop his gun. Almost dying and shooting someone was something not quickly forgotten, nor was the kiss, our kiss moments before the gunfight.

I paced the small floor inside my house, trying to convince myself to go over and talk to Abby. I knew she wondered why I hadn't said anything about that kiss. Actually, if I were in her shoes I'd be wondering if it meant anything, too.

Kissing her had just complicated our relationship. I hated the nagging voice in the back of my mind, hinting I wasn't sure who I'd actually kissed. I felt like a heel. I wanted to tell her how incredible it was. Our kiss made all the other women I'd kissed pale in comparison. Every time I closed my eyes, I saw a strikingly beautiful face. Lolita's face. Even though everything about her personality was a turn-off, the shallow part of me wondered if her perfect body turned me on. But the more I got to know Abby, talked to her, thought about her, the more I knew I was in love with the woman inside, not the body outside.

I interlocked my fingers on the back of my head and let out a frustrated breath.

Maybe I was just making up excuses. Maybe I was afraid of what I was feeling. Abby wasn't like all the others. The idea of making love to her and not having a real relationship, like with Pam, didn't sit right. Where did that leave us when we returned home? If we returned home. We were going to live across country from each other. States apart. It wasn't like I could just drop in on weekends. However, maybe a love born across time and space could survive a long-distance relationship until I finished med-school. There had to be a way to work it out.

I'd never felt this conflicted before. I had to be sure about how she felt about me. Maybe Abby was as conflicted as me, even if for different reasons, hers being in Lolita's skin, mine being outside, looking at the body and wanting the woman within. I needed to say something. I had to suck it up and go over there. Determined to talk to her, I opened the door and stepped outside.

An overcast sky greeted me. Soon the camp would be lit with campfires. Men would sit around and talk about their finds or their failures. Banjos and harmonicas would rise above the chatter. It would be so easy to pull up a log, sit, and pretend no earth-shattering revelation had rocked my world.

I stared at the blanket flap serving as Abby's door. *It's just a couple of steps. Walk in. Get your feelings out in the open.*

Why was I so nervous? Women never made me nervous. I wiped my clammy hands on my pants then took a step toward her home. My thoughts jumbled, my courage waned, and I turned around. "Abby, it's like this..." I mumbled. "No." I shook my head. "Abby, I've got a thing for you." *That sounds lame.* I wrung my hands. "I really care about you." *Yeah.* I pivoted. I could start with that. It was the truth. I did care...a lot. I squared my shoulders, stepped forward then...*nope.* I veered left into Benjamin's tent.

He looked up as I entered.

"Sorry for just barging in."

"Come join me." He gestured to the chair beside the table where he sat.

"I need to talk to you," *about me being a freaking coward.*

"I'd be more than obliged to listen."

"I...hmm." I rubbed my stiff neck. "It's like this..." Stalling wasn't helping, but I wasn't sure talking would be helpful either. Spilling my guts to another guy wasn't something I was comfortable with. The only locker-room talk about women was who got lucky, and did you see the tits on that cheerleader?

"Wyatt, my friend. Sit. Let's put to rest whatever worries your mind."

I sat. Where to start? My foot tapped the floor. I wanted to ask, *Hey, did you see the big game on TV last night?* I wanted to talk about anything except my mixed-up feelings.

"Old Judd had a hefty find a few days back." Benjamin poured clear liquid into two glasses and slid one toward me.

I lifted the glass and breathed in the strong fumes that smelled like pure alcohol. "Lucky man." I took a swig. The fire-like booze burned its way down my esophagus. I coughed. "Whew, that's got some kick."

Benjamin smiled. "Made it myself."

Moonshine, of course. I raised my glass. "To you then."

Glasses clinked, and another chug of liquor burned down my throat.

"Heard Judd laid down two thousand dollars' worth of gold dust on the faro table. Word around town says he doubled his money." Benjamin poured another round. "Monty was angry enough to eat a skunk."

Was she as effected by our kiss as I was? Thinking about how those lips felt pressed against mine, the warmth, the taste of her tongue was driving me crazy.

"And you, my friend, how do you fare?"

"I've had better days before I shot someone. How did you get over killing a man?"

Benjamin looked at me with troubled eyes. "I must confess, I have yet to forgive myself. Sometimes I confess out loud in my sleep."

"I understand."

"When my mind is troubled by past events I cannot change, I lose myself in my music. You must find something you can escape into."

Centering myself with meditation usually eased my mind, but it wasn't working. "I guess it's going to take some time."

"Time, and a good stiff drink." Again, he filled our glasses.

We toasted and took a swig. "Benjamin, what do you think about Lolita?"

"She is a fine, good-looking woman."

"Yes." And that was the problem. Abby looked nothing like the woman I saw every day, and as much as I wanted to believe I had feelings for Abby, how was I to explain my confusion over their personalities without sounding like a jerk.

"What are your intentions toward Miss Lolita?"

"My intentions?" I studied the moonshine in the bottom of my glass. Benjamin's question rolled over and over, and my thoughts began dissipating like a wave sinking into the sand. Over the rim of my glass, I saw him studying me, waiting for an answer.

"I don't know."

"Therein lies the problem. Figure it out."

I sat in silence, mulling over Benjamin's words. It was Abby I wanted, the alluring redhead with a smile that lit up those incredible green eyes, the smart, vulnerable woman who I looked forward to getting to know really well, especially if and when we get back home, but winning her over without involving Lolita was going to be a challenge.

Abby's secret revealed

As I walked out of my home, Wyatt stepped out of Benjamin's tent, and my heart leapt. I couldn't get our kiss out of my mind. An unexpected kiss I didn't want to end, a kiss so wonderful that I hadn't heard a peep out of Lolita since. I shouldn't have been surprised; I'd been studying those lips for weeks, all the while she had been coaxing me to go for what I wanted.

"How is your shoulder?"

"It's killing me."

"Maybe I should help you change the dressing." Any excuse to see his shirtless chest.

"That would be appreciated."

We walked the few steps to Wyatt's cabin, he ushered me in, and delicious nerves fluttered in my stomach. "I checked in on you yesterday, but you were sleeping." Seeing him shirtless lying asleep on his bed, his arms and chest tan against the white sheet made me want to walk over and slide my body next to him.

"You should have woke me up. I would have enjoyed your company."

"I thought about it, but you needed to rest." I thought about a lot of things: kissing him again without the threat of death looming over us, or wondering what our future held. "Sit." I pointed to the chair and he sat.

The anticipation of undressing him, of touching him sent heat to the junction of my thighs. "I heard the Sheriff arrested Blackjack."

"That bastard deserves to rot in jail. I just hope he didn't cause some catastrophic rip in the course of world history."

"I'm sure he was arrested for something somewhere along the line." I leaned in and touched his chest and felt his breath hitch. "Off with your shirt..."

He reached out and traced the side of my cheek then ran his fingers over my lip. I shivered at his touch. "Your skin is so soft."

His warm breath caressed my face. The intimacy in his eyes triggered a retreat I refused to give in to, despite a lingering fear of being hurt all over again. It was strange...frightening. How had I gone from hating him to being completely enamored by him?

He cupped my cheeks and our lips met. He smelled like smoke and cleanly shaven skin. His lips were soft, strong, and his tongue urged me to open up for him. With a small moan, I accepted the tip of his tongue, let it caress mine, and my instincts flowed with an ease that surprised me. With his warm lips still pressed against mine, he stood. His arm encircled my waist. One hand cupped the back of my neck, his fingers intertwined with my hair as he eased me closer.

My arms embraced his body, and I ran my finger in the tender spot where his hair touched his ear.

"Oh, Abby..."

What am I doing? My heart did a flip and I pulled back. "Wyatt," I whispered, my voice breathless. "Who do you see?"

"I see you. Abby. You. I see a woman who, despite her fear of heights, crossed a steep cliff and risked her life to find me." He leaned back and took my hand. "I see a woman who hauls wood and stands over a boiling pot in hundred-degree weather, wearing layers of uncomfortable clothing, who never complains, and an angel who sat by my side when I wavered in and out of consciousness." He planted a kiss on my neck.

A gush of warmth flowed through me.

"You have beautiful eyes...four season eyes," he murmured in my ear. "White for winter, green for spring's new growth, and specks of golden summer sunrises. I watch a lot of sunrises here. Those brown specks in your irises remind me of autumn leaves."

"Why, sir..." I batted my eyes and smiled, touched by his words. "I never knew you to be such a prolific poet."

He studied my mouth as he ran his fingertips along my jaw. His intense desire heightened my own.

"And, little lady," he said with a slow southern drawl, "you got a pair of killer legs, and yes, I saw them peeking out from under your white-lace cover-up the first time I saw you at the beach."

He nibbled my ear. Frisson revved, releasing tension, awakening every nerve.

"You're smart, determined, the kind of woman who fought apprehension and rode a horse to prove she could." He planted another kiss on my neck. "You're a fighter who battles a temperamental Spanish maiden inside you. You have a big heart, and even though you don't believe it, I think you're sexy."

I chewed my lip, begging myself to believe him. He was looking at Lolita, kissing her neck, not mine. "I can't compete with her." I hated the insecurity that had to take one last shot at our relationship.

"There's no comparison."

"And our kiss before the gunfight...what was that all about?"

He sighed. "Maybe the kiss was a fearful, I'm gonna die, goodbye reaction, but I didn't want to regret letting go of you without that moment of closeness that I've wanted for so long."

"You wanted to kiss me...not Lolita?"

"That's why I'd always held back. I told myself I wouldn't kiss you the way I wanted to kiss you until we were back home in our own time when you were you, and not Lolita." He huffed. "But who knows if or when we'll ever return. In that moment, all I lived for was that kiss, and since then, all I've thought about was that kiss." His voice dripped with emotion.

His tender heartfelt words began to untangle all my apprehensive knots. I watched breathlessly as his eyes studied me with silent intensity.

"I wanted to tell you how I felt without Lolita hearing what I say." He leaned in. "You've got to believe me," he whispered against my skin. "I'm in love with the woman within."

"Even if I see ghosts?" I blurted out, not thinking. My heart hammered as I waited for his horrified reaction, sure he'd look at me as though I was crazy, a loon.

"Ghosts? Really?" His eyes met mine and I saw skepticism that made me regret having said a word.

Anxiety sprang to my chest and squeezed. "I know it sounds crazy. If I were you, I wouldn't believe me, but it really happens. I saw Cattie and Joseph's ghosts at the river, even talked to them before our trek back in time. And I've seen other's too. Please don't be angry at me for not telling you earlier. Cindi doesn't even know."

He just stared at me like his brain had just winked out.

I turned away and muttered, "I shouldn't have told you."

Wyatt placed a finger on my chin and turned my face back to him. "Your sixth sense is more than just premonitions."

"I didn't want to say any more in front of Benjamin."

His eyes morphed from dark doubt to a bright desire that shot heat through my body, chasing away the cold fear that I'd just ruined any chance of a future for us.

"That couldn't have been easy to tell me, but sharing that part of you makes me love you even more. I believe you, but I'll confess, I have no idea what it all means. After all we've been through, I want to stick around to learn what it's all about." He ran his finger along my jaw. "But it might take me a lifetime."

"You don't think I'm weird?"

"Maybe I like weird curvy redheads."

His smiling eyes promised a love I could believe in, and all doubt passed, as if it were just a fleeting fear I'd never again revisit.

Wyatt's in love

I traced the bridge of Abby's nose then ran my thumb over her luscious lips. At first, I wasn't sure she believed me when I said I loved her, but looking into her dreamy eyes and the contentment on her face softened the knots in my chest.

"I love you, Abby, and I'm not wasting another day to tell you that." I'd never said those words before, and the powerful feelings running through me excited me to my core.

Her breath caught. I wondered if she would say something. Anything. Sitting here waiting and wondering made me anxious all over again.

"Oh, Wyatt..." She pressed her mouth against mine.

I could taste her salty tears on my lips as our tongues met and explored together. My heart pounded. I looped her waist and drew her close to the heat of my body. The soft feminine feel of her form against me made me dizzy with want. Her hair smelled of sweet flowers. The contentment I felt holding her settled my worried heart.

"I love you, Wyatt." Her smoldering eyes lit with mischief as she kissed me again with a fiery passion that took my breath away. And then she was back to business. "Now let me see your bullet wound."

She lifted my shirt over my head, and I ignored the sharp pain in my shoulder. The heat traveling through my body was not from pain but from a desire to feel her touch that part of me that was throbbing with need.

She trailed her fingers down from my shoulder to my ribcage, her fingertips causing sensual delight over my bare skin as she touched every muscle. We stared into each other's eyes while she unwrapped the cloth covering my wound. Every gentle touch seduced me. She planted a kiss on my collarbone above my wound, then another on each side then one underneath. And as her lips trailed lower and lower, I heard myself groan. If she didn't stop, there'd be no turning back from the need pulsating through me. I closed my eyes, loving the way the long silken strands of her hair felt as they brushed along my nipples, loved the way her warm lips felt against my bare chest.

"Abby..." I said her name slowly as if savoring every sweet letter then drew her up to meet my eyes.

"We have to stop."

"Your shoulder?" Her brows shot up with concern. "Of course."

"That's not the problem right now."

She blushed. "So..." Her fingers inched down my stomach. "Is the problem down here somewhere?"

I caught her hand and kissed her fingertips. "I want to make love to you. But not now. Not here. Do you understand what I am saying? I don't want there to be any doubt in your mind who I'm making love to." I knew her well enough to know she'd wonder if I was making love to her or Lolita.

She nodded.

I kissed the warm flush of her throat and she groaned. "You're killing me." She smiled.

I pressed my lips firmly against hers, and kissed her slowly, savoring her taste, then pulled back. "That kiss is a promise for more to come, and when we get home, there will be no stopping us."

Abby has second thoughts

Wyatt was right to stop us. As much as I wanted him to pick me up, carry me to his bed, and make passionate love to me, Lolita would be there under those sheets with us. Oddly I hadn't heard her press for that union.

Pushing aside my disappointment, I slipped free of his embrace and walked to his door. "There will be a blue moon in two days," I said somberly and sighed. Not knowing what was destined to happen soured my stomach.

Wyatt walked up behind me and wrapped his arms around me. "We're gonna save them."

I rested my head on his good shoulder. "What if we can't?" I'd told him nothing he could have done would have changed Emanuel's fate. Now that Horace was gone, would the children's fate change or would Monty or his hired guns get to them before we could prevent their deaths? My eyes clouded with tears. Or would Lolita do the deed herself, as the legend had said she did?

"Abby, look at me."

I swiped tears from my face and turned.

"You and I are going to do everything we can. Do you understand?"

"What if I'm wrong? What if we're not here to change the

past in order to fix something in the future?"

"No." He stepped back and shook his head. "I believe you. We were sent here for a reason, to stop a murderer. That's what you said."

"I've had second thoughts. What could be so wrong with the future that we need to fix it?"

"It's not for us to know, so I'm not going to stand here and debate the issue."

"Wyatt, you're being unreasonable."

"Damn right I am. Nobody else is going to die on my watch."

I understood and shared his frustration, but deep in my heart, I feared we'd fail.

Chapter Twenty-Two

Abby's number-one suspect

I got up bright and early. We had so much to do and so little time. It was the thirtieth day of July. Tonight, the moon would be big and bright but not yet a completely full moon.

The children were still sleeping as I quickly and quietly set a table with fruit, slices of bread, and big glasses of milk. Thinking about my conversation with Wyatt brought tears to my eyes.

I sniffled and walked to my trunk. If tomorrow night I'd be seen wearing the red dress, I would not wear it. I threw open the lid, picked up the dress, and buried it under layers of clothing. Legend be damned. I slammed the lid shut.

"Good morning, children."

"Morning, Mamma," they both chimed in.

I walked over and hugged them. The thought that anyone could cause them harm formed a knot in my chest. I helped them dress, and though I desperately wanted to get to town and spy on Monty, I shared a meal with them.

"Abby."

"Come in, Wyatt."

He pushed aside the blanket door. "I'm going to ride into town and talk with the Sheriff about our mystery man, the guy with the beret, then see what he learned about Doble."

"Good idea. I'll go with you. Benjamin can stay with the kids until we get back." I turned to the children. "You are to stay inside and play." I hurried to the shelf and pulled out a few books. "Cattie, these should keep you and your brother occupied."

"Yes, Mamma."

"Cattie, Joseph. I love you both."

Joseph smiled.

"We love you too," they said in unison.

My heart lifted.

"Wyatt, let's go. There's no time to lose."

After we stopped at Benjamin's and he agreed to look in on the kids, Wyatt lifted me onto Jack, straddled the animal's back, and wrapped his arms around me. I leaned into his chest and rested my head on his shoulder. We had one day to learn all we could before tomorrow night's blue moon. Would anything we learn help? *It's gonna be all right*, I kept telling myself as Jack trotted toward town.

Wyatt stopped Jack in front of the jailhouse. He jumped down, reached up to me, and I slid into his arms.

After a quick kiss, we rushed through the door. A young man I'd never seen before sat at the Sheriff's desk with his feet on the desktop.

"Who are you?" Wyatt asked.

He swung his feet off the desk and stood. "Name's Luke. And as of yesterday, I'm the acting Sheriff."

"Where's Samuel?" Wyatt's voice reeked of impatience.

"Took Blackjack to the Coloma courthouse and said he'd be back tomorrow."

"Damn it. Abby, let's go."

He took hold of my arm, and as we stepped outside, I noticed a man wearing a blue beret.

"Wyatt. Look." I pointed across the street.

"Hey, you," Wyatt called out as he practically dragged me across the street. "Frenchie."

The man turned and stopped. "Bonjour." He tipped his beret as we met up with him.

"Good day to you, as well." I smiled. "Thank you for the drink you bought me the other night."

"What drink you say?"

"The port...at the saloon."

"Non, mademoiselle."

"He doesn't know what I'm talking about, Wyatt." I shook my head. "It wasn't him. Merci, Monsieur."

He nodded and walked into the saloon.

"We have nothing. Nothing." I wrung my hands. "And why

is Lolita so quiet? She hasn't been in my head for two days."

"Maybe she wants our relationship to grow without her."

"A romantic at heart, you think?"

"Horace hurt her. Maybe acting like the town floozy is her way of coping."

"I know what she's going through. Rejection isn't fun."

"The important thing is, we are a team now. If the Frenchman didn't poison your drink, someone else did, and we are going to find out who." He took my hand. "Come on. Let's have a word with the bartender."

Wyatt and I spent a frantic day asking people if they saw who ordered the drink. The barkeeper gave us nothing, other than it was busy and he couldn't remember. Daisy was nowhere to be found, so I figured she was upstairs entertaining a man. We kept a close watch on Monty's hired guns, but they stayed close to the saloon. As far as we could tell, Monty never left the building.

After running around all day, Wyatt insisted we take a breather before we continued. We sat in rockers near the door of the mercantile. The oppressive evening heat beat down with unbearable intensity. My head pounded, and anxiety made me queasy.

"Wyatt, we have so little time." I reached for his hand.

"I know." His hand covered mine. "Let's go through this again. We know Lolita never accepted Monty's promise for a better life. She loves her kids too much to give them away and Horace is gone, so there's no reason to believe her part in the legend."

"So that leaves Monty." We had infallible proof that Lolita didn't kill her kids, but I'd seen their ghosts, so someone killed them.

"What does the legend say about Monty?" Wyatt rocked back and forth, and I found the repetitive movement calmed my tense nerves.

"Nothing, but we know he has the most plausible motive. Maybe in retelling the legend over time, his name got dropped from the story."

"Yeah. Monty is definitely the killer."

Chapter Twenty-Three

Abby's Blue Moon

On July 31st, the sun rose over a partly cloudy sky. If the weather held, tonight's full moon would be clearly visible; the blue moon of legend would finally arrive.

Wyatt met me in the street in front of my home. Jack was saddled and raring to go.

"You ready to confront Monty?" Wyatt asked and planted a kiss on my cheek.

"Let's go."

He hoisted me up on Jack, but as if on cue, Monty strutted toward us from his parked wagon. Dressed in his usual black suit, he avoided a muddy hole, and I couldn't help but notice the shine on his boots. The rim of his hat cast a shadow over his eyes. He was a man who demanded attention, a man others scurried away from, someone no one wanted to cross.

"Lolita, get on down from there. You're coming with me."

Wyatt put his hand on my leg protectively. "We were just on our way to see you."

Monty stopped in front of Jack. The horse whinnied and stepped back as if instinct told him to be wary of this human.

"So? You've seen me. Now, Lolita, my wagon is over there. Beats riding into town on a smelly horse."

Jack snorted.

Wyatt stood his ground. "She's not going anywhere with you, but I have a few questions." His expression was dark and threatening. He kept his unwavering gaze on Monty. Who was going to blink first?

The veins in Monty's thick neck bulged. "She will do as I demand."

"She doesn't answer to you," Wyatt said, his voice firm.

Testosterone hung in the air like a thick blanket of fog.

"Stop it, both of you." I slid down from Jack and slammed my hands on my hips. "I can speak for myself. Thank you very much."

A lopsided smile lit Wyatt's face in approval. Monty's eyes widened in surprise. Cleary Lolita had never stood up for herself when it came to her boss.

Wyatt faced Monty head-on. "What's so pressing she has to go with you this instant?"

"I am to host a party for some out of town guests this evening, so her services are needed." Monty's tone was steely.

"I hope you're referring to her singing services." Distaste crunched Wyatt's brow.

"That is none of your concern, but yes, she is to be the entertainment."

I closed my eyes and pinched the bridge of my nose. Tonight, was the night, and I needed to be near Monty since he was our only suspect. He had to stay away from my children, and even though I wanted to be there to protect them, I didn't dare let him out of my sight. I exhaled, pulled myself together. "Monty, please excuse us a moment."

He nodded.

I grabbed Wyatt's wrist and we stepped into my home.

"You're not thinking about working tonight, of all nights."

"I have no choice but to go." I put up my hand before he could argue. "It's the party where some say Lolita was singing that night. I'm not going to let Monty leave."

"And how are you going to keep him there?"

"Oh, I don't know, but I bet Lolita can come up with a few ideas." Despite my angst, I smiled and watched his neck turn red. I ran my finger along his jaw. "You're so cute when you're jealous."

"I'm not jealous. I'm worried."

"You take care of the children while I'm at work. Tuck them in bed. With you watching over them, they'll be safe."

Wyatt let out a deep pent-up breath. "Fine. Go. But keep an eye on his hired guns, too."

Wyatt's babysitting job

I watched her walk off with Monty. I wanted to follow and punch the smug, triumphant grin off his face. But Abby was right. Since he was the murderer, keeping an eye on him was our best shot at keeping those kids alive.

Benjamin stepped out of his tent. "I'll be needed in town, as well."

"Do me a favor. Keep an eye on her, will you?"

"But of course. I'll not let any harm come to her."

"Thanks, Benjamin." I watched him ride off in his buggy. All kinds of scenarios went through my mind as I tried to figure out who tried to poison Abby. She was certain Monty wouldn't have done it. If the Frenchman didn't order the drink for Abby, why did Daisy say he did? And why did he acknowledge Lolita when the drink was delivered? Did he misunderstand her gesture to him? Did the bartender indicate to Daisy the wrong patron who'd purchased the drink, or did the bartender drop the poison in the wine? Why? What would he gain by killing their top attraction, or was he ordered to do so by someone else, like Blackjack Hardington? Maybe he'd cut the reins on the wagon, as well. That made more sense than anything.

And what did any of this have to do with the legend? Was it because of something we did just by being here? We had already changed the future. We never would have fallen in love if we hadn't come here, so when we go back, the future will have changed.

Since I was no longer going to town, I tied Jack to a tree between my house and Benjamin's tent then walked across the road and stepped into Abby's place.

The children were sitting on their cot. Cattie was brushing Joseph's hair.

I was going to miss them when we finally left this place. I swallowed a lump of emotion. "Cattie, you are quite a young lady."

"Thank you, Mister Wyatt."

I walked up to them and patted Joseph's shoulder. "You're the man of the house, so make sure to look out for your sister and listen to her and your mamma, okay?"

"Are you going somewhere?" Cattie asked.

I wished I knew the answer. "I'm staying with you for a while."

"Promise?"

"Scout's honor."

"What's that?"

"Where did you come from, Mister Wyatt?"

"Alabama." Just popped into my head.

"Where's that?"

Oh, brother. It was going to be a long night.

That evening, we played in the road, tossing a ball back and forth and laughing. As the sun set, the full moon rose, a blue moon, as beautifully white and bright as could be. I found it impossible to believe this night had ended with the murder of these two wonderful kids.

"Come on, guys. It's time for bed."

After I tucked them in, I sat at the table, lit the oil lamp, and made sure my gun was loaded, just in case Monty slipped away from the party and showed up here to do the deed. Sometimes I stood and paced for several minutes, walked to the door and looked outside. Campfires flickered about, and the clouds glimmered with silvery moonlight. Other times, I checked to see the kids were asleep then paced again. I even sat with Hans Christian Anderson and read a bit of *The Little Mermaid*. My mind kept slipping to the party. What was Abby doing? Singing? Dancing? Flirting... What was I doing here babysitting when I should be with Abby? I shouldn't have let her talk me into splitting up. Not tonight. I should be with her, making sure she was safe, making sure that creep Monty kept his hands to himself. Damnit. Again, I checked my loaded gun.

A commotion rose outside, horses riding in, a whinny, and fast-approaching boot steps.

The Sheriff charged in. "Wyatt, you were right."

"Shhh." I ushered him outside so our conversation wouldn't wake the kids. "Right about what?"

"The fire. The wanted poster."

"That son of a bitch killed his wife, didn't he?"

"Yup. The wife's oldest brother, Eunice Christen, saw the

whole thing. The brothers been looking for Monty for some time now."

"Yeah. They found him at the hotel the other night. Made quite a scene. I thought they were going to shoot it out right there."

"They came to me for help, on account of the hired guns, verified Monty's last name was Doble, just like you said." Samuel tapped his hat against his leg, which loosened the accumulated dust from his ride to the camp. Shadows passed over his face.

I glanced up and saw part of the full moon before it disappeared behind a cloud. "Why didn't Eunice say something back then, have Monty arrested?"

"Monty beat him unconscious, damn near killed him. By the time Eunice recovered, Monty had skipped town. The brothers decided to handle it on their own. A family matter, they figured." Samuel plopped his hat on his head. "Now it's in the law's hands. I'm going to the saloon to arrest him right now, just me and the brothers, but going up against Monty's hired guns, I sure could use your help."

The landscape brightened. I glanced up again to see the cloud had passed to allow the full moon to shine down on us. Its bright silver surface drew and held my unblinking eyes. The blue moon of legend, so beautiful, so deadly—

"Wyatt. What do you say? You ridin' with us?"

I blinked and thought of the children asleep inside. With Monty locked up, they'd be safe. Abby, on the other hand, might not be, especially if word got out we were gunning for Monty. Who knew what kind of trouble would go down? She could be caught in the crossfire.

"Sheriff, let's go put that son-of-a-bitch in jail where he belongs."

Abby's legend

Music and laughter filled the crowded saloon. The party was in full swing. Men I didn't recognize played faro. The whiskey flowed. Women gave lap dances, and men, their eyes glazed with lust, fondled breasts. Two of Monty's hired guns stood by the door, bouncers meant to keep the unwanted out of this private party.

Monty had insisted I change into something sexy, so I chose a yellow gown, not red, with ribbon ties in the front. There'd be no mistaking where I was and what I was wearing this night.

I rushed out of the dressing room and over to Daisy, happy to see her. "I was hoping you'd be here."

"Did you think I wasn't good enough to be invited?"

"No. I—"

"Don't think just because Monty has eyes for you that you're better than me."

"What?" My jaw dropped. Why was she so angry? "What did I do?"

"Watch this."

Her comments were so out of character I couldn't think of a reason for her anger as I watched her storm through the crowd to Monty. She looped her arms around his neck.

Why is she coming on to him?

"She is jealous of me," Lolita said.

Monty pried loose Daisy's arms. He looked angry, but she threw herself at him again.

"What's that all about?"

"She was his gal before I came along."

I couldn't hear what they were saying but Monty stepped back and pointed toward the bar where I stood. Were they talking about me, or was Monty telling her to get back to work and serve drinks? This time his rejection was more forceful; he turned her away and booted her in the ass.

Daisy spun around and our eyes met. Her glare was narrow and hard. It lasted only a second, but long enough for me to wonder what she was trying to prove.

"Monty will never take her back."

"Why take it out on me? We're friends."

Lolita *sighed. "I thought so too."*

Daisy stood at a card table, her expression sullen. I'd smooth things over with her later. Right now, I had more pressing things to worry about than Daisy's bitter jealousy. I had to concentrate on Monty. I looked up at the mirror behind the bar, didn't see him, turned and scanned the room. No Monty. Shit. My heart beat double-time. Oh my god. Had he left? Again, I surveyed the room but didn't see him. The children...I had to get to my children. I sprinted across the room toward the door.

Just then, Monty strode out of the back office like a king expecting his subjects to pay him court as he walked by them with a fresh cigar, smoking.

I stopped short and took a calming breath. The children would be fine. Wyatt was there to protect them.

Monty stopped at the piano. "Benjamin, play something sad for Daisy." He laughed.

The sad melody, *Thou art gone from my gaze,* filled the room. I hurried up on stage and started singing. "Thou art gone from my gaze, like a beautiful dream, and I seek thee in vain by the meadow and stream. Oft I breathe thy dear name to the winds floating by, but thy sweet voice is mute to my bosom's sigh."

It was as if Lolita were singing the lyrics to her own story. Her heartfelt sorrow flowed from her throat in a wash of emotion. I thought about her children and agonized over what had happened to them. But not now, not if I could stop Monty.

"In the stillness of night, when the stars mildly shine, my heart fondly holds a communion with thine. For I feel thou art near, where e'er I may be, that the spirit of love keeps a watch over me."

My tears reflected how I felt, how Lolita felt, each word tightening my chest. A nagging worry in the back of my mind kept repeating: *you can't change the future.*

Monty rested his hand on my backside, and I flinched. If I could, I'd peel this sexy body off of me and give it back to Lolita. Being beautiful was taxing. I was so sick of men who only saw the curves they hoped to manhandle and lips they wanted to kiss. They didn't give a damn about the person inside.

The sound of applause broke into my miserable thoughts.

"Well done, my dear." He wiped a tear from my cheek. "You have all the men eating out of your hand, including me." He kissed my palm.

I wanted to jerk away, but I had to keep him close.

"Come, let us dance." He took my hand. "Benjamin, a

waltz."

I could see all eyes were on us as we moved across a floor now clear of tables and chairs. Like a marionette held up by tight strings, I swayed slowly to the gentle rhythm. I wanted to escape, but those invisible strings held me captive. I hated the ogling looks, hated Monty's possessive hand in mine, and I reminded myself I was here to keep him in sight. This was the night, the legendary night Lolita danced and sang while her children were murdered, and I was going to make sure he got nowhere near them. A quick glance to the door assured me his hired guns were still standing guard. It comforted me to know Wyatt was watching over the kids, keeping them safe.

A commotion at the front door made Monty stop mid-step. Two men had entered and pointed guns at his hired gunmen.

Benjamin stopped playing. The chatter ceased.

"What's the meaning of this?" Monty's voice boomed across the room. His arm held me tight around my waist.

"Monty Doble."

I recognized Sheriff Townsend's deep voice.

"You're under arrest."

Monty's grip pinched my side as the Sheriff stalked toward us. Behind him, Wyatt stepped into the saloon. My breath hitched. What was he doing here? Who was watching the children? An ache in my chest inflamed like a fireball. I tried to break free from Monty. I had to get home to protect the children.

Despite my frantic thrashing to get away, Monty pulled out a gun with his free hand and pointed it at my head.

I froze.

His eyes bulged with anger. The veins in his forehead pulsed. He cocked the gun with his thumb. "Stop or I'll kill her."

The Sheriff stopped. Wyatt stopped beside him. They were only two steps away but helpless.

Blood drained from my face. Did he know I'd been in his office, that I knew his real last name? Why was he looking at me with such loathing? Did he? Oh, God. He did. He knew... Every breath hurt as I stared at Monty's gun. "Please don't."

"Lolita. You did this to me," Monty shouted. "You ruined everything. All I ever wanted was for you to love me."

Out the corner of my eye, I saw Wyatt charge forward.

Before Monty had a chance to duck, Wyatt landed a punch to the side of Monty's head. The gun went flying as he stumbled, crashed into a nearby card table, and hit the floor.

"Get up." Wyatt stood over him, fists balled. "Get up, you murdering coward."

As he stood, Monty eyed the gun he'd dropped, but Wyatt kicked it away. "You heard the Sheriff. You're under arrest."

Monty started swinging at him, but Wyatt blocked every jab and landed a counterpunch, this time to Monty's gut, buckling him over. "That's for bullying Lolita." A side-sweep with his foot sent Monty to the deck; he landed on his back. "And that's for ordering the murder of her children."

"My children," Lolita screeched. *"What is he saying?"*

"It's okay, Lolita. They're safe."

Monty huffed. "You're crazy." He struggled to his feet. "Sheriff, you just gonna stand there and do nothing?"

Samuel crossed his arms in front of his chest. "Don't mind if I do."

Wyatt grabbed Monty's lapels. "I heard you give your goons the order to get rid of the brats." Wyatt pinned him against the bar. "Admit it."

A murmur rippled through the crowd of stunned partygoers.

"Now wait a minute," Slimbo bellowed despite the gun held to his head by one of the brothers. "He ordered us to kidnap Gilles' young'uns, but we refused. We ain't hangin' for him."

Wyatt shoved Monty toward the Sheriff. "Get him outta my sight."

The Sheriff grabbed Monty. "Did you set fire to Gilles' place?"

"I admit to no such offense." Monty straightened his coat. His gaze shifted to his gunmen held at gunpoint. "They did it."

"We were following Monty's orders," Buckeye shouted.

"You imbeciles. I told you no such thing."

"Our word against yers."

Monty put his palms out to the Sheriff. "Now Samuel, you can't believe him. He's just saying that to keep from swinging at the end of a rope."

The Sheriff pointed at Monty. "You got three counts

against you, attempted kidnapping, arson, and murder."

"Murder? I didn't kill anyone."

"Liar." A voice like cracking knuckles drew all eyes toward the door. The room went dead silent. Simply dressed in overalls and a red wool shirt, the elfin man stepped into the saloon and let the doors swing behind him.

I recognized him from the hotel dining room. Eunice.

He marched over to my boss, stretched to his full height halfway up Monty's chest, and put an accusatory finger in his face. "I saw you kill my sister, your wife. You thought you'd beaten me to death, but I survived to bear witness against you...for murder, Monty Doble."

The crowd gasped.

"Let's go." The Sheriff rammed a gun into Monty's back and shoved him forward. The volume in the room rose to its usual loud chatter as Monty and his hired guns were escorted out the door.

My knees shook. I propped myself up on a nearby table.

Wyatt walked up, calm as could be. "Are you okay?"

"Are you crazy?" I screamed at him. "You left the kids alone?"

"They're fine. The murderer was here the whole time. You were in more danger than the kids."

"No. We're missing something."

"Relax. It's over. We stopped the murderer and ended the legend of the Weeping Woman."

My sixth sense was completely freaking out. "Then why do I feel so edgy, like...I don't know..." I couldn't put my finger on it. The sensation felt like that day in the river...the foreboding...the sense something else was going to go wrong that I had no control over. A creepy feeling in the bottom of my heart told me the legend was still very much alive. *The brats. The brats? Something about the brats?*

"My children are not brats," Lolita hissed in my head.

"That's it. Wyatt. The brats Monty referred to, they were Gilles' kids. Not Lolita's. The killer is still out there."

"The killer? What killer?" Lolita screamed.

Camila rushed in through the swinging doors, white as a ghost and breathing heavily. "Wyatt." Her face was red and slick with sweat, and as she approached us, her gait staggered on the verge of collapse.

Wyatt held her up.

"Los niños..." she said, her eyes wide with fear.

"What about the children?" Wyatt's voice held a note of impatience and alarm.

"Ellos están perdidos."

"They're missing?"

Alarms went off in my chest. "We have to get back to camp." I raced to the dressing room to get my cloak. It was gone. My throat tightened. Someone took it. Who would want it? I'd have to go in this skimpy yellow dress. I pivoted and, in my haste, I knocked over the rack of Daisy's dresses. The stand crashed to the floor. Glass shattered and the smell of almonds wafted up. Cyanide?

"Daisy? No. It couldn't be..."

I sprinted back to the barroom, saw Benjamin at the piano, his eyes wide with shock, but no Daisy. "Benjamin. Get the Sheriff. Meet us at the river."

Wyatt took my arm. "Let's ride."

As we rushed outside, I saw a town illuminated under bright moonlight, high above, the infamous blue moon of July, 1852. Wyatt pulled me toward Jack tied at the post. "Let's not panic. Maybe the kids just went outside to look at the moon."

We were up on Jack in nothing flat and galloping down the road toward camp. Wyatt kept me firm in the saddle as the terrifying pace whipped up my dress and tangled my hair.

I wanted to shut my eyes and wish this nightmare away.

Jack jumped over a ditch. We flew in midair. I couldn't breathe, and nausea rose in my stomach. He landed with a *clip-clop,* hooves again beating on dry earth. Wyatt kept Jack at top speed by clicking his tongue and swiftly tapping the horse's neck with the reins.

Jack barely stopped in front of my home before Wyatt dismounted. His arms reached up, and I was off before I knew it.

"Check inside. Maybe they've returned." He pointed to my home. "I'll go check Benjamin's place."

I rushed inside to find it empty. Panic attacked my chest like stab wounds to my heart.

The dress...

I ran to my trunk and flung open the lid. Everything was in disarray. Frantically I dug through the garments, yanking out clothing and tossing it all aside. The legendary red dress was gone. *Daisy?* "Oh my God...oh my God. The children..." Two blue-eyed stone necklaces lay on the table. They might have had the power to ward off evil spirits, but they were useless against a woman scorned. I whirled around, headed outside, and nearly collided with Wyatt. "It's Daisy."

"Daisy?"

"She tried to poison me." I clenched my fists on my quivering lips. "And she's got the children. I know it."

Wyatt grabbed my hand. "The river. Let's go."

That same feeling of horror that had overtaken me the night my mother died, smothered me to the core. The tightness in my chest made breathing difficult. I ran, barely able to keep up with Wyatt.

"You and Daisy are friends."

"Daisy and Monty were an item before Lolita came along." I stumbled over the hem of my dress.

He caught me and threw his arm around my waist. "Why would she be the murderer?"

It was Daisy. Daisy. Suddenly it all made sense. "She'd lost Monty's affection, any promise of a future in San Francisco, of course she was angry at me. But why take it out on my children?"

"She wants to hurt me in the worst possible way," Lolita cried. *"Hurry."*

Puffy dark clouds hung in the sky, their shadows masking the rough ground and making our steps treacherous. The clouds drifted across the face of the full blue moon that I would have admired, all a-sparkle on the roiling river, if not for its deadly presence; it was now an eerie celestial orb haloed in cloud. Dark gray craters stood out against the intense white glare until another cloud turned off the greatest nightlight in nature.

At the river's edge, we stopped. I saw a wooden rowboat caught in the grip of the current upstream and barreling toward us. Three dark figures stood in the rocking boat.

Wyatt stripped off his shirt, yanked off his boots, and

kicked out of his pants. I was surprised to see he'd been wearing his swim trunks as underwear. He dove into the river. I pulled at the front ribbons of my gown, shoved it down past my hips then stepped out of the dress, leaving me in my bloomers.

As the moonlight returned, I saw a woman in a red dress and cloak, struggling with Cattie as Joseph dropped low and gripped the side of the boat. Daisy. In my red dress. Of course. She wanted me to be blamed for the murders. Maybe even hanged...so she could get another shot at Monty...

Wyatt was swimming like a crazy man toward the boat.

With shaking fingers, I unlaced my shoes, and dove into water so cold it sucked the air from my lungs, but I started swimming toward the boat with all the fury of a mother protecting her young.

Cattie's screams echoed down the canyon and tore into my heart, prompting me to swim harder and faster than I'd ever swam before. In my haste, I accidentally gulped in water, causing me to choke and cough, but I kept up my frantic pace.

The small boat pitched back and forth, spun in the current, and was floating past me sideways. Daisy was trying to throw Cattie into the river, but my little girl held onto the gunwale with all her might.

I ignored the frigid water flooding my mouth and nose as I dug through the fast-moving current as fast as I could.

Every second or so I caught glimpses of Wyatt in the moonlight. He was close to the boat. "Jump," he shouted. "Cattie, Joseph, jump. I'll catch you."

Joseph shook his head and stared at the dark water as though his feet were chained. Cattie was holding on for dear life while Daisy tried to dislodge her.

The boat rocked and twirled as Wyatt fought the whitewater and grabbed the boat and struggled to haul himself over the rim.

Daisy stomped on his fingers.

The boat dipped in a rapid swirl. Wyatt lost his grip and went under.

I swam with every ounce of strength I had to reach him. A second passed, the longest second of my life as I desperately searched the dark water for his head to pop up. "Wyatt."

His head broke the surface and relief washed over me.

My overtired legs cramped in the cold water, but I pushed on, frantic to get to the boat before the current sucked it downstream. Caught in the rapids myself, I thrashed and flailed wildly then went under. Ice-cold water gushed down my throat. Memories of my last drowning flashed through my brain. I couldn't see anything, felt like a rag tossed about in a washer. The river held me in its rippling grip. I propelled myself upward, broke the surface, swallowed water, and gulped in air.

"Abby." Wyatt clasped my waist.

Ahead of us and now out of reach, the boat spun in the roiling current. One by one, Daisy tossed the children into the rushing water. They went under and never resurfaced.

"No," I screamed.

The boat plunged downstream, its only passenger the woman in the red dress clearly visible under the bright blue moon. Anyone who saw her would undoubtedly blame Lolita for a crime she didn't commit. Daisy screamed. The boat slammed into a patch of rocks and disintegrated, and that was the last I saw of her.

The fast, turbulent stretch of the river flowed into a bend where the foamy surface curled upward and fell back on itself, forming a treacherous whirlpool of currents that sucked us both under. I was torn from Wyatt's grip, and the force of the water slammed me against the rocky bottom and held me down until nothing mattered anymore.

Chapter Twenty-Four

Abby's back home

"Abby. Abby. Wake up."

Hands nudged me. I struggled to open my eyes. A face appeared over me. Cindi's face. "Abby?"

I coughed and spat up water. Gasped and choked. The sun shone down in my eyes, the moonlit landscape of 1852 now gone to history. My brain felt fuzzy, and my body felt like I'd been trapped on a runaway wagon, but I was alive. I was back, but with that revelation came dread. Had we changed history?

"Abby. Come on. Talk to me."

I was soaking wet, again wearing my one-piece black swimsuit. The crowd around me stared with narrow eyes, firemen, medics, beachgoers...not a single gold miner in sight. Everyone's mouths were set in hard lines as they watched me breathe deeply and look around with disbelieving eyes. No holes dug, no tents pitched, no campfires burning.

"She's okay," someone said.

Their faces gave way to relief, smiles, pats on the backs. I must've given them all a big scare.

The piercing wail of a siren and flashing red orbs drew my attention to the road where the red Ferrari was parked.

"Wyatt?" I tried to sit up, but Cindi held me down. Panic ricocheted through my chest. "Where's Wyatt?"

"He's with the paramedics getting checked out." Cindi placed a reassuring hand on my shoulder. "He almost drowned saving your ass."

"Saving me? What...what happened? How long was I in the water?"

"Chill, sis." She hugged me. "You almost drowned, too."

I grabbed her by the arm. "The Weeping Woman legend? Is it—?

"Give it a rest, will you?"

"Oh my God. Those beautiful children died anyway."

"You're delirious."

The crowd made me feel claustrophobic. I took several quick breaths. If I didn't calm down, I was going to hyperventilate.

"Lolita? Are you there? Lolita?"

Silence.

Two men, dressed in navy pants and white shirts, hooked their arms under me and turned me on my side. They patted my back, and I coughed up more water. I stared at their black shiny shoes. For some bizarre reason, I thought of Wyatt's new boots. He'd bought new shoes for Emanuel, too. He was always helping someone. Always looking out for me. Tears blurred my vision.

The medics put a breathing mask over my nose and mouth, and I felt cool oxygen brush my face. I wanted to tear it off and scream for Wyatt. The medics turned me on my back and lifted me to a gurney, strapped me down, and as they wheeled me from the beach, Cindi held my hand like I was a long lost friend. I had so many questions to ask her, questions that would sound as ridiculous as the Weeping Woman legend. Did I appear out of nowhere? How long was I gone? Did I really time travel, or had my near-death experience made up the journey in my mind? I could only hope Wyatt remembered what had happened to us.

It was a bumpy ride up the road, past the red Ferrari, to the waiting ambulance. The back doors opened and out popped Wyatt wearing those familiar swim trunks. "Thanks, guys." He turned and locked eyes with me. "Abby. Abby." He ran to my side. Gone was the long blond hair and tanned rugged face of a cowboy. "Looks like you're going to be okay."

"Okay?" I pulled the mask up onto my forehead. "Is that all? Okay? After what we've been through?"

"Yeah. She's a feisty redhead again." He turned to Cindi and the paramedics. "Give us a moment alone, will you all?"

"Sure."

They cleared an area around us.

"Abby," he whispered. "They can't know what happened

to us." He cupped my face with his hands. "They'll never believe it anyway."

"So you do remember Dry Diggins and the camp—"

"All of it, including the good part...where I fell in love with you."

"You love me?"

"You heard right."

"But look at me, my tummy flab, pale skin, red hair. I'm not Lolita anymore."

"Yeah. Now you're perfect."

I smiled. I was far from perfect. Though I never felt ugly, I was always overly critical of my body. I saw what I feared others saw. I let my perceived view of how they saw me color my perception of myself. If I'd learned nothing more from our jaunt back in time, it was that beauty was only skin deep. I was more than just my body. Even when I had the perfect figure, it didn't define me. I was still me. From now on I was going to concentrate on my positives.

Then a sadness crept over me. "The kids didn't make it."

He pressed his forehead against mine. "At least you now know the truth about the legend."

I sighed and closed my eyes, holding back tears. "Then we didn't fail."

"Nothing has changed, well, except us. I learned to get my hands dirty...and we fell in love."

"We did, didn't we. I love you, Wyatt."

"I love you, too, Abby." He leaned in and kissed me.

"Hey. What's going on here?"

I recognized Pam's annoyed voice.

"What does it look like?" Wyatt snapped at her. "I just kissed Abigail Stewart."

Pam stared at him with contempt in her eyes. "I don't appreciate my boyfriend kissing this fat pig."

If I could have sat up, I would have decked her myself, but I had Wyatt now, she didn't, and I had nothing to prove. "Pam?"

"What?" She crossed her arms in spite.

"I want to thank you for that nasty trick you played on me in high school."

"I-I don't know what you're talking about."

"Sure you do," Wyatt said. "The phony date I had with Abby on prom night."

"I don't get it," she huffed, all full of herself. "Why thank me for that? It was mean and humiliating and *so* much fun." She laughed.

I filled her in. "If Wyatt hadn't stood me up, I never would have hated him so much. Turns out, hate can turn into love once misunderstandings are cleared up." I interlocked my fingers with his. "And I love this man more than you ever could...with your perky boobs being in the way, and all."

"Give me a break," Pam spat. "He saved you from drowning. This hero-love thing you got for him now won't last."

Wyatt straightened. "It's more than that, Pam. I'm through with you."

"Nobody is ever *through* with me. You'll come crawling back. Wait and see."

"I never want to see you again."

Her jaw dropped. "But—"

"Go." He turned to the medics. "Give Abby a good check up, boys."

"I'm all right," I said, not wanting to be prodded and poked. "Undo these straps so I can get up."

"You sure, lady?" the medic asked while unbuckling me. "We should take you to the hospital."

"I decline." I sat up. "Give me the form to sign."

"Oh, great," Wyatt said. "Here comes my dad."

I got off the gurney and saw a tall, overweight man dressed in a suit and tie pressing through the crowd. No wonder he wanted to live football vicariously through his son. He was in no shape for it.

Cindi brought me my sandals and cover-up.

"Thanks. I'll call you later."

She smiled at Wyatt. "I don't know how you did it, Abby, but you go, girl."

Wyatt's dad stopped in front of him, huffing and puffing. "What happened? I hear you saved some woman's life?"

"Not just some woman, dad. My woman." He tilted his head to me. "Meet Abigail Stewart."

I smiled at him.

He afforded me only a glance. "That's fine, son. A redhead. But why did you risk your life? You could've ruined your football career."

"Thanks for the concern, but I'm not going pro."

"What are you talking about? Of course you are."

"No. I'm going to med-school."

"Y-you're obviously delusional. Let's go. We'll finish this conversation at home...after our doctor looks you over for head injuries."

"Wyatt," a feminine voice called out. A beautiful blonde woman ran up and wrapped her arms around him. "Are you all right?"

"I'm okay, Mom. Really." In his mother's arms, the angst on his face softened. He broke from the embrace. "I finally told him."

"Good for you." His mother smiled.

"Your son is talking nonsense. Not going pro? Bull."

"Look, Dad. Going pro was your dream. Not mine."

"This is ridiculous. And we shouldn't be having this conversation in front of strangers." He shot a glance at me.

Wyatt took my hand then turned back to his dad. "I'm going to med-school, and before you tell me you're gonna cut off my funding, it doesn't matter. I'll get a job."

"You? A job? Don't make me laugh."

"Try me."

Mom jumped in. "He's made his decision, dear. Let's go home and I'll make you a martini." She steered her grumbling husband away.

I snuggled up to Wyatt. "I'm proud of you for sticking up for yourself."

"After nearly drowning twice and taking a bullet to the shoulder, I realize life is short, and I'm gonna choose my own path. Dad's just going to have to live with it."

I ran my finger over Wyatt's shoulder. There was no sign of a gunshot wound. "I'm glad our legendary journey changed us both."

"For the better, Abby, and for a long time to come."

My dad emerged from the crowd. "Abby?" He ran up to me, and I stepped into his open arms where he held me tight.

"What do you mean you're not going to the hospital?"

"I'm fine, dad. Really."

"You almost drowned." Tears welled in his eyes. "Don't you ever scare me like that again." He examined me up and down. "Are you sure you're all right?"

"I've never been better." I glanced lovingly at Wyatt.

Dad looked him over. "I see."

Wyatt held his hand out. "Hi. I'm Wyatt Beaufort."

My dad accepted the handshake. "Nice to meet you, Wyatt."

"Do you mind if I shadow you at the hospital sometime? I'm going to be a doctor."

"I look forward to that. And Abigail, I'm taking some time off. You and I are going to have some father-daughter time."

"That would be nice."

We waved goodbye to my dad. The paramedic walked up with a release form for me to sign. "You all good now?"

"We are more than good," Wyatt said as I signed the form. "In fact, there's something I have to ask you, Abby."

The medic took his form and headed toward his ambulance.

"What's that, Wyatt?" I added a coy grin for effect.

"Will you go to the prom with me?"

"Prom?" I furrowed my brow. "A little late for that, don't you think?" It was cute and sweet, him asking. That had been my dream, to wear the gown my mom and I had picked out, just so I could dance with Wyatt. A sudden chill enveloped me, and I sensed my mother's presence standing next to us. I fought back tears and took a deep breath.

Wyatt grinned then his expression turned serious. "Well?"

"Wyatt, we're not in high school anymore."

He took my hand. "My mom organized a summer social at our old high school. It's tomorrow night. What do you say?"

I stared into his bright blue eyes filled with love, and my heart felt secure. Wyatt saw me. He loved me. And he was patiently awaiting my answer. "It's about time you asked me for a date."

His eyes glinted with joy.

Chapter Twenty-Five

Abby's date with Wyatt

S tepping into the El Dorado High School gymnasium was like stepping back in time. Flower-filled cowboy boots sat on cream-colored tablecloths. Blue tulle and string lights hung from the ceiling, and an old wagon filled with hay bales sat in a corner. We could take our pictures at the jailhouse façade or in the swinging doors of the saloon. A country-western band, dressed in Western duds, played a lively beat. Wyatt glanced at me and I smiled. "Let's dance."

After a fun Virginia reel, the music slowed. With our arms wrapped around each other, Wyatt and I danced among the high school students and alumni. Young girls wore corsages similar to the pink roses on my wrist. The green gown my mother and I had picked out fit a little loosely but felt perfect. Wyatt and I had come full circle, and being here with him tonight felt so surreal.

When the song ended, the band took a break and Wyatt took my hand. "Let's go for a walk."

I nodded and we hurried through the throng and stepped into the hall. "Where are we going?"

"What do you say we get a little privacy in the library?"

Anticipation of privacy revved my heart.

We ran through the hallway to a room I was very familiar with. Wyatt flung open the door and we rushed inside. The woody scent of books made me feel right at home.

He pressed me against a book rack, and a book fell with a thud to the floor behind me as he planted kisses along my neck, sending delightful tingles throughout my body.

"Can you feel them?" Wyatt asked as his lips traveled to my ear for a nibble. "The stories, the characters nestled between the pages. This place feels so alive."

"Shhh." I giggled. "The janitor may hear you."

"No one is here but us." Wyatt went back to nibbling on my ear, and my body shuddered in submission. The delicate touch of his warm lips on my neck pushed any thoughts of being caught by the janitor from my mind.

Our lips met and he kissed me long and deep. He whispered my name and I moaned. His skilled hands roamed my body and heated my skin. Peace filled my heart.

A childish giggle broke the mood.

"Wyatt?"

"Who was that?"

The room suddenly felt chilled. A flash of movement caught my eye. "Over there." I pointed to the end of the book shelves. "I think I saw them."

"Who?"

"Wait for it."

At the end of the row, luminous lights flashed and sparkled. The glow solidified as the spirits of Cattie and Joseph materialized, dressed just like before.

Wyatt's eyes widened and I sensed his excitement as he held me tighter.

"It's okay."

The children giggled then ran down the aisles, darting and ducking, playing catch me if you can.

Wyatt gasped. "I see them."

Joseph glided our direction and floated before us, shimmering. "I tried to tell you our mamma didn't do it."

"Yes, you did. That first time I saw you on the riverbank."

"My sister wanted you to see for yourself."

Cattie swung in. "Mister Wyatt..." She gazed at him lovingly. "Thank you for trying to save us."

Wyatt nodded.

"And you too, Abby."

"What happened to your mother?" I squeezed Wyatt's hand.

"The Sheriff found her on the shore downriver," Cattie said, her voice sad and echoing through the room. "She was in her underclothes again."

I remembered taking off the yellow dress before diving

into the water. "And Daisy? Did he find her?"

"He never looked cuz he saw Mamma in the boat."

"Now we know that's not true."

"She cried a lot after that," Joseph added.

"Yes, she did, and history remembers her for the love she had for you."

"We love you," Cattie sang and took her brother's hand.

"We love you, too," Wyatt and I said in unison.

The children turned, flew a few laps between the bookshelves before their essences dimmed and disappeared. The sound of their laughter echoed down the hallway...then silence.

I looked at Wyatt and smiled at the awe in his eyes.

He drew me in close. "I kinda like this sixth sense thing you got goin' on."

"They are happy now, and so are we."

Wyatt's lips met mine with a passion that, I swear, sent sparks flying. Held in his arms like this, I felt strong and loved. My entire body craved him, craved more of his loving, so I wrapped my arms around his neck and melted into his embrace. This man was my past and my future, and I thanked God for the timeless river that brought us together, that ignited the fire of love in his eyes, and breathed life back into my wounded heart.

A Note from the Author

I hope you enjoyed reading about Abby and Wyatt's journey back in time as much as I loved writing their story.

Writing about the past is my passion. I enjoy researching and learning about the men and women who left home and friends to pursue their dreams of adventure and riches.

I did my best to portray all the hardships and hours it took to pan for gold, and how difficult it was to live in a mining camp with so many different nationalities and races, where the lust for riches sometimes overshadowed human decency, and greed blinded ordinary men and women.

For those Forty-Niners who struck it rich, a promising future awaited, but for most others, their reward for a hard day's work was blistered hands, weathered, mosquito-bitten skin, and disappointment. Nevertheless, these men and the few women who followed them are part of our colorful history.

I know the song, *Sweet Betsy from Pike* was written in 1858 by John A Stone, in San Francisco, but I chose to take an author's artistic license to use it here, since the song fit in so well with my scene. Interesting facts: the mining town of Dry Diggins (or Dry Diggings) was renamed Placerville in 1854. In 1856, a fire destroyed most of the original buildings.

Thank you for choosing "Timeless River" from the countless books available. With so many authors to choose from, I am honored that you picked me. I would be grateful if you would take a moment to write a review at Amazon.

Please visit my website to read the excerpts of my other books or browse through my extensive research links at: **www.mariannepetitbooks.com** Please feel free to blog with me or drop me an email. Sign up for my occasional news, contests, and upcoming books. I'd love to hear from you at: **riteromance@aol.com**

Thanks again from the bottom of my heart.

Marianne

About the Author

Marianne Petit is a past President of the Long Island Chapter of the Romance Writers of America. She is currently the District Governor of the Suffolk County Lions clubs, a service organization that raises money for the less fortunate - especially the sight and hearing impaired. Ms. Petit was also the chairman for their New York State Reading Action Program which promotes literacy around the world.

Her love of writing stems back to high school. She spent hours reading Nancy Drew, Alfred Hitchcock, and historical romances. At the age of fifteen, she wrote a short story for children, as well as numerous works of poetry. Her love of history stems from her father, Roger, a Frenchman, whose love of American history greatly influenced her writing interests. A Native American time-travel was her first book, published in 2000.

Long Island Newsday and several local newspapers have written articles on Ms. Petit and she was interviewed on television for her time travel, A *Find Through Time.*

Marianne lives on Long Island, has two sons and four grandchildren, and is happily married to the real hero in her life, her husband Steve.

Other books by Ms. Petit available at Amazon.com:

A Find Through Time: A Native American time-travel
https://www.amazon.com/dp/B004VS6WEU

Rebecca's Ghost: Set in the 1700s in Virginia
https://www.amazon.com/dp/B00BFG1W3M

Amulet of Darkness: A mythological fantasy
https://www.amazon.com/dp/1533121826

Behind the Mask: Set in France during WWII and based on true stories.
https://www.amazon.com/dp/1494749920

Amore Moon Publishing

http://www.amoremoonpublishing.com

an imprint of

http://www.twbpress.com
Science Fiction – Supernatural – Horror - Thriller